Ebook ISBN: 978-1-964658-06-3

Print ISBN: 978-1-964658-07-0

Cover Design & Book design by Peter J. Wacks.

First printing edition 2012.

Second printing edition 2024.

www.kevinkauffmann.com

10 9 8 7 6 5 4 3 2

MURDER OF CROWS

The Icarus Trilogy
Book 1

KEVIN KAUFFMANN

Murder of Crows

Kevin Kauffmann

*For Grandma E. She wouldn't have liked it,
but she would have been proud.*

Stage One
DENIAL

Prisoner's Dilemma

Ryan Jenkins sat on the cold, metallic bench in the Crows' locker room, the world on mute around him. It was a dingy place—the hinges of each door caked with rust and dirt mired between every tile—all because the apathetic and underpaid janitorial staff could not be bothered.

It was just as well; Jenkins hadn't noticed even after he had taken off his utilitarian, almost featureless helmet to reveal a short crop of brown hair and an innocent face. There were no scars or wrinkles, he was just a boy, really. His adolescence had extended well into his twenties, just like his jury of peers. All manners of grime covered his armored hands, but Jenkins could only focus on the splashes of blood decorating his gloves. He remembered how they had been stained.

Roberts sat a few meters away and watched Jenkins while scratching at the brown fuzz on his scalp; his hair had not had a chance to grow back, yet. Though two years Jenkins' junior, Roberts' tired eyes betrayed several lifetimes of fighting on the fields of Eris. Roberts wore a weary frown, but he knew the physical and emotional trauma that came with the first game. Roberts had spent four years on this prison world and had seen so many supposed athletes come and go, but none of them had been heroes from the start.

It seemed like Jenkins was not cut out for this kind of work. Nobody really was, but Roberts' new teammate had already been gaping at his hands for ten minutes. Roberts had to guess it was because of the dried blood covering the grey power armor, which—aside from the crimson and black crow on his shoulder plates—was plastered with corporate logos and mottos, most notably the iconic image of McCoy's crescent moon painted onto the left of Jenkins' chest plate.

That was expected, since the fast-food chain was their major sponsor, but it was an odd choice. Whenever Roberts saw the icon on his armor, it hardly made him want one of their cheeseburgers.

Roberts sighed at the rookie's shell-shocked behavior, but some paternal instinct kicked in and he knew that he would have to help Jenkins get over this trauma, whatever it was. Roberts stood up—freshly dressed in off-duty, standard-issue khaki fatigues—and walked over to the rookie, maintaining a reasonable distance. Sometimes the new soldiers would snap, and Roberts did not want a recruit to break his nose again just because he was being too friendly.

"Jenkins, you okay?" Roberts asked, wishing he was better at this. He would have used the rookie's first name, but he hadn't had the chance or desire to learn it. It was much easier to yell last names over gunfire, and there was no reason to break the habit outside the battlefield. Most soldiers would either be retired or traded away, eventually.

At first, Jenkins didn't answer him. Not verbally, at least. He looked away from his hands and slowly turned his head and gazed past Roberts, making him uncomfortable in his own skin. Jenkins breathed in and out deliberately, as if breathing was no longer involuntary.

"He died."

Roberts had no idea which *he* Jenkins was referring to. There were a dozen likely suspects—their fight against the Warthogs was quite the bloodbath—and Jenkins had been present for a few of those deaths. Shifting his weight to his other foot, Roberts contemplated his approach.

"Um... who's *he*?"

"Warner. He died right in front of me. He was yelling at me for something and... and..."

Roberts had witnessed that particular act of stupidity. Warner had been standing above cover and yelling at Jenkins when a soldier on the other team took a lucky shot that had promptly landed in Warner's temple.

Hopefully, the violent convict would learn from his lapse in judgment, but Roberts would make sure Warner did not take any more chances like that during the next games. That kind of behavior could end up getting Roberts killed, and death was usually something he tried to avoid.

"Hey, look..." Roberts awkwardly patted Jenkins on the shoulder with his delicate hands, which should have been rough and weathered after four years of combat. Though he briefly considered how many bodies he had used since his arrival on Eris, Roberts tried to console his new teammate.

"That wasn't your fault. Warner's an asshole a lot of the time. I've had my own fair share of stupid behavior... even before I landed myself on this rock. We all make mistakes we pay for," Roberts said before falling back into memories of another life. After banishing the past from his thoughts, he turned to see Jenkins had shifted on the bench.

"I know, I know. It's just the first time I've seen it up close. I've watched the games since I was a kid but it didn't seem so... real before." Jenkins offered an exasperated smile.

Now that he was finally talking, Roberts had to change his mind about the new Crow. Jenkins would be salty and experienced soon enough; it would just take him a little more time.

Roberts did nothing to hold back his sigh at the realization. Getting used to Eris wasn't exactly a good thing.

"Just wait until your first kill. That'll be something." Roberts' statement was warped by a grunt as he sat down on the bench beside Jenkins. The first death in the games was always a little traumatic; the first kill always depended on the person. But when Roberts looked at his new teammate, it was as if Jenkins had been startled awake.

"Actually, that really wasn't a problem. I got two or three guys today. Warner, though, I *knew* him. I've been *eating meals* with him for a month, now. Then he just went and died in front of me. I guess it's affecting me more because I knew the guy. The people on the other team could've been robots or aliens for all I care." Jenkins pinched the bridge of his nose as if he felt some sinus pressure, but it was a relic of a time before the Commission had made it so he would never need glasses again.

Robert could only stare at his new teammate; usually the new guys would take a few matches until they could hold their own. Roberts himself had not killed anybody until his third game, and *War World* had called him a prodigy at one point.

Kids these days, Roberts thought, *starting way too young.* The modern gladiator ran his hand along his scalp and then propped it up against his chin, trying to figure out how this rookie would adapt. Obviously more comfortable, Jenkins looked back at him and chuckled before letting out an anxious sigh.

"It's going to be so weird to see Warner tomorrow."

JENKINS SHUFFLED FORWARD in the line, staring at the unappetizing food displayed in front of him. He was dressed in the standard issue fatigues—a far cry from his battle gear—but for some reason he was still uncomfortable. The material didn't breathe right, the beige cloth was just a little too starchy, and it made his skin itch terribly. Jenkins thought it was the Commission—the organization responsible for the day-to-day operations for all the soldiers on Eris—trying to keep them on edge. Comfortable gladiators were not very entertaining.

Jenkins grabbed a processed chicken sandwich and placed it on his metallic tray with all the other food, a smattering of oily vegetables and easily-produced foodstuffs. The constant training for the gladiators really built up his appetite, but it seemed like he was the only one who seemed to crave more than a few bites of anything. Every other soldier on the Crows had a modest amount of food piled on their trays, enough for survival and little else. It forced Jenkins to wonder why he was the only one with an appetite.

After loading up his tray, Jenkins walked over to the few soldiers he recognized. There were about two dozen people sitting in the three rows of benches—mostly men—but Jenkins was still a rookie and only knew a handful of the people in the brightly-lit room. As he trudged to the second row of benches, Jenkins tried to ignore the buzz of the fluorescents above him that were seemingly designed to keep him on edge, and he eventually sat down next to Cortes and Feldman.

Cortes—a sorrowful man whose only trace of Spanish lineage was black hair and slightly darker skin—gave Jenkins a bit of a glare, but Feldman didn't look away from his tray. Feldman was a titan on the battlefield, but in the barracks he usually kept to himself. The giant soldier was more than two meters tall and had a humble crop of black hair, but after just five days without shaving, his beard had outgrown the rest of his scalp.

Jenkins knew better than to talk to either of them; he had not earned the right to speak to them as equals and neither one of the Crows were exceptionally friendly. Glancing around, Jenkins found Roberts sitting further down the dining table, just lifting his gaze after poking a piece of broccoli with a plastic fork.

After shrugging and giving Jenkins a half-hearted smile, Roberts lifted the overcooked vegetable to his mouth and munched on it without enthusiasm, doing his best to avoid eye contact. Jenkins knew the smile was just an awkward show of courtesy, but it was a comfort. To a degree, one of his teammates accepted him.

After a minute of silence, one of the Crows at the other end of the table snorted and almost choked on a piece of synthesized meat before looking over at Cortes in excitement. Jenkins had seen the red-haired Englishman a few times during his training, but had never learned his name. He had never had a chance to ask.

"What, Norris?" Cortes asked their smiling teammate, noticing the look but refusing to make eye contact with the red-haired soldier. Norris grinned even wider at the reaction and picked at his green beans, which were being stubborn and rolled around his tray.

"Nothin, mate. Just remembering that chainsaw fellow from the Vipers game," Norris said, finally able to spear a bean on the flimsy tines of his fork. Cortes had to search for the memory in his head, but eventually he looked back at Norris and twisted his face in discomfort.

"The one you shot through the knee?"

"Yeah, bastard never saw it coming. Fell on his chainsaw. Just thought it was funny and I wanted to relive the memory with you. He just couldn't get back off it, no matter how hard he tried," Norris mused with a smile before turning back to his tray. Giving up on the green beans and cutting into his synthesized protein, Norris used the edge of his fork instead of bothering with a knife that would likely break in his grip.

"You're hopeless, you know that?"

Cortes didn't expect a response, and it was just as well; he wouldn't get one. Norris went back to eating his mystery meat with a smile and Cortes went back to his rice with a sigh. Most of their meals were like that, just like all the other teams in all the other barracks. The only things these men had in common were their debts, their crimes and the experience of killing men and women for sport.

Jenkins was chewing on his bland sandwich when another soldier walked into the far-too-bright mess hall. Though he was oblivious for a moment, once the silence fell over his teammates, Jenkins glanced up to see Warner, his partner in the last game against the Warthogs. Warner stopped mid-step when a hush fell over his audience, but after a moment's hesitation he continued to the lunch counter.

In contrast to how he had looked yesterday, Warner was almost bald, gaunt and worn-out, as if he had substituted caffeine for sleep for too long. Although Warner usually sported thin, sandy-brown hair, after every resurrection each soldier had to start with nothing. They would still age in the stasis cell, but the fresh clones would emerge without foot-long nails or manes of hair. It was one of the first problems the Commission had needed to solve when the games were introduced.

Jenkins could see the anger hiding behind Warner's eyes, the perpetual scowl on his face, but there wasn't much he could do about it. Warner had killed men even before he had come to this rotten asteroid, and Jenkins did not want to provoke him. He just watched as Warner progressed along the line of sub-standard food, but by the end of it the convict had only filled up a quarter of the tray.

Resurrection had apparently killed the man's appetite.

Warner picked up his lunch and headed to the table closest to him, scowling at those who dared to look at him. Midway through his journey, Warner stumbled and almost emptied his tray onto the floor, only just keeping it from flying from his hands. Quickly, he recovered and jerked up to his full height before scanning the room for any person foolish enough to laugh. After scowling at his teammates, Warner shuffled forward and sat down at the far end of the table. Warner stared at the dull, bland organic material, and he did not seem to want any attention.

He was getting it, anyway. Masked in sidelong glances and the craning of necks, nearly everyone had their eye on Warner. Resurrection—while commonplace—was not something to be taken lightly, and the Crows needed *something* to occupy their thoughts.

Roberts, however, had his eye on their newest teammate. He could see a yearning; a dumb, foolish, *idiotic* desire to *make things right*.

Minutes passed at an unbearably slow pace. Roberts already knew what was going to happen and the delay was only making him anxious. He almost breathed a sigh of relief when Jenkins stood from the bench and started toward Warner's position, his breathing and steps light so he could minimize how much noise he was making. Though Roberts was about to speak up and talk Jenkins out of it, a deep voice rumbled and took the responsibility from him.

"You shouldn't."

No one recognized the voice at first, but they didn't hear it very often. Jenkins looked behind him to find Feldman looking at him under droopy eyelids, as though he was staring right into his soul. Jenkins sighed, his defiance born from obligation rather than the desire to do the right thing.

"I have to." Jenkins forced a smile for the giant staring him down. Feldman held his heavy gaze for only a few more seconds before looking back to his tray and picking up a stale biscuit covered in soy-based gravy.

Feldman had said his piece; he didn't presume to have any control over his teammate's actions.

And so Jenkins continued toward the newly-resurrected soldier trying to eat his meal in peace. A thousand thoughts and scenarios rushed through his mind, but Jenkins felt like he had to do something. He had to acknowledge that Warner might feel he was responsible for his death. The world slowed down as Jenkins approached the ruthless killer; time expanded and even Warner's lazy chewing seemed to take minutes. After an eternity, Jenkins reached the end of the table and stood close to Warner, whose plastic knife trembled in his hand.

"What do you want?" Warner asked, setting his knife and fork to the meal in front of him and avoiding eye contact with Jenkins. He viciously cut into his synthetic steak, which could have been cut easily by a spoon, and raised a piece to his mouth before slowly chewing the artificial beef. His eye twitched as pain raged at the muscles of his jaw.

"I'm just... I just wanted to say I'm sorry," Jenkins mumbled, shoving his thumbs inside the waistline of his slacks. He felt more awkward than he had ever been back on Earth.

"Sorry? Sorry for what?" Warner let out a harsh sniff as he cut his steak into smaller bites. He had still not made eye contact with Jenkins and that unnerved him.

"Because you... well, you didn't make it," Jenkins blurted out, finally realizing that every Crow was watching their interaction.

"Kid, sometimes we don't make it. If that's all you wanted to say you can go sit back down. I don't need to hear your apologies," Warner said dismissively before picking up an orange and starting to peel the rind away. Once he was finished, he faced Jenkins and popped a slice into his mouth, determined to act unaffected by his teammate's apology. Although Jenkins looked slightly taken aback by Warner's reaction, he soon regained his composure and nodded at his former partner.

"So... we're good, right?" Jenkins asked. The convict's eyes flashed with anger at the question and he stood up, knocking the table with his knees. He practically spit out the orange along with his fury.

"*Good*? No. No, we're *not* good. Because of you I *died*. *Again*," Warner said with an icy tone, shoving his index finger against Jenkins' chest. "I was finally starting to *earn* money and in a couple of games I might have been able to start making a profit and get off this fucking planet. But now, with all these resurrection costs, I'm in even *more* debt!

"*You* are the reason I'm in the red," he said, punctuating it with another tap of his index finger.

"I was able to pay those fucking bloodsuckers back, but now the dream's gone. I'm probably never going to have another chance. We're in prison, kid. Only the lucky buy their way out. And *you*?" Warner asked, a frustrated smile on his face as he backed away from Jenkins. "You've given me an awful case of bad luck. Get the fuck back in your seat."

Jenkins felt years' worth of repressed rage pouring out, poisoning the air they all breathed. Warner was angry at him, certainly, but even more than that, he was angry with his life. As he plowed through his tirade, telling everyone exactly what Jenkins had done to him, there was little movement from the other Crows. They fully expected Warner to find some reason to kill their newest teammate.

When Warner finished talking and focused on his tray, Jenkins almost breathed a sigh of relief, since it seemed like nothing more than angry words. The young soldier had almost made it through his penance unscathed, but in yet another poor decision in a long chain of poor decisions, Jenkins opened his mouth again.

"I'm sorry."

Warner whipped around and threw a right hook into his jaw. His form was off and he didn't follow through, but Warner had made his message known. Jenkins staggered from the initial hit and tried to regain his footing before Warner was able to follow up with a haymaker.

He didn't regain his footing.

Warner connected with the next blow and almost knocked him out, forcing Jenkins to fall to the ground as he reclaimed his senses. Only years of scrapping in the dens of New Chicago saved him from further punishment.

As Warner came down on him with his next assault, Jenkins threw up his forearms and blocked the blows before pushing the older man off with a powerful shove from his legs. After claiming some room, Jenkins threw himself up to his feet just in time to see Warner preparing to tackle him.

However, by that time, Feldman and Cortes had gotten out of their seats. Before Warner could connect with his tackle, there were three other Crows between them. The fight was effectively ended, but Warner's rage was hard to contain.

"You're a sack of shit and I swear to *God* if I ever get traded to another team I'm going to hunt your ass *down!*" Warner roared his threats and sounded unintelligible by the end of them; civility was clearly the last thing on his mind. The situation seemed almost irrecoverable until an authoritative baritone broke through the noise, causing each soldier to stop mid-action.

"Warner, back off. It's not his fault."

Warner craned his neck to see the speaker, and even within that short span of time he had calmed down noticeably.

"It *is* his fault! I was yelling at him to cover me before it happened! That *fucking* rookie has my blood on his hands!" he shouted, breathing heavily and pointing at Jenkins with a shaking index finger.

A man looking to be in his late fifties broke through the crowd of warriors and walked deliberately to the side of the Crows. Jonathon Carver was gruff, to say the least, and a fair amount of salt was mixed in with the pepper of his hair. His face was tired and the elasticity of his skin had long since given way, but the blue-eyed veteran still looked formidable. He walked right up to Warner, who no longer had to be restrained, and breathed out in a disappointed huff.

"Organize your support *before* you break cover. It's a simple idea. You can't blame the kid because someone took advantage of your incompetence. Sit down."

"But..." Warner almost seemed to whine, and Carver reduced his eyes to slits.

"Just sit down and stop embarrassing everyone here. The only reason this is a big deal is because you *made it* a big deal. Eat your goddamned food. It's gonna get more unappetizing by the minute," he said, his stoic face daring Warner to disagree.

The convict looked like he wanted to say something to Carver, but the words would not come. When Warner eventually turned to the rest of his teammates, shame flashed over his face and he let out a labored breath.

Pushing past the men in the crowd, Warner sat back down at his solitary place at the table. He was tempted to throw his tray on the ground as an act of rebellion, but eventually decided against it; it would accomplish nothing. Instead, he lowered his head and went back to eating his cold lunch.

After watching Warner for a moment to see if there was still a threat, Carver turned his gaze to the rest of the Crows and lifted an eyebrow.

"What? Is this a party? If you're done eating, head back to your rooms. All this standing around nonsense is just that." Carver looked around so he could stare down anybody who would object, but no one took him up on that offer. Within a few moments, the two dozen men and women shuffled back to their seats and became grazing cattle just like before.

The old soldier then turned to Jenkins and grunted after looking him over.

"Alright, kid. We're going for a walk."

JENKINS FOLLOWED three steps behind the older man, feeling like he was back in grade school and due for a scolding. It was an odd feeling to be this close to a legend. Carver had done so much in his time with the Crows that *War World* had even aired a retrospective of his career. Jenkins remembered watching a much more youthful Jonathon Carver on the giant televisions in New Chicago; all heroics and symbol for all that was man. The athlete had been larger than life, but as Jenkins took in his surroundings, he had to remind himself that he was just three steps behind that very same man. Carver's back wasn't as straight and his skin was weathered, but the old man was still intimidating.

Those blue eyes of his had not faded in the slightest.

They had walked out of the mess hall and down the dingy hallways toward the training yard—the empty center square the barracks had been built around—and then up into the battlements, which were little more than hip-high walls skirting the roof. From there they could see the charred and blasted landscape of Eris, their home covered in a perpetual haze of clouds and smoke.

Jenkins had not seen a truly sunny day since he had arrived at the barracks, and it was hard to think that only half of the planet was covered in that warzone, that there was a place outside the constant destruction and death. The other half of Eris was devoted to supporting the games, covered in satellite cities for the staff and agricultural communities to help feed them all.

As he looked out on his new home, Jenkins wondered if he would ever visit one of those fabled cities. Neither he nor Carver had said a word on their way up to the battlements, but after a few moments of gazing at the war-torn and pockmarked landscape, Carver turned his head slightly to face his new recruit. The veteran still looked toward the horizon, but it was clear he was watching Jenkins out of his periphery.

"You didn't owe him anything," Carver said in his gruff voice.

Looking back at his arms, which he had folded on top of the wall in front of him, Jenkins tried to resist the urge to pinch the bridge of his nose. Although he was unnerved by the distant din of gunfire and artillery—even after a month of training—Jenkins gathered his resolve and responded to his elder.

"He died, sir. I felt like I should say something," he said in a clipped tone, as if he was talking to a superior officer. Though they held no ranks in the Crows or any of the other teams on Eris, Jenkins felt like he owed Carver a certain level of respect.

"It's not the first time. Warner's died forty times now, or something like that. Comes with the territory." Carver watched the horizon in front of him, and a gust of wind brought in the smell of gunpowder to accent their conversation.

"But—"

"But nothing," Carver interrupted, turning to face Jenkins directly. "That kind of man has to save face. He has to be the top dog. *Thing is*, he just doesn't have it in him, so he has to have excuses. You were his excuse and then you walked right up to him and owned up to it."

"But—"

"Stop it," Carver interrupted again, brow furrowing as Jenkins struggled against his lesson. "It only encourages people like him, and he doesn't need any more of that crap. The only thing you should ever apologize for is friendly fire. Everything else doesn't really matter."

"Oh..." Jenkins muttered before looking back up to the piles of dirt, rock and broken roads spreading out around the barracks. The Trade Union had done a decent job with this false planet, and it made him wonder about the other seven false moons in Earth's orbit. It was hard for him to tell that he was on an asteroid that had been reconstructed into a serviceable colony for the ever-expanding human race. Anxious at the thought of being a day's space travel away from Earth, Jenkins looked over at his elder and could see no discomfort in Carver's expression.

He looked like he belonged.

"Sir, I have a question," Jenkins started, but the old man's eyes twitched at the title.

"Don't call me *sir*, rookie. That's the second time, and you're not gonna like what happens after the third."

"Um... okay. Just... I was going to ask why you're telling me all this," Jenkins said, forcing Carver to break his staring contest with the sky and look at his newest compatriot. His gaze softened when he looked directly at Jenkins.

"I know all that out there seems scary, so I just wanted to give you a tip or two. I have a bit of a soft spot for you new guys."

"Because we remind you of when you were young?" Jenkins

laughed as he spoke, but immediately regretted saying anything once the veteran's eyes flickered with annoyance.

"No, you *child*. I'm not that old." Carver resumed his gaze toward the endless hills of battlefields, seeming to sink into himself. "Shit, who am I kidding? I *am* that old. It's just ... nobody deserves this."

Jenkins thought it inappropriate to interrupt him, but his curiosity would not let him be.

"Sir—I mean, Carver..." he quickly corrected himself. Luckily, Carver's mind was still focused on something else. "How do you keep doing it? I mean, how have you been doing this for so long?"

The old Crow looked back at Jenkins, his unfocused eyes betraying a tortured view of the world. "I don't really have a choice, do I?"

ROBERTS RAN AS FAST as he could, his feet flying past jagged edges of steel and nets of barbed wire. Even with the assistance of power armor covering his entire body, which allowed the man to run faster for longer, his lungs burned from a mixture of exertion and smoke inhalation.

As long as he was moving, Roberts felt in control, but the empty nature of his surroundings definitely put him on edge. He could see wreckage and trash throughout the steel meadow obscuring the dirt and mud of Eris, but none of it would help him if he ran into an enemy soldier. None of that would allow him to hide from the ammunition they would fire his way.

Roberts breathed easier once he reached his teammate's position. Cortes was laying down suppressive fire on a nest of the opposing team, which was holding out in a ruined shack.

However, Cortes was not trying to hit anyone with his automatic weapon. He just spewed rounds into the derelict building in the hopes that Feldman, his partner, would be able to rush them with his plasma sword.

Resting for a moment to catch his breath, Roberts huddled close to a ruined steel support. With all of the desensitization he had experienced on Eris, Roberts wasn't particularly interested in watching the coming display of violence, but he was safe hunched over near the infantryman. He just watched as Feldman rushed up the ridge and rounded the corner of the building, cries of warning rising from their opponents inside. Though Roberts did not have the angle to see what happened in the shack, the flash of light and screams of pain were quite telling.

Soon after Feldman's initial strike, an unfortunate soul fell out the back door in a panic. Roberts trained his rifle on the frightened man—his crosshairs centered on his terrified face—but before he ever touched the trigger, another bright flash filled his scope. When Roberts brought down his rifle, he saw Feldman standing over the still-screaming soldier, his massive plasma sword moored in the ground where he had cut the man in half. It was a heavy thing—seventy kilos of machinery, batteries and shielding—and McCoy's not-so-inconspicuous fast food logo was plastered over the side. The familiar yellow crescent was half-covered in the blood of those poor soldiers.

Even after getting cut in half, their opponent was still trying to crawl away; shock had yet to set in and he was obviously in denial about his predicament. Feldman sighed, walked over to the man and brought his boot down on the soldier's head, settling his weight on his helmet and crushing it like a tin can.

It was testament to how heavy Feldman was in all that power armor when Roberts could hear the sickening crunch from thirty meters away. A gruesome death, certainly, but it was better than the alternative of bleeding out after the scarred tissue gave way. It was the least Feldman could do for the miserable creature.

Turning to Cortes, Roberts found the man scrounging around for a clip. He had apparently spent most of his ammunition on being a distraction.

"You guys staying here?" Roberts strained his voice as he tried to yell past the barrier of his helmet. He didn't feel like using the Comms system from so close.

Cortes shrugged and gestured to the giant walking toward them.

"Up to him. Might head east to meet up with Carver and Warner.

They were calling in for support earlier." While he spoke, he replaced the empty magazine in his weapon.

East was largely relative on Eris. There was no magnetic north on the asteroid construct; the instruments in their Heads-Up-Display just used the nomenclature as a stand-in. The Commission found that it made it easier to coordinate between the soldiers if they had something familiar on this gladiatorial battlefield.

Roberts looked to the "East" after Cortes' suggestion, but knew Carver would be just fine even though he had Warner in attendance. The newly-resurrected Crow was decent enough when he wasn't standing above cover like an idiot.

Jenkins was another story. The last thing Roberts had heard over Comms was that he and Abrams were running around looking for the enemy, and Abrams had a habit of doing whatever she needed to do to survive. She was hard-hearted and ruthless, but that wasn't necessarily a bad thing.

Roberts sighed before looking over Cortes and Feldman—who had just arrived—and nodded to the north.

"Think I'll go check on Jenkins and Abrams," he said wearily, grunting as he stood up and readied himself for another long-distance sprint. Roberts looked to the giant to find Feldman nodding in approval, his sword settled into the dirt by his side. When Roberts turned to his other teammate, Cortes shrugged and cocked his head to the side.

"Hey, weren't you paired with Goldstein today? Where is he?"

Roberts looked back the way he had come and pointed in the general direction of his drop point.

"Corpse is back that way. Couple of the Boars hit us with grenades about five minutes after we landed," Roberts said, laughing in dismay. "Goldstein didn't even try to jump out of the way. He just grabbed his crotch and told them to go fuck themselves."

"Well, what can you do?" Cortes asked before sniffing and looking at his grenade belt. The explosives were the leading cause of death in the games. Most soldiers armed grenades just before dying just to see if they could take anyone with them.

"Yeah, what can you do... Anyway, I took 'em out and then headed this way. Guess I'm a free agent today."

He might have said that, but Roberts looked toward Jenkins' beacon on the horizon and knew where he was going.

JENKINS HAD GONE into this day's battle with the impression that he had garnered enough experience, that the tension from pretend warfare would no longer affect him.

This was not the case.

After the two of them had landed in the drop zone, his partner sprinted away and left Jenkins to follow. Abrams was more experienced and *far* more aggressive than Jenkins would ever really be. She was one of only three women on the Crows, and she had to work harder to keep up the act for the people watching at home.

After five minutes of jogging, Abrams huddled behind a ridge and motioned for Jenkins to follow. Relying on his partner's experience, he hunched down and joined the soldier in front of him, oblivious to the why of it. Abrams had a revolver in her holster, but at that moment she was holding a razor-sharp knife in her left hand. When Jenkins reached her side, she put her right index finger to her lips.

Abrams wasn't especially happy that she was paired with the rookie. She hated babysitting, and this Jenkins didn't seem to be more than a child in power armor. When she saw that he understood her gesture, Abrams turned back and raised her head above the ridge. There were two enemy combatants right in front of her and Abrams had to hold in her disgusted sigh. These Boars were *strolling* through a war zone, and they did not belong on the battlefield with real soldiers.

Immediately, Abrams spun the situation in her mind and found that she appreciated her luck. These two kills would garner a hefty bonus for the match, and she would be that much closer to buying back her freedom. That was all that mattered. It would only be a dozen or so matches without dying and she could be on a space travel back to Earth.

Back to living without blood on her hands.

After the Boars passed by, Abrams crept over the ridge and soundlessly slinked over to the soldier on the left. She took care as she stepped in the gaps between the trash and the metal, her armored feet sinking softly into the dirt underneath. When she was within a meter of the men, an artillery shell blew up in the distance.

It would be her best chance.

Abrams planted her foot and then sprang at the man on the left, bringing her right hand up and grasping at the bottom edge of the Boar's helmet before jerking his head back. She didn't let the man say a word before she plunged her knife into his throat and pulled out. Blood sprayed from the new opening and covered the grey and black landscape with red, but Abrams did not pause in her work. She left the first soldier gurgling as the other Boar turned to meet her and brought up his automatic to ward off this new predator.

Abrams' face was empty of emotion as she kicked away the man's weapon with her right foot and fell into a rush attack. The momentum of the strike was enough for the man to turn and Abrams thrust her knife into the man's upper back, near the spine. The man went rigid with pain and Abrams felt a pang against her conscience, almost regretting the action. The last thing she wanted to do was cause more agony, so she twisted the knife and pulled it across his spine, cutting the nerve tissue like it was nothing.

After he fell to the ground, Abrams leaned down and brought the blade across his throat so death would come sooner. As he died, she had to remind herself why she had forged herself into this kind of warrior, why she had denied her former life of studies, books, dating and all the other things a woman in her twenties would normally do.

Only a dozen games without dying and Jessica could make it back home. When she looked down at the dead men beneath her, she thought about how these Boars were just the stepping stones that lined her path.

"That was impressive," Abrams heard from the ridge behind her, and she turned to see Jenkins holding his rifle and advancing. "They didn't even see it coming."

"That was the point. I'm not going to waste a bullet if I can cut their throats." For that remark, Abrams looked down at her prey and apologized without words before deciding to head northeast. She didn't want to speak to her partner; he was nothing. Jenkins was probably just a convict or another kid hoping to make money off the games.

It was another half hour before they ran into anything noteworthy. The war-torn landscape—filled with scattered sightings of rotting clones dead from other games—was somewhat disturbing, but the lack of combat was more unnerving to Jenkins.

In his mind, every ridge they passed hid a number of Boars ready and willing to take his life. His apprehension came to an end when Abrams was jogging along and then quickly fell to the ground, instantly changing the nature of their afternoon.

Jenkins was confused at first—he hadn't heard a sound—but as Abrams scrambled to the cover on her right, she frantically waved at him to get down, an order he was more than happy to obey. After slamming down on the ground, Jenkins crawled over to the veteran and waited for her to say something.

When he reached her position, she looked back and let out a heavy breath. He wondered what her expression was like underneath the mask; he wondered if she even looked nervous.

"There's two, twenty meters ahead of us. I think they might have seen me, but I haven't heard anything since. We... we might be able to sneak around them. Do you think you can keep yourself from fucking up?"

"I can try," Jenkins said without confidence.

Abrams sighed at her partner, but then readied herself for what was coming.

"It'll have to fucking do," she said before bringing out her revolver. The riflemen would make short work of her if she brought a knife to their showdown.

When she sprang out of cover, she instantly cursed herself but stepped forward anyway. The riflemen were still standing off to the left, but there were two other Boars to her right that she had not seen.

All four noticed her sudden appearance.

Abrams knew that staying in this position would yield her death even if she ducked behind cover again, since they probably had more than enough grenades. She jumped and ran forward into the shooting gallery, using the kinetic motivators in her armor to enhance her speed as much as they could. Her only hope was to reach the dugout twenty meters ahead of her and launch some sort of counterattack.

Abrams was running at full speed when she realized she had left Jenkins behind without so much as a word. That meant he was going to die, in all likelihood. Bullets hit the ground around her and she could feel them heating the air as they streaked in front and behind her. Though she had no hope for a response, Abrams thumbed the button for Comms and prayed she would make it to the dugout in front of her.

"This is Abrams and Jenkins and it's a shitshow. We're up against four and would appreciate the assist," she yelled as she ran, sending a poorly-aimed bullet at the pair of soldiers on her right and trying to force them behind cover. The dugout was only two meters away, now, and she didn't think the Boars would allow her much longer to appreciate her life.

When Abrams dove at the pit in the landscape, she wondered if she would die airborne.

Abrams hit the ground hard and rolled into the ditch. It hurt, but at least she knew there weren't any bullets lodged in her body. She was thinking about what she was going to do—all alone and surrounded by four soldiers—when she heard a second impact behind her. Jenkins had somehow made it to the position with her and rolled down to the bottom of the dugout, momentarily relieving Abrams of her fear of grenades. Still, it changed nothing.

The two of them would die here surrounded by false earth.

"So, what now?" Jenkins asked after a tense few seconds.

Abrams looked at him and he could almost feel her disdain for him, which was made more apparent when a fragmentation grenade landed in their dugout and she just grabbed it and lobbed it back over her shoulder.

"Well, we call for back-up, unless you have any better ideas…"

Jenkins craned his neck and imagined what was happening beyond their cover. The shattered wasteland was wreaking havoc on his radar, which he could see on his helmet's display.

"Well—"

"That was *rhetorical*, you cock-knobbler," Abrams interjected, shifting in her mechanical armor. The standard issue allowed for greater strength and mobility, but it was uncomfortable and never fit quite right. At first, Abrams had thought the Commission was just not prepared for a female athlete, but then she looked at the team rosters and found there was a sizable female population on Eris. Then she asked the other Crows and found that *none* of their armor fit perfectly.

Apparently, that was not a priority for McCoy's or the Commission, the organization that dictated every moment of their lives and futures.

In any case, the heat was stifling under her helmet and Abrams just wanted it to be an hour from now. She wanted the match over and to be safe in the barracks. She wanted to talk to her sister, especially since her first effort that morning had been rewarded with atmospheric interference.

Most of all, she really wanted the new kid to stop bugging her while she was trying to think. Abrams opened the team channel and pinged their location, mentally crossing her fingers in case any Crow was listening to them.

"This is Abrams. Jenkins and I made it to cover but we're under fire from both flanks and need assistance. Broadcast when en route," she said with a resigned tone, leaving the channel open while bullets flew past their cover. Dirt and rocks fell down the ridge as countless shells sank into the false earth above them, but luckily, no grenades followed after. The Crows waited like that for a minute, but there was no broadcast from their teammates.

Abrams looked back at her partner and found him looking expectantly back at her. After noticing the attention, she realized that she couldn't blame him for that, especially since she had just barked at him for speaking.

Pursing her lips, Abrams came to the conclusion that they were the only two people that would be helping them out of this situation, so she started to think about their options. Every scenario had a grisly and inevitable conclusion, but Abrams turned her head up at the rookie and steeled her nerve, knowing she would not let the men above them decide her fate.

"Okay, kid. It's not going to be long before those bastards realize they can just cook the grenades and I won't be able to throw it back. We have to get out of here. What we're going to do is we're going to rush over this mound and shoot *every* motherfucker we see. Try to focus in that direction, though," she said, nodding to her right. "We're gonna try to use their cover against those other assholes. You might die, I might die, but it's the best we can hope for."

She waited for him to object, but he breathed in deep and looked at her, pretending at eye contact.

"Well, we all have to die eventually. Might as well get the first one out of the way," Jenkins said as he checked his rifle and looked at the crimson crow emblazoned on his upper arm, rubbing his thumb along the design. It seemed like he was already saying goodbye to this body, which was shocking. Just from that little detail, Abrams decided she actually liked the kid, but it was far too early to let him know it.

"Alright, on my mark," Abrams said before grabbing the last grenade from her belt. It was a chaff grenade, since outright killing their opponents was less important. Even if she had a fragmentation grenade, she would have wanted to use this one in order to scramble their sensors, just enough to give them a chance. She pulled the pin and started cooking the grenade, but before she threw it, she sent one last message over the private line.

"Sorry 'bout the cock-knobbler, kid."

ROBERTS GOT THERE way too late. He had heard Abrams' message over Comms and had broken out into a full-out sprint toward their beacons, and he must have been going over thirty kilometers an hour. Even with that sprinting prowess, Roberts was still a hundred meters from the dugout when he saw the chaff grenade float up into the air and sail toward two of the Boars. Abrams had timed it perfectly and it burst into light a few feet from the ground.

The Boars didn't take kindly to having to deal with the static on their visor outputs and opened fire haphazardly in the general direction of their opponents. Fortunately for Jenkins and Abrams, the erratic gunfire forced the soldiers on the other side to take cover.

Abrams took care of one source of gunfire fairly quick, taking aim with her revolver and sending a bullet into the man's ribcage. The hand cannon was more than enough to power through the plates of armor covering the man's vital areas and burst through his torso and out his back with a trail of blood. He screamed in pain and fell to the ground.

One soldier still remained on that side, however, and the chaff grenade's effects were not going to last forever. Jenkins tried to take up as little room as possible as he lined up his shot. Once he brought the rifle up to his shoulder, he framed the soldier inside the crosshairs and took just enough time to breathe and calm his nerves. Then Jenkins gripped the handle and pulled the trigger.

The bullet flew at the Boar just as the static cleared from his visuals, and the poor soldier only had enough time to see the Crow's muzzle flare before feeling an enormous amount of pain on the left side of his neck. He went to touch the source of the pain as warm blood flowed out of the wound and was confused when his senses started to go numb, his fingers unable to find where he had been struck.

As he fell, the gladiator had enough time to wonder if he was fainting.

While it was certainly a good thing for the Crows that they had swiftly removed two opponents from the field, the absence of friendly fire was enough for the other Boars to pop up from cover. Roberts only had enough time to yell over Comms before they started firing at his teammates.

"Your six!"

Abrams was able to wheel around before the first bullet hit her. She had learned long ago to trust anything over Comms and didn't even think about her actions. The impact of the bullet staggered the woman, but from the dull ache in her chest, Abrams guessed the rounds had not pierced through the combat armor.

It was a lucky thing, but she was by no means safe. She fired a quick burst as she rolled to the ground and then flattened her body. If nothing else, it would make her a smaller target.

Meanwhile, Jenkins rushed behind a cement wall that was somehow still intact, and once he finally reached relative safety, he breathed in quick and jagged bursts. He needed just a couple seconds to gather himself for these new opponents.

He had half a second. One of the Boars pelted his cover with a hailstorm of bullets, content with keeping Jenkins there and out of the fight while his friend took care of Abrams. The arrogant Boar had faith his teammate would finish off Abrams in no time.

Neither of them had noticed Roberts flanking them. He was still two meters away when one of the Boars stopped to reload, momentarily halting his assault on the grounded Crows. The man who had been firing at Abrams bent down to grab the clip at his ankle and twitched when he heard heavy footsteps approaching. Turning his head just in time to see a boot connecting with his helmet, the Boar was caught completely unaware, and he didn't even hit the ground before Roberts sent a pistol round into his temple.

The other Boar spun to greet Roberts and was about to open fire when he was knocked off balance by a couple of rounds from Abrams' revolver, which had only been glancing blows. Though they did not pierce the Boar's armor, it gave Roberts more than enough time to sink three bullets into the man's ribcage, causing him to sink to his knees and crumple into a heaving pile of flesh and armor. Roberts thought about granting him a soldier's mercy, but decided against it; he might need the bullet. Instead, he just stepped on the man's carotid artery and watched as he stopped breathing.

Roberts grabbed the man's automatic—abandoning the corpse— and walked over to Abrams, who was busy inspecting her armor for bullet holes. After seeing the four pockmarks on her chest plate, she sighed and looked back at Roberts.

"Well, thanks, I guess. Doesn't hurt to have you around," she said apathetically, determined to stay aloof. No one needed to know the insecurities she harbored.

Glad that Roberts had showed up, Jenkins picked himself up from behind his pile of rubble and started to approach his veteran team-mates. Jenkins finally felt at ease, now that the bullets had stopped flying, but then there was a click behind him and a muffled percussive sound. Then a pinch and an explosion of pain in his torso.

Jenkins staggered a bit and then looked down at his chest plate, which was starting to blur. He didn't see anything, but that burning in his torso was certainly real.

Then it started to fade. Then everything started to fade. He heard Abrams shout something as Roberts unloaded his magazine into the space behind Jenkins, which he did not entirely understand. Then he remembered the soldier they had abandoned at the beginning of the firefight; they had assumed Abrams' revolver had ended his life.

Jenkins fell to his knees as his compatriots charged toward him, their guns still drawn in case there was further threat. Darkness rapidly filled his field of vision, and he could barely make out Roberts' small body kneeling down to catch him. Before the darkness completely overtook him, Jenkins thought he heard Roberts saying "sorry."

Then he was gone.

Even though he had already been avenged, Jenkins' body hung limp in Roberts' arms. He had meant to give the rookie some words of consolation before the life left him, but that explosive round had ruined any chance of goodbyes; Jenkins' insides more closely resembled jelly than human organs.

Dropping the corpse, Roberts hauled himself to his feet so he could look at the fresh cadaver. After a moment of scrutiny, however, he thought better of his actions and knelt back down to give their team-mate some dignity.

Taking little time, Roberts laid out the body and folded Jenkins' hands over his midsection; he couldn't just leave it sprawled out like that. Then—after picking himself back up—Roberts looked again at the corpse lying in the grey dirt. He wondered if such respect for the dead really meant anything.

Roberts looked over at the Boar who had forced him into that awkward situation and saw how the man's helmet had been completely dismantled by Roberts' vengeance. It only took one look for him to realize that he had gone overboard trying to save an already-dying soldier. This Boar, whoever he was, did not deserve Roberts' animosity.

Dying was a lonely journey, and this man had just been trying to take someone with him.

Roberts was just about to speak with Abrams and make a point out of it all when a flashing announcement came over his visor feed. A lovely artificial woman's voice accompanied the message scrolling across the bottom of the display.

"Round over. The Crows win. Repeat, the Crows win. Make your way to your respective rendezvous points and return to your base. Repeat, the Round is over. The Crows win..."

Abrams scoffed at the situation before turning to face her teammate, waving at the dead body they had been guiding through this modern Purgatory.

"Poor fucker almost made it."

2

Life After Death

Jessica Abrams sat down into the plastic embrace of her desk chair and looked at the photos on her desk, the fatigue from battle flowing out of her as she stared at the pictures. They were the only things that she had chosen to decorate her bland grey room, and Jessica tried to remember how she had convinced herself on Earth that she didn't need to take any mementos with her.

Luckily, she had been able to download pictures of her family from the computer terminal in the library. They were black and white—the Commission was too stingy to pay for color ink—but they were still a comfort. Jessica grabbed the family photo tacked onto a piece of cardboard and traced her fingernail along the face of her mother. It was the last picture they had taken together, twelve years ago in St. Louis, and it hurt Jessica to know that.

Sniffing back a tear, Jessica set the photo back onto her desk and grabbed one of the others, this one showing an older version of her father and a sister who was no longer a child. Rebecca had grown up so much in those twelve years, and even though she looked weak and spindly hooked up to that oxygen tank, Jessica could now hope that the young woman would bounce back. According to the doctors, it would only be a few more months until Rebecca would be able to walk.

Although she was crying freely at this point, Jessica smiled as she set the picture back onto her desk. Her throat hurt when she realized she would not be there for that echo of Rebecca's first steps, but at least the poor girl would have them. Jessica opened the drawer of her plastic desk and drew out the small communicator Goldstein had given her so many months ago. It was a small thing—barely more than a keypad, small display and an earpiece—but it was Jessica's singular treasure.

With this, she could hear her sister's voice.

Praying that the atmosphere would not interfere, Jessica pressed a few buttons on the menu and waited for a signal. As she did, Jessica looked at her arm and saw a rash had developed from wearing her ill-fitting armor. It had only been twenty minutes since the transport had landed back at the Crows' barracks, and only ten since she had been able to remove the military shell.

Recalling the experience, the pain in her chest came back in force. The impact of the four shells had not killed her, but they were certainly not pleasant. At least she was still alive, unlike her partner. Before she could feel bad about Jenkins dying, a familiar voice stole her attention.

"Hey!" a soft voice came from the earpiece, and Jessica's mind immediately discarded thoughts of the battlefield.

"He—"

"This is the Abrams' residence. Sorry we're not here!" Rebecca's cheerful voice continued, causing Jessica to feel like an idiot. The message had been recorded five years ago—before Rebecca had gotten sick—and even though their father had wanted to change it due to grief, Jessica had forced him to keep it. She had told him that Rebecca needed hope that she could return to being a normal girl.

Now, as she heard it for the umpteenth time, Jessica realized that she needed it more than her sister. She listened to it as tears streamed down her face.

"We're probably out having crazy adventures. Or, well, more likely we're all working like dogs, but you know how it is! Go ahead and leave a message, and one of us will get around to hearing it. *Maybe.* If you're *lucky.* We *are* busy, you know. Haha! Just wait for the beep!" she exclaimed, giggling at the end. Jessica let the tears run down her cheeks, tasting the ones that happened to fall into the corners of her mouth.

Jessica had missed her window while they waited for her call earlier in the day, and so the best she could do was leave a message. When she heard the beep, Jessica almost couldn't react, but she soon cleared her throat and tried not to sound sad.

"Hey, guys. It's me. I... umm, I'm sorry I didn't talk to you earlier. You know how the atmosphere fu—screws with everything on here. I..." she said, pausing as she tried not to include the terrible parts of her life. Rebecca did not need to hear any of *that.*

"We won the game today. I know that's not that much of a surprise, considering that *I'm* there to save everyone," she bragged, laughing weakly.

"It shouldn't be much longer until I see your faces, guys. Becca, I hope the PT's going well, even though I know it is. I'm so..." She halted, wishing she could say these words in person. "I'm so proud of you, kiddo. We'll play soccer or something when I get back, alright? Dad... Just you wait. When I come back, I'll help you out with the bills.

"Alright, guys, I'm not so good with the one-sided conversation. I'll try to catch up in a couple days. Be good," Jessica said, burying her head in her free hand. "I love you both...*so* much. Have a... nice week."

She was just barely able to stop herself from sniffing before hitting the cancel button on the communicator.

Once the line was cut, Jessica set the communicator on her desk and let the tears fall freely, crossing her arms in front of her and holding her sides while she rocked back and forth in her chair, wracked with silent sobs.

Just a dozen or so games without dying and it could be over.

RYAN JENKINS DIDN'T SEE any light. Everyone had lied to him all along. All those people with near-death experiences must have been seeing something else, because Ryan knew he was dead and there was only darkness.

On the other hand, he *heard* quite a bit. He did not feel his ears anymore, so *hearing* might not have been the right word, but he sensed something. He could feel whirring and clicking and ambient noises he could not quite pick out. The ambient noise reminded him of machines and gears, but that was based on what he had seen in movies and shows.

He had never been too keen on technology and advanced toys; that was the realm of the tech geeks and the cyber witches of the digital world. He had lived his days on the streets of New Chicago, and there was little tech to be found in the gutter.

Ryan had run in a gang just like everyone else in his position. Nobody could even find jobs anymore, so most people resorted to crime, and Ryan couldn't even afford to spend time on technology or entertainment. At the very most, he would watch the games every once in a while, to satisfy some bloodlust and watch commercials for things he could never really have.

The TV spots about the resort planets were the best. Just a quick day of space travel and he would be able to experience something other than dirt, rampant pollution and garbage covering his everyday world. Ryan had dreamt that he could smuggle himself aboard one of those space cruisers and find some job on Solaria or Elysia. Living the life of a pool boy seemed like paradise.

He chuckled to himself, or at least thought he did. How appropriate that he ended up off-planet at the one place worse than the overpopulated, desiccated husk of Earth. Twenty-four years of selfishness had landed him on a moon devoted to war, and now it seemed like he had found himself in Limbo.

Ryan had always assumed consciousness ended after death. He had thought that it wouldn't matter if he died a thousand times and kept getting resurrected. There wouldn't be any real consequences. He would just keep fighting.

How horrible to think that he might be like this forever; that every one of his clones would end up just like this. He had doomed his soul to purgatory just to be on television. Whining in the darkness, Ryan cursed himself and just wanted it to end. He had not meant it. He would rather go back and choose twenty years in the slave yards on Demeter instead of brief bouts of warfare punctuated by an eternity of ellipses.

Although he bemoaned his fate, he soon felt himself moving. No longer was he trapped in a tomb of sensory deprivation. He felt things happening to his body; he *existed*. This couldn't be purgatory, the whirring and clicking he heard had to be from *something*. He just needed to focus on it, focus on that instead of the panic still flooding his brain.

That was when he saw the light. It hit him that they might have been right after all. Maybe it just took his soul a little time to get used to being dead. Maybe eternity was just starting.

The light grew. It expanded and became brighter. It was almost pink, rather than the white he expected. As Ryan approached it, he realized that the slight pink hue was from his eyelids. He was not some disembodied consciousness; he just had his eyes closed.

Ryan opened them—slowly, at first—but soon enough he could see. He could actually *see*. Something was touching his eyes and it stung, but he didn't care. He was alive, or something like it, and he was about to find out what was going on. Ryan couldn't move his head, but he was not afraid anymore.

All of a sudden, the light was too much for him to handle. He had a splitting headache and his eyes burned. The light came faster now and within moments he was completely enveloped, and he could not help but wince and shut his eyes to keep the light from overwhelming him.

He felt himself jerk to a stop and then felt his legs swaying through whatever surrounded him. Although he was still very much numb, Ryan's sense of weight reminded him that his legs still existed. He was about to open his eyes and allow some light in when he felt something start rushing down alongside his body. Before he could react, his head was exposed to cool air and Ryan finally realized he was surrounded by liquid, and he felt it drain away from his body.

Ryan felt awkward and cold afterward and forced his eyes to open.

Things were blurry at first, but he could notice figures moving about in front of him. He did his best to blink away the rest of the water—which felt thicker than it should be—and tried to bring his hands up to wipe away the rest, but they were too weak to move.

He suddenly realized what was happening. Ryan had been too busy fighting his disorientation to realize it, but he had a solid grasp on what was happening now. He hadn't died, at all; at least, not really. His consciousness had been transferred to the organic hard drive of his current brain. All his memories, behaviors and quirks had been digitally moved to a clone. Ryan had a new body now, and he was waking up in a clone of himself.

It made him nauseated to think about it. He *had* stopped existing, even if it was for just a moment.

THE BIOTIC FLUID encasing the soldier inside the cell had emptied out, causing Dr. Hawkins to push himself off his desk chair and walk to the resurrection chamber and the cell containing the toy soldier.

Hawkins thought he was clever when he called them toys, action figures or dolls, especially since the cells reminded him of the packaging companies used to wrap up their collectible figurines. They were his direct foil, as the men inside these particular cells were in better shape than the doctor would ever be. Peter Hawkins had quite the paunch, his light-brown hair was already receding, his eyes were framed behind thin glasses and he had a permanent crease along his forehead.

However, he did not give one thought to his unpleasant appearance. The middle-aged scientist cared more about his brilliant mind than anything in his life, and *that* was as sharp as ever. He sighed and hit a few buttons on the computer display, which was a touch-screen interface woefully behind the times; other doctors in other clinics probably had holographic displays by now. It was just one of the few things Hawkins resented as he whiled away his time taking care of the Crows.

The loading arm holding the new soldier lowered the resurrection cell into the proper position and then retreated into the darkness of the storage bay. It was only a few seconds before the front half of the vessel popped open with a hiss and rose to the open position.

The naked soldier—whose name escaped Hawkins at the moment —was lying against the back of the cell, covered in electrodes and wires and ready for his attention. For formality's sake, Hawkins looked at the display again and read the action figure's name.

"Jenkins, Jenkins..." Hawkins murmured to himself. There were studies that showed soldiers had less chance of a resurrection episode if they were coaxed back into the world with their name, and the Commission had asked him to try, at the very least.

What foolish, little creatures, Hawkins thought. The scientist did not much care for the men and women under his care.

Peter Hawkins only had to work eleven more years in this hellhole and he could retire to Elysia. Then he could find some gold digger with enormous breasts and contribute to the overpopulation problem. That fantasy—as well as his experiments—was one of the very few things that motivated him, though his experiments were far more important.

There was just something about playing God that appealed to him.

His assistant shuffled through the door behind him, the door hissing closed behind her. She was a troublesome thing and was often clumsy with her bookkeeping, but Dr. Charlotte Kane had that pesky bedside manner absent in a man like Hawkins. The woman had only been in Hawkins' clinic for a couple of weeks, but things were already looking better for the scientist.

Tolerating the woman allowed him more funding for his work, so it was a necessary annoyance, but it didn't hurt that she was reasonably attractive. Her shoulder-length black hair framed a pleasant round face, which was a welcome sight during Hawkins' solitude. Her eyes were a rich coffee brown and gave off an air of kindness, especially when she smiled.

Although Hawkins would never admit to her that he enjoyed the view, as it were, sometimes his thoughts did wander in the middle of the night, as he played with the pain thresholds of his human guinea pigs.

"How are you today, Hawkins?" Charlotte asked, picking up her lab coat and throwing her arms through the sleeves.

Hawkins' appreciation for aesthetics fell away as reality broke back into the scientist's mind; the good doctor had a habit of asking questions for which he had no use. Instead of answering those useless questions, Hawkins grunted and checked the readings for his newest patient. The subject's brainwaves and vitals were off standard specs and that annoyed Hawkins, and that allowed him to avoid actual conversation with his assistant.

Meanwhile, Charlotte moved to the box of gloves and sighed.

"Okay, then. What's this man's name?" she asked, stretching the latex over her fingers.

"Jenkins," he responded, watching the aberrant readings on his display.

"And his *first* name?"

"What does that matter?"

"Peter, the man just died. I would say it's pretty important," Charlotte scolded him, setting her uncovered hand on her hip and looking at him in disapproval.

"Ugh, fine, it's Ryan, I think," he conceded, turning back to his display and hoping the woman would abandon her questions. Charlotte sighed again and walked over to the terminal to check the patient's name, putting the other glove on her hand as she did so.

"Let's check here, yes, Ryan Jenkins," she said with a slight smile and a nod of her head. Hawkins looked over at his assistant with a scowl.

"I *said* so, didn't I?" he said, rolling his eyes and wondering why the readings on his display didn't go along with his freshly-resurrected action figure. As he did, Charlotte walked over to their newest patient.

"You said *you think*. I'm not traumatizing a patient because you had a hunch. And furthermore, *ah*—" Charlotte squeaked.

She might have been in the middle of a rant, but the soldier's wide-open eyes had startled her. They were filled with fear or shock or a number of other reactions and emotions.

More importantly, they were not supposed to be open *at all*.

"Hawkins! Why are his eyes open?"

This grabbed Hawkins' interest, and he looked at the young man in the resurrection cell. Hawkins had been so caught up in the routine and the subsequent distractions from his assistant that he had not bothered to actually look at the soldier, who was clearly conscious.

The readings were no longer mysterious.

"Huh, that's odd," Hawkins said before initializing the revival procedure with added sedatives. He was supposed to have started the process long before the man had woken up.

"*Odd*? That man is *terrified*! We need to get those wires and machines off him! Fix it!" Charlotte urged before trying to soothe the man reclined in his resurrection chamber.

Hawkins scowled at her for getting caught up in the moment.

"What do you think I'm doing? It takes a bit for the process to start up," Hawkins said as the equipment and syringes moved into place, followed by the machine unlocking the restraints holding the man in place.

"How was he even awake? They're not supposed to reach consciousness for an *hour* after leaving the vault." Charlotte implied the accusation, relying on what Hawkins could only assume were her emotions.

"Shush. It happens sometimes. The clone memory retrieval isn't a perfect process, yet. Probably won't *ever* be perfect. Besides, you've seen this before. There," he said after hitting a button on the interface and watching the needles puncture Jenkins' flesh. "As soon as the drugs kick in, I'll take out the rebreather. Then you can console him like the sick puppy you want him to be."

Hawkins could feel her fuming from a meter away, and he would readily admit to loving this display of power.

"You bastard. It's not the same. We could have another headcase on our hands because of this. Do you understand that?" Charlotte asked, her hands on the poor man's arm.

Hawkins walked over to Jenkins, who was now fully under the effect of the tranquilizers and could barely lift his head from the resurrection cell. The scientist then proceeded to pull out the breathing tube from the newborn man's mouth with an indelicate touch.

"Maybe you don't understand..." Hawkins said while turning to her with a smirk.

"That's *his* problem."

RYAN DID NOT like being in restraints while the two doctors were fighting. That Hawkins was clearly an ass and Ryan didn't really want him to be in charge of anything, much less his recovery. He certainly felt on edge when the automated needles lanced into his skin and filled him with drugs, disorienting him as they worked through his system. Ryan felt out of control, powerless.

Afraid.

When Hawkins pulled out the breathing tube, Ryan choked and coughed, feeling the plastic tube tear away at the lining of his throat. A good amount of synthetic amniotic fluid came with it and his throat hurt like hell.

It was the first time he was really breathing with this body and he did not like the feeling. He felt blessed that he didn't remember the first time he was born, but then cursed once he realized that this was the first of many more experiences just like it.

Ryan breathed in sharp and hyperventilated, anxious as to what would come next. Though it took some effort, he could move his neck and was thankful for it. From what he could see, it almost looked like he was in a regular clinic room. The only special pieces of equipment were the machines responsible for his resurrection.

Otherwise, it felt like it was a good room to come to if he had a bad cough.

He noticed the raven-haired woman walk up to him with compassion in her eyes. Although Ryan was still nervous and scared, her soft gaze seemed to help. She seemed to care, even if the other one did not have any empathy to speak of.

"Ryan, I am *so* sorry about this. Normally this is supposed to be a better experience. Unfortunately, you suffered a premature Consciousness Retrieval. My name is Dr. Charlotte Kane. Do you know where you are?" she asked, clearly concerned. Ryan coughed again and tried to breathe normally—much more difficult than it should have been—but eventually he looked at the doctor and tried to speak. A weak rasp is all that came out, but she nodded at his efforts.

"Hmm, sometimes that happens. But if you keep trying, it will work. Your vocal cords aren't used to moving yet. Do you know where you are?" Charlotte's hand settled on his wrist.

Though he normally did not appreciate that kind of familiar touch, Ryan realized he craved some sort of affection in the moment. He looked at her again and decided that he was *going* to speak. Steeling his nerves, Ryan forced his throat to cooperate.

"Clin—ic. I... died. I'm... ba—ck." Ryan felt tired, but he was proud that something came out, at the very least.

"*Good.* That's right. You should count yourself lucky. Something went wrong with the personality transfer and your brain was primed before it was ready. Basically, what makes you *you* was adopted too early," Charlotte explained, trying to use language a normal person would understand.

"Again, I'm sorry about that, but if it makes you feel any better, many patients in similar situations encounter incomplete transfers or mental dissolution. That you retained some small measure of yourself is... kind of a miracle," she said, a warm smile playing through her pleasant features. While he wanted to smile along with her, Ryan's thoughts returned to his consciousness retrieval.

He did not quite understand his predicament, but he certainly did not feel *lucky*.

"Thought... pur—gatory. I... *lucky*?" he asked, trying to punctuate the question with a laugh, but it hurt too much for him to succeed. After hearing his attempt, Charlotte tried to suppress her criticism for his antiquated ideas.

"Well, it shouldn't have happened and I'm sorry. If it's any consolation, it wasn't *purgatory*." Charlotte offered a weak laugh, feeling silly just for saying the word, even if she was trying to lighten the mood. "We're going to move you into the training room. Are you ready?"

Ryan looked at her like she was an idiot, and she almost felt like she was.

"Want... sleep. I want... to sleep. The last hour... or so... was pretty rough," he said, determined to speak without stopping. Charlotte looked at her patient and sighed; her conscience was heavy, but she was on a timeline.

She had to get him back to the Crows' barracks within the day.

"I know, Ryan, but we have to get that body moving. It's been sleeping too long already," she argued, handing the young soldier a pair of briefs.

However, it did not take her long to realize Ryan was still suffering from disorientation. Charlotte helped him place his legs in each hole and brought up the garment to his waist. Feeling slightly more comfortable now that he was clothed—even barely—the good doctor helped Ryan to his feet and they started toward the training room.

It was a slow process. His steps were labored and he was not used to his new legs, which were more than just uncooperative. Charlotte kept out her hand for whenever he lost his balance, but as they made their way to the training room, his steps became more sure, his stride more confident. Soon enough, Charlotte didn't even have to keep out her hand for support, but she looked ahead and dreaded what was to come in the training room. She was still so new to this place and the terrible acts that she had to perform for the job.

Ryan looked at the doctor lost in her thoughts, but then became distracted by his own. As he regained his ability to walk, Ryan examined the room to his right. He could tell from personal experience that the machines humming on the other side of the doorway were massive computers. His crew had stolen ones just like them and made quite the profit, though he had never known how to use them.

This close to them, now, Ryan wondered what kind of data they held. He assumed that along with maintaining the clinic and the clones held in storage underneath the facility, the computers held something much more important. Jenkins assumed that they held his life, his memory and personality in those lines of code.

He was right.

In order to maintain the soldiers' memories and personalities after death, each soldier was tagged with a sub-dermal microchip that constantly uploaded to satellites in orbit around Eris. The machines would then transfer the data to the computers and, upon death, would immediately transfer the data to the new clones.

It was efficient, but it relied on the satellites maintaining a constant connection. A few years prior to Ryan's arrival, one of the satellites devoted to the Mastiffs was destroyed by space trash. After half the team was killed in a battle, they were unable to transfer their memories and the Commission had to rely on old data to revive them. Half the resurrected soldiers suffered mental dissolution and had to be retired.

It was a bad year for the Mastiffs.

Ryan remembered hearing about the tragedy; it was one of the few horrible truths War World Entertainment had not been able to keep from the public eye. In any case, Ryan hoped that he would not suffer something similar in his time on Eris. His premature adoption worried him and he did not want to experience it again, but the newborn Crow looked ahead and realized he was almost in the training room.

He wondered what he would have to do once inside.

RYAN'S LEGS felt like they were on fire. All he wanted to do was lay down, but he kept being subjected to brutal calisthenics. Charlotte was standing behind a one-way mirror while he ran on the treadmill, keeping track of his progress. Although he felt as if he had already run a marathon, the display on the treadmill told him he had only run a few kilometers.

His lungs disagreed. It felt as if some witch doctor was squeezing his chest with the malice of an inexperienced child.

On the other side of the glass, Charlotte monitored the readings from the miscellaneous medical equipment in the observation room. Ryan was effectively in a suit of machines promoting muscle growth and stamina while he ran on just one of the treadmills that filled the training room. The complex was equipped to accommodate three quarters of the team at any time, which was more than enough. It was only on very rare occasions that the team would be butchered past that degree.

Though she disliked the process, Charlotte watched as Ryan continued to run on the machine. The running was more to provide blood flow to all affected areas rather than for any actual exercise, and within a couple of hours he would be sent back to the Crows in an acceptable condition for battle.

Charlotte did not envy the poor man. The next few days would be filled with almost intolerable pain from the conditioning and he would still be expected to play in the next game, where there was every chance in the world the process would begin all over again. So many soldiers were stuck in an endless cycle of painful death and rebirth, having no chance to ever exist in a world without agony.

It was no wonder there was a steady flow of black-market painkillers to the athletes of Eris.

Charlotte hated the games and what they did to these men. The aspiration of making it big and walking away with a fortune was a cruel joke; a carrot hanging from an impossibly long stick. Even the criminal offenders were undeserving of this constant cycle, and Charlotte wished she could do something about it.

Unfortunately, she was left to monitor readings and provide a friendly face to the newly-resurrected. The games were the most popular form of entertainment in the entire system. Along with the games themselves, there were movies, shows and video games based on the whole ordeal.

A corporation like War World Entertainment could hardly be expected to deny a dollar for a simple thing like empathy.

People had tried, of course, and Charlotte had thought about joining them. Luckily, she hadn't. Most protests—like the riots in St. Louis only a decade before—had ended in bloody massacres by the

Earth Orbit Security Forces. The *defenders of the populace*, they were called. In reality, they just defended the interests of the corporations who owned them.

And they were all interested in the games.

Charlotte sighed at the thought. The worst part was seeing the soldiers' faces. After the second or third death they all wore the same expression and she could *feel* their despair. They could do nothing to change their lives, and even suicide was out of the question. If they tried and were not forcibly retired, they just woke up enraged the next day.

It was even worse for them.

When she broke out of her thoughts, Charlotte found that Ryan had stopped running. He was bent over, shakily holding his legs above the knees and panting. Checking the display, Charlotte saw that he had only run 8.3 kilometers, which was not nearly enough. He had to run twelve before he could move onto the rowing machine.

She flicked on the intercom and hated herself all the more.

"Ryan, you need to keep running. It's almost over." Charlotte often lied in her line of work, but it was never enjoyable.

"I can't," Ryan answered when he wasn't panting. He had tried, certainly, but he was sure he was past his limit. Charlotte seemed like a nice woman, so he didn't want to mess up her job or anything, but he felt like he was about to pass out. The urge to throw up was unbearable, but he had literally never had anything in his stomach. The most he could do was dry heave.

Charlotte did not have a choice. She flicked the intercom again.

"I know, Ryan, but we have to keep going. The longer you stay still, the more it will hurt. And I don't want to," she said before taking a deep breath, "but I'll be required to shock you if you don't continue."

She flicked the switch and sank back into her chair, breathing out as she watched Ryan's face. Charlotte could see his opinion of her change through the one-way glass.

Ryan felt betrayed, but he understood. He should have guessed this would happen; he should not have expected kindness. However, he did not have the ability to run, so he breathed in and out for what seemed like an eternity. Ryan needed to catch his breath, and some curious part of him almost wanted to get shocked just to force the point home.

Nothing happened to him. Ryan felt that maybe the two-faced doctor was showing him mercy, or maybe she could not pull the trigger. Maybe this was just something she was forced to do, and after all this pain, Ryan wanted to believe that. He stood up and forced his legs to cooperate, every muscle in his body raging against him. His world was pain, but it seemed easier when he tried to think better of her.

On the other side of the glass, Charlotte took her finger off the button that would have electrocuted her patient. She had already waited a few seconds too long to comply with her own threat, but Charlotte let out a sigh of relief and leaned back in the chair once Ryan picked up a steady pace.

This, she thought, *has to be the worst part.*

RYAN TOOK a deep breath as he exited the clinic. In the small medical complex, the air was heated to perfect conditions for resurrected soldiers, but there was no mercy as the soldiers walked to their home in the barracks. The crisp air was almost painful, but what he saw was enough to shake Ryan from his thoughts.

As he walked the short distance to the barracks, he could see Earth in all its faded glory. It was a few hours past Earthrise—what counted for night on Eris—but the ground and most of the sky was still clearly visible, the clouds and haze having dispersed at the beginning of the night cycle.

There was never any true absence of light on Eris. Even when the sun was eclipsed by the planet or any of the other orbiting moons, the reflected light would always end up illuminating Ryan's new home. It was beautiful when paired with the absence of light pollution. Ryan almost felt like he could reach out and touch the stars.

As he moved forward, Ryan could see the shattered moon off to the left. It was mostly intact, really, but huge swaths of the rock had been blown off and still hung about. The moon was the first attempt at colonization more than two hundred years ago, but the intellectual elite had not perfected the process yet. Instead of making the rock habitable, the scientists ended up causing the Moonfall, the catastrophic explosion that caused thousands of high-speed projectiles to fall to Earth's surface.

That's what happened to Old Chicago. That's what happened to a lot of places.

Now Ryan was living on a real scientific marvel. Overpopulation and pollution had become so bad that even the mass casualties involved with the Moonfall didn't really help the problem. Humans still needed someplace to go, but had never fixed the problems involved with interstellar travel.

As a result, the next batch of scientists had turned their eyes to the Kuiper Belt. The asteroids were close enough that travel would not be too much of a problem; just a few years there and back. The scientists figured they could drag a bunch of asteroids into orbit, add the trash from humanity's rampant pollution, give them an atmosphere, add some new-fashioned scientific *voodoo* and turn them into little planets. To a degree, Earth's ecosystem had to be sacrificed to make these new homes, but it was a gamble humanity was willing to make.

It had worked, surprisingly. A Trade Union had been formed and funded the creation of eight reformed moons, built from the ground up for specific purposes. Gaia, Zion and Midgard were the first, purely for residential purposes.

Then came Osmos and Demeter, which the scientists had forged into agricultural phenomena. While each world did its best to support itself, these two were meant to feed the entire system. The scientists were almost magicians when considering those two; the gravity was different and allowed plants and animals to grow even larger in hydroponic systems.

No one could blame the Trade Union for making the first five moons, but *then* they built Elysia and Solaria as resort planets for the rich. The Trade Union didn't mind sacrificing more and more of the Earth if the wealthy could be accommodated on these new planets.

The poor were not too happy about that, but their opinions didn't matter; there was no voice without money and by that time every world government had lost its voice. The planets belonged to the Trade Union and the people were just allowed to live there. The lower class and freedom-concerned citizens would have been upset—possibly would have started an uprising—but then the Trade Union built Eris. It was not long before the people lined up to give their support. No one even called it Eris; they just called it by the name of their favorite television show.

It was *War World* to them.

Ryan kicked a tin can as he made his way up the pathway, it helped distract him from the thoughts flooding his brain. When he caught up to it, Ryan kicked the can again, but this time he sent the piece of trash flying off the path by a few meters. He sighed as he looked up and saw the Crows' barracks, a massive complex built for everything the soldiers needed. From here, he could see the Crows' crimson and black banner flying over the barracks and wondered how long he would have to be on Eris. Ryan even wondered if he would ever make it back home to New Chicago. For now, he would just have to deal with this new home he had chosen for himself.

It was strange to see the barracks from the outside. Before his first death, he had spent a few nights staring out from the structure to see his former planet and home. Now Earth dwarfed the barracks, offering Ryan a new perspective. In that moment, the ruins of the moon were just to the side of the building, and it was a sight he never thought he would witness just three months ago.

With those two broken things floating above him, Ryan thought about all his plans for when he was released from this prison. He thought about the kind of luck it would take to leave Eris behind. Then he realized he had never had that kind of luck, and maybe Warner had been right all along.

Ryan Jenkins realized he might never go home again.

Stage Two
ANGER

1

Coming To Terms

Ryan's body didn't hurt as much as he expected it would. A few minutes after the morning alarm, he rolled off his bed and started putting on clothes. The strain made the pain return, but it was a lesser torture after a night's re st. He bit his lip to distract himself from the agony in his legs, trying to avoid memories of the day before.

This pain was sharper; he could focus on that instead.

He looked around the barren room and sighed, his mood as dark as the cloudy sky outside his window. The Commission hadn't bothered to give anything special to their gladiators, as there were far too many men and women under their care. The subsidiary of *War World Network* did everything it could to cut corners.

Ryan had a small bed, an empty desk and a chair, which almost seemed to blend into the walls surrounding him. If he ever wanted to write something, he could, but he didn't see that happening. Ryan had never tried to foster any talents during his brief years in school, before the law could not keep him from abandoning his education. Sometimes he regretted dropping out of secondary school—he actually liked to learn—but the school system had been hopelessly underfunded in New Chicago. It had been more logical to get into a gang early and get started with his *real* life.

The same *real* life that had eventually led him to indentured servitude on a prison planet.

With great pain, Ryan limped toward the mess hall and tried to forget the life that he had left behind on Earth. Ryan didn't have a strong appetite yet—his stomach was still quite small in comparison to the one in his last body—but he needed *something* to make it through the day.

Once he arrived at the doorway, Ryan could only stare at the dull metal of the double doors, trying to gather his courage. Every one of his teammates would be sitting along the benches just past that door. He didn't understand why he was so nervous about this confrontation —it was not so different from what Warner experienced the other day —but Ryan was nervous all the same. Convincing himself that no one would care, Ryan braced himself and pushed through the door.

He was wrong. Only a few seconds after Ryan entered, almost every soldier was staring right at him. The only one who kept his gaze to himself was Carver; the old Crow kept eating his powdered eggs like he had every other morning for thirty years.

Everybody else in the room was looking at their new comrade for some sign or some action. They wanted something from him, but Ryan didn't have a clue as to what he could give. For too long of a moment, Ryan felt compelled to say something profound, but he had nothing to say. There were no grand words hiding away in his mind; his canvass was blank.

Thankfully, the moment passed. His arrival was really nothing more than a curiosity and most were satisfied after a glance. Cortes went back to sullenly poking at his sausage; Norris smiled as he played with his oatmeal, making conversation with himself because everyone else ignored him. It was business as usual, after all.

Everyone died during the games.

Ryan stood at the entrance for a moment before heading to the lukewarm food stewing in their containers, finding that breakfast held little appeal after resurrection. He grabbed a modest portion of eggs and some toast before picking up his tray and turning to his compatriots. What little food was on his tray was merely theater, to show them that he was dealing with his first death with dignity.

Now, Ryan was keenly aware of Warner's reasons for acting up. Even if death was commonplace, Warner wanted his loss to be acknowledged. The convict had *wanted* Ryan to talk to him and become the subject of his misplaced rage. He had wanted to fight, wanted his death to mean more than just another tally mark on his record. Ryan could sympathize.

He had died, and no one had cared for more than a few seconds.

Noticing an empty spot on the bench next to Roberts, Ryan felt relieved, visibly sighing as he walked over to the young man. Even if he was older than Roberts, the boy soldier had unwittingly become a sort of mentor for Ryan. When he finally reached the bench opposite Roberts, Ryan cleared his throat and gestured with his tray at the empty space on the table.

"So, uh, do you mind if I sit here?"

The eternity it took for Roberts to acknowledge him made him uncomfortable—he had not expected such a cold welcome—but just before he was about to speak, Roberts wiped his mouth with his napkin and grunted.

"Don't see why not."

There was just indifference; no hospitality from the boy soldier he respected. Ryan sat down beside his supposed teammate and picked up the fork from his tray, wondering why the Commission had denied them real silverware and left them with plastic substitutes. Letting the thought flit away, Ryan looked at his food and then back at the fork in his hand, considering that he may not need silverware, after all. The yellow loaf of powdered eggs was unappetizing, at best, and Ryan had not recovered his appetite. He found it difficult to bring any of it to his mouth.

"The first time is always the worst."

The statement tore Ryan from his apprehension and he focused on the small man across from him.

Roberts had not shifted his gaze from his tray, but that didn't mean he hadn't noticed his teammate's behavior. He felt bad for his new companion, who had been staring at his plastic fork for a solid minute.

Distracted by the plasticware, Roberts remembered when they had made the switch from metal. There had been a rash of suicides, and the Commission had deemed it necessary.

"Really?" Ryan asked, the tone of his voice making him seem like a dog called in from the rain.

Roberts could see the hope that filled the recruit's face and wanted to lie to him, let him avoid the truth for a bit longer, but hope had never helped anyone on Eris. After considering his words, Roberts sighed and looked at his own loaf of eggs, which were almost melting on his plate.

"No, not really."

JOSEPH WARNER GROANED as he woke up for the second time that day, his new body still unfamiliar and a roadmap of aches and pains. He hated having to wake up like this, the moon high in the sky and surrounded by clouds, making their version of noon closer to twilight than anything. He hated that he would spend the rest of his life here, that the dream of making it out was gone.

He sighed once he realized that it was foolish to hope for freedom in the first place. When he had discovered that he had gone positive on his debts, momentarily free, Warner should have quit as soon as possible and gotten himself off this secondhand planet. If not for his greed, he would not be waking up to this half-lit sky.

It made him angrier since it was his own fault; his death and incarceration had nothing to do with the new kid.

He swung his feet around and planted them on the ground—waiting for a moment as he gathered his resolve—and then pushed himself to his feet. Once he had overcome the weakness in his legs, Warner looked at the crack in the wall in front of him.

That spider web of violence was not the product of one bout of rage; the wall had been punished for more than three years, innocent as it was. Throwing out his fist lazily, Warner felt the wall sink in and the skin of his knuckles pinch at the impact. The pain resonated through his arm, traveling along his bones and muscles, then faded.

Warner inspected his knuckles and saw two of them were already bleeding, having caught one of the jagged edges from the numerous cracks. He huffed in annoyance as he realized that this clone's hands would never be as strong as the hands from his original body, the one that had carried him through decades of travel between Earth and the slave yards of Demeter.

Warner trudged over to his desk and sat down in the nearby chair, which squeaked at his weight. He rifled through the papers sitting on top of the cheap desk and found the list of scribbled names of friends, colleagues and former cellmates.

Some were scratched out, like Mike Perlmutter, who had died of a lung infection on Demeter, or Rizzo Johnson, who Warner had stabbed seventeen times with a shiv made from a toothbrush. The list would be rather incriminating if law enforcement still cared about him, but Warner kept the list around so he could remember his former life. Even though he had killed Rizzo, Warner remembered a few months where the two of them had been thick as thieves.

Warner set the sheet of paper aside and grabbed a blank page from the stack to his left. After diagnosing him with anger issues, his last therapist had suggested he keep a journal. Warner had left the man bleeding from three severed fingers after just a month of visits, but writing in his journal had become a habit. He could pour his feelings and mindless anger into the words on the page instead of hurting the people around him. If he had kept track of all the pages, his journal would probably be the length of a short book, but Warner had never cared about that.

That journal had been the first way he could truly express himself.

Warner had been able to develop his self-control as the journal had grown in size. Over the years since the therapist had suggested it, Warner had developed a nice writing style, which might have seemed chaotic to an outsider. He enjoyed drawing some of the words, sometimes spending a minute on just seven or eight letters, and his script would adopt a visual tone in line with his current mood.

When he had found himself in the black and out of debt, his words had taken on an airy quality, light and practically amorphous. After his last death—his freedom taken from him—the words had seemed to scream off the page, deep gouges cut into the paper and single words taking up four lines of space.

Now, as he was sitting down in his room and experiencing the ache of resurrection, the words were muddy. They fell on the page and seemed to sink into the background, barely legible in his apathy. Warner continued for only a few minutes before he realized that he had nothing to express.

Looking at the words he had spilled onto the page, Warner snarled in disgust and crushed the piece of paper in his fist. He threw the page at his wastebasket—already full from other crumpled pages—and then cleared the top of the desk with one sweep of his arm, scattering white paper across the tiled floor. After a few harsh breaths, Warner collected himself and realized there was no reason to be angry at a few pieces of paper. His frustration was because of his own failure.

Feeling the gurgle of his stomach, Warner decided that maybe hunger was the problem. He had missed the alarm for breakfast—having decided that lying in his bed was a better idea—but lunch would be ready in just a few minutes, if it was not already laid out underneath the heat lamps. The food, if it could be called that, would be a suitable distraction, and maybe in an hour or so he would be able to sit back down at his journal.

Warner exited his room and walked down the hallway, gritting his teeth as he dealt with his frustration. Though he was angry at his own behavior, he wanted to strike outward. He wanted to hurt someone and maybe that would solve his problems.

Warner was thinking violent thoughts when he saw the new recruit in front of him. Before Jenkins could notice the footsteps behind him, Warner slowed his pace and watched the back of the partner who had let him die. His eyes narrowed as he remembered their scuffle in the mess hall and the embarrassment he had felt when Carver had put him in his place. The blood in his veins pumped faster and Warner's thoughts drifted to fantasies about tearing off Jenkins' arm and stuffing it down his own throat, his teeth scattered on the floor around his head.

Warner realized halfway through the fantasy that the imaginary violence would give him no satisfaction, which made him even more frustrated. Although he held a grudge for his last death, Warner did not wish outright harm on the oblivious soldier walking in front of him. Jenkins was not at fault for his own incompetence.

Warner had to wonder if he would ever escape this eternal prison. To overcome his debts, he had killed quite a few people. In the past, he had even enjoyed quite a few of those kills, but now that he thought about it, Warner realized he did not appreciate the bloodshed the same way. Remembering the days before he had come to Eris, Warner regarded it as the best time of his life; each cold-blooded kill was a mark of respect.

Now it was all hollow.

Warner thought about the Commission and War World Entertainment and how they had ruined everything. Not only was he trapped in this endless cycle, but now he couldn't even enjoy his bloodlust. They had taken that from him, and as Warner shook his head, he wondered if there was any way he could take revenge on the organizations.

The Commission, let alone its parent company, was largely untouchable. The bureaucratic organization regulated the games and the different outposts of civilization on Eris, and the Crows were part of the Northwest Quadrant. Warner set himself in a fantasy where he escaped the battlefield and caused havoc in the support cities like McClellan just to screw with Maxwell Garrison—the director of their quadrant—and the Commission's bottom line. Warner had only met the balding man once, but the thought of throwing his fists into that weak jaw and setting jowls quivering was enough to make him smile.

He almost didn't notice Jenkins looking back over his shoulder, watching Warner a few meters behind him. Without realizing the malicious smile was still on his face, Warner was confused to see Jenkins increase his pace and shove his hands in his pockets, clearly nervous.

After realizing *he* was the reason for the rookie's behavior, Warner chuckled.

"I ain't gonna hurt you, pretty boy, though I do appreciate the respect."

Although Warner had distanced himself from that post-mortem fury, he felt satisfied that Jenkins was scared of him. He loved to intimidate people whenever he had the chance, though he had no intention to follow up on it.

It was Warner's version of harmless fun.

WARNER TOUCHED the skin around his right knuckles with his other hand and tried to resist wincing. His hands stung from where the skin had been worn off, but Warner wanted to feel what he had done to himself. His touch was delicate, but he didn't resist letting his fingers glide against the injuries so they could set off a cascade of pleasant stings.

The pain was something else to focus on. He had eaten a solid meal after following Jenkins to the mess hall, and afterward he had a satisfactory workout in the yard, lifting weights without the help of a spotter. There was a sense of accomplishment for a few minutes, but soon after that, the void had set in.

Warner hated to read or to watch reruns on television and he still was not in the writing mood, so he was left with nothing to occupy his mind. There was a need for a distraction, since he knew he would just start thinking about the Commission again, if left to his own devices.

So Warner started his assault on the walls of the barracks once more. He liked to start out by punching the concrete walls in the training yard to get the pain going, earning scratches and abrasions that would only tear wider on further impacts. Seeing the crimson he left on the grey walls made him feel powerful and in control. In his mind, Warner was so much man that it didn't matter if his body could not take it. He was the boss of his body, and he could push it as far as he wanted.

Warner moved from that patch of wall to another, and then to another after that. The soldier's bones ached underneath the skin, likely earning microfractures at each impact, but Warner didn't care about any of those temporary injuries.

He would have brand new bones, eventually.

After he finished a session of striking the wall in his room, the surface splintering even more, Warner sat on his bed. He could see the bloody marks over the broken plaster—some of which had been dried over the course of years—and smiled at the fantasy of it all.

During this session, he had imagined that he was sinking his fists into the doughy body of the male receptionist in the lobby. Warner didn't have to think too hard to justify his anger, as the insufferable man would always talk down to the Crows, sneering at Warner whenever he needed information. It would have been enough to drive the old Warner to violence.

However, the Warner sitting on his bed and nursing his bloody knuckles wasn't going to beat up a receptionist. It wasn't worth the fine, not when every other day he could take out his aggression in gladiator combat. In the afterglow of his pain, Warner wondered what it would be like to pound away at Jenkins. The convict smiled at the thought, but soon felt guilty about it.

Warner looked around his room and sighed, the satisfaction from his self-inflicted violence finally ebbing away. The paper for his journal was still scattered around his desk and Warner did not have the energy to pick up any of the pages scattered on the tiles.

He would have nothing to pour on them if he did.

JENKINS MUST HAVE EXPECTED Carver or Roberts on the other side, but when he swung open the door, Warner was glowering in the hallway. It took Jenkins considerable effort to hide his initial fright, but after the shock abated, he mustered his courage and crossed his arms.

"Hey, Warner. What's going on?"

After looking everywhere but at Jenkins' face, the veteran sighed and shook his head.

"I wanted to say that I'm sorry," Warner admitted, avoiding eye contact the entire time.

Jenkins furrowed his brow, obviously wondering what the soldier was playing at. Warner did not seem the type to apologize for *anything,* much less violence.

"Sorry for what?"

"Well, a lot," Warner started, covering the back of his neck with his hand, "but in regards to *you,* I'm sorry for beating on you. I was out of line. I shouldn't have done it." After he finished his apology, Warner looked up to find that Jenkins' gaze had softened.

"It's okay. I understand where you're coming from. I just got back from a resurrection this morning. I get it."

At the assumption, Warner gave him a quick glare; the kid had no *idea* what it was like. Then Warner realized he was being brash again. Jenkins had just died and had to make that lonely display of courage in the mess hall for the first time. This new soldier was allowed to think that he understood, even though he had not yet been exposed to all Eris had to offer.

"Well, I just wanted to make sure there wasn't any bad blood. We need to be able to fight together." Warner realized it sounded like it had come from his old coach, but the words were out of his mouth before he could stop them. Warner would snap the kid's wrist if he decided to take advantage, but he was deprived of any potential retribution once Jenkins gave him a slight smile.

"No bad blood," he agreed, offering his hand.

Warner looked down for a second before realizing Jenkins was going for a handshake, but then he realized that might be awkward. He raised the back of his hand and pointed at the torn knuckles before shaking his head.

"I... don't think you want to," Warner said, taking Jenkins' swift nod as a tacit agreement, and then turned awkwardly toward his room.

As he walked down the hallway, Warner tried to think about how he had come to this point, apologizing for just getting into a fight. Eris was making him soft, it seemed, and he felt a distinct feeling of injustice at the realization. While he could agree that he might have been too violent back on Earth, he did not appreciate what War World Entertainment had done for him, had done *to* him.

Warner's fingers itched as he realized he could pick up the papers from the floor of his room. He had plenty to write about.

A FEW DAYS after the mental transfer, Jenkins' body was no longer a testament to pain. His new muscles were familiar; his body felt his own. He had even participated in the last game against the Mastiffs. That was remarkable, even if they had become one of the lowest-ranking teams after the satellite tragedy. His conscience took a hit every time he sent another soldier to the Hell he had experienced after death, but they were professional athletes.

Dying was part of the job.

Today, Jenkins had even held his own in the training yard. The Crows had already started to file out of the area, but Jenkins and a few other stragglers stayed behind. Since Jenkins was still having difficulty adjusting to his new body, Feldman had chosen to help him with his bench press.

That made it seem like the brutish giant had taken a liking to him, for which Jenkins was grateful. Although Feldman didn't offer many external signs, Jenkins knew that even his smallest actions held significance.

Across the yard, Norris and Abrams were sparring, as they did most days. Norris had a dozen centimeters and twenty kilograms on his partner, but to call Abrams scrappy would have been an understatement. Jenkins' repetitions were often backed by the sounds of impacts and groans from the two fighters.

Feldman stood over him without a sound, which made Jenkins feel oddly comforted and scared at the same time. Impressively large by any standard, Feldman dwarfed the young man beneath him, but that was not the reason Jenkins preferred him as a spotter over anybody else. There was just something about the gentle giant that eased him.

Deciding that he shouldn't waste more time, Jenkins focused on the task at hand and continued his exercise with a grunt. His arms swayed from the effort, but he regained control and started counting out with every push.

Feldman had almost reached out for the bar after he noticed the bar swaying in the rookie's arms. Jenkins was in decent condition, considering, but Feldman didn't want the kid to strain himself and hurt his new body. It was part of Feldman's paternal streak. With the exception of Carver, he often thought of everyone as children.

The young soldier lying on the bench beneath him was a toddler in power armor; Abrams and Norris were teenagers refusing their feelings for each other. It was painfully obvious to Feldman, but most of his fellow gladiators didn't notice or care.

If that was the case, as it so often was, Feldman felt like he needed to be the one to take notice. So many of his comrades were filled with apathy; so many dominated by a void in their soul. To him, it felt like they were all skirting on the edge of oblivion. They were slowly forgetting they were human, slowly forgetting they were capable of so much.

Feldman didn't want to end up like that, and he certainly did not want to forget all of those connections and experiences. The giant was observing Abrams' frustration in her fight against Norris when Jenkins faltered again. Before the rookie could ask for help, Feldman had already put out his hand and lifted the bar up on the rack.

After Jenkins realized the bar was in place, he breathed a sigh of relief and let his limbs go limp on the ground. Feldman looked down at the child lying on the bench—eyes closed from exhaustion—and smiled in approval. Jenkins was a good kid; he still had some life in him. Feldman guessed that was why he liked the little man. This mausoleum of living people hadn't corrupted him yet.

Feldman walked over to the stack of weights and began replacing Jenkins' weights with larger and larger plates of steel. His young partner was alarmed by the clang of metal against metal and opened his eyes in alarm, but quickly figured out that the new weight wasn't meant for him. He sat up and wiped the bench, trying to clean up after himself.

"I—uh... I'd spot you if I could, but I don't think I'd really be able to help here," he said with an exasperated sigh. Feldman looked down at the smaller man and chuckled.

"I appreciate it, Jenkins, but I can't say you're wrong." He looked over the overgrown teenager before sitting down on the bench, lying on his back and staring at the sky.

"My name is Ryan, by the way. In case you cared," he said while putting out his thin arms below the iron bar that Feldman held in his grip. The act was enough for a smile to break through Feldman's stoic expression.

"Caring doesn't really help on this asteroid, Ryan." Feldman pushed hard, lifting the hundred kilograms he would use as a warm-up. Jenkins' disappointment was written all over his face.

"Yeah, I see what you mean," he replied, but Feldman cleared his throat after lowering the weight onto the rack.

"Stop. I'm not going to be rude. I'm Gregory. Nice to meet you, Ryan," Feldman stated before pushing up against the bar so he could then bring it down to his massive chest.

Doing his best to avoid direct eye contact, he could still see the child was relieved. Jenkins looked so young and naïve like that.

Feldman knew it was only a matter of time before that changed.

2

Anger Management

Jenkins was nervous as he stared out of the loading bay, the roar of wind and engine turbines playing havoc with the knot in his stomach. He had just watched Goldstein fly out with Norris—his partner for this game—and knew they were plummeting to the battlefield below. Jenkins wondered when he would be paired with either soldier—the Commission tended to shuffle around players whenever they died— and remembered what it was like to watch the games. The constant changes helped keep the games fresh and exciting.

Anything to draw in more viewers and advertising revenue.

Jenkins could feel Feldman breathe heavy behind him. With the extra armor and kinetic motivators, Feldman was a good two and a half meters tall, making Jenkins feel like he was completely outclassed. Although Feldman's size should have comforted him, Jenkins was uneasy with the prospect of having this titan as a partner. Feldman was certainly accomplished, but Jenkins was a rifleman.

He had no idea how to play with a berserker.

He didn't have much more time to think about it before the drop point came up and the green warning light blinked by the back of the cargo bay. Jenkins took a breath and prepared himself for the jump, trying to steel his nerve. After five games, he thought that he should be used to flying through the air, but his body was still fighting his every action.

Jenkins jumped out of the plane. anyway.

The ground rushed at him impossibly fast and he could see more and more detail in the landscape as he approached terminal velocity. The scream of the wind flying past him made it hard to focus, but in that first month he had been trained to release his parachute at forty meters. It was almost automatic as his hand drifted to the plastic at the end of the ripcord. All Jenkins had to do was just make sure he wouldn't land on a spire or jagged line of barbed wire.

Manipulating the air resistance against his body, Jenkins directed himself to a patch of clear ground and released his chute. It fluttered behind him and caught the atmosphere, reversing his acceleration and yanking him backward. Although it slowed down his descent considerably, he was still falling toward the surface faster than he would have preferred. At five meters, he flicked the release switch and prepared for the landing.

Jenkins met the ground with a thump and dispersed his momentum in a forward roll. Although the suit took the brunt of the impact, he still needed to do something to compensate for the freefall.

When he got to his feet, Jenkins inspected his body to see that he had not come to harm. His bones ached, but that was a fairly common occurrence on reentry.

There was a crash behind him, and he thought he had been ambushed before realizing it was just his partner making a dramatic entrance. The brute had released his parachute at twenty meters from the ground, just like every other game. His suit was reinforced for all the extra weight and a great deal of his fan base was enamored with his juggernaut style, even if Feldman had no use for such theatrics.

It was just part of his contract.

Usually, Feldman landed on his feet and tried to seem like a behemoth, but in this instance, the giant fell onto a pile of trash and metal and promptly landed on his back. He groaned for a moment—already knowing one of his ribs had come out of place—and lay on the ground for a few seconds before sitting up and rising to his feet. After a deep breath, Feldman closed his eyes and pressed against his chest plate, feeling his rib slide back into place with a considerable amount of pain.

Ignoring his ordeal—sadly commonplace—Feldman focused on the present and wiped mud from his armor before looking around for his sword. The overseers of the battlefields placed the more expensive weapons at the drop zone instead of sending it along with the soldier, as there had been too many mishaps and problems involved with reentry. It also made it more entertaining for the viewers to have some of the soldiers virtually unarmed until they could find their weapons.

Feldman had long since stopped caring. His weapon was usually tucked away nearby, and in the few times he had been ambushed before being able to claim it, he had adapted. Most soldiers had a hard time reacting to an armored giant rushing at them.

In those circumstances, Feldman felt fortunate for growing up on an asteroid farm. His genes had taken full advantage of the lesser gravity and the Commission had replicated that in his clones.

As Feldman dealt with his distracting thoughts, Jenkins looked around the clearing and found the giant's sword on top of a patch of grating to his right, the handle pointing skyward. Feeling proud of himself, Jenkins waved at the weapon with his rifle and pinged his partner.

"Over here, Feldman. It's just missing the shiny pink bow," he said, turning from Feldman and taking in his surroundings. As the giant lumbered toward his plasma sword, Jenkins scanned the horizon for his teammates' beacons.

Goldstein and Norris were still alive and setting up camp along a ridge. They would probably stay there for the whole game, just so Norris would snipe any of the Hawks that came their way. Although guarding the sniper was not the most glamorous job, it would keep Goldstein out of trouble, which Jenkins assumed was preferable. After that grenade ambush in the last game, Goldstein deserved a break.

Feldman was trudging back toward Jenkins when he heard a few rocks fall down the ridge behind him. He turned quickly for his size, but a flurry of shells pelted his armor before he was able to gain his bearings and bring up the flat of his sword to block incoming fire. He was undamaged from that first assault, but it was still somewhat jarring. Once he was able to think, Feldman heard Jenkins yelling something over Comms, but he didn't pay attention.

He was already rushing the source of the gunfire.

There were two men from the Hawks above the ridge, and Jenkins laid down suppressive fire as Feldman drove forward. Their opponents were already retreating to the other side of the crest, and Feldman brought his sword to the right so he could sweep it across their bodies. He did not smile when he prepared for the coming violence, as Norris or Warner might have done. He took no pleasure in killing men.

Feldman was only a meter away from the crest when he activated the armor's kinetic assistance and was jerked forward by the extra speed. Though he already had a giant's strength, Feldman was grateful for his armor's assistance, as his armor and sword together weighed upward of a hundred kilos. Without the boost, Feldman would have died in every match, but he was able to clear that crest with a graceful leap.

However, that boost would not help him survive against four men with blue Hawks emblazoned on their shoulders, who had been standing on the other side of the ridge and waiting for him to land. Feldman cursed himself for falling into the obvious trap—he should have known better—and braced himself for what was coming next.

In concert, the four Hawks unloaded their magazines into Feldman. Most of the bullets glanced off harmlessly—automatic weapons weren't particularly adept at breaking through Feldman's modern plate mail—but others sank right into the joints of his armor. He could feel the shells tearing through his kneecaps, his unguarded torso and his shoulders. The bullets reversed his momentum as they pushed him back to the ridge, where he landed and collapsed into his armor.

Although he was still alive, the suit was the only thing that kept him from falling to the ground.

All four Hawks kept firing until they spent their entire clips, the empty clicks of their weapons signifying the end. At that point, Feldman was only clinging to consciousness and confused as to how he was still alive. Just by chance, one of the soldiers should have sunk a few rounds into his helmet, but Feldman kept kneeling, his life steadily flowing out of him.

There was an odd quiet as the four soldiers stared at their broken opponent in the forty-kilogram suit. Feldman didn't know if they had hit any vital organs, but it didn't matter. In a matter of seconds, Feldman was going to bleed out. He was already dead; his brain just refused to admit it.

When the giant let out a ragged breath, he tasted metal in his mouth. With that breath came the compulsion to cough, but he did not want to drown in his own blood and resisted the urge. Feldman guessed that he only had a minute left to live and that he was about to go into shock, so he looked at his opponents.

They were all children from the look of it; new recruits who feared death. Feldman could tell they had never looked that boogeyman in the eyes. In a way, Feldman thought them an odd mix of fortune, as they still had so much growing up to do. At the realization, the giant swallowed the blood filling his mouth and knew that he did not need the minute.

He knew this would only take a few seconds.

Feldman forced himself forward using the kinetic motivators, which were somehow still functional. His bones and joints were useless things—damaged beyond any hope of repair—but the suit would move forward for him if he tried. It was pain beyond enduring, but he pushed himself past the surface feelings. Feldman already knew he was hurt, knew he was dying, and pain was unimportant.

The broken titan rose and lunged at the four children not prepared for his attack; they had thought he had died kneeling. Feldman's sword was heavy, but he had enough strength left in him to propel his weapon in a wicked arc from right to left, the air sizzling as the sword burned through the atmosphere. The poor boy on his right only had enough time to look down before the plasma passed through his armor. The coil of energy literally burned through the man's breast plate and sealed the man's wounds as it passed, a pop coming from the super-heated air in the man's lungs once that gave way.

The Hawk was still alive as his two halves fell to the ground.

They had started to fire on the giant again, but it was no use. The only hope they had to survive was if they could detach Feldman's arm from his body, and that wasn't going to happen. Their fates were beyond even Feldman's control, as he had started to fade midway through the swing. His arm sailed on in its own momentum.

The sword bisected the next Hawk just below the diaphragm, continuing on its downward arc and cutting through the next man just above the waistline. Those two men died quickly and did not last very long once they fell to the ground.

The last soldier was another story. The blade passed through his thighs, relieving him of his legs and causing him to fall to the ground screaming, Feldman right beside him.

Feldman was fading, but he could still hear the child screaming his heart out less than a meter away. If nothing else, Feldman just wanted the noise to stop. He reached out his hand and found the man's helmet before wrapping his fingers around the mesh covering the man's neck. Pain lanced through Feldman's fingers, but it was becoming dull as blood left his body.

After a moment, the pain departed, and he could tell the infernal screaming had stopped. He decided he wanted to sleep, but before Feldman closed his eyes, he looked to the ridge that had been his doom. A shadowy figure was walking toward him with the sun framed behind him, a sight that made him feel merciful relief.

Then Gregory Feldman closed his eyes and died.

THE WHOLE TIME the Hawks had unloaded their clips into Feldman, Jenkins had hidden behind the ridge like a child. Although he would have wanted to fight, he could not follow over that ridge. Jenkins would just end up dead or dying alongside him. Obviously, staying behind was the smart play.

That didn't stop him from feeling like the worst kind of coward.

After the gunfire stopped and the screams died down, Jenkins peered over the ridge to see what had happened. He saw the carnage Feldman had wrought with just one swing and was more than just impressed. The display made him violently ill.

Fortunately, he had nothing in his stomach to throw up.

After climbing over the ridge, Jenkins ran to the side of his fallen comrade. He noticed the bloody titan had one of the Hawks grasped by the throat and was dumbfounded by the fact that Feldman had been able to do anything at all. By the time Jenkins reached the deadlocked opponents, the Hawk was already gone.

So was Feldman.

Jenkins sat back on his feet and tried to figure out what he was going to do. If he was going to live through this match, it would be a complete accident. Feldman was supposed to protect him—the man was a glorified security blanket—but the Hawks had seen fit to shred him within the first few minutes.

Jenkins lost himself to despair for a few horrible moments. He contemplated shoving his rifle under his chin and pulling the trigger, but he remembered his resurrection and pushed the thought from his mind. He wouldn't be able to take that pain again. Not this soon.

That was when everything fell into place for Jenkins. His priorities were clear: he was alive and he did not care what he would have to do in order to stay that way. He scanned the horizon, looked for the indicators of his teammates and found that there were four ID beacons still active on his helmet's display. Three were to the south, but only one mattered.

He left to join Carver.

CARVER WAS tired of it all. He was always tired, but he was getting particularly annoyed at these new rules and handicaps they had now forced on him and the other Crows. The worst part was that War World Entertainment had not bothered to notify the supposed *athletes* who were about to die for *their* profit whenever one of those handicaps was active.

The old Crow despised the men in charge, though Garrison, for all his bureaucratic sensibilities, wasn't particularly awful. The Director was one of the only constants Carver had during this decade-spanning career, and certainly not the worst. Over the years, Carver had been dealing with the Commission and so many middle-men that he did not bother keeping up with the date, anymore. He guessed that he had been on Eris for thirty years or more, but it didn't matter.

Jonathan Carver would be a Crow until the end of his days.

The veteran was walking east with Warner and Cortes. There had been six Crows in their group at the beginning of the match, but the Hawks had a high concentration of soldiers in each area, steadily whittling away at Carver's troops.

Now he was left with stragglers.

He noticed Jenkins' marker moving toward him and that there was another ID tag four kilometers to the northeast just sitting there. As soon as he realized he didn't recognize the numbers, Carver realized the soldier was not worth knowing. The Crows he did not remember were the ones who would be traded away, eventually.

As they walked, Carver wished that Abrams had not died. Cortes was a decent enough kid for a gangbanger, but he was a poor shot and it was his fault that Carver didn't have Abrams backing him up.

He wasn't going to say anything to Cortes, but Carver was allowed to *think* whatever he wanted. His thoughts wouldn't hurt the coward's feelings.

Carver knew why Abrams had not made it, but he had no idea what had happened to Warner's partner. He had shown up without Corrigan and had not said a word about why, but Carver knew well enough not to push it. After the game—if he still cared—he could look up what had happened on the highlight reel. Maybe see why Warner's arm had a bullet in it.

For now, the only thing on Carver's mind was survival. He had been through the resurrection process more times than he could remember, but he would rather find his way off the battlefield intact. In order to survive, the best thing he could do was keep moving and perhaps run out the clock. Hopefully, Jenkins would catch up and add his weapon to their arsenal.

From time to time, they would hear the distant explosions of artillery, which put them all on edge. There were at least seven other games on Eris at any given time, allowing for plenty of highlight reels on *War World.* The people loved their war and the Commission made sure to give it to them.

Strangely enough, constant warfare did not help morale among the athletes.

After twenty minutes of wandering, Carver's group saw Jenkins running toward them from across a littered landscape. Their teammate was winded when he arrived, but he did not make them wait on his account. Between breaths, Jenkins briefed his compatriots.

"Feldman's dead."

"He's not the only one," replied Warner. Any indication that he was ever mad at the rookie was absent, since this was his usual tone. He was bitter, of course, but that most likely had something to do with what had happened to him earlier in the battle. Carver eyed the convict, but then turned to Jenkins with a grunt.

"Figured. Guessing he took a few of 'em with him?"

Jenkins scoffed at the question and regained his full height once he had caught his breath.

"More than a few. Greg's still *dead*, though."

"Happens to the best of us. Any trouble on the way here?" Carver asked, keeping his eyes on his surroundings rather than the soldier he was debriefing.

"One Hawk out there. Took him out before he even knew I was there. Didn't feel too proud about it." Jenkins cradled his rifle at the memory and saw the blood still on the barrel of his weapon.

"Good. Only cretins take pride in a coward's actions."

Carver was tired of aimlessly moving around the battlefield; something odd was going on. If there was a time limit, it should have been long past gone, and that worried him. He spotted a war-torn building off to the south and motioned to his comrades.

"Time we hole up somewhere and talk. Somethin' ain't right." He was already walking toward the decrepit building.

"Time to rest your old bones, old man?" Warner verbally jabbed, but still followed behind their de facto leader.

"*Careful.* My bones are old and brittle, but I still have enough fight in me to break all of yours. Shut your mouth."

Carver didn't even look at the man as they made their way to the dilapidated house. He walked up the exposed staircase—the creaking of the stairs had covered the sound of his creaking bones and joints—and settled up against a broken wall, sliding his back down the plaster before settling on the uncomfortable armor of his backside. However, he refused to complain. Carver was past his prime, but he did not want his teammates to hear the evidence.

The Crows settled throughout the second floor, doing their best to cover each avenue of approach. The atmosphere wasn't conducive to high spirits and there was an itch in the back of their minds they just could not scratch.

Then Jenkins gave voice to the question on their minds.

"Hey, Carver, why's the match still going? It's way past the hour limit."

Carver stared at the young soldier for a moment before turning to the others, trying to find the right words. He wanted to reassure them; he wanted to ease their minds.

He couldn't.

"I don't know, kid. It's bugging me, too," he trailed off, looking outside their house toward the other Crow's beacon. The digital mark on his visor was still floating above the same patch of ground, as if their teammate was hiding from his enemies. Grumbling at the thought, Carver realized he would have to slap that boy around before the next game, whoever he was.

With a sigh, the old Crow looked back at his team and noticed Warner, who seemed to be making eye contact even with the barrier of their helmets between them. As soon as Carver realized this, Warner confirmed what the veteran had been dreading.

"We're in an annihilation match."

"AND WHY DIDN'T you fucking *say so*?" A large part of Carver wanted to strangle Warner, but he restrained himself. They would lose all cohesion if *he* lost control.

However, that did not stop him from blurting out a number of obscenities. Warner was calm and took the verbal abuse. Once Carver was finished, he lazily rolled his head back.

"Look, it doesn't *matter*. We're *all* dead. They fucked us from the beginning."

Carver was angry at him, but that did not change the fact that he was probably right. Watching their interaction, Jenkins stood near the two and looked noticeably confused.

"Wait, how do you know?" he asked, causing Warner to take his eyes off Carver and turn to the naïve Crow with a shrug.

"When Corrigan and I were hit, I heard the Hawks talking about it. Dumbasses thought they killed me with a bullet to the shoulder and started gloating. Made sure they regretted *that* when they turned their backs." He grinned at his revenge before refocusing on the conversation. "So anyway, yeah. We're done for."

There was no more fighting once they took in the reality of the situation. All four men settled into a desperate silence, each of them coming to terms with their impending doom. The Crows were at a disadvantage, and the worst part was that they had no control over their situation.

"Goddamned handicaps on an annihilation match. Those corporate fuckers." Warner cursed, and no one bothered to argue.

When Jenkins looked around the room, he felt more frustrated than helpless. These men were supposed to be fighting with him, but they were giving up before it was over. They had resigned themselves to death so easily and, as a result, they were taking Jenkins with them.

That's what made him angry.

"Listen, you assholes," he said, his grip tightening on his rifle as he looked at each of his teammates. "We're not dead, *yet*. I don't know about you, but I have no interest in training another body. Sure, the team's practically broken and held together with safety glue, but we've killed everyone we've fought, right? There can't be that many of *them*, either. I say we hunt those assholes down and earn our way home!"

When Jenkins finished shouting at his teammates, he tried to gauge their reactions. His heart was pounding from the surge of adrenaline and every second seemed to pass by slowly, but from their reactions, he almost felt like he had made a mistake. When he turned to look at Carver, the old man's gaze burned into him.

"Whaddya suggest, kid?"

Jenkins breathed a sigh of relief, if only because his hero had not completely shut down his idea. Then he realized he had not thought that far ahead and searched his brain for a possible suggestion. After a moment, his gaze fell to the lone Crow's beacon a few kilometers away from their position.

"Well, that soldier out there..." He paused, forgetting the new soldier's name.

"Roth," Cortes provided.

"...yeah, Roth. He's been there since the beginning. I say we grab him and then figure it out from there. Five guns are better than four, right?" Jenkins looked to his fellow Crows for approval. "We could probably change things with him around."

Warner was apathetic at his plan; Cortes only shrugged. On the other hand, Carver nodded.

It seemed like a good plan.

PERCIVAL ROTH WAS DYING and he knew it.

He looked down and could see the stumps where his legs used to be. The sound of chainsaws tearing through his knees still resonated in his ears, and he could feel the life flowing out of him. This was his first death and he was terrified.

Percival had joined the Crows for fame, glory and money, not realizing—just like most of the population—that being part of the games was not all it was cracked up to be. He had come from a middle-class family and was destined for a life of accounting on Gaia, just like all the men in his family. He had been provided a reasonable education; his father had used his connections to get him into the best schools. If Percival had just followed through with it and let his father make his decisions for him, he could have lived a life of mediocrity and died an easy death.

However, as he painfully realized while dying in the dirt, Percival had been an idiot. He had wanted to show his sister and their father that there was more to life than sitting in a cubicle and punching numbers into a computer display. It made no difference that Percival's brain had seemed to be built for quick calculations. In his mind, just because he was good at something did not mean he had to spend the rest of his life doing it.

As he looked around the small clearing, Percival could see his legs off to his side. The bastard Hawk who had done this to him had come up from his left and taken Percival out of the fight without really trying. He had then rushed up to his partner, Templeton, and dug his meat-threshers into the man's chest. Percival had already started to go into shock from losing his legs, but he still heard the gurgling coming from his teammate's throat.

That Crow was in pieces now, but that was his own doing. While the soldier wielding the chainsaws was busy tearing apart Templeton's chest, he had pulled the pin on his grenade. Both soldiers had burst apart and pieces of their bodies were scattered around Percival, the scenery for his slow death. He had not been surprised when the other two Hawks had left after the explosion.

They must have assumed there was nothing left living in the area.

As he lay there, Percival wondered how he was still alive. From all the movies and shows he had seen in his little suburban town, it seemed absurd that he had not bled out by now. He hadn't considered that the suit itself had tried to stem the flow of blood from his wounds, but that was because Percival had not read the owner's manual.

The new recruit wept as he slowly died. He couldn't do anything in this situation; he couldn't even crawl away. It seemed like such a cruel death, as he and Templeton had been fine shooting at the two Hawks coming from ahead, but neither one of them could have expected the man with the chainsaws flanking from their left. It was just not fair. Percival was supposed to be an accountant and now he was dying.

He was angry. He was angry at the situation, he was angry at the chainsaw-wielding maniac and he was angry at his father. If not for Tobias Roth, Percival could have just been happy working somewhere safe. If his father had not pushed him, Percival would never have pushed back and hopped on a spaceship to the other side of the system.

Percival's consciousness started to fade and he realized it wouldn't be much longer before he was dead. The suit was no longer able to hold back the blood pouring out of his arteries and the polymer had given way. As the blood poured out of his stumps in earnest, Percival realized that this was somewhat peaceful. He could slip away and no one would criticize him, not his father, not his sister, not anyone; not on his deathbed. Best of all, it wouldn't be long before he came back in a brand-new body.

He smiled just before an explosive shell hit his midsection and burst him to pieces.

CARVER HAD BEEN GETTING ready to lend his support behind Jenkins' idea when they were interrupted by a massive explosion to the north. That artillery was definitely *not* in a different game, but it only took a few seconds for the soldiers to realize they were still alive. Cortes looked over the broken wall by his shoulder and tried to find Roth's beacon, just like everyone else.

There was only smoke where it had been.

"Oh, *c'mon!*" Jenkins shouted, frustration coming through his voice. Carver looked at the young soldier with a bemused grin no one could see.

"*Sudden death artillery*, kid. Yet another lesson that life ain't fair."

Instead of surrender, Jenkins stood straighter and breathed deep, his fists clenched with resolve. He grabbed at his rifle and gripped it until his hand hurt.

"The new plan is we're going to hunt down every last one of them or die trying." Violence permeated through his tone. "We're going to give the audience a fucking show. I'll be damned if I'm going to be blown to bits by artillery because I wanted to take a nap in a trash heap of a house."

Jenkins then turned away from his comrades and walked to the stairs, pausing at the first step.

"Come with me or don't, just don't be surprised when I use my new body to kick your fucking asses," he said before walking down the stairs with determination. Carver smiled at the rookie's antics and rose to his feet, his bones creaking in protest.

"Well, yes, *sir*. We wouldn't want that." He followed after their teammate, but before disappearing from sight, Carver looked at the stragglers and shrugged.

"Might as well get up, boys. You have nothing else to do." He stared at the other Crows for a moment before Warner angrily sighed and picked himself up with difficulty, favoring the gunshot wound in his shoulder.

It was not helping his sunny disposition.

"Fuckin' souvenir from those cunts. I guess I can give 'em some payback. You know what they say about freedom, yeah?" Warner said as he hobbled to the staircase.

Carver smiled and shook his head as Warner walked past him and used his good shoulder to knock into the old man. When Carver turned to Cortes, he knew exactly what the coward would do. He didn't even raise his head.

"Yeah, I figured. Don't complain if things go sour, though," Carver said before walking down the staircase. He joined his comrades, already aware that this was not going to go well for any of them.

A good part of him could sympathize with the coward he left behind.

JENKINS WAS ABSOLUTELY TERRIFIED. He might have acted tough back in their makeshift base, but he didn't have any semblance of that false confidence left.

Luckily, Sudden Death rules made it much easier to find his opponents—each ID beacon had become visible to everyone on the field—but he still felt iffy about his plan.

That could have been because there *was* no plan. Jenkins would have much preferred to follow Carver around—he was the hero of the Crows—but leadership had been thrust upon Ryan Jenkins, and the crown did not rest easy.

It didn't help that there were only three of them running toward the blast site and that the Hawks were likely running there to meet them. Jenkins had considered arguing with Cortes and slapping him around, but it had only taken Carver's hand on his shoulder to convince Jenkins to leave the coward behind.

There was no use wasting words on a man who would not fight for his life.

The artillery shells continued to fall in different parts of the war zone. They were in a random pattern at first—enough to scare the remaining soldiers into killing each other—but now it seemed like they were closing in on the remaining soldiers.

Maybe Roth had been unlucky to get caught in that first blast, or maybe the powers that be had decided to make an example of the man, but Jenkins just hoped the shells would keep falling *around* him instead of *on* him. They did not have much time, and they needed to kill the four remaining Hawks who were now only six hundred meters away.

They broke off their rush toward death a hundred meters from their opponents. It hadn't taken long to reach them, since the Hawks were also sprinting toward *them*, but now they were at an effective stalemate. Neither team wanted to poke its collective head out first and have it blown off, and that was double true of the new soldier who had led them here. Although Jenkins' courage had gotten him this far, he was too nervous to even think about volunteering for scout duty.

Jenkins was perched on a small outcropping of cement and glanced anxiously in the direction of the Hawks. There was a pile of wreckage in the way, and Jenkins half-expected them to vault over and kill him and his teammates at any second.

The rotting corpse to his left didn't even register in his mind, as he was so distracted by the soldiers on the other side of the pile. Jenkins had run into plenty of corpses in his short time on Eris—five games meant five battlefields full of discarded bodies—so he had become desensitized, to a point. When it came to the corpses, the only thing that made him anxious was the prospect of finding his own dead body, but that was because he just did not know how he would react.

Thankfully, he had not yet died enough to make that a possibility.

There was a tense quiet peppered with artillery explosions as the teams prepared for their final battle. The explosive shells were getting closer now, since the Commission—and thus the public—had become impatient and would not be entertained for much longer.

Although this had been his operation, Jenkins shook his head and desperately wanted Carver to take command from him. Seemingly reading his mind, Carver cleared his throat and craned his neck toward Warner.

"Hey, you sweep around left and try to figure out where they're holed up. Jenkins and I will follow and flank from the right. Got it?" That made Warner cock his head to the side and tap his helmet with his right hand.

"You kiddin' me, old man? Why the *hell* would I do that?"

Carver sat back, tapped at his left shoulder and tilted his head in response.

"You still object?" He knew full well that the convict understood the subtext, and Warner looked at his left shoulder and did not hold back a growl that came from his throat.

However, he soon picked himself up from the ground and started to go around the left side. Before breaking cover, he turned his head back to look at his teammates.

"Make sure it's worth it, you faggots." He almost seemed to spit inside his helmet, but as soon as the expletive was out of his mouth, he was gone.

Warner reported nothing for thirty seconds and there was no gunfire, so Carver took it as a sign to head forward with the pincer maneuver and patted Jenkins' back as he passed. The young soldier followed, but not without trying to settle something in his mind.

"Why did he go? And what was the arm thing about?" he whispered, causing Carver to trip on his way out. The old man regained his footing and crept forward, wishing he could avoid the explanation.

"He got shot in the shoulder," he said as he climbed over a pile of rebar, taking care not to step on any scattered pieces of trash as he came down the other side.

"So?"

"*So* he's dead, anyway."

"It didn't look like it'd kill him," Jenkins argued, and this time Carver turned back to look at him and motioned at the broken house forty meters ahead of them.

"Probably wouldn't get the chance to. Enough questions, kid, we got better shit to worry about." Carver grunted out as he climbed over one last pile of steel. "I'll get into specifics when we get through this."

"*Why* is he dead, Carver?" Jenkins asked, suddenly feeling very angry that Carver kept leaving out pertinent details. Jenkins was not a child—no matter what the living legend said—and so he decided that he was not going to move until Carver answered him.

Noticing his stubborn behavior, Carver huffed in annoyance as he walked back to stand over him. "Look, kid. It doesn't *matter*. This whole thing is a suicide mission and we're all dead anyway. Now, you sanctimonious *sack* of *shit*, get ready for everything to go to hell and stop fucking talking."

Carver turned back to the ruined building, which seemed as ominous as the dark sky above them. Even if Jenkins would stand there in the open for the rest of the match, Carver was finished talking.

Though frustrated at the old man's refusal to answer simple questions, Jenkins realized he agreed with Carver; this was not the time or place to talk about the *next* terrible thing that Jenkins had to learn. The very nature of this fabricated moon made him furious. He was angry at the situation, he was angry at the people in charge, but most of all he was angry that he was probably going to die for no reason except that eight worlds worth of humanity wanted to see him bleed.

For now, he was going to give them what they wanted.

Jenkins approached Carver's position and tried to find the Hawks in front of him, seeing their beacons but not the soldiers who owned them. The display in their helmets showed their enemies were only twenty meters away, but perhaps their equipment was faulty.

Once the bullets started flying, the Crows realized they should have died right where they were standing. The Hawks had been lying down in the center of the clearing underneath piles of garbage, watching their enemy approach.

Luckily, they had decided to focus on Warner first, as Carver and Jenkins were further away and could be killed afterward. Warner had almost stepped on one of the soldiers before they had started firing— they had been trying to wait until all three Crows could be killed easily —but when Warner had come so close, they had been forced into action.

Soon after they revealed themselves, bullets tore through Warner and killed him where he stood. It was a painful death, but the sacrifice afforded Carver and Jenkins the opportunity to make their stand.

Jenkins would have cursed himself for a number of mistakes and for Warner's death, but he was trapped in his own bloodlust and rage. He didn't even know what he was yelling; he just knew he could not stop.

There were four Hawks scattered around the clearing; three were on the ground while another was perched on the second floor of the ruined building nearby. Because of his vantage point, Jenkins considered that soldier the most dangerous and sent a few rounds at the Hawk before the man ducked out of sight. Carver clucked his tongue at his teammate's shooting and threw a grenade near the support of the building, and shortly after that sent rounds into the beam supporting the corner of the second floor. Soon enough, the second floor collapsed and caused the Hawk to fall to the ground and onto the grenade.

The explosion underneath their teammate was enough for the three Hawks to turn their focus away from shredding Warner's corpse.

One of the men stood and turned to face the Crows, foolishly thinking their numbers would intimidate their opponents. In response, Jenkins shot him in the knee and followed that with a shot to the visor.

He was not playing nice, anymore.

Unfortunately, neither were the Hawks. The one on the left threw a grenade right between Jenkins and Carver and his teammate threw one onto the ground on the veteran's other side. Although Jenkins was able to jump to the side behind cover, Carver prepared for his death and could only try to jump forward and out of the way.

Try was the operative word; the grenades flung the old soldier forward once they exploded behind him. Carver's right leg was blasted from his body, but the force had already killed him and it was just a corpse that fell between the Hawks.

Not taking any chances, one of the Hawks kicked Carver's body over to look at their work, but he was met with a surprise. Jenkins popped out of cover long enough to see Carver's body roll over and expose the grenade he had primed before he had been launched airborne, and that grenade exploded in the Hawk's face.

After the dust settled, Jenkins realized he was alone with the last Hawk and it was up to him to finish the match. He could no longer rely on his teammates—they had already done plenty—and victory depended on killing this last soldier. Jenkins steeled his nerve and stood out of cover, trying to end it all.

He felt rounds tear into his chest plate and drive the air from his lungs. Jenkins had tried to fire, as well, but the impact of the shells ruined his aim and he doubted the accuracy of his shots. In just half a second, Jenkins realized that he had failed his teammates, the very men that he had led here to die.

That realization was quickly followed by the explosion of an artillery shell directly between the two soldiers.

Jenkins died from the blast almost instantly—the heat wiping him from existence—but his opponent did not last much longer. The explosion launched a piece of hull plating along the ground, and it tumbled and cart-wheeled toward the Hawk who could do nothing to avoid it. After bouncing along the ground, it spun through the man's groin and relieved him of his left leg, sending arterial spurts into the dirt below him.

The Hawk bled out soon afterward, with no one to witness but the cameras.

HECTOR CORTES WONDERED what was taking so long. He had heard the explosions all around him, but could not be bothered to move, as he was not the type of person to run to or from danger. There was no reason to rush things.

Hector felt bad for disappointing Jenkins. He seemed like a good guy—no matter what was in his past—but Hector's heart just wasn't in this fight.

It was never in any fight. Hector had the worst kill-to-death ratio on the team, and that was while ignoring his records from the other teams that had thrown him away. He hated the whole idea behind the games; he had never wanted to kill anyone or force pain on his opponents. Usually, he would aim around the other team and let the others get the credit.

After all, Hector was not on Eris for money or bloodlust; he was here to atone. Dying painfully over and over again seemed like the best way to alleviate his guilt and make up for what he had done.

Hector sank against the wall and looked at the broken ceiling above him. He could see grey clouds overhead, just like every other day cycle. It always seemed like it was about to storm on Eris. In his thoughts, the coward always called the unnatural moon by its true name. There was no reason to give in to the advertising; Eris did not need to be sullied like that.

Looking back at his feet, Hector sighed, sick of all this waiting. If he did not care about what the Commission thought, he would have run to one of the blasts at the beginning of Sudden Death.

However, Cortes was paranoid that those resurrection scientists would mess with his head if he showed he was suicidal in any real way. He had seen what they had done to Norris and how they had treated

Washington way back when. Norris used to be a friendly guy, but now he was a bloodthirsty sociopath. The lab coats must have done something to the man.

Washington was another matter completely. There was no way Hector was going to kill himself and end up like Carver's old student.

Hector heard his brother's laughter echoing throughout the derelict house. It only took a moment for him to realize that it was *not* his brother laughing; Hector understood he was hearing things. As always, he hated that his grasp of reality was based on knowing his brain was lying to him, telling him that something was there with him. He wanted to yell at his own brain; he wanted to strangle it and shout that he knew he should feel guilty. There was no need for the constant reminder that he had killed his brother.

It was an accident, of course. Hector had been running in the Sidewinders and the gang was putting him through initiation. All he had to do was kill his target—Miguel Garcia—outside of a convenience store, but Hector ended up holding his own brother while he died. After the tragedy, his parents disowned him, and he couldn't blame them. Hector had decided that he did not deserve to live, even if it was slave labor on the asteroid farms, so he chose his punishment accordingly.

The penitent killer had never regretted that choice. Hector was more than willing to atone endlessly for killing his brother. Hell was an abstract to him, but Eris was as close as he could get with certainty.

Still, this infernal waiting was getting on Hector's nerves. He should have been blown sky high by now, or discovered by enemy soldiers, at the very least. Failing that, Jenkins should have made his desperate gambit and killed everyone or die trying. Instead, Hector was left sitting on the second floor looking at the torn supports in the ceiling.

He threw away his gun in disgust and sighed inside of his helmet, which was stifling. He was just about to unclip the protective gear and throw it away to join the gun when the announcement flashed across his display, bringing a smile across the soldier's face.

Jenkins, that fool, had done it; he had won the game for the Crows.

Cortes was walking over to his gun—ready to sling the strap over his shoulder—when the AI's feminine voice shocked him.

"Results of the Annihilation Round. Hawks: 0, Crows: 1. Congratulations, Crows. Head back to your Rendezvous point."

Hector could not believe it, at first. Whatever Jenkins and the others had done, Hector was the sole survivor in the annihilation round. At the realization, his shoulders dropped and he stared blankly at the floor. He was ashamed of himself and could not comprehend the twisted logic that seemed to operate on this world.

Jenkins had gone and taken care of the threat and Hector had waited to die. It was not fair, and even Hector could see that. He struck out with his fist against a nearby support beam and heard the bone crack, but he did not care. His only focus was on the injustice of his continued existence. A voice came to mind, his father's this time, but Hector knew that this was no hallucination or delusion. He remembered when his father had first said it, the family credo.

The coward lives on.

Hector could not stop the tears pooling at the bottom of his eyes. He wouldn't have wiped them away if he could. The saying was about him, and he finally understood; it had always been about him. He was just afraid to die, and this was another act of cowardice that had allowed him to live while brave men sacrificed everything. Hector sniffed and tried to regain his composure before heading to the stairs, knowing there was nothing he could do. The beacon for the airlift was four hundred meters away, and he needed to get there, eventually.

Halfway to the beacon, Hector saw his younger brother in that same orange shirt he had worn on the last day of his life. Sam looked disappointed in him and Hector could think of a thousand reasons why his subconscious mind would do this to him. Taking a deep breath, Hector tried to convince himself that Sam was not there. He tried to walk by and ignore his brother, but the vision decided to make that difficult with a verbal barb.

"Why is it always *you*?"

3

So Much for the Afterglow

"Welcome to the best show on television! It's *War World* with Eric Jones, Samantha Bishop, Franklyn Stone and, of course, our senior game correspondent Patrick McEwen!"

Douglas Finnegan hated his voice, hated these people and particularly hated having to praise them on international television. Being the announcer for the most popular program in the system was unfulfilling work. His compensation wasn't nearly as high as those talking heads in front of him, but Douglas couldn't complain. He had the voice for it, after all, even if the focus groups hadn't preferred his real name.

The disheveled announcer for the sports program was wearing loose-fitting clothes and a four-day beard, as he never had to step in front of a camera. His ruddy, brown hair could have used a comb, and his gut—which he had acquired through heavy drinking and pure laziness—was bunching up beneath his shirt. As Douglas sighed in self-loathing, he looked at the talking heads just as the worst of the lot nodded back at him.

"Thanks, Sean, we'll take it from here," Eric said, donning his plastic smile and ready to lie through his teeth. He was picture-perfect; nicely combed light-brown hair and athletic body in a trim suit.

Douglas' eye twitched, and he wondered yet again what was so bad about *Douglas* that the big heads had decided to call him Sean.

"So today we're gonna talk about a few games. We had a great one with the Tigers and the Wolverines and I can't wait to talk about that later on," Eric said before Franklyn chimed in, the token Black anchor smiling from ear to ear.

"Real bloodbath there."

It was just to make noise. Douglas could see a flicker of annoyance on Eric's face, and that made him smile. While Douglas wasn't exactly Eric's biggest fan, he hated Franklyn for a variety of other reasons. Eric was a shallow man-whore who lived the celebrity lifestyle, but Franklyn Stone was an intelligent man who played the stereotypes just so he could have a bigger check.

"Haha, sure was, Frank," Eric said, trying to regain control. "We also had a crazy match between the Grizzlies and the Hammerheads with some full-on mech-suit action."

An image of a monstrous machine piloted by one of the Hammerheads flickered on the television behind him to highlight the game. Before Eric could continue, the blonde woman by his side spoke up.

"Some great plays in that one," Samantha commented, not realizing the canned answer made her seem vapid. The woman was only there to serve as the network's backhanded answer to activism from women's rights groups. Technically, they complied, and now they had another way to keep their male viewers captive.

Douglas was almost grateful when Eric continued despite her interruption.

"Not wrong on that one. But we'll get to those in just a bit. We have to talk about this game between the Hawks and the Crows. Fan-*tas*-tic game, here. And I *know* what you're all thinking at home," Eric said, pointing at the camera. "The Crows have a much higher ranking than the Hawks, but the Commission decided to give those underdogs a *huge* boost."

One of the greatest actors of our generation, surely, Douglas thought before turning his attention to Patrick McEwen, who seemed to have woken from his stupor.

The old soldier's mind had steadily deteriorated over the years, but he had been a big winner in the games and had retired after a long career. On massive TVs around the planet, McEwen had devastated his opponents and been responsible for untold carnage.

That's how the former Crow had paid his way off Eris and had been offered the opportunity for a permanent spot on the program.

It was too bad his brain was addled from the numerous resurrections, and now Patrick was a shade of his former self. To add insult to injury, the producers of *War World* shoved medication down his throat so he wouldn't say anything inappropriate on air. When Patrick sat at the table on set, he seemed to melt into the chair. His hair was white and—if not for the people in charge of makeup—his beard would be scraggly and his liver spots would show. Sadly, his blue eyes only held a small spark of what he used to be.

When he spoke, Patrick was rocking back and forth in his chair.

"Damn fine game. Handicaps weren't around back when I was fighting, but it's nice to see the hustle out there." Patrick grumbled, adding his supposed wisdom to the commentary.

"Sure was, Pat. Great plays on both sides and you couldn't ask for a better annihilation match. Only one athlete walked off that field," Eric agreed, but Franklyn did not let that go without his own comment.

"Couldn't get any closer to a draw, Eric."

Douglas could positively *feel* the contempt from Eric. The smirk remained on Doug's face as Eric wore his plastic smile.

"That's right, Frank, and no one wants that. Well, let's go ahead and dip into some of those highlights. Sam, take it away," Eric said in a rare display of politic. Samantha beamed at the opportunity and read from the teleprompter while clips of the fight were shown on the screens behind them.

"Well, first, Eric," she said with a smile, batting her big brown eyes. "We have the ambush of the Crow's sniper."

While she spoke, images of Norris and Goldstein flickered about the room. Norris was clearly messing around with his compatriot, jostling the man by the shoulder.

"A total surprise on the part of the Hawks," Franklyn started, pausing while he shifted in his seat. "Norris and Goldstein don't have a clue and then boom," he said just as three Hawks swept around and surrounded the two soldiers, "Santiago, Yokoi and Aerin hit 'em hard."

"A good maneuver, to be sure, but my favorite part..." Patrick said, pointing at the center screen as the soldiers fought in the background. Yokoi had stuck a knife in Goldstein right from the start, but it hadn't stopped the middle-aged Crow from turning and spraying a few rounds into the Hawk's helmet in return. Norris was fighting off the remaining Hawks when Patrick wagged his finger at the screen and continued, "...is right here!"

Norris grabbed Aerin by the neck while the other soldier shot at him, but the sniper threw his opponent down the hill and ran after him while the Hawk's bullets took turns glancing off armor and sinking into Norris' flesh. After tumbling halfway down the hill, Norris fell to a spot close to the Hawk and seemed to be having a fit on the screen. Then he finally unstrapped his sniper rifle while the other man groaned and pushed the barrel against the man's helmet.

It was only a moment before he blew the man's head off, causing Patrick to throw up his arms and whoop.

"That's the *good stuff*, people! I tell ya, most of the time when I was playing, us soldiers were just looking for the most stylish kills," Patrick said with a silly grin on his face, his mind clearly mired in the past.

Douglas shook his head. Even after seven years of working with the man, Patrick's bloodlust still surprised him.

"Well, in that case Norris has a pretty decent score with that one," Eric said as the clip continued. Norris was turning with his rifle to take out Santiago, but the other soldier had an incendiary RPG waiting for him.

"Unfortunately, he didn't get to enjoy it," Eric concluded as the Englishman burst into flames behind him.

"Haha, it's still a great image for the fan club. Everyone knows Norris isn't afraid of going down in flames, so long as it's pretty." Franklyn shook with fake laughter before he playfully slapped the counter. "Now, do we get to talk about the best woman in the games?"

"We're getting there, Frank," Eric said with a chuckle.

Douglas rolled his eyes at Franklyn's behavior and wondered how he could stand himself. Franklyn was there for the urban demographic, but *Douglas* had more of a colorful background than the ethnic stereotype on display. Franklyn Stone had gone to Hawking University with full honors, and that creature up there was just smoke, mirrors and plastic.

"Well, we better. I could talk about Jessica Abrams the whole *show*," Franklyn said in a mock serious voice, any sense of self abandoned.

"Hah, since you seem so enthusiastic about her, I guess we can get it out of your system," Eric said as flashes of war flitted about behind them. Eventually, it settled onto an aerial view of Abrams, Cortes and three Hawks pinning each other down.

"Now, this starts out normal enough with a firefight." Samantha relayed the teleprompter script in a serious voice.

"Mhmm, but it stops being that way in a second," Franklyn interrupted. "Now we all know Cortes is a support soldier and the two of them are a good pairing, but the way that Arthur, Blankenship and Baaj have the two covered, they can't really work like they want to."

"Yep, but this is where that starts to change," Eric said as Abrams stayed out of cover to wait for a Hawk to raise his head. When Blankenship rose above cover, he was met with a round from the woman's revolver.

"Hah!" Franklyn laughed as Blankenship fell to the ground, "*That's* because my girl's there. She's all about evening the odds."

"Sure is, Frank, but then things go south here," Eric said as the Crows sat behind cover. "Abrams is out of ammo and they have two Hawks sitting there with guns."

"That's a sorry position if I've ever seen one," Patrick added with a grim nod.

"Yeah, but don't forget that Abrams will surprise you," Frank said with a not-so-sly smile. They all laughed at the statement and Douglas had to fight the urge to run on stage and strangle the fake people in front of him.

Instead, Douglas watched as Abrams broke cover and sprinted toward the Hawks. Baaj and Arthur were shooting at her, but it didn't matter; the gladiator juked and tumbled in all the right places. Cortes popped up enough to give a slight distraction and provide cover fire, but Douglas was focusing on the warrior woman. Abrams vaulted over the Hawks' cover and her blade soon found its way to Arthur's aorta, although she was shot in the belly for the effort.

Abrams then drew out the knife and plunged it under Arthur's chin again just as Cortes' grenade flew between Baaj and the couple embraced in death.

A credit for your thoughts, Douglas thought before the soldiers were ripped apart by the grenade. After it was over, Douglas turned his attention back to the people who made five times his salary. Franklyn had finished jumping around in his seat and the mood had become somber, or at least as somber as the stage of *War World* could be.

"Always a tough call when you have to sacrifice one of your own, but Cortes made the right decision," Patrick said with morose approval.

"Seems to be the theme of this game," Samantha proclaimed, to no one's surprise.

"Pretty much," Eric started, "but we'll get to that in a little bit. Let's focus on the Hawks for a while. They were pretty smart with their deployment this time around and you can see that with their treatment of Templeton and Roth."

"Oh yeah, that was good stuff," Franklyn said with a nod.

"Classic skirmisher play," Patrick declared while shifting in his seat, drawing a nod from Eric.

"Beautiful execution, too. Two rangers and a melee berserker are such a powerful team. They didn't even get the drop on the Crows this time, but they came out ahead." Eric was always careful when explaining the plays to their, presumably, simple viewers.

"Right," Franklyn said, trying to pick up where Eric left off. "So we have Morimoto and Sachinsky with rifles paired with Williams, who just so happens to have the chainsaw gauntlets."

"Even though I only had a few years to deal with them, I'll be the first to say that no matter what equipment I had, the chainsaws always scared the crap outta me," Patrick said with a nervous chuckle.

"You're not the only one, Pat," Eric said with an understanding nod. "It certainly unnerved the Crows in this play."

"That's a way to say it!" Samantha exclaimed. "Morimoto and Sachinsky set up a great diversion with their stand-off while Williams flanked the Crows."

"That's all they needed to do," Eric interrupted with a smile. He permitted the woman her own highlight, but he could lend his grace to the occasional explanation. Samantha returned the smile and then continued, just as Williams rushed the two men in the background.

"They played that part well, it seems. As you can see here Williams gets to Roth first and literally sweeps the legs out from under him," she said as the man ran up to Roth's side and cut upward through the gaps in the armor behind the Crow's knees. The man fell onto his back as gore flew out from the wounds.

"Way to take advantage of that blindside," Frank said in a more serious tone, almost slipping into his actual personality.

"Yep, Roth didn't even see it coming. Now watch this, Williams uses the opening to get closer to Templeton and then," Eric said as he started a controlled wince, "...*wham!*"

He slammed the table just as Williams slid both chainsaws into Templeton's ribcage. Blood gurgled out through the openings as the weapons ground Templeton's organs to liquid.

"Horrible way to go, but at least Templeton had the right idea and pulled his grenade pin. You can see it happen in just a second," Samantha said, and true to her word, the soldiers exploded into pieces. Franklyn nodded and cleared his throat.

"Say what you will about the Crows, but they sure know how to make everything count. Roth and Templeton are rookies, but they did what they could to balance it all out," Frank said in approval.

"Right, nothing to be ashamed of there," Samantha said while nodding. "In fact, if things hadn't worked out the way they did in Sudden Death, it might have been Roth who was the last man standing, well... so to speak..."

Samantha trailed off once she realized what she had just said, but tried to push forward. "The guy laid there and Morimoto and Sachinsky moved on. Just poor luck with that first artillery shell."

Douglas had smiled when he heard her poor choice of words, and most smiled along with him. Patrick, however, shifted in his seat before speaking.

"I wanna go back to how the Crows make everything count. I just wanna remind people that I actually used to play for the Crows. Now, I've only actually played with one of these guys…"

"Carver," Eric interjected.

"Right, but there were two of these athletes that made me proud to be a Crow, today."

"Oh, I can guess who those are," Frank said with a fake smile. Patrick looked at him with mild annoyance, clearly regarding his co-anchor with little respect.

Douglas wished the old man still had his mind; he would probably like whatever the retired Crow would say.

"I'm sure you could, Franklyn. It's pretty obvious that I'm talking about Feldman and Jenkins. Those two were quite the pair," Patrick said in approval and with a loud sniff, Eric nodding along the entire time.

"They definitely were. I'm not sure who was more impressive today."

Douglas thought he saw the head anchor being *genuine* for once, but he shook his head at the consideration. As he did, Franklyn let out a loud boom of a laugh before launching into his so-called opinion.

"My vote has to be with Feldman. That guy is a *monster*. I'm sure he's a nice guy—the way he talks—but with all that stuff he hauls around, he is a *huge* target. And here he gets absolutely *destroyed* by four of the Hawks," Franklyn started as the screen began the prepared footage of Feldman as he stood against a hail of hundreds of bullets.

"Then," Franklyn continued, "the guy picks himself up and kills the *four* guys who had already killed him and he does it with *one* swing! He is just a *monster*. I would *never* want to fight that guy!"

The explanation drew a smirk from Eric on the other side.

"Pretty sure you won't have to. But you have to consider Jenkins." Eric waved his hand in an empty gesture, just to catch the public's attention. "He's only been in five games so far and he's still considered a rookie, but he showed his mettle today. He really stepped up and led the Crows in their standoff in Sudden Death. Sometimes things just click and then we get to see something like *this*. I cannot *wait* to see what Jenkins becomes with just a little more experience."

As he spoke, the background televisions were showing how Jenkins had killed the lone Hawk he had encountered on his way to his compatriots. Across ten screens, Ryan Jenkins grabbed the soldier's neck from behind, bringing his rifle up to the man's back before pumping a few rounds into the soldier's torso. As the Hawk fell and Jenkins moved on in silence, the anchors were more concerned with their conversation.

"Yeah, but Jenkins had Carver and Warner backing him up the whole way. It's easy to be brave when you have a veteran athlete giving you support and—well, to be honest—one of the craziest men I've ever seen. Feldman was all alone," Franklyn replied.

Looks like he identifies with the asteroid farmer who has nothing in common with him, Douglas thought. *Or he **really** likes the muscles.*

"Backup from Carver or not, Jenkins stood up. He got them to move and keep fighting, and in the thick of it you don't get a chance for composure or rational thinking, Frank," Patrick started with a tone of disapproval, the pronunciation of his words becoming clearer.

"That he was able to get them to pull together with so little experience is a true testament to his character. And, because of their gamble leaving Cortes behind to live, they were able to grab victory even with the odds stacked against them. Jenkins was a true soldier out there today. That doesn't come from mindlessly killing the people who had already shot you. Feldman's act *was* impressive, but Ryan Jenkins showed us potential while taking victory."

Sometimes Patrick had a lucid moment and he would speak his own brand of wisdom, showing the world what he used to be. Douglas loved it when the soldier shamed them all.

"Yeah, but Feldman's *all* show business." Franklyn tried to break the silence with laughter and threw his hands up. "Not saying Jenkins didn't show his stripes, Pat. I just like to side with my man, Feldman."

His plastic smile gave no hint to the apprehension he felt, but everyone knew Franklyn was nervous. Patrick scowled at the man, but soon enough turned his gaze down to the table and huffed. Douglas could see the production managers soundlessly screaming at each other and trying to cue up some sort of commercial break, but his eyes were on one man in particular.

Jamie Caswell, the lead producer, was glaring at Eric as if to tell the lead anchor to take control. The false man nodded with his eyes and then turned to the camera.

"Well, we can always bring this to the people. How about you guys call in or message us and tell us your favorite part of the match. We'll start answering them on air right after these commercials. And don't forget, we have an exclusive interview with Alexandra Quayle from the Eagles. She's going to talk to us about her career, including her time on the Harpies, the all-female team!"

All of the anchors' faces were beaming except Patrick, who was looking sullen with his hands clasped together on the table.

Douglas was almost too distracted by the spectacle to notice that Jamie had turned and was motioning for him to read off the announcement on his screen. Noiselessly, the announcer cleared his throat and then read off the display.

"We'll be right back with the best show on television. Be sure to send your messages to our website or call in to the *War World* phone line. You better not change the channel. You don't want to miss what happens next. This program is brought to you by McCoy's, *Feeding The Whole System*, and Future Bionics, *The Future is **You**.*"

After he finished, Douglas sighed and watched Jamie Caswell walk over from the office to scold Patrick for his outburst. Douglas couldn't blame the old man for speaking his mind, not when it was something worth hearing.

Unfortunately, Jamie Caswell—with his slicked-back black hair and his tailored suit—decided if anything was worth hearing.

They'll probably cut it out of the broadcast tonight, Douglas thought. *Fuckin' shame.*

He watched as Caswell walked back to the assistant production manager and chewed him out for not preparing McEwen properly for the broadcast. As he considered the state of his world, Douglas shook his head and walked over to the break room, stopping at the coffee machine. He could see through the window that Patrick was still sitting in his chair, looking at the blank screen that had just shown the team he had left behind on Eris.

Poor guy must miss it, Douglas thought.

Patrick was the only one that Douglas liked. He absolutely despised Franklyn, who was currently ignoring Samantha's advances, and both of them had been on Doug's nerves for some time. Samantha was trying really hard to bark up the wrong tree and get into Franklyn's wallet, and Douglas knew that nobody else liked her, either.

If that wasn't the case, somebody would have told her that Franklyn was gay. Instead, they just laughed at her for not noticing.

Douglas was in the process of stirring cream and sugar into his coffee when he felt someone walk up behind him and stop at his side. When Douglas looked out of the corner of his eye, he saw Eric making his own cup of coffee.

"Damn shame when that happens," Eric said in a rare display of courtesy. Douglas had to restrain the urge to roll his eyes.

"The thing with Patrick?" he asked. Douglas was stuck in the conversation, anyway, so he might as well help it along.

"Mhmm, I hate it when they talk down to him."

You're one to talk, you asshole, Douglas thought.

"Yeah, well, they have to make sure he says all the right things."

"Sounded like the right thing to me," Eric said while stirring his own coffee, which caught Douglas by surprise. Eric lifted an eyebrow once he noticed the reaction. "What, I can't agree with the man?"

"Sorry, I just didn't expect that from you. My impression was always that you care more about the paycheck," Douglas half-heartedly criticized. He had his own guilt-soaked paycheck to cash.

"Of course, I care about that, but that Jenkins kid reminds me of a cousin I had once. I just sympathize for the guys down on that fucked-up asteroid," he said while looking at Patrick, who was waving away an intern holding a small cup of pills.

Douglas joined his gaze to watch the old man in his protest. Patrick was a half-formed relic, and it was sad to think this poor veteran was one of the few success stories for the games.

"They do have it pretty bad. But like I said, I just don't expect that from you," Douglas said before sipping on his coffee. He had made it too sweet, but he wanted the caffeine anyway.

"You don't have to hate me, you know. I'm not as bad as Jamie. I just talk up there. *You* know the difference, I think," Eric said before heading back.

Although Douglas did what he could to come back to his senses, that last comment stung, considering the source. After taking a moment to recover, Douglas walked to his own station to wait for the end of the commercial break.

The makeup people were buzzing about the talking heads now and trying to prepare them for the next segment. As the old man was patted down with makeup, Douglas could see the wistfulness in Patrick's eyes fade. It made him think about the whole situation in the studio. Then it made him think about all those poor souls down there on Eris.

It's just stupid, that's what it is, Douglas thought before reading off the next sponsor's message.

DARKNESS AGAIN. He was engulfed by it. If Ryan could move, he could not feel it. His senses were absent and all he could do was think.

At least he knew what happened this time.

Ryan waited for his cell to be brought to the loading bay and to start the painful process all over again. It was a jarring and uneasy awakening, but at least this time there was no religious experience; no crisis of existence. He knew he just had to wait and the light would break and he would be reintroduced into the world. There was no purgatory for him.

At least not the abstract kind.

The newborn Crow had no concept of real time in his prison. He could have been awake a minute, maybe ten. He had no real way of knowing, and the torrent of thoughts racing through his mind did not help. It was interminable, and he started to doubt his assertions. Maybe he *was* feeling true death this time around. Maybe that sense of security was being proven false.

With the doubt came the panic.

The light came eventually, and he felt much more at ease with its presence; he felt fortunate and grateful for that light. Dread soon followed, since the whole painful process was coming around again and there was nothing he could do to stop it. A small part of him did not want to leave his cell.

But Ryan realized he did not have a choice.

He was angry he was in this situation. He was furious that he had been tricked into this perpetual cycle of dying and painful rebirth. He was livid that he had no chance to escape.

The worst part was waking up in the darkness. It seemed especially unfair that he had to suffer this twice, as Dr. Kane had told him it was rare. She told him that she was sorry and that it would not happen again. The first time was just a statistical anomaly, she had said.

Even the nice ones were lying to him. Ryan wanted to scream. He wanted to throw his fists against the glass and fight the world. Ryan could not scream; he had a breathing tube stuck in his throat. He could not break the glass; his arms were too weak. He realized there was nothing worse than being angry and not being able to do a thing about it.

Ryan was a grown man and had no agency in his own life. His last stand on the battlefield seemed so silly now. He would always end up here, so he continued to wait for the growing light in front of him. He hung there in the restraints of his Plexiglas tube, each minute passing by unbearably slow. It was his only option, or, at least, that's what he thought.

However, he realized that was wrong. There was something he *could* do, even if it didn't make sense. It was not rational, but he had all these thoughts about how he could have brain damage and not even know it. Dr. Kane had said that these premature adoptions—or whatever they were called—likely ended in mental dissolutions, or whatever *they* were called. It might be better just to try again.

And it was *something*; it was in his control. He could assert himself into his life, into his deaths. He had a choice.

He grabbed at the breathing tube, or tried to. His arms were weak and he could barely muster the effort to raise them, but after a strenuous moment, he brought them behind his neck. He felt around his head for the straps and restraints. It was a trial—he could barely feel anything—but even in his numb and desensitized state he could sense the pieces that were not part of him. He grabbed at the strap and lifted it around his head.

He wanted this.

Ryan Jenkins yanked out the tube and prepared to drown.

CARVER HAD a unique flair to him. Even with his new body, absent facial hair or calluses, the old man gave off a gruff and weathered air. Charlotte wondered at the living legend, who was more than twice her age. He had been through the resurrection process so many times that he denied the usual treatment; he would want to leave as soon as he exited his cell.

If nothing else, Charlotte enjoyed the change of pace. Carver seemed to accept his position and the process. It made her job easier, her conscience lighter.

Before Charlotte had ever started to work at the clinic, Carver had made it clear he would never take any of their sedatives or drugs. Early in his career, Hawkins had made the mistake of trying to administer Carver with a tranquilizer against his will. Carver had thrown the smaller man onto the floor and stepped on his throat, and since then Hawkins had not forced anything on the older man.

When she had heard about the incident, Charlotte had laughed at the image. It was just another act that endeared him to her.

Charlotte was outlining Carver's upcoming exercise program to him when the alarms went off in the resurrection chamber. The smile on her face disappeared once she could see Hawkins scrambling with controls through the clear windows, and she felt anxious even before Carver spoke up.

"You better go. Wouldn't trust that guy for anything."

Charlotte agreed under her breath and rushed to the other room. When she burst through the doors, she found Hawkins furiously tapping the display overlay.

"What happened?"

"One of those damn soldiers screwed up the process. Messed up his airway somehow." Hawkins was more focused on trying to move the cell into the chamber than the conversation with his assistant.

"Which soldier?" Charlotte asked while trying to read the name for herself on the display. She figured it would be faster, given Hawkins' proclivities.

"Does it matter?"

The loading bay opened up in front of them and Hawkins seemed to calm down slightly, tapping the screen in front of him to prepare the resurrection machines.

"You idiot, don't get that out. Get the crash unit out instead," Charlotte urged.

Hawkins glared at her, but quickly started the process for the crash unit even though he was unwilling to admit he had been wrong. The machines that had been coming out of the wall started to retreat back, more slowly than Charlotte would have preferred.

Even though she had that sinking feeling in her gut that she already knew the patient's identity, she continued to scan down the screen. Most of the Crows had already been through the resurrection process and were already in physical therapy.

"Oh, no," Charlotte murmured once she was proven correct. Ryan Jenkins' miserable face was staring back at her from his picture on the overlay.

If she had gods, she would have cursed them.

"What?" Hawkins asked in a clipped manner. He was already annoyed with her for pointing out his mistake with the resurrection equipment and didn't want any more unpleasant blows to his ego. Only now were the mechanical arms and medicine caches sinking within the walls, and the last cell was just becoming visible in the blackness of the storage area.

It was unlikely the crash unit would be ready for the soldier.

"It's Jenkins," Charlotte murmured.

"Who?"

"He was the last premature adoption, Hawkins! Don't you remember?"

"Oh, him," Hawkins said, suddenly more curious than angry. "He certainly has bad luck."

Charlotte was furious at that point. Hawkins was a callous sort, but sometimes the man seemed to have no humanity left. She wheeled around to the entrance to the chamber and half-ran to the loading deck, her lab coat catching the wind as she made her way.

The crash unit was still slowly extracting itself from the wall, causing Charlotte to scream profanities at the people in charge of making the thing. Ryan's cell entered the room, clipped into the intermediate stage and the biotic fluid started to drain from the soldier's container, but Charlotte knew it was not fast enough.

"C'mon, c'mon, c'mon," Charlotte willed the machine under her breath. The now nearly-empty cell sank into the loading deck and the loading arm returned back into the opening behind it. The cell hissed as it opened and revealed Ryan lying limp with his breathing tube hanging to the side.

"Shit!" Charlotte shouted. "Hawkins, get in here!"

"Wait a bit," Hawkins said over the intercom. He had lost his sense of urgency when he saw the breathing tube lying outside of the action figure's throat. As long as it was the soldiers' fault they had died, Hawkins didn't have to worry about any liability fines. He could take his time, and the Crow was most likely brain dead from the premature adoption, anyway.

Charlotte cursed Hawkins along with her pretend gods, looking in desperation at the crash unit that was even now coming out of the wall.

"Shit," she said again, knowing she had to do something. Left without options, Charlotte rushed to Ryan's side, lifted his chin and pressed her hands to the man's chest. She pumped three times, then placed her mouth to his and tried to get his lungs to work. The process was archaic, but the human body had not changed.

Hawkins laughed as his assistant was hurriedly attempting CPR. Doctors only learned it in medical school as a formality. Compared with all the technology of the day, it was crude, at best.

Hawkins shrugged as he started to tap on the display again, completely giving up on saving the soldier's life. Charlotte had found an appropriate pet, it seemed, and he did not want to get in the way as it died.

Even with all her efforts, Charlotte tried for about a minute and had no idea if she was even performing it correctly. Throughout the process she looked at Ryan's vitals and what she saw did not encourage her. His brain activity was almost nonexistent.

It was a mixed reward when the man sputtered back to consciousness. A stream of biotic fluid spurted out of the man's mouth onto Charlotte, covering the front of her lab coat and the white blouse underneath. There was more, but the rest of the fluid just drained out to his side as Ryan sputtered toward consciousness. It was disgusting, but Charlotte was more concerned with his life than her comfort.

He coughed up the rest of the fluid and opened his eyes. When he looked up at Charlotte, Ryan was completely lost.

"Ryan, are you okay?" Charlotte wiped off the biotic fluid and tried to be as compassionate as possible.

He looked up at her with eyes filled with sadness and pain, and he shook his head.

Well, look at that, Hawkins thought as he sat in the Control Room. He had not expected it to work. After seeing the soldier come back to life, Hawkins tapped a few more times at the screen to move the resurrection equipment back into place.

He had to laugh at how the crash unit had just now slid into place, shaking his head at the action figure's suicidal antics.

"What an idiot," he muttered to himself.

"Seems like."

It startled Hawkins and he whipped around to see a mostly-naked Jonathon Carver standing behind him, still staring at the people in the resurrection chamber. The veteran looked down as Hawkins made too much noise and slid away from him.

"Oh, relax, you pansy. I'm not here for you," Carver said dismissively. He turned to walk through the door of the chamber, and Hawkins didn't even think about stopping him.

Ryan was having a rough time coming back to the living. Even though Charlotte was trying to talk, the words felt muddled as he continued to drift toward consciousness. Ryan could not quite hear her, but he could see that she cared. She looked pretty.

"Are you okay?" she asked, and he could finally hear her. Ryan hurt quite a bit; his throat even more than the last time. In response, Ryan shook his head. He didn't feel the need to lie to her.

"Do you know who you are?"

Ryan thought about the question. He knew who he was. At least, he knew his name and where he was, and so he nodded at her. Charlotte visibly relaxed after his answer, but soon after that he noticed a shadow above her. Ryan panicked at first before he recognized that it was Carver's elderly face. He relaxed, confident he was safe.

He was not.

Ryan felt Carver's strong hand close around his throat and suddenly he was off the table and thrust against the wall. Although Ryan could hear Charlotte say something, his focus was on the old Crow who held up his entire body just after being resurrected, himself. Atrophied and weak, Ryan could not help but listen to Carver.

"I know you can't speak, yet. Your vocal chords are new and unpracticed. That will not stop you from hearing what I have to say. In fact, it's better because you can't interrupt.

"*Never.* Never do that again. I know you're angry, but that's *not* a solution. They will save you, or they will *stop* you. Even if they can't, they'll just bring you *back*. If you'd been gone for any longer, the next body would have woken up and *that*, my friend, would have been a problem. *Think*, Ryan, before you decide something like that."

Carver had not hurt him; he had just held him against the wall. After shaking him one more time, Carver let Ryan go and started out the door, Charlotte glaring at him as he went. When he noticed that anger, Carver turned to her with a shrug.

"Coddling the suicides doesn't help them. They need to know their situation."

"That couldn't wait five minutes?"

"It could have, but he could understand me. He wasn't dying anymore. And now," he said, turning to look back at Ryan. "Well, now he has something to think about."

With that, Carver walked back out of the resurrection chamber.

Charlotte was angry at the man. There was plenty of time to knock sense into a soldier after a near-death experience, but grabbing Ryan immediately after bringing him back to life wasn't a good way to go about it. This was the second time in a row Ryan had a premature adoption, and Carver, even if he was a living legend, needed to respect that.

Then she remembered the medical condition they had in common.

Immediately, she stopped being angry. Charlotte looked down at Ryan and felt sorry for both of them, kindred in their misery. After helping him back to the table, Charlotte grabbed a syringe and manually gave Ryan a sedative, not bothering to rely on the machine that had just come out from the wall. The soldier closed his eyes and let tears fall down the side of his cheek, and Charlotte only just had the ability to stop her own.

Carver walked through the control room without looking at Hawkins. If he had, he would have seen the wicked smile twisting the scientist's face.

"I rather liked that speech."

Carver had been at the doorway of the room—ready to leave—but he stopped after Hawkins' smug statement. He turned slowly and faced the smaller man.

"Oh really? Well, I have a few words I would share with you. Would you like to hear them?" Carver made sure venom was dripping from every word.

Hawkins flinched ever so slightly, but soon he was bolstered by his over-inflated ego. The soldier dare not touch him; not after the fine from last time.

"*Sure*, Carver. What words would you like to say?" Hawkins *wished* the soldier would do something, and then the Commission would give him carte blanche to do whatever he wanted to the veteran. Carver merely shrugged at the question and eased the tension from his shoulders.

"When you're dying, you'll be ready to hear them," he said before turning and walking through the doorway. His confidence forgotten, Hawkins forgot to breathe until well after the soldier's departure.

When he did, it was not with relief.

RYAN HAD THOUGHT about what Carver had said, but his sadness had quickly turned to anger. He resented the old man for that lesson in shame and started to feel sorry for himself. Carver should have held only compassion for the new soldier, since he had to deal with entirely different circumstances. These premature adoptions made Ryan angry and he was *allowed* to be angry; he was allowed to rage against his situation.

The old man had stepped into his life and out of bounds.

Yet it was a quiet resentment. Everything Carver had said to him was completely true, and it didn't take long for Ryan to realize it. What really bothered him was the *way* Carver had relayed the message.

It was only made worse that Carver was by his side throughout the therapy process, since the massive scale of the annihilation match and the timing of their deaths meant that the two of them had to undergo their therapy together.

Ryan's strained thoughts during that time had been filled with fantasies of tackling the older man and beating him within an inch of his life. It wasn't *completely* out of the question. Ryan was young, after all, and that was something Carver certainly had going against him.

The old Crow would get some licks in, certainly, but in his fantasy, Ryan would have bloody knuckles and little else. Those thoughts of violence helped him through the calisthenics regimen; those thoughts of revenge were enough to push away the pain.

He had someone to be angry toward, and that was enough.

The entire walk back to the base was uneventful. Ryan had actively tried not to look at Carver on the way to the barracks, as he wanted as little interaction as possible with the veteran. That did not stop his curiosity, however, and every once in a while, he glanced. From just a few steps behind, Ryan watched the elder soldier gazing up at the ruined moon.

During their walk, there was only one time where the old soldier looked away from the broken satellite. At the time, Ryan had increased his pace to get in front of the man, but had ended up at Carver's side. The veteran didn't even turn his head; he just looked out the corner of his eye at the young soldier beside him. Carver was asking a rhetorical question with those blue eyes, and he already knew the answer.

Ryan wanted blood.

ONCE THEY WERE inside the building, it was only a couple of minutes before Ryan finally snapped and tried to grab at Carver's neck from behind.

He quickly earned Carver's elbow slamming against his stomach, and pain spread throughout his abdomen. He didn't even have the time to spit out the air in his lungs before Carver swept the legs out from under him and followed with a palm thrust determined to pass through his chest and into the floor.

It didn't quite make it, but Ryan's ribcage creaked from the effort.

Ryan retched as Carver stood over him. He had no food in his stomach before the counter—which was quite the blessing—but biotic fluid ended up covering the floor in front of his bleary eyes. Once Ryan rolled onto his back, he saw Carver looking down at him.

He was not angry; the old man was practically apathetic. Only the slightest lowering of his eyelids betrayed the lurking sympathy behind them. After a moment, Carver stepped away from the vomit and reached out his hand.

"C'mon. No funny business. We're gonna talk."

Ryan wasn't mad anymore, but he was still wary of Carver's intentions. He let the Crow's hand stay floating in the air, which drew a sigh out of his old teammate.

"Just talking, Ryan. I need to tell you something."

Ryan almost thought about grabbing the elder's hand, dragging him downward and smearing his wrinkly face in the vomit beside him. He very quickly realized he did not have the willpower or strength for it, so he reached for Carver's hand. Once he did, the old man dragged him to his feet and led them to the mess hall.

The fluorescents were not filling the room with artificial light as usual, which created a strange effect. They were able to see their surroundings well due to the light bouncing off the Earth, moons and other floating objects, so the room lights weren't *necessary*, but it was quite different from the usual atmosphere.

Ryan decided he preferred it this way.

Carver walked over to the second table, sat down on the bench and promptly seemed to deflate in front of Ryan's eyes. His shoulders sagged; his legs went limp. For the first time, Ryan saw the legend and thought he was actually *old*. Carver didn't just have years behind him, he had all the aches and pains that came with them. Taking a moment to gather himself, Carver eventually looked up at the young soldier and beckoned him to take a seat on the bench across from him.

Ryan was wary, but he did not know how long those new legs of his would allow him to stand—the pain was already creeping through him —so he sat down and eyed the old man across the table. Carver let out a tired breath and tapped his chest twice.

"How's the..."

Ryan squinted at the old soldier and looked away, unable to make eye contact. He never thought he would see Jonathon Carver look awkward, but his newly-acquired resentment wasn't going away anytime soon.

"What do you *expect*? You know just as well as I do that a pat on the back isn't going to make it better," he said, sniffing as he crossed his arms and glared at the window at the end of the room. Carver sighed and put his hand up to support his head.

"Sorry about that. I've always been a fan of ending troublesome things before they start. So," he said before pausing for emphasis. Ryan had turned back to glare at his superior, finally able to make eye contact.

Carver was staring right back, which reminded him of the gargoyles of New Chicago. Those twisted sculptures held endless promises of mystery for Ryan as he grew up, and he had spent afternoons staring at the creatures outside the public buildings. As he glared at Carver, Ryan felt that his gaze was the same, except for the bright blue eyes.

"Speak your mind, kid," Carver muttered, rubbing through the stubble already forming on his new face. At the offer, Ryan thought about screaming a thousand curses and maybe suggesting Carver stick his head up his ass.

However, he only thought about it. Carver had heard all of it and worse by people much more intimidating than someone like Ryan Jenkins. In addition, Ryan really couldn't blame Carver for anything. Everything the old man had done to him was in retaliation against his foolish actions.

At the realization, Ryan looked down and huffed, as he had nothing to say.

"Well, if you don't want to, I'll talk," Carver said, his gaze softening as he shifted his head to the other hand and continued. "I can understand your frustration. I've felt the same anger. I have no idea what it was like for you on Earth, I'm guessing—or wherever you came from—but I know all the misery you could ever experience here on Eris. You're not alone."

Ryan heard the seemingly empty platitudes and felt offended. To him, it was just another leader speech. What bothered him most was offered in that last statement. It was enough for him to growl at the older man.

"Okay, I get that you're trying to play father figure, but you do *not* know what's happened to me!" he snarled, slapping the table and gesturing wildly with his right hand. "Sure, we *die*—some of us more than others—but every time they bring me back, they fuck up the whole process! I wake up completely numb and drugged up and I can't even see anything because it's all pitch black. The first time I didn't even know if I was alive or if I'd gone to limbo or someplace even worse! They strand me in the darkness with no ounce of comfort. I'm alone in there. You can't understand."

Carver merely sighed. No shock; no awe. He just looked at his young teammate.

"Yeah, I figured. It's not common, but you're not the first one this had happened to. Eventually, you'll get used to it."

Ryan only scoffed at the veteran before looking away. "You can't tell me that."

"Sure, I can. I can say whatever I *want*, but this just so happens to be the truth. After the first few years, I almost looked forward to it. It's quiet in those few hours. You can't really get that here too often," Carver said as he looked at the window. "It's almost ... precious."

Ryan eyed the old man with suspicion. When Carver turned back to look at him, a wry smile spread across his wrinkled face.

"That was my not-so-subtle form of confession, kid," he admitted, propping himself up on the table.

"What..."

"Honest, kid. Not something I'd lie about."

"Every time?"

"Think so. Memory's starting to drop out on me."

"But you've died so many..."

"Hundreds. Thousands, maybe. Again, memory loss is common with men my age."

"How do you deal with it?" Ryan asked, unable to comprehend that someone else had experienced this problem before, and—even more ridiculous—that Jonathon Carver was that man.

Ryan had given into despair and assumed he was in for a thousand lives of misery, but Carver was a *legend*. He had played in the games before Ryan had been born and he had died countless times.

And Carver had somehow learned to manage the darkness.

"Well," Carver paused as he shifted on the bench, "at first, I was like you. I was angry at everyone and everything. Eventually, I just couldn't keep it up. I couldn't keep spending all of my energy being angry. It was exhausting. Besides, it's not exactly like they could really help me from being a fluke. They still don't know why it happens. Probably why you came down with it, too.

"I started trying to get out of here at one point. I was just desperate to make it stop. I took one look at my balance sheet and promptly forgot about any of *those* dreams. Even after a few resurrections, the debts are just too much to overcome. You're already screwed, if you haven't figured that out," Carver said, interrupting himself. "Without that sentence of yours, you might have gotten out, but you've got— what, six months of the games to play?"

Ryan nodded at his new role model.

"Yeah, you're done for. That's the usual sentence and at that point you're never getting out. Might as well forget about it. Warner wasn't too out of line when he barked at you after that first fight. Kid almost made it," Carver said before sighing and then scratching the back of his neck with new nails.

"Anyway, after I found out about my debts, I basically stopped caring. I was just floating through the games. I died more than a few times in that period. The more apathetic I became about the whole ordeal, the less the early adoption bothered me. I knew it would always be like that and that I had nothing to be afraid of. I ended up just flexing my muscles to get ready for the physical therapy. It was a good way to pass the time and it really helped out. I whole-heartedly suggest it, since you're in the same situation."

Carver looked down and coughed into his hand, and Ryan felt bad for this older version of himself. Whatever hope he had gained upon finding a kindred spirit had been dissolved; he had nothing to look forward to.

"You just... stopped caring?"

"Yeah, well, kinda. It just doesn't affect me anymore. There are always other problems to focus on, and sitting by myself in the darkness for a few hours isn't much of a problem. If I was a prick, I'd say you'd understand when you're older, but I'm sure you're plenty old enough to understand that."

Carver seemed to have finished his explanation. What had seemed like such a major development for Ryan had been worth nothing more than a sympathetic nod from the veteran, and Ryan let out a heavy breath.

"So, what's the deal here? Are we modern-day unicorns? How many of us are there?" Ryan asked with a half-hearted wave of his hand.

"I really have no idea. Thought I was the only one around, but it's definitely possible there's more out there. When the scientists figured out that I was destined for premature adoption with every resurrection, they basically swore me to secrecy at risk of permanent death. We used to have another one on the team but he's... he's gone," Carver said before turning away, obviously affected by a powerful memory. He looked back up and shrugged at his compatriot.

"No use in really worrying about it, though. We're stuck here with ourselves. None of them will be able to ease our minds," Carver said as he started to twiddle his thumbs. He kept surprising his young compatriot with these unexpected behaviors, but Ryan was more concerned with taking it all in.

"Wait, you said they threatened you with permanent death?" Ryan asked while lowering his gaze. Carver nodded and leaned back on the bench. "If you were so miserable, why didn't you just take that route? I mean, I know the feeling."

"Kid, honestly, that's a different situation. No matter how terrible your life is, when actually faced with a certain decision about letting yourself die, it's difficult as hell to make it. In that Plexiglas tube it's pretty easy to think death could be better. When Garrison sits you down at a desk and talks about taking away your very existence like it's a trade agreement ... it's a little intimidating. Even the worst circumstances aren't enough to stop you from clinging onto any hope that things could be better here where you know how the world works. That afterlife thing the churches always promote seems like quite the fairytale."

"It could be better."

"Could be worse. Could be *nothing*. It could be *just the same*. You can't know. But this," Carver said as he tapped his arm, tapped his chest and felt the wrinkles around his eyes. "This is a little more concrete than a sky fairy that tempted its creations into betraying it."

Ryan looked at the old Crow in appreciation. He had never been the biggest believer in anything, and he had always preferred the asphalt below his feet or the money in his pockets. It was not difficult to understand where Carver was coming from.

"I guess I get it."

"Sad fact of life. We're all children of Thomas, in a way. Doubt thrives in any circumstance," Carver admitted, sinking into his own sorrow.

"That's... pretty depressing." Ryan had a lot to digest, and he watched as Carver shook his head and wiped the fatigue from his eyes. "So did we lose the match?"

Carver could not help but laugh at his colleague. He shook his head and ran his hand through the light fuzz on his scalp, thinking there were worse things than Ryan showing up in his life like this.

"You certainly have a way of changing topics. If you really care, I talked to Dr. Kane about it. We won," he said, wearing a dry smile. At that, Ryan raised an eyebrow.

"*How*? I didn't kill that last Hawk..."

"Artillery shell killed the both of ya. Poor kid got sliced up by a bunch of steel plating."

"Then why did we win?" Confusion was evident in Ryan's voice. He didn't understand how it could have turned in their favor. Even if that Hawk had died, he had still died *after* Ryan had been destroyed.

"It's because I was still alive."

Alarmed by the new voice in the room, Ryan turned quickly to see Cortes standing in the doorway.

His anger came back like it had never been gone.

HECTOR WAS STARING at the ceiling and his head hurt quite a bit. He forgot why he was down there until he saw Ryan's face appear above him, his brow furrowed and teeth exposed in anger. Then the rookie drove a fist into Hector's face with a right hook.

It hurt.

Hector briefly thought about letting Ryan beat him to death, but his survival instincts kicked in and he shoved the man off him with his legs. The rookie rose two feet in the air, but he soon fell back down to slam his fist into the coward's jaw. In his daze, Hector allowed Ryan to get two more hits in before he bucked his hips and launched him past his head.

Once clear of his attacker, the smaller man scrambled to his feet and looked warily at the enraged soldier.

Hector had meant to ask forgiveness and explain that Ryan should have lived—not him—but his teammate had rushed him before another word had passed his lips. Ryan had knocked out Hector for a split second with a haymaker and had followed the man down to the ground, continuing his assault until this current stalemate.

Now the two were staring at each other while Carver watched. Hector thought that wasn't right, and without taking his eyes off Ryan, he yelled to Carver.

"So are you going to help or not, old man?" Hector asked, his speech slightly garbled as he noticed the metallic taste on his tongue. The veteran sitting on the bench just smiled and propped his head up on one of his hands.

"As I recall, he promised to kick your ass with his new body. I can't really get in between that, can I?" A deep chuckle issued from his throat.

Hector breathed out in exasperation as he prepared to fend for his life. Although he didn't want to fight Ryan—especially since he felt so guilty about living through the game—he also didn't want to end up dying there in the mess hall. Hector lowered his hands and tried to look Ryan in the eye.

"Look, I know I screwed up. I know I didn't help you guys out. I'm taking the blame for that. If that means you have to kick my ass, fine. But I'm not gonna fight back. I feel like shit about it, okay?"

A whine crept into his voice by the end. A part of Hector wanted to atone, but the rest of him desperately wanted his speech to change Ryan's mind. Hector could see his brother sitting two meters away from Carver and shaking his head, and he did his best to ignore Sam.

The distraction was enough for Ryan to cover about half the distance between them and when Hector turned back, Ryan buried his knee in his gut. His abdomen seized as the knee forced the air from his body, and Hector crumpled halfway to the ground.

On his knees, he looked up to see Ryan standing triumphant and angry. Hector saw a god; he saw an angry father; he saw punishment incarnate.

He blacked out halfway once Ryan brought a hammer blow across his face. His head landed on the ceramic tiling and—way back in the corner of his mind where he was still conscious—Hector knew there would be a bruise tomorrow. It would be one of many. He expected much more pain, he felt like Ryan wouldn't stop, but there was no other blow.

After a lull, Hector turned his already swollen face to see Ryan standing above him and breathing heavy. He was still angry, but there was no true malice in his eyes. With one last huff, he looked to Carver, who shrugged. He had no power over the rookie's vengeance.

Ryan turned his head back to the broken man beneath him and offered his hand. Although Hector didn't quite understand why the assault had stopped, it was a welcome turn of events. Upon bringing Hector up, Ryan looked at his handiwork and realized his face would be a wreck for a week.

"I'm sorry," Ryan said before looking down at his feet.

It was the last thing Hector expected. He had betrayed the man, let him die and lived to be the coward. *Hector* half-wanted to kill himself just out of shame. A beating was the least he deserved, and yet this man in front of him was feeling guilty about providing discipline for him. Ryan felt *guilt* for helping Hector atone.

The hallucination of Hector's brother just looked at him, sighed and turned to the window. Although he tried not to let the tear fall from his eye, Hector couldn't help it. Luckily, the lighting was poor enough that nobody could notice.

"It's alright, I deserved it," he said, his speech warped by the already-fat lip Ryan had given him.

"No, you really didn't. It's no one's fault. But maybe next time..." Ryan said as he resumed eye contact with the smaller soldier. He tried to smile, but it flickered now and then, betraying the awkwardness Ryan felt.

Seeing that, Hector decided to help him out with his request.

"I'll help you out, don't worry. The beating I can take, but it's a little rough on the soul to be the last one left," Hector said as he, too, tried to smile. He could tell the soldier was still furious, but not at *him*, so that was enough for them to try to be cordial. Ryan offered his hand, which Hector took, and they awkwardly shook hands.

Carver scoffed, shaking them out of their preoccupation. The two soldiers had completely forgotten they had a live audience.

"We done here?"

Ryan dropped his gaze while Hector tried to look around.

His brother was gone, but he knew Sam would be back eventually. The apparition liked to kick him while he was down. Instead of focusing on it, Hector looked back to Carver, who had shifted his head to his other hand.

"Well, if that's over and done with I suggest that we all get to bed. We have quite the day ahead of us," Carver said as he lifted himself to his feet and resumed his full height. With Hector present, it seemed like it was time for the old man to stop letting his age get to him.

"What happens tomorrow, Carver?" Ryan asked at the old man's back as he made his way to the exit. Carver paused near the door and looked at Ryan from his side.

"We live or we die. I can't give you any other guarantees. Try to get some dreams in, gentlemen. They're the only things they can't take away," Carver said before disappearing through the doorway, Ryan looking after him the entire time.

After shaking his head, Ryan looked briefly at Hector and sighed involuntarily, clearly regretting what he had done to his teammate. He looked down and then walked after Carver, figuring that time was the only way to completely remove his guilt.

Hector watched Ryan follow the veteran and could not bring himself to move. He was not the same as them. There was some bond there that he could never hope to have with either man, and it made Hector feel uncomfortable in a way he did not quite understand. They were too close already, they were kindred, and Hector did not belong with them in that hallway.

"They're just like us," said a small voice at his side. Hector looked down to see the boy in his orange shirt with just a splash of red below the ribcage. All the guilt he felt for the last game was replaced by yet another wave of guilt from his perpetual crime.

"You need to shut up," Hector said, looking away.

"They're family, just like us."

"They're different," Hector said, unable to stop talking with the fabrication at his side. He looked down at his delusion to see the young boy looking at the spot of red. Then his brother turned back, a sad smile on his too-young face.

"The feelings are the same," Sam argued, speaking words Hector did not want to hear. He let the tears fall freely this time. There was no one to keep him from feeling anymore.

"I didn't mean to. It was an accident."

"I know, but you did. You can't take it back."

At the remark, Hector looked away and could not escape his self-loathing. It was his constant companion. "I love you, Sam."

"I know, Hector. I know."

Looking down to get another glance at his brother, Hector realized quickly that the hallucination had gone. He cursed his mind and walked to the doorway, pausing by the double doors. He struck his hand against the frame as he walked by, hearing another crack and feeling the pain in his second broken knuckle. Hector looked at his hand as it started to swell, but then shook his head and walked down the hallway to his room. Though he laid in his bed and tried to sleep, he knew that it wasn't possible. Hector Cortes cried as he remembered his family.

He would never be able to atone for what he did to them.

Stage Three

BARGAINING

1

Merchant of Eris

Jessica Abrams woke from her slumber and felt the warmth of light coming through the window of a room that was not hers. It was at least twenty minutes before the morning alarms and she had some more time to curl up if she wanted to. Instead, she let the sheets fall from her as she sat up on the bed. She looked to her left to see Norris sleeping soundly, his gangly limbs spread across his just-big-enough mattress.

Taking in the sight of her erstwhile lover, Jessica wondered, as she always did, why she had chosen *him*. Most of the time Norris annoyed her, but there was something about the sniper that drew her attention. It was not attraction—Jessica disliked his looks and behavior—and it was difficult to imagine any other situation where they would end up together. As Jessica remembered why she shared his bed, she had to sigh at herself in disgust.

Norris just didn't care about his lot in life. This dirty, dark asteroid did not hinder his joy or ruin his view of the world. Although he used to be different, the personality that he now showed all of his team-mates was the true Edward Norris. There was no going back to the shy, sweet man he used to be when he had first arrived on Eris.

Jessica thought about whether or not she would still sleep with him if he was still that awkward Englishman who was forced to kill men and women, if he was still the same guy who nervously smiled at her with a set of crooked teeth. She shook her head as she walked to her clothes, finding that man in her memory even less appealing.

After walking over to her discarded clothes, Jessica slid her shirt over her head before raising her khakis up around her waist. After she was finished covering herself, she looked at the snoring sociopath on the bed, hating the fact that this was the kind of man she looked to for comfort.

Jessica walked out the door with fifteen minutes left before the morning alarms, not saying a word to the man who had held her all night.

As she walked down the East Hallway, Jessica absent-mindedly peered in the windows of each room to see the occupants inside. The only one who had survived this last game was that coward Cortes, her incompetent partner.

Fucker got me with that grenade, she thought, anger at her rising debts hardening her expression. When she passed by his room, hoping to scold him, Jessica was able to see that his face was swollen and covered in cuts and bruises. At the sight, anger departed from Jessica's mind and she decided to keep walking.

Someone had gotten to him first.

She walked past another room, *P. Roth* etched onto the plaque by the door, and heard the new kid moaning in his sleep. The first death was usually the worst—Jessica remembered her first vividly—but she could not see Roth staying on the team. He had only been with the Crows for his month of training and a week of battles, but he would probably get traded away fairly soon.

He doesn't belong with us, Jessica thought as she watched him writhing, the blond fuzz on his head gleaming with perspiration. His eyes were closed, but his mouth was open in agony. *This'll be just one of many.*

Halfway to her own room, Jessica felt a familiar cramp and her spirits immediately sank.

God damn it. Really? Why can't they just get rid of this shit?

The warrior woman hurried to her room to try to find one last tampon from her last cycle, hoping she hadn't run out already. The pieces of cotton weren't exactly commonplace on Eris.

She entered her room and went to her desk, desperate and already dreading what she might have to do. As she tried to rummage around one of the drawers, she looked past the photo of her and her sister from their trip to Australia. In the photo, she had her arm wrapped tight around Rebecca's shoulders while the young girl had her eyes shut, but Jessica was currently too distracted to smile at it.

When she found the box of tampons, Jessica was momentarily elated before shaking the box and realizing there was nothing left inside. That knowledge made her groan, and after throwing the box into her trash can, Jessica knew she only had one real option. She sat down in her chair and buried her head in her arms, muttering to herself all the while.

"Last thing I need is to deal with that fucker."

ZACHARY GOLDSTEIN SAT by himself in the mess hall, and he certainly did not mind. The rank and file usually kept him at a distance, which allowed him to feel superior and retain some sense of importance. During his stay on Eris, all Goldstein really wanted was some free time to call his own; time he could use to keep track of all the debts and accounts of the Crows and support staff who were foolish enough to deal with him.

The Crows' resident merchant saw Roberts walk by his table, making Goldstein consider getting the weekly shipment of painkillers into circulation. He hated Roberts' situation and the part he played in it, but Goldstein still had an appreciation for the boy's addiction.

After the side-betting from the support staff that funded most of his operation, Roberts was one of his biggest sources of income.

As Goldstein absent-mindedly poked at his breakfast, he glanced at Feldman walking by. So far, the titan had neglected to use Goldstein's services, but that just meant the big guy was an untapped market. The merchant failed to consider that Feldman would not associate with him for other reasons, or why the giant might not appreciate his business.

Goldstein was still trying to think of new ways to manufacture debts when he saw Abrams approaching his table, which made him anxious. Goldstein never could tell what she wanted, so that meant he had to keep a larger inventory on hand. Though it was a bit of an inconvenience, he tried to remind himself that it provided more in the way of opportunity.

She sat down across from him and avoided eye contact while Goldstein ate his home fries.

"Never too late to practice safe sex, Jessica." He always started by pushing her buttons. Abrams didn't barter well when flustered, if at all, which was always a good development.

"No reason to start, jackass. I need tampons." She stared at Goldstein while rubbing her forehead with her fingers, where wrinkles were just starting to form. It was a shame, as the woman was only in her late twenties.

"That time of month, eh? Shame they don't get rid of that for ya here. Anyway, why don't you just go to medical? You've never asked for 'em before," Goldstein argued, mostly because he *didn't* have any tampons hidden away.

The rest of his clientele were of the opposite persuasion—the two female Crows who had practically lost their minds, Elba and Sargasso, did not use his services—and it would look awkward if anyone found feminine hygiene products in his room.

Abrams just sighed as she ran her hand through what little hair she had.

"Oddly enough, you're less of a pain in the ass. Hawkins or Kane would probably make me go through a bunch of tests and a lot of other bullshit. Last time I was in there was just a little too much, and I think you can understand *that*. With you, I just have to pay, and I'm guessing you'll stay quiet and not tell stories to the other boys." Once she was finished, Abrams wiped sleep from her eyes.

"Why would I do that? The boys *love* their stories." Goldstein liked giving her a rough time, just like all the others. It was how he expressed affection.

"Because that's your business, *ass*," Abrams said, curt.

Goldstein laughed; he appreciated that kind of behavior in a woman. It gave him hope that he might find someone like her for himself. This dream girl would have to be prettier than Abrams, of course; maybe just a little more top-heavy and more swell to her hips.

After dwelling on thoughts of this fantasy girl for a moment, Goldstein shook his head and brought his wits back to the business at hand.

"Fair enough. I'm guessing you need 'em pretty soon?"

"Like five minutes ago." Abrams pursed her lips, and Goldstein looked to the clock on the wall and sighed.

His partner wasn't supposed to deliver his shipment for another hour.

"Well, I'll see what I can do. Gimme a minute," he said, placing a napkin over his tin of water and getting up to leave. He turned his back to Abrams and did not really care what she did after that, as long as she didn't follow.

After walking down the hall and entering his room, Goldstein found himself looking at the false floor underneath his bed. He wondered for a moment if he *did* have a box of tampons down there, but he pushed the thought from his mind. As there were only three female Crows—and only one of them talked to him—he knew it was unlikely.

The merchant grabbed the communicator from his drawer and keyed in the number for his contact in the clinic. It rang four times before he heard Hawkins' voice on the other end, his clipped, nasal tone enough to annoy Goldstein, already. The merchant took mental inventory and then spoke to his supplier, pretending to like him for the sake of business.

"When you bring that shipment of pills go and grab me a box of tampons... Nope, it's for a nosebleed, stop being a dumbass and just bring 'em with. ...I'll let her know. If you can be here a little sooner, I'd appreciate it," he said before clicking off the communicator.

Once Goldstein wrote down a few scribbles onto his notepad, he started back to the mess hall. He was gone for only a few minutes, nothing too suspicious about it; none of the staff watching the camera feeds would know that Zachary Goldstein was really the king of the black market unless they were in on it. As he made his way back to his tray, Goldstein couldn't stop smiling at his own genius.

To his surprise, Abrams was still sitting across from his seat, apathetically shoveling breakfast into her mouth. She had a tray of food, at least, but, for appearances, it was still inconvenient. When Goldstein sat down, his glare was filled to the brim with annoyance.

"You know how it works, Jess. There are plenty of other seats. I can always come over to you, instead," he said, trying to lay on the subtext in a way that was easy enough for her to comprehend.

She didn't even look at him. She scoffed while poking her fork through fake sausage.

"I know how you work, Goldstein, but I don't much care. I want to know if you can deliver," Abrams said between bites, the synthetic meat doing nothing for her palate.

Goldstein sighed as he watched her eat; he had always found the act of eating somewhat disgusting. It almost made him want to empty his own tray into the trash bin and go hungry for the rest of the day.

"It's currently en route. Can you pay?" he asked before grabbing his fork and poking at his own links of sausage, ignoring his disgust. The "meat" was not kosher, but neither was he. He had left all those traditions behind him with his family on Zion.

He never much cared to keep either the traditions or the family.

"I can pay, but you need to tell me how much."

"Seventy-five." Goldstein watched for her reaction, which didn't take long. Abrams coughed as her food went down the wrong pipe, her fork clattering to her tray as she focused on trying to survive Goldstein's offer. After she cleared her throat and drank some water, Abrams spoke again, her voice low so the others could not hear.

"You're kidding, right?" Her voice was barely above a whisper. Although it was slightly cruel, Goldstein had to smile at his power play.

"Price of convenience," he said while looking away from her. They were starting to attract attention from the other soldiers, which wasn't particularly desirable. Roberts looked at him with a silent question, his eyes full of pain, and Goldstein's heart sank. The poor boy probably just wanted to know when his fix would come in, and he would likely visit after Abrams had left Goldstein alone.

"The price is *pretty damn inconvenient,* Zach. You know they're just *thirty* at the clinic commissary," Abrams said as she set her tin of water back on the table. Goldstein turned his gaze from Roberts and then shrugged.

"Yeah, but *my...* tampons," he said, smiling briefly as he considered the statement, "do not come with tests or any experimentation by Hawkins. I can imagine he's quite interested in *you.*"

He noticed a slight shudder rippling through her body at the man's name. Even if Hawkins had never laid a hand on the woman—which he undoubtedly had—that shudder should be the natural reaction. Hawkins was a moral disaster, and nobody liked waking up to see him tapping on displays.

That was probably why Dr. Kane had gotten hired in the first place.

"Ugh, fine, I'll get you the money when you get me the damned things," Abrams said before picking up her tray to join the other soldiers.

"Always a pleasure, my dear. Should be here within thirty minutes or so."

As he watched her depart, Goldstein made a mental note to actually charge her eighty when she came to pick them up. The woman was quite desperate.

He could use that.

RYAN WATCHED as Abrams and Goldstein chatted at the other table. He was wondering what the two could possibly talk about when he noticed that Roberts was also looking at the pair of Crows. *That* got him to look around more, and soon enough he noticed three or four of the soldiers—men who usually kept to themselves—stealing glances at the two. Even Corrigan and a pair of men Ryan had never spoken to were watching intently, waiting for something.

Wondering what was so important about Goldstein, Ryan leaned over to Feldman on his left and nudged him with his elbow.

"You need something?" he asked, his eyelids half-closed.

"Yeah, do you know what they're talking about?"

Suddenly, Goldstein stood up and covered his tin with a napkin before leaving, exiting the mess hall while Abrams sat there watching his back.

"Probably business," Feldman said after glancing at the scene.

"What kind of business?" Ryan asked in his naïve way, watching Abrams approach the chafing dishes for their food and then assemble a meal for herself. Feldman sighed as he realized that his young friend still did not know anything.

"Anything that Goldstein would want to sell," Feldman said before stuffing his mouth with food, his tongue scratching against the stale biscuit that had probably been re-heated three or four times.

Ryan's brow was furrowed as he turned his attention back to Abrams, who had set her tray opposite Goldstein's seat. Ryan was still trying to figure out what Feldman had meant when they heard Roberts from across the table.

"He's in charge of the black market here, rookie," Roberts said as he looked anxiously toward the entrance of the mess hall. Ryan looked at his compatriot and suddenly the entire exchange at the other table made sense.

"What kind of black market?" Ryan was curious as to how Goldstein was able to sell anything, since he was trapped in the barracks with them.

"Anything you want. I think the only thing he can't get a hold of would be ordnance, and I think we've all got enough *that*. If you ever need anything, you just need to go to Goldstein," Roberts said with a small amount of distress in his voice, his eye twitching slightly. He anxiously looked over to the other table to see Goldstein sitting back down to negotiations with Abrams.

"I might do that sometime," Ryan said absent-mindedly, more to himself than either of his teammates. He couldn't think of anything he would really want, as he was as comfortable as he could really be on a moon devoted to slaughter.

The Crows had a library; they had a television. They were just distractions, but Ryan thought they all needed a distraction now and again, even if he had spent very little time in the library.

The three of them ate in relative silence until they noticed Abrams leaving Goldstein's table with an air of disgust. Though Ryan noticed out of curiosity and Feldman was trying to ignore it, the other Crow was just waiting for his opportunity.

Roberts gave Abrams a minute to sit down at the other table before he left to talk to Goldstein, his first few steps halted and staggered.

"What do you think he needs?" Ryan asked, not bothering to look at his giant friend.

At the question, Feldman stopped ignoring his teammate. When he looked at Roberts, his head twitching and his leg pumping up and down in anxiety, Feldman's heart was filled with sorrow. He turned his gaze back to his food, which had suddenly become even less appealing, and placed his fork back on his tray.

"Some of us feel a little more pain than others. Some of us want to escape it more. That child has both problems, unfortunately."

After Feldman's revelation, Ryan could see that it had all been an act. Roberts just pretended to be tough, pretended that he was not afflicted with a terrible addiction. Ryan had seen it before plenty of times in New Chicago—where a third of the city's population was enslaved by their dependencies—but it seemed so much worse for Roberts, as he was already living through hell.

Poking his fork at the home fries on his tray, Ryan tried to take in all of this new information while broaching another uncomfortable topic.

"Hey, I've been meaning to say something." Ryan hesitated, but Feldman only raised an eyebrow and waited patiently.

"I just wanted to say... I'm sorry I couldn't help you in that last game. I felt terrible after you fell into that trap, but I just—I didn't want to die," Ryan said before grabbing his tin and filling his mouth with orange juice concentrate.

Sometimes he just wanted to stop himself from talking, and maybe the bitter liquid could help with that. There was no real way to apologize for his cowardice, and he didn't know why he was compelled to do it anyway. Perhaps it was the giant's influence, but Ryan couldn't be sure.

Instead of anger or annoyance, Feldman let out a low chuckle.

"No need to be sorry. No offense, but I didn't expect you to help me. I've always had to bear my own fate." Then he patted the little soldier's back before picking up his tray and leaving the table.

Ryan looked after him and certainly felt offended at Feldman's seemingly patronizing comment. He *wanted* to be respected. It wasn't out of the question that he could help out on the battlefield and Feldman shouldn't talk down to him like that. Then Ryan realized the titan was just in a different league and he truly had not meant any offense.

Feldman was part of the Crows, but only on the scoreboard. Out on the fields of Eris, swinging his massive sword at those who did not deserve to die, Gregory Feldman was by himself.

He was always by himself.

GOLDSTEIN ARRIVED at the reception area to find a package waiting for him, the receptionist's fingers tapping along the top while he wore a shit-eating grin. Evans reminded Goldstein of a reptile and—when he spoke—his voice was oily and treacherous.

"Another care package from *Aunt Marie*, Goldstein. Seems odd that you would have any family left, and that they would love you so much that they would give you care packages every two weeks!" he exclaimed, a sneer on his narrow face.

Goldstein knew exactly what Evans was getting at, but he decided not to make a show in front of the cameras.

"She's a tough old gal, Evans. Even moved to McClellan just to be closer to me," Goldstein said as he placed his hands on either side of the box, attempting to drag it off the counter. Its movement was halted by the hand Evans kept on the top of the package.

"I know what this is, Goldstein," Evans whispered, leaning in close so the watchers would not pick up on their conversation. "And I would like some funds so that I might... look the other way."

At the implication, Goldstein leaned in and sneered back at the receptionist.

"Careful. Remember the debts you owe me," he growled, keeping his voice low. A smile spread across Evans' face and he shrugged menacingly.

"Those were illegally obtained, Goldstein. Just like this package. All the friends you have aren't going to stop the Commission from stepping in if any of this," he paused, backing away and waving his hand at the package, "comes to light."

"Hmm, well, you have me there." Goldstein let out a heavy breath before propping his arm on the counter and setting his chin on his outstretched hand. "But, hmm, you know, all those *friends* I have?"

"Yeah?"

"See, I have a *whole lot*, Evans. I have some on the staff here, I have some higher up in management, and, well, I have a *whole bunch* that live in McClellan. They're pretty tough guys. And, something's... something's coming to mind... Oh yeah!" Goldstein said, snapping his finger and wearing a broad smile.

"You live in the *Green District*, right?"

He studied the receptionist's expression as Evans lost his confidence, realizing Goldstein's veiled threat. He stepped back, frowned and then huffed before sitting back in his chair on the other side of the counter.

"Just go," he said, already turning back to his terminal and logging back into whatever social networking site had claimed his public life. Goldstein laughed, winked as he grabbed the package off the counter, and then started back toward the dormitories.

Once the merchant made it to the relative privacy of his own room, Goldstein set the care package down on his bed, cursing Hawkins for using *Aunt Marie* far too many times. He opened it up to find a number of kitschy items the scientist had provided for cover. The teddy bear at the top was a nice touch, even if he was going to throw it all away.

Goldstein grabbed at the false bottom of the box to find outrageous quantities of prescription painkillers, a case of tampons and other assorted items. His eyes wandered to the comic books Norris had requested and the titles alone were enough to make Goldstein laugh.

The issue on the top of the pile was named *Bimbos in Brazil*, and the cover showed three artificially-endowed women throwing sun lotion at each other while the local hunters looked on from the bushes. It was just one of the many comics that were so dirty the library terminals did not have access to them. As a result, Norris had asked the merchant to supply him with his heart's desire.

Goldstein smiled and shook his head, thinking he might read one or two of them before handing them to his client. Considering that a decision for later, Goldstein grabbed a box of prescription painkillers and the package of tampons and threw them into his pockets. After doing so, he laid the rest of the contraband into the hole in his floor and replaced the false tile once he was done. Once his room was presentable, Goldstein walked through his doorway and set off on his rounds.

He walked by Roberts' room and placed the pills in the desk drawer. Roberts wouldn't be able to pay until after the next game—he had said as much in the mess hall—but Goldstein knew that the soldier was more than willing to sacrifice his future wages for the painkillers.

Even if he never caught up, Goldstein would provide them for him, anyway. He wasn't going to let Roberts go without pills even for a few days. Deep down, he would have preferred to give them to the boy for free, but Goldstein's greed was stronger than his conscience, or at least it was when they had made the initial deal.

Goldstein looked around Roberts' room and sighed. No one could know the man was an addict except for the occasional sweaty forehead and shaky hands; most of the watchers were completely oblivious.

When Goldstein thought about the torture that boy had to go through, he wondered what kind of Hell was in store for Hawkins.

Goldstein shook his head as he left the room and continued toward Abrams' quarters. The Crows had a game later that day, but that was later, and she would *probably* want her tampons before going off into battle.

Goldstein appreciated these pre-battle hours, even if his compatriots would be consumed by anxiety and depression for the carnage ahead. For the time being, Goldstein could peddle wares and think about all the money he was making off his two dozen compatriots. It was an odd position, as he never had to worry about the costs associated with death.

Even when Goldstein died, he still had the money to get out at any time. From the beginning, he stayed only so that he could earn enough money to grab a solid mansion on Solaria. Then Goldstein could send mean messages to his family from his house on the hill and show them everything they had never been able to afford.

Goldstein wanted almost nothing more than to laugh at their relative misfortune.

When he arrived at Abrams' door, he found it shut tight. *The woman does love her privacy*, he thought as he knocked, in rhythm with *Shave and a Haircut*.

It was necessary to be polite when it came to his fellow Crows, and he only had to barge in on Warner's room once to learn that lesson. Warner had been very involved in his diary, and he had not appreciated the interruption.

Goldstein's scars were gone with that body, but he had been forced to live with an ugly face for a few weeks, and the merchant had no intention to suffer a repeat incident.

After a moment, he knocked again and was rewarded with rustling behind the door. When it suddenly opened, Goldstein saw Norris standing there wearing a bemused grin on his face and nothing else. Even that fell away once the jester grasped the situation.

"Way to ruin a surprise for me, Goldstein. I thought you were the girl." He leaned against the door frame, not bothering to conceal any part of him.

"I could be, if you bought me flowers, first." Goldstein pouted and acted hurt, and that made Norris laugh.

"Oh, but I *never* buy flowers, mate. Gives the ladies the wrong impression. So what you want with my dancing partner?" he asked before walking backward to the side of Jessica's bed. After he settled down onto the white sheets, Norris crossed his legs out of comfort rather than decency.

Goldstein entered the room and closed the door behind him, still carrying his box of contraband underneath his right arm. Though he had been prepared to hand them off immediately, now that he was in for a conversation, Goldstein did not appreciate being out in the open.

"A door-to-door salesman, aren't ya?"

"You know me, always looking out for *the people*," Goldstein said as he placed the box on Abrams' desk.

"How much she owe you?"

As he realized what Norris intended, Goldstein did not hesitate.

"Ninety or so, nothing too harsh," he said without looking the Englishman in the eye. He didn't want to betray himself or his act of deception.

"Those *little cottony things* are worth *ninety* credits? Bloody rip-off, that is. Here," he said, smiling at his own wordplay. Norris leaned down, grabbed at his pants and then pulled out the wallet from his pocket. After picking out a wad of credits—Norris was the only Crow who bothered to keep cash on him—he found he had nothing smaller than a hundred mark.

"I don't suppose you have any change?" he asked, shaking his head since he already knew Goldstein's answer.

He didn't offer more than a shrug.

"Figures, you bloody salesman," Norris said as he gave the mark over. "Let's call her debts settled, my friend." He fell back to lie on Abrams' bed, and Goldstein looked over the mark, smiling on the inside as he realized how much he had profited.

"Nice doin' business, Ed." Goldstein turned to leave, grateful at how well the drop-off had turned out.

"Go on. Get out before my balls shrivel up. I wasn't particularly planning on greeting you naked." Norris winked as he propped himself up on his elbows, earning a laugh from Goldstein.

There were plenty of terrible things to say about the sniper, but he *was* a character.

Goldstein left down the hallway room and felt a small pang of conscience once he was a few meters from Abrams' room. He had completely forgotten about Norris' comics or how he was going to tell him they would be on the next shipment. Instead of turning back, the merchant shrugged off his guilt and continued toward his room.

If nothing else, Goldstein would get to see what was so dirty about the bimbos in Brazil.

RYAN DIDN'T REALLY KNOW how he was supposed to go about requesting his records. Fifteen meters away from the receptionist, his mind was chaos as he considered all the possibilities. Evans was the only person in the building who wasn't one of the soldiers or the janitorial staff, other wage slaves who never bothered to speak. For all his faults, Evans was the only link Ryan had to the corporation that owned him.

Every movement stiff and awkward, Ryan walked up to the man sitting at the counter, who looked like he had never done an honest day's work. The blond-haired receptionist was just listening to music and looking at his computer monitor, scowling as he clicked away. Evans didn't even look away from his distractions until Ryan was standing over the counter. When he did bother to look up, the man's eyes radiated spite.

"And what would you like today, Mr. Jenkins?" he asked with venom.

The very idea that he had to work must have been reprehensible, and he reminded Ryan of a small iguana. This receptionist gig must have been an easy job for him, where he could do whatever he wanted as he wasted away the day. Evans probably commuted every day from the support city of McClellan and spent most of his days arguing on the internet or writing his memoirs, which were so terrible his girlfriend wouldn't even read them.

At least, this was what Ryan had made up in order to connect with him. It made it easier to talk to Evans if he had a back story. He wouldn't be a completely uncaring person who wanted nothing to do with him.

"Umm, well, I—uh..." Ryan stammered, wondering if Evans even had access to his records.

"Take your time, Jenkins. We have all day." Evans made sure the statement was drenched in sarcasm.

"Well," Ryan replied, trying to take control of his rebellious mouth. He took a breath, looked him in the eye, and suddenly realized he had nothing to fear. Ryan was a soldier who had already experienced death, and Evans was just a small obstacle.

"I'd like to have my balance sheet to see how much money I'm making," he said, puffing out his chest slightly.

The statement took Evans off-guard, and he made no attempt to stop the bark of laughter that escaped from his throat. Setting to the task, Evans smiled and shook his head as he clicked through a few menus on the display in front of him. When the printer nearby spit out a piece of paper, Evans handed it to Ryan without bothering to look at what it said.

"Here's how much money you're making, big man."

Ryan's skeptical gaze lingered on Evans before he decided to read his balance sheet, confused as to what the man would find so funny.

It was like he had been hit by a transport. Ryan had been through five games and been paid well for them, but the cost of his two deaths and resurrections were taken right out of his account. The fees were atrocious and put the soldier far past the red, claiming all his income and then some. Doing some calculations in his head, Ryan quickly realized that he would have to survive through fourteen more games just to break even.

It was more than just unlikely.

Ryan remembered Warner's outburst in the mess hall, how the man had roared and screamed at his lost chance at freedom. Finally, he could empathize with the other convicts.

Willing it to be different, Ryan looked down at the sheet again. He wanted the ink to rearrange itself and tell him a happy story this time around, but he knew that wasn't going to happen. However, he kept reading over the page and—on the third try—realized there was a mistake.

Although he had only died in two games, he had been charged for three resurrections. Ryan felt relief as he realized that if he got that death taken off his record, he might have a better shot at maintaining a positive balance. He turned back to the receptionist and pointed at the three resurrection charges.

"This is wrong. I've only died twice. I shouldn't be charged for this," he said, Evans' face twisting in misguided fury. The receptionist sighed and looked back down at his computer screen, reading through the miscellaneous charges on the file.

"You've died three times. That's what it says."

"Yeah, well I'm saying there's been a mistake. I've only died twice. I remember it. *Vividly.*"

Ryan wasn't going to have a reception monkey throw him to the wolves just because he wanted to be lazy. After one more look, Evans sat back in his chair and crossed his arms.

"The system says you've died three times. That means you have died *three times.* Even if I believed you—which I *don't*, by the way—*even* if I believed you, *I* can't do anything about it. You would have to talk to one of the accountants."

Disdain was evident in Evans' voice, and Ryan's eyes narrowed at the dismissal.

"Well... can you get in me in touch with one of them?" he asked, tapping his finger on the white counter. Evans looked at the childish act and did not respond for a few seconds. When he did, it was without enthusiasm.

"I would have to have a good reason to take up their time."

"I think *this* counts. It sounds like an accounting problem to me."

"Unfortunately for you, it doesn't sound like one to me." Evans' eyes flared to express his annoyance, and then he turned to Ryan with a yawn.

"They've charged you for three deaths. In your contract it says you hold ultimate accountability. Every time you die, they charge you for resurrection. If they've charged you three times, it's because you've died three times. Their system is perfect. Your living situation and my wages? All of that doesn't matter, but when it comes to *their* money, the system is flawless," he said, grooming his nails the entire time.

Ryan thought about what he would have done to Evans if he had wandered onto his turf back in New Chicago. He thought about what the man would look like without teeth.

"You realize I've been trained to kill people for a living, right?" Ryan asked, unable to resist implying the threat.

If it affected Evans, it did not show. The receptionist didn't even shrug.

"Goodbye, Jenkins," he said dismissively as he turned his attention back to the computer terminal. Evans wasn't going to entertain the soldier anymore, as he had done what little of his job there really was.

Although Ryan stood there for a moment and fantasized about ripping the man apart, he realized quickly that the punishment would not be worth the satisfaction. He turned and walked down the hallway back to the barracks.

Dwelling on his misfortune, Ryan tried to figure out how many games he would need to survive through if there were only two deaths on his record. Soon after that, however, he remembered that his stay was not so temporary.

He was not stuck paying for an *accounting problem*. He had to stay for his entire prison sentence of six months, which had seemed so short when the judge offered him the option. It was a *fact* that Ryan was going to die over and over again as long as he stayed on Eris. Two or three deaths may have been possible to overcome, but with a game every other day for six months, Ryan was looking at insurmountable odds.

Ryan walked in a daze toward his room. He did not concern himself with any of the people he passed or the things he could see. Reality was fully sinking in, now, and he cursed his decision to ever come to this hellhole. There was never going to be an option to leave— and, at best—Ryan was going to end up like Carver.

Now that the tables had turned, Carver's version of survival was no longer the goal. Carver was now everything he never wanted to be.

When Ryan regained his senses, he found himself in the library. He had never been inside the complex and his first thought was about how the room was practically a museum. If people read anymore, it was on a computer display, not from a dusty moth-eaten relic.

That was the very reason the library was so well-stocked, as no one wanted to fill their bookshelves anymore.

It was perhaps too large—considering the need for such a room— but most of the plastic bookcases were empty. All the books that belonged in them were scattered around in stacks on the tables and the floor.

For most of the Crows, the main draw for the room was the set of three computer cubbies near the entrance, but otherwise the room was devoted to relaxing and enjoying a quiet read, and it seemed like someone was getting use out of that. Pieces of antiquated furniture were scattered around the area devoted for that purpose, and although they were falling apart and the material was torn off a few pieces, the furniture seemed to have retained its comfort.

Ryan threw his balance sheet into the garbage can as he passed the set of computers. He sat down in a slightly-worn cushioned armchair near one of the smaller book stacks. Though he had expected springs to poke into his back, the chair accepted him easily and only creaked in protest.

The corporate masters allowed them some luxury in this room, it seemed.

Mindlessly playing with the edge of the material by his fingers, Ryan fell into the chaos of his thoughts for a few moments. He couldn't tell how time was passing; it just felt like quicksand.

All he knew was that he was sitting in the arm chair by himself one minute, and in the next Feldman appeared between stacks of books, holding a dusty tome. When Feldman looked up from the book in his hand and noticed Ryan staring from his chair, he merely nodded and then sat down in the bigger armchair across the table.

There were a few moments of uncomfortable silence as Ryan took turns watching and trying to avoid watching Feldman. Although they had spent a few afternoons together, Ryan somehow didn't know how to interact with the man, and he had never expected the giant to be such an avid reader. Ryan almost started to speak several times, but every time he opened his mouth, the initial sound was followed by nothing.

Eventually, it was too much for him to bear.

"Sooo... do you read in here often?" Ryan asked, adopting an informal tone and trying desperately to fill the silence. Feldman looked at his young friend, dog-eared the page he was reading and then set the book down on his lap. After a moment of consideration, the giant raised an eyebrow.

"Sounds like a bad pick-up line."

Ryan instantly felt stupid. He could have tried to play it off like that was the joke, but he couldn't muster the false bravado. Instead, he laughed and shrugged.

"It... really does. I just didn't know what to say."

"Plato once said: *A wise man speaks when he has something to say, a fool when he wishes to say something,*" the giant quoted from the arm chair, the fingers of his hands becoming interlaced as he set them over his book. Ryan had not expected such intelligence from someone so large, and promised he would make no more presumptions about his new friend.

"I guess I'm a fool after all," he conceded, but Feldman shook his head and scoffed.

"Well, we're all fools. We don't need Plato to realize that." He nodded at their common ground, which brought a smile to Ryan's face.

Before that game against the Hawks, Feldman had said almost nothing to the new recruit, and afterward would only provide answers to the questions Ryan wanted to ask. In what seemed like his element, Feldman was finally opening up.

"I didn't realize you were such the brainiac. Someone your size..." Ryan said before slapping himself mentally. However, Feldman's voice remained friendly and calm.

"Hah, we're all big, dumb gorillas over on Osmos, I'll admit. And I'm not that special, Ryan, I just know more than most. On Eris, I have a lot of time to read, especially since I can't be bothered with television or extra training. And, honestly, these books help me deal with all... *this* around us," he said while waving his hand suggestively.

"So all the fighting *does* get to you. I thought you were superhuman about all that stuff."

"The fighting doesn't get to me," Feldman replied abruptly.

"Then what's *all this*?" Ryan asked, waving his hand in the same way.

"All of *you*." Feldman looked his compatriot in the eye, and Ryan felt even more vulnerable.

"And what's wrong with *us*?" Ryan asked accusingly, his confusion apparent. He didn't like Feldman talking down to him, even if the brute had almost half a meter on him.

"You're all stuck in here. You're all miserable. I want to help you get through this," he said while looking down at his hands. "But sometimes I just need time for myself. I need time to get away from your problems. The books are how I get by."

"Everybody wants to escape in their own way, I guess." Ryan didn't know how he was going to get by, himself, as he had no way of retreating away from his life like the others.

"It's not... *escape*, really," Feldman replied before pausing to consider what he was saying. "It's just a way for me to hope for better. In these works of fiction—even some of the historical tomes—I can see that there were some dark times."

"And how does that make you hope for better?"

"The dark times *ended*. It gives me hope that this is temporary. I know it's hard to consider when you're new to the games, but this is *not* forever. Eventually, the games go on without us. There are always new players to take over for the old."

Feldman rose out of his chair and dwarfed the other Crow. Then he walked over to his small friend and placed his hand onto Ryan's shoulder.

"We don't *have* to turn into Carver. We have other options," he said before starting toward the door with his book in hand.

Ryan didn't know what to say. In his despair, he had not even considered that all the old men left the games, eventually. Now that he thought of it, he remembered plenty of days staring up at televisions and seeing Patrick McEwen's wrinkly face on *War World*. That old man was living proof. Although Ryan's fear of becoming Carver was still very real, the prospect didn't give him as much anxiety as before.

Thankful for this change in perspective, Ryan called after Feldman, catching the giant right at the doorway.

"I have a question for you." His voice already sounded lighter, almost like a child's. Feldman turned sideways so he could look at the rookie.

"And that is?" Feldman asked, his hands clasped over the book held at his hips.

As he stood there, Ryan thought about the question he really wanted to ask. It burned away at him, the desire to know why this kind giant—who seemed to have a solid head on his shoulders—had ended up here with the rest of them. Ryan was a criminal and so were many of the people here; others were here for the fool's gold they were promised in the advertisements.

Gregory Feldman was not the type of person to belong to either group.

"What are you reading, anyway?" Ryan asked with a smile, banishing his real question to another conversation. Feldman looked at him for a moment, analyzing his friend with skepticism, but soon lowered his head and laughed.

"*The Neverending Story*. Always loved it when I was a kid. I'll see you on the battlefield, Ryan," he concluded before turning the corner and disappearing from view.

Left on his own, Ryan sat against his arm chair and looked at the ceiling, thoughts of the giant's past slinking away to the back of his mind.

Ryan had six months to ask those questions, and there was only one hour before the next game.

JENKINS FELT EXHAUSTED, barely able to pick up his feet as he trudged onto the transport, which, from the outside, resembled a box with rounded edges and two stabilizing wings along the length of the vehicle.

On the inside, it was a metal box with benches along the walls.

The game was fairly uneventful for Jenkins. For the entire match, he had only run into three soldiers with his partner, Templeton. He had killed two of them; Templeton got the other.

At this point, Jenkins did not consider himself an old hand—and he certainly didn't think he had as much skill as the veterans—but Templeton didn't meet *his* standards. It seemed sometimes that he wasn't even trying. Even then, he was more competent than Roth, who was still performing terribly.

At this point in his career, Jenkins thought both the new soldiers were rather pathetic.

The Crows had fought against the Dragons, which were one of the lowest ranking teams in the circuit. After the last match, they needed an easy opponent to even things out, as none of the Crows were ready for another resurrection.

Unfortunately, five of them would have to face that misery, yet again. Roth had been killed again, but this time it was a bullet instead of a chainsaw and an explosive shell. Surprising no one, Cortes had been killed by an enemy grenade, and Feldman had been caught in the crossfire of two enemy soldiers.

Corrigan, an average soldier who did his duty, had found himself on the wrong end of a rifle, and Elba, who was just as unremarkable, had been burst apart by her own remote mine. There were a dozen drones just like them in the Crows' roster; men and women who had given into their depression or addictions and accepted their fate. It was hard for Jenkins to remember all their names, but he knew he was not the only one who had that problem.

Jenkins was one of the first to sit in the return aircraft as soldiers came back from the field, since he had been much closer to the rendezvous point. A few straggled in while he was trying to remember the names of his silent teammates, but what caught his notice was Abrams' arrival.

She wasn't wearing her helmet but instead held it in her hand. When she sat down, she set the equipment next to her on the bench and then crossed her arms and closed her eyes, determined to mind her own business. Jenkins had no intention to deny that wish, and so he returned to his own thoughts.

When Goldstein arrived at the transport, he didn't seem to appreciate the silence. He sat across from the woman and hunkered himself into a position so his knees supported the weight of his upper body. Once he took off his helmet, Goldstein cleared his throat and addressed his fellow Crows.

"Well, that was pretty easy money, right, gentlemen? And lady, excuse me," he added toward Abrams, wearing a wry smile. Aware of the violence she could cause with just a knife and a revolver, Jenkins had to wonder why Goldstein would antagonize the woman.

"Very easy money. Let's just leave it at that," Abrams replied, refusing to look at Goldstein. She just peered out the loading bay and tapped her armored fingers against the curved plates covering her upper arm.

Goldstein sat back and leaned against the hull of the transport, cradling his helmet between his knees.

"Fair enough. Gentleman doesn't ask and a lady never tells, as they say. Did you get the *care package* from your sister?" he asked with a small turn at the corner of his lip. Even Jenkins knew that there was a load of subtext underneath the question, but he waited to see Abrams' response.

"Yes, it was quite nice. *Thanks for asking.*" Her tone was clipped and her green eyes flared at Goldstein's verbal abuse.

"How is she doing, anyway? That condition of hers stabilized?" Goldstein asked, and it seemed like his voice was momentarily colored with compassion. Though she had been angry just seconds ago, Abrams' expression softened a bit before she glared at the merchant and then out the cargo bay.

"Yes, she's fine. Best money I ever spent."

Jenkins didn't know what they were talking about, but he could tell the merchant had diffused the situation.

"Good. Wouldn't want you to regret it," he said before joining Abrams in looking out the cargo bay. There was something going on that Jenkins couldn't possibly understand, but it was getting to the point that he did not *want* to know anything else. The information would likely come at too high of a cost.

An awkward quiet fell over the soldiers as more of them fell into ranks in the transport, filling up most of the benches running along the sides of the hull. Those Crows who had been there to witness the conversation between Abrams and her antagonist were keeping to themselves and looking at their feet, which seemed odd to Jenkins. For a moment, he thought that maybe it was just him who had noticed the entire exchange, but he knew the two of them had been far too obvious.

Soon enough, noise started to fill the loading bay, courtesy of their resident jester. Norris had appeared sans his partner and was trading stories with some of the other Crows, though it was an uneven trade. He only waited for them to finish their stories before he set off into his own.

"So there I was with Roth and the two of us were sitting around waiting for a Dragon or two to show up," he said, gesturing wildly at each turn in the story. "I figured we could lay low for a bit and maybe get a good nap in. Then the bloody idiot sees one of them and instead of letting me—*the sniper*—know about it, he gets it into his head that he should shoot at the bloke.

"Of *course*," he exclaims, slapping the forehead of his helmet with the palm of his hand, "the tosser misses with the RPG and then he gets his head blown off by someone who has *clearly* spent more time on the battlefield.

"It gave me enough time to plant a bullet in the guy's face—so I can't really complain—but it was just silly," he said, shaking his head. As he recalled the experience, Norris started laughing and pointed at the drone across the aisle from him. "I tell you what, though. Roth got shot in the shoulder right before his head popped off and I swear he did the best pirouette I've seen from a man. Downright graceful. Right bloody dancer, he is."

Throughout the story, Jenkins looked at the soldier skeptically. He didn't get the humor, and it seemed like he was far from being an outlier. The Crows just pretended to laugh at the Englishman's stories because they didn't know what else to do, and Norris was far too pleased with himself as he relayed his tales of light-hearted warfare.

In dismay, Jenkins looked over at Abrams, who apparently shared Norris' bed from time to time. When he turned to look at the woman, he found her eyes had instantly focused on him, making him nervous. Because of that attention, he tried to play the eye contact off by continuing his head movement past Abrams and toward the other side of the loading bay, hoping that she had not noticed. For a few moments, Jenkins continued to look out to the bleak landscape beyond their transport, but his curiosity soon got the better of him and he glanced back.

She had not averted her gaze the slightest bit. Abrams' green eyes were peering right into his.

RYAN WALKED down the hallway and pretended he was wearing blinders, since he was afraid Abrams would try to catch up with him. All he wanted was to go back to his room and try to sleep, try not to be awake. If he failed at that, he would just stare at the ceiling. Solitude was his highest priority.

No one tried to stop him in his efforts. Ryan made it to his room and sank into his bed, letting the tension fall from his shoulders as he realized he was finally alone. The eye contact with Abrams had not lasted very long and she hadn't said anything, but just that one look was enough for Ryan to be nervous during the entire trip back to head-quarters.

Ryan let everyone else dominate the conversations—especially Norris and Goldstein—and made sure to keep his head down. When the transport landed, he tried to keep to the middle of the group, and in the locker room, he discretely took off his armor and kept his eyes to the wall.

He had done his best to close his eyes in the showers, but Ryan had mistakenly looked around after he had washed the soap from his eyes and saw Abrams standing off to his side. Although he desperately tried not to look her over, weeks of living on a prison moon had been difficult.

Abrams was not unattractive, and the cloning system didn't allow for high percentages of body fat, which was incredibly distracting for a wandering eye. After his indiscretion, Ryan was about to look away when their eyes locked again. Instantly, Ryan cursed under his breath and went back to washing himself. When he finished prematurely, soap still clinging to his skin, he threw on a light outfit and then rushed out the door.

Now he was staring at the ceiling of his room. He was still sore from his resurrection and the match against the Dragons certainly didn't help with that. Back on Earth, Ryan rarely had a decent night's sleep, but here on Eris, he had yet to have one. The pain of the resur-rections, the discomfort of the bed and the constant background bombardment were enough to make sleep a difficult prospect, even if he had grown up in the dens of New Chicago.

Ryan closed his eyes and decided to think about how his life ended up like this. He tried to think about what he could have done differ-ently so he would not have to live in a perpetual limbo. Deep in those thoughts, Ryan was almost unable to react when he heard his door swing open with a slight whine. He propped himself on his elbows, and when Ryan was able to look at his surroundings, Abrams was standing right next to the doorway, arms crossed in front of her. She leaned up against the wall and let the door close slowly.

"What do you want?"

She was curt, as always. If nothing else, Ryan appreciated her direct nature; it was nice to know that she meant everything she said.

Unfortunately, he had no idea how he was going to respond to such a question.

"Umm, what do you mean?"

"You've been looking at me or," Abrams said as she walked over and sat down in his desk chair, "deliberately *not* looking at me since the transport. What do you want?"

She stared at him with those green eyes, which reminded Ryan of the planet-wide forests of Elysia. This woman was definitely intimidating, but Ryan thought the color flattered her.

"N—nothing. I just heard you and Goldstein talking and was a little curious. Then I realized it was none of my business and got all nervous about the eavesdropping. Sorry…"

Ryan figured if he came clean, Abrams would leave and then he could have his solitude, which was all he really wanted. Ryan certainly didn't dislike her, but he felt uncomfortable around her after this series of events.

Instead of leaving right away, Abrams sighed and looked at him.

"Damn straight it wasn't your business… but that's not your fault," she said before looking down at her hands. "Zach pokes and prods at people just for fun. Tries to make 'em weak so he can get more money out of them. You couldn't help that you were in the audience." She looked to the door, then sniffed and turned back to him. It was obvious she was holding back tears.

"You wouldn't believe it, but he's not entirely a scoundrel. He helps sometimes when he doesn't have to." She shook her head for a long moment, eventually looking back at the rookie in front of her.

"Alright, introductions. Name's Jess," she said, obviously considering a handshake before she abandoned the idea and looked at him, as if she was the anxious one.

"Why are you here anyway? You seem like a good kid," Jessica said as she sat back in the chair, drawing up her legs to cross them on the seat.

Confused by what was happening, Ryan could not figure out how to react. He had expected her to be angry; he hadn't expected her to try to get to know him. Picking himself up from his elbows, Ryan sat up on his bed and tried to have small talk for once.

"Umm, well, first off, my name's Ryan. I got caught stealing a bunch of tech. Used to run in a gang and they threw me under the bus," he explained, glossing over the specific details. She didn't need to know about Jack or Tommy or the street value of a shipment of megaprocessors.

However, when he recalled the incident, he realized he wasn't bitter or angry anymore. The day after it had happened, Ryan could have killed any of them with his bare hands. Now, he realized it was in the past; he had moved on. The story—*his* story—had become boring.

After the realization, Ryan shrugged and waited for her to comment.

"Never pegged you for that. I'm guessing Earth?"

"New Chicago. It was a shithole, but it was my shithole," Ryan said with a sigh, drawing a laugh out of the normally-stoic woman.

"Usually how that works. St. Louis was my shithole." She looked back at the doorway, her fingers worrying the fabric covering her knees. "My sister was dying."

Her voice was a little softer, now. Ryan would have expected a tirade on the trade embargo with the Siberian Underground before hearing those words come out of her mouth. After the statement, there was a moment of silence, and Ryan didn't want to be the one that broke it.

"The reason I'm here," Jessica provided, swallowing back the ache in her throat. She was obviously tempted to look her teammate in the eye, but did not have the nerve. "My sister was dying and my family didn't have the money to pay for it. My mom had made most of the money back when we were young, but she died in a riot a few blocks away from our home. My dad was barely making ends meet and when

I was old enough, I tried to help out too. Even got to have a few vacations, but then my sister got sick."

Jessica wasn't trying to hold back her tears, but she was not sobbing. Her voice did not shake, and Ryan admired her endurance. Ryan had never been close to his family and it was one of his secret pains. His parents had not been the kind of people he wanted to know —he had left their house as soon as he had left school—but he had always been jealous of that kind of connection.

Ryan had not realized that connection made people vulnerable to this kind of pain.

It was almost enough for Ryan to want to reach out and give her shoulder a sympathetic touch, but he didn't know how she would react to personal contact. She sniffed again and looked at the floor before wiping the tears away from her eyes.

"She got... *really* sick. And we just didn't... we just didn't have any money to help her. It was Higgins-Scott's disease. Rare genetic disorder. Her body was rejecting itself. Only thing that could be done was gene therapy, but it cost more than we'd ever seen." Jessica laughed in despair at the last comment, her voice becoming more serious afterward.

"That's when I thought about the games and the big payoff. I went to the recruiting station and told them my situation. They said they'd front the money for the therapy and I could make it up in the games." She scoffed at the memory. "It was a dream come true, in a way. Rebecca would get to live. My little sister wouldn't have to die. I'd have to leave, but I thought I could live with that.

"Well, you know what happens here. Been waiting a long time to get out." Now that she was finished, Jessica leaned back in her chair and unfolded her legs so she could let them fall to the floor.

Ryan didn't know how to respond. The woman in front of him was so completely altruistic—giving up her life for her sister—and Ryan had done nothing but avoid a prison sentence on Demeter. A big part of him didn't feel like he was worthy to be on the same team as this woman, but Jessica could clearly sense his awkwardness and decided to take the burden of a response from him.

"I—I really don't know why I told you that. I just wanted someone to know other than Goldstein, honestly. The guy can be such an asshole, even if he has that decent streak. He found out about it from digging through my records. Believe me, I was pissed," she said as she wiped the last tears from her eyes and then scanned over Ryan one last time before offering judgment.

"You're a good kid, even if your eyes wander a bit too much for my preference."

Remembering the awkwardness in the showers, Ryan instantly panicked and tried to think up a few excuses for why he had accidentally ogled her, but she laughed when she realized was going through his head.

"Relax, kid, it's fine. I'm the only girl here who can still string words together, so I'm used to all the horny soldiers. Half the reason I attached myself to Ed was so that I didn't have every one of you guys chasing me," she said as she smiled at the man on the bed. "I swear, I'm not even that pretty, but the bunch of you are fucking desperate."

Ryan had to laugh at that, and she laughed with him. Although he was sure he wouldn't want to sleep with her, if she wasn't offended, then he did *not* need to correct her. He wiped his hand across his forehead and smiled at Jessica, forgetting how hostile she had been in the past.

"I think desperate is a bit of an understatement," Ryan said, shifting on his bed. When he looked at her face, he noticed that half of her was still far away. "So your sister's therapy is going well?"

Coming back to the present, Jessica looked back at him and nodded.

"Yeah, seems like it was worth it. The doctors got her going strong. Makes me happy. Should be able to walk soon," she said with a sad smile on her face. Ryan was glad she was content with the decision, but his conscience still ached at the consequences of her sacrifice.

"Admirable. I don't know if I would have been able to put myself into slavery like that. I guess I'm pretty selfish, after all. I'm just starting to realize I'm not getting out of here. It must hurt to realize that you sold yourself into this just to find that out," Ryan said offhandedly. When he stopped speaking, he noticed her brow had furrowed.

"I'm getting out, kid," she stated, her voice low and dark.

"What are you talking about?"

"I'm *getting out*. I figure if I only die one or two times in the next twenty games, I'll be able to get out. I'm not staying here for the rest of my life."

From her tone and her facial expression, Ryan could see that she believed it. He wondered where that came from.

"Jess, I know you're a good soldier, but you have to know how ridiculous that sounds. That's going to be impossible." His words were heavy and simple, as if he was explaining a difficult concept to a child. He didn't quite understand how she was able to delude herself like that, but her eyes flashed with anger, anyway.

"It's not impossible. I'm getting out of here. Just because you're dying all the time doesn't mean I'm going to die, too. You know what?" Abrams said as she picked herself up in a hurry. "I don't know why I told you any of that. We're done, here. I'll see you around, asshole."

She opened his door and slammed it behind her, and the chair at his desk wobbled over and fell to the ground.

Ryan was noticeably confused. Abrams had been around for so much longer than him; she should know the down and dirty facts of the game they played. He thought back to his record sheet that showed how he owed the Commission for three resurrections and the indignation he felt for being overcharged. That, in turn, brought to mind his vain plan to get off Eris if only he could survive through however many games. After that consideration, Ryan realized he had just recently overcome his *own* denial. Maybe Abrams was just taking longer to realize her situation.

Maybe she never would.

RYAN STARED down the sights of his fake rifle. It wouldn't shoot real rounds, but it would simulate it well enough. Each soldier had to spend at least an hour down at the shooting gallery on their off days, though some of the more simple drones would remain in the galleries for much longer than that.

In order to simulate real battle, the different sets of lights throughout the room would create realistic holograms and the soldiers could shoot at them with their fake rifles. Most of the time, the targets would move and the room would simulate the different sounds on the battlefield, including chatter over Comms and screams from their opponents. The Commission tried everything they could to make the experience more immersive, though it wasn't much different than anything Ryan had seen on Earth.

These galleries were just a few generations more advanced than the models they put in shopping malls.

Ryan trained his sight onto a moving target in front of him, watching it maneuver around the fake battlefield. If the light construct turned to shoot at him, he would get a bad score, but he didn't care about those meaningless numbers. Instead, Ryan watched the man made of light run about his holographic surroundings.

Soon enough, the soldier turned and red lights went off above him. Ryan sighed and fired his fake rifle at the construct, his aim perfect. The soldier made of light disappeared and then another simulation appeared in the middle of the gallery, running to a different piece of cover. As exciting as the experience would have been back in his old life, on Eris it was a rather boring way to spend an afternoon.

Ryan was grateful when the air horn went off behind him, meaning that his hour was up and he could leave for his conditioning in the training yard.

He exited the shooting gallery and walked down the sterile hallway, his hands in his pockets. Ryan didn't know why the corporate masters decided to make the whole thing white or, rather, just off-white. Maybe there was some research that said that inmates would be calm and less violent after being exposed to the lack of color.

Ryan was about to exit the doorway out to the southern hallway when he heard a loud grunt from the last door on his left. He looked in the window to see Feldman in his battle armor and wielding a safe mock-up of his massive plasma blade. The batteries inside the weapon were replaced with weights—the giant didn't need to swing around a miniature fusion reactor inside the barrack—but Feldman's artificial opponents wouldn't know the difference.

Those batteries were one of the few reasons the Commission salvaged anything from the battlefields. Along with suits of armor that had not been absolutely destroyed—usually headshot victims—the plasma swords were picked up after the carnage was over. The tech was too valuable to keep lying around. Little attention was given to the soldiers themselves and, inevitably, the salvage teams left the corpses to rot.

In the training room, Feldman was hacking and slashing at the same kind of simulated soldiers Ryan had just finished shooting, and the giant had to react quickly to avoid the laser show that was unleashed by the virtual soldiers. Though some of the false bullets scored hits on his body, Feldman launched his sword in dangerous arcs and quick movements, scattering the mock soldiers into the air before moving on to the next batch.

If nothing else, it was quite theatric.

After a few minutes of watching, the holographic soldiers stopped appearing after each swing, and Feldman lowered the sword until it hit the ground. He shifted his weight and started to support himself with the massive instrument, breathing heavily. Taking this opportunity to walk in without getting a plasma sword to the face, Ryan opened the door and stepped through.

Feldman stood there huffing for a moment before realizing his young friend had entered the room. The giant then straightened up to an even more impressive height and set about releasing the clasps around his helmet with one hand. Ryan waited throughout the process and then smiled at Feldman as the giant let the helmet fall to the ground.

"How are you today, Ryan?" His breath was already under control. Taking this as an invitation, Ryan and walked toward the giant.

"Doing okay. Better than you, at least. How's the resurrection treating you?"

"A little better this time around, but it's still rough. The arms are a bit sore," Feldman said as he flexed his arms. Chuckling softly, Ryan patted the false sword that supported his comrade.

"I bet. You do heave that thing around for hours. How much does this thing weigh, anyway? Can't imagine it's fun to carry around," he said as he inspected the modern marvel, Feldman laughing at the remark.

"Weighs more than you can lift, my friend. And no, it's no fun at all. I wish I could shoot people like the rest of you. I actually hate the damn thing."

Tilting his head, Ryan looked at his friend skeptically.

"Then why do you use it? I know there's a bonus and everything, but it can't be that much."

"It's not. The bonus barely counts for anything. I use it because I have to. It's in my contract," the giant said before heaving the sword onto his shoulders. Ryan's brow furrowed at the mention of a contract.

"It's in your *contract*? Why would you sign up for that?"

Instead of responding immediately, the giant walked over to the wall and placed his sword in its mooring.

"I didn't have much of a choice," he said, sighing over the memory.

"I'd rather not talk about it. I'm going to take a shower," he said as he walked out the door without so much as a look in Ryan's direction. "I'll see you at dinner."

Almost offended, Ryan felt like he had struck a nerve for his comrade, but pushed it from his mind for the time being.

He still had a great deal of exercise left to do in the training yard.

2

Property Rights

Jenkins had an uneasy feeling about this game. He had been paired with Goldstein, and the merchant had a reputation for taking advantage of every situation. The pair had been midway through the deployment queue, so—after landing—they were doing what they could to strike out on their own. Once they had patted the dust off their uniforms and walked off the shock of landing, Goldstein took point and led Jenkins into unknown territory.

It was a bit of an odd pairing. Usually, the Commission tried to partner soldiers with different specialties so they could work off each other's strengths, but both Jenkins and Goldstein were riflemen. They were specialists in mid-to-long-range fighting and trading bullets would be the most interesting thing that could happen. However, that was not any of Jenkins' concern.

It was his job to survive.

He hoped there would be little enemy contact with the Tigers. After that annihilation match, the last thing he wanted was anything exciting, new or deadly. Even though it had been more than a week since he had died in that game with the Hawks, Jenkins guessed that Goldstein would likely agree. He didn't seem the type to stage heroics for anyone else.

After ten minutes of walking, Goldstein hunkered down near a tall pile of scrap metal and motioned for Jenkins to do the same. The rookie knelt down and tried to guess as to why Goldstein would have stopped in the middle of the battlefield—maybe the older man had heard enemy movement beyond cover—but he tossed that idea aside once Goldstein plopped onto his butt and leaned against the scrap pile.

Goldstein unclasped his helmet and set it in his lap, his black hair shining from sweat, and let out a contented sigh. The man then took out a cigarette and ignited the end with a lighter that seemed to appear from nowhere. After taking a long drag, Goldstein opened his mouth and sent out a plume of smoke that rose to meet the grey sky.

"Did you want one?" the merchant asked to the cloudy sky, noticing without looking that Jenkins was staring at him. Instead, Goldstein watched the smoke from his lungs fade away into the bleak cloud cover above.

More out of bewilderment than an actual response, Jenkins shook his head.

"No, and what *the hell* are you doing?" He was starting to get annoyed, but Goldstein raised an eyebrow and shrugged, flicking his thumb against his plastic lighter to create sparks to contrast their bleak surroundings.

"Smoking. Thought that was obvious," he said before taking another drag. He looked at the cinder at the end of the cigarette and shook his head. "Mental addiction, that's what it is. My body hates me every time I smoke one of these things. I don't even get the nicotine high, and sometimes I even feel sick to my stomach. Yet, *somehow...* I'm *compelled*," Goldstein said as he took one last drag and threw the dying cigarette into the wreckage.

"I'm not complaining, in any case. Just thought it was weird. It's not like cancer's gonna get to me anytime soon." He chuckled at his own cleverness, and Jenkins regarded him with contempt. That was enough for Goldstein to laugh and focus on the helmet in his lap.

"*Oh*, don't you judge me for this. I don't like to start killing people without getting a smoke in." Goldstein then stretched out his arms and put them behind his head, crossing his legs in order to be more comfortable.

"All our teammates are playing. Why don't *you* pitch in?" Jenkins asked while cradling his rifle and standing rigidly over his partner. Goldstein seemed like the laziest waste of training he had ever seen, but the merchant disarmed him with a scoff.

"Why are you in such a rush to die? You're not going to get much money for killing those Tigers out there. If you die, you'll owe even more money. I would think that you would be more likely to run away and hide," he claimed, tossing his lighter between his hands. "It doesn't much matter if I die again—I'm swimming in money—but just the same, I'd rather not go through another resurrection. Even when playing the long game, it's good to have short-term goals."

He looked at the sky above him as if he could see past the haze, and Jenkins could see a slight smile on the man's face.

"Swimming in money?" Jenkins asked as he crouched by the veteran's feet. Goldstein looked at him skeptically for a moment before bringing his hands back down to his helmet, stowing the lighter in a satchel at his hip as an afterthought.

"Indeed. I'm sure you've heard by now that I have a fairly lucrative side project going on here."

"I've heard something like that, yeah."

"Well, let's just say I don't really need to worry about the games anymore, as long as I don't fuck up too bad. It's almost just something to pass the time," Goldstein said as he tossed his helmet from hand to hand.

"Then why are you here?"

"I guess I'm just greedy. I want a nice beach house on Solaria and some servant girls. I think that'd be pretty fun," Goldstein said with a wink. "And believe you me, kid, that is a *pricey* dream I have."

At the mention of Solaria, Jenkins thought about his own dreams of escape to the tropical moon. Jenkins had only aspired to be a pool boy.

Goldstein wanted to own the pool.

"So I have a question..." Jenkins said, trailing off toward the end.

"I might have an answer."

"So you run the black market, right?" he asked, and Goldstein rolled his eyes.

"Well, if you want to call it that, sure, but make sure you write a letter to the local EOSF station, too. Wouldn't want our boys in black to be clueless," he said sarcastically, referring to their so-called police. Jenkins felt silly at the man's verbal jab, but since Goldstein seemed to be joking, he continued with his line of questioning.

"Well, how do all the soldiers pay you? Aren't we all in a ridiculous amount of debt from all the resurrections?" he asked, the barrel of his rifle falling as his grip relaxed. Goldstein laughed before uncrossing his legs and bringing his left knee up to his chest.

"Haven't read your contract, have ya? Basically, we have an outstanding balance with the Commission. As soon as we get a positive balance, we can buy ourselves out, but that doesn't mean we can't spend what we make. They don't really expect us to ever pay them back. The balance is just there to say that they own us."

Goldstein drew out another cigarette and fumbled around in his satchel to retrieve the lighter he had just stowed away.

"Anyway, whatever we earn in the games we're allowed to spend. Basically, on whatever we want. Extra rations, Earth provisions... you name it. Anything that's approved, that is. For the things they don't approve—some entertaining bets or things you don't want them to know about," he said before finding his lighter and setting his cigarette ablaze. "Well, you talk to me."

Jenkins looked at his rifle, tapping against the dirt as he tried to think of anything he might want. He tried to think of his favorite things on Earth when he was growing up, but it all seemed so trivial. Now, the only thing he wanted was to be far away from Eris and his growing debt.

He was shocked out of his internal process by Goldstein's voice.

"You need anything, by the way? I could set up a ledger for you..." Goldstein suggested with a smile, but he figured Jenkins wasn't going to take his offer. He wasn't surprised when the rookie scoffed.

"Nothing you can get me, Goldstein," he said, looking at their surroundings. As Jenkins scanned the horizon for enemy Tigers, Goldstein laughed and took a long drag from his cigarette.

"I wouldn't be so sure of that, my friend," he said before taking a sharp breath and then exhaling hard, ridding his lungs of smoke. He looked at the cigarette for a moment before grimacing and throwing it away.

It was a testament as to how little he cared for them.

"My lungs hate me for that shit. Nasty little habit," Goldstein said, climbing to his feet and clasping his helmet back onto his head. He then turned back to his compatriot and nodded north.

"You still in a rush to die?"

After Jenkins picked himself up from the ground, he shrugged and shifted his weight to his right foot.

"I guess I can go either way."

Goldstein laughed before turning around and heading north, his rifle by his side.

"That's the spirit. Apathy is the way to go, kid."

FIVE MINUTES LATER, Jenkins was still walking behind the merchant. They had taken out three of the Tigers already, mostly because Goldstein had been able to sneak up on them and throw grenades at their feet. One fell to the ground missing a leg and the other two had been scattered from the explosion, easily picked off in their confusion. It didn't seem right to Jenkins—these cowardly tactics—but he had to consider the fact that he was still alive.

There were obvious things that Jenkins didn't like about Goldstein —his arrogance and teasing grated on his nerves—but he had obvious experience on the field. Walking through these steel meadows, Jenkins never felt like he was in constant danger as he did in the other games, as if enemies were lurking behind every corner.

Goldstein's leisurely attitude was almost enough to make him feel like he was not on the same moon.

As they were walking between two piles of discarded transport parts, Goldstein peered over his shoulder, past Jenkins, and then turned to look at the empty field beyond the two piles. Jenkins was curious as to why Goldstein had done that, but he didn't have long to wonder.

"Just makin' sure no one's following us. Don't worry your head off," Goldstein said lazily over the private channel, not bothering to turn to his partner.

"I wasn't." Jenkins had tried his best to avoid sounding like a pissed-off teenager, but the sentiment came through, anyway.

"Sure, sure. So," Goldstein said as they walked along a makeshift pathway through the wreckage, eventually bringing his rifle up to look through the scope and observe the open ground. "You have five months to go on your sentence, right?"

"Yeah, close enough... why do you care?" he asked, jostling the rifle in his hands as he stood between the trash heaps. Goldstein lowered his rifle and then stepped back to their junkyard cover with a shrug.

"I make it my business to know that kind of thing. What's your balance looking like?"

Jenkins thought about withholding the information, but he realized it didn't much matter if Goldstein knew his debts.

"Not good. Not sure what it's going to look like once my sentence is up."

"Ugh, I hear ya. If I didn't have the side-business, I'd probably just kill myself and hope they don't bring me back. Those resurrections costs are killer," Goldstein said before heading back to the edge of their cover.

In tacit agreement, Jenkins followed and sighed wearily. He shook his head and stepped around a spur of scrap in the pathway, almost tripping on the outcrop of metal.

"Pretty shitty, more like," Jenkins said, feeling more at ease now that he could gripe about his situation. "And to top it off, they hit me with an extra resurrection and I can't override it." He continued down the pathway to open ground, but he was stopped in his tracks by Goldstein.

"What?" Jenkins asked, holding his rifle with some anxiety.

"They can't do that. Well, I mean, they *can*, but they don't care enough to do it. What are you talking about with this extra resurrection?" Goldstein asked while squaring up to his partner.

It surprised Jenkins, as he had not realized anything he had said was all that important.

"Well, I've only died in two of the games but they've charged me for three resurrections. The guy at the front desk... Evans is his name? He was pretty rude about it," Jenkins said, noticing that Goldstein was looking up and down his body. Then he shifted his weight and let his weapon fall to his side, supported only by the strap draped around his shoulder.

"Oh, fuck. You don't know."

At the claim, Jenkins' brow furrowed underneath his helmet and he was suddenly very curious as to what Goldstein would say.

"What are you talking about?"

Goldstein stood there for moment before bringing up his hand to his helmet and shaking his head. Then he made what eye contact he could and put his hands on the man's shoulders.

"Ryan. *Trust me.* You've died three times."

"No, I haven't. I only died twice in the games," Jenkins stated, sure of the truth. Although Jenkins would admit there were secrets no one had told him, he could remember his *own* deaths.

"Oh, I *believe* you. But I'm saying you've died *three* times," Goldstein said before Jenkins shrugged off his hands and adopted a hostile stance.

"I think I would remember that."

"That's the thing. They don't *want* you to remember that first one." Goldstein hoped to get this over with quickly, as they were not in the best area for this kind of conversation.

"What are you talking about?" Jenkins asked, an undercurrent of rage coursing through the question.

"They killed you before you ever got to this planet, Jenkins." Goldstein took a deep breath, waiting for his partner's reaction. Eying the older man, Jenkins motioned for Goldstein to continue. "They took a sample of your DNA and mapped your brain on planet. Then they sent all that code to the clone banks up here on Eris. Then they killed you on Earth. In a few ways, you're officially dead."

At the revelation, Jenkins' mind became a maelstrom of anger, despair and denial. He just could not understand what the other man was saying and questions filled his thoughts. Why would they have killed him like that? What could they have gained?

This was not the deal he had in mind when the judge offered six months on Eris.

"What? Why?" Jenkins' voice came out, surprising even him by how weak it sounded.

Considering the truth of their situation, Goldstein looked at his feet and sighed.

"Well, it cost less, that's for sure. They wanted perfect synchronization between your brainwaves and your clones. It was easier just to grow some shells for you that were specifically made for the process. As for your body on Earth, you had some stuff wrong with you, right? You were fat or something?" he asked, grasping at straws.

Ryan raised his hand to his head, trying to remember his former life.

"I used to have pretty bad eyesight. They told me they put me into surgery to fix it," he said, suddenly skeptical about the entire memory.

Now that he had time to focus on it, Jenkins had actually almost forgotten that he used to wear glasses, at all. His habit of pinching his nose at sinus pressure seemed to have disappeared, and he couldn't quite remember the last time he had even tried.

"Well, that's how they got you under, at least. They didn't operate on your eyes. They fixed the genetic code in your clones so they wouldn't *have* bad eyes. They weren't going to spend money cutting up your body on Earth and then shipping it to an asteroid. It's so much easier to send data instead. Unfortunately, your first body..." Goldstein paused; he was trying to avoid completely breaking the mind of his new comrade.

"It was... trash. They probably burned it up and added it to a compost pile or something. Try to remember. Did you have any scars from growing up that had disappeared by the time you started training? That's because they never happened to that body," Goldstein explained, wishing he could glance around the field at his back. He would have stepped back between the two piles and into cover, but he was nervous his partner might lash out.

Jenkins could not catch his breath for a moment, as he had not mentally prepared himself for the idea. Although he tried to remember his body during his month of training, he knew that he would not find his answer. In that first month, Jenkins had not worried about the beauty mark he had once received from a broken bottle, or if it was even there. Its absence hadn't even been considered.

Jenkins wondered what else the Commission might have lied about.

"So..." he said before realizing it was just a noise. Jenkins had nothing poignant to say. His brain was flooded with a thousand thoughts and he couldn't express a single one of them. It was just as chaotic and useless as the field of trash around him.

"So they have effectively resurrected you three times. I'm sorry," Goldstein said, placing his hands back on Jenkins' shoulders.

He didn't shrug them off or brush them away this time, instead welcoming Goldstein's touch even if there were layers of power armor between them. It was enough to feel something concrete touching him, to feel like he was not entirely alone in the universe. Jenkins took a deep breath and sat down against the pile of broken chairs to his right, trying to compose himself.

Though he would have preferred getting into a better position—one that was less exposed—Goldstein was grateful that he had the opportunity to move away from the open field. The guilt of revealing the truth to Jenkins was starting to get to him, but he was more concerned with getting back into cover after being out in the open for so long.

Except he didn't have the chance.

Goldstein felt the first bullet enter his chest cavity just above the diaphragm, the shell hotter than hell and burning everything around it. It didn't hit anything vital, but he didn't feel all that fortunate. Then the second bullet hit him right above the kidney and tore through his right side, causing him a great amount of pain as it passed through his intestines, only to be stopped by the power armor covering his midsection.

He let out a groan before falling beside his comrade.

"Goddamnit," Goldstein muttered before trying to turn and look at the soldier who had shot him.

There were two Tiger riflemen swooping in from a ridge thirty meters away, across the very field that had given Goldstein all of his anxiety. Although ridden with pain, he mustered enough energy to bring up his rifle.

Luckily, the gunshots had also shaken Jenkins out of his daze and his partner trained his sight on the approaching gunmen.

Bullets whizzed by them as the Tigers closed the distance, causing Goldstein to curse his luck. They were obviously new soldiers; they tried to shoot at the Crows while running, ruining their aim.

Goldstein rolled his eyes as he planted a shell between the eyes of one of them. Though he was more concerned with his black market, Goldstein had spent plenty of time on the field and he had the skill to back it up. After his counter, the other Tiger looked at his fallen comrade and tried to get the man up, shaking the newly-made corpse. Goldstein sighed in disgust at the behavior and could not believe this had happened to him.

He was about to shoot at the stupid Tiger when Jenkins tagged the boy in the leg, sending their enemy to his knee as he yelped in pain.

At least the kid is worth **something**, Goldstein thought as he looked back at Jenkins and smiled.

He saw his comrade rise to his feet and was about to say congratulatory words when he saw Jenkins' shoulder whip around, which brought him to the ground. Looking back at the Tiger, Goldstein was able to see that the soldier had trained his own rifle on Jenkins. He was hunkered down on one leg since the other one was useless, but that didn't stop the weapon in his hand from working.

Goldstein's eyes narrowed as he lifted up his rifle and sank a round into the boy's eye, the Tiger's neck snapping back before the corpse fell to the ground.

The pain was starting to fade from his torso, but Goldstein knew that was just shock, so he huffed as he brought himself up to lean against the pile of scrap furniture to his right. He could tell that nothing vital had been hit. He was going to bleed out and it was going to hurt the entire time.

Knowing that he was finished, Goldstein sighed and looked at his comrade. Blood seeped from the wound in Jenkins' shoulder, but otherwise he was unscathed. However, Goldstein bit his lip in anticipation for what was to come for his partner.

His hands closed around his lighter and cigarettes and he brought them out onto his lap. After unclasping his helmet, he threw it toward the corpses twenty meters away. Goldstein then brought a cigarette to his lips and tried to use the lighter, his thumb weak from blood loss. For all his practice, Goldstein couldn't quite get his fingers to cooperate and he was debating on just throwing it away, but Jenkins came to his rescue.

The rookie grabbed the lighter with his left hand and flicked it on for his comrade, seeing the flame waving about in the slight wind. Smiling at his partner, Goldstein lowered his mouth and then took a drag from the last cigarette he would have in this lifetime. He tasted metal along with the acrid smoke filling his mouth and lungs and had to resist the urge to cough, but he still made sure he seemed grateful when he patted the ground next to him.

"Sit, sit. We have some time, you and I," he said, his voice scratchy and weak. Jenkins looked at him warily, but eventually sat down where Goldstein had patted the ground.

"Sorry about all that. I know that must hurt."

"Don't worry about it. Comes with the territory. Besides," Goldstein said before filling himself with smoke again. He could feel it burning its way out of his lungs and into the cold air of Eris. "I kinda hit you hard with the stark truth there."

Jenkins looked at his compatriot briefly before turning back to look at his feet, trying his best not to think about the pain in his shoulder.

"Thank you for telling me," Jenkins said under his breath. "I'd rather know they did that than think it was an accounting problem."

Goldstein laughed up blood as he considered his partner's perspective. He supposed it was certainly a different way of thinking about it.

"No problem, my friend. Always willing to give you guys information. I'm playing the same game, you know," he said before turning to look at the boy. "I just have a few extra rules I have to play by."

"If it makes you feel better, I don't think you're as horrible as they say you are," Jenkins said with a light grin Goldstein could not see.

"*Hah!* Yes, you do, but it's kind of you to say so." He took one last drag, then a gust of wind flew past him and scattered the ashes of the cigarette away from him. The fire departed with the ashes, which brought a smile to Goldstein's face before he looked back at his comrade. "Well, I guess I have one last request."

"What's that?"

"Would you be a doll and sink a bullet in my brain for me?" Goldstein asked, shuddering slightly as the shock from his dying body waned on him. Jenkins was obviously surprised by the request and fell away, which only made Goldstein laugh harder.

"Oh, get a hold of yourself. It's a simple request. I just don't want to bleed out here."

"Why do you want *me* to do it? Why can't you just shoot yourself?" he asked, shaking his head the entire time.

Goldstein shrugged and pain lanced through him, making him wish that the shock still flooded his system.

"God, you really don't know anything. Whenever there's a suicide, they try to analyze the soldier's mind and run a lot of diagnostic tests. They basically hold 'em in stasis until they figure out what went wrong. I'm not a suicide risk or anything, so we don't need to involve them. I just don't want to die slow," Goldstein admitted, keenly aware of the blood pumping out of the twin holes in his back.

"It's a pretty terrible way to go, honestly. If you just grab one of their weapons and shoot me it looks like they just got another round in me. Win-win, as they say," he continued, smiling as blood dribbled down from the corner of his lip. Goldstein was doing his best to act nonchalant about it, but Jenkins just stood there as his willpower faded.

"Look, I'd really appreciate it. I'd rather die quick, that's all," Goldstein urged, letting the veil fall and showing Jenkins the man underneath the façade. Maybe if the rookie saw the serious side, he would actually grant his request.

After just another moment, Jenkins sighed and then ran over to the corpses, trying to avoid jostling his right arm. He grabbed the rifle of the Tiger who had put a bullet through his shoulder—over-thinking their story slightly—and then ran back to his teammate.

Goldstein was not smiling when the rookie came back.

"Thanks, kid. I really appreciate it," he said, gulping down the blood rising up to ruin his last words.

Watching the man in pain, Jenkins let his shoulders fall as he remembered the promises of fame, fortune and glory that *War World* claimed. Now that he was closer to it all, Jenkins didn't feel like a war hero out here in between piles of scrap metal. He brought up the barrel of the stolen rifle to point at his partner's head, hesitating slightly. Jenkins was about to pull the trigger when Goldstein brought up his hand.

"One last thing, kid," he interrupted, Jenkins keeping his finger on the trigger as he pointed the gun at his compatriot. "I'm sorry about the shoulder."

"It's not your fault," Jenkins said, but Goldstein tilted his head and bit his lip.

"Yeah, well, I'm sorry, anyway. When I see you back there, I owe ya something. Whatever you need. I know how terrible it is when you get tagged like that," he claimed, causing Jenkins to look at him skeptically.

"What are you talking about?" he asked, the mesh of his armored finger gliding along the trigger. Although he now had a sense of respect for the merchant, Jenkins didn't appreciate how many secrets Goldstein kept hidden inside his head.

"You'll see. On the other side, my friend," he said as he closed his eyes, his face full of resolve. Jenkins decided the man was going to be cryptic no matter what.

He pulled the trigger and felt little more than recoil.

JENKINS WAS WALKING to the rendezvous point and trying to think about what Goldstein had meant. For that last walk, he had slung his rifle over his left shoulder since he didn't want to irritate the gunshot wound. Jenkins felt guilty for killing his partner, but Goldstein had asked him to do it, and he was in no position to deny a dying man's wishes.

The Crows had won yet again, which was to be expected in a traditional game. It wasn't an annihilation match and there were no handicaps, so it was as fair as it was going to get. In their league, the Tigers had a lower ranking, but the influx of new soldiers on the Crows' roster—namely Roth and Templeton—were enough for the Commission to think it was a fair match.

To Jenkins, the victory felt especially hollow. He wasn't fighting for anything he believed in; he got nothing from team statistics or shallow pride. From his perspective, it was all luck. The two of them could have easily switched places and Goldstein could be walking toward the rendezvous point with a bullet in his shoulder.

Jenkins could have been the one to bleed out from his temple as the veteran walked away.

Because he had to, Jenkins shook the thought from his head. Goldstein would have been perfectly fine with shooting him if their positions were reversed; he wouldn't have wavered, at all. It made Jenkins a little uncomfortable that the man was so callous about these things, but in the back of his mind it made a certain sense.

Jenkins wondered if he would end up the same way.

The transport was sitting above a ridge nearby, a trail of Crows leading up the ramp to the cargo bay. Grimacing as his shoulder plate jostled against the wound, Jenkins walked toward the ship and prepared for an uncomfortable flight.

He could tell the bullet hadn't hit an artery—he would have already bled out otherwise—but that didn't stop the wound from hurting. The hole in his arm was seeping blood onto his clothing under the armor as well, and that was not particularly comfortable now that it had started to clump together. For the last ten minutes, Jenkins had wished he could teleport to the clinic and skip ahead to his recovery. He really just wanted to stop worrying about it.

When he arrived, Jenkins discovered that most of the surviving Crows were already sitting down in the transport. Jenkins sat on the left side toward the middle of the bench and looked at his comrades, watching their behavior. There was not a single joke or discussion and his somber teammates were just sitting on their benches. Jenkins checked his visor to see if there were any other Crows out on the field and he could see three more ID tags closing the distance.

He started to feel anxious at the silence and looked across the aisle of the transport. Cortes—he could tell from the ID tag in his display—was sitting there, staring at his own gun. Resolving to end the silence, Jenkins thought about what he could possibly say to him. The last time they had spoken more than a few words to each other, he had beaten Cortes beyond dignity, but he couldn't avoid the Crow forever.

"How are you, Cortes?" Jenkins asked, setting his rifle down on the bench to his right. Although Cortes tilted his head at Jenkins, he was obviously confused at the question.

"I'm... okay, I guess. Alive at least. Can't say the same for every-body," he muttered, already trying to avoid the interaction. Jenkins was about to let the whole idea drop when Templeton piped up from further down the aisle.

"Hey, Cortes, weren't you paired with Norris today?"

"Umm, yeah."

"Where is he? He has the *best* stories."

Templeton's praise confused Jenkins. Norris may have had stories, but Jenkins had rarely thought any of them were *good*, and especially not *the best*.

"Norris ain't here, rook. Leave it at that," Carver said from the other end of the transport. He hadn't bothered to look at the other soldiers and instead gazed at the wall in front of him.

Silence followed after the elder's remark, as Templeton was not brash enough to venture his opinion again. After some time, Jenkins forgot that his shoulder was hurt and shifted in his seat, which in turn sent a spasm of pain through his arm and torso. He regretted it instantly and let out a small gasp in reaction.

Cortes looked up from the floor and saw a trickle of blood flowing out of the bullet hole in Jenkins' shoulder plate. He squinted through his display and hoped he wasn't right, but he wasn't going to rely on his display to leap to any conclusions. The coward unclasped his helmet and put it in his lap, leaning forward to judge Jenkins' shoulder with his own eyes. Without the mask in the way, he could see the broken metal for what it really was.

"Jenkins, did you get hit?" Cortes asked as a formality. He just wanted to hear what the rookie would say about it.

At the question, Jenkins looked at his teammate and was put on guard. From Cortes' face, he could tell that there was genuine concern, so he nodded and gestured with his left hand.

"Yeah, but I don't think it's that serious. I can't really move it, but I haven't bled out yet. I think I'm safe."

Jenkins had tried to play down the pain he felt, but it seemed to have the opposite reaction. Cortes looked down and rubbed his eyes before breathing deep, whispering a wordless prayer. He then turned his head to the end of the aisle and stared at Carver, waiting for an answer to a question he did not verbally ask. Jenkins started to worry as the old Crow broke out of his train of thought and looked back at him.

"Damnit, kid. Where'd you get hit?" Carver asked before taking off his helmet and walking down the aisle. Jenkins was confused enough to stay where he was, and merely waited until Carver propped himself on his knees and inspected his armor. The old man immediately noticed the blood trail coming from Jenkins' shoulder and touched it gingerly with his gloved fingers. For a few moments, he tilted his head back and forth, inspecting the wound from a few angles.

Then he wrapped his fingers around Jenkins' forearm and yanked down hard.

The pain was unbearable. Jenkins almost blacked out as the agony resonated throughout his body, and he didn't notice Carver back away, put his hands around the back of his helmet and let out a deep breath.

Half a minute passed after Jenkins fell to the floor, writhing about on his left side, and it was only after the pain became a dull ache that he was able to regain his senses. In all his lives, Jenkins had rarely experienced pain like that, and he was certainly not prepared for a friendly hand to cause it.

Once he was able to think clearly, Jenkins tried to pick himself up, but he only ended up staggering to his knees. In order to help, Cortes leaned down and wrapped his hands around his good arm, heaving him onto the bench as their leader stood by. After concentrating on breathing for a few moments, Jenkins face turned to stone once he realized that Carver was still standing over him.

"Why the *fuck* did you do that?"

"I was testing whether or not it was a flesh wound or something deeper," he said, crossing his arms. Jenkins growled beneath his helmet at the man and wished that he was in enough shape to hit him.

"And what did you find, you *ass*?" Jenkins had to resort to sarcasm since he couldn't physically do anything about it.

Carver stood there in a defensive stance for a few seconds before sighing, dropping his arms and then sitting down on the bench beside him.

"You're screwed, kid. I'm sorry," he admitted, his elbows on his knees. That was enough for Jenkins' anger to slip away from him, curiosity taking its place.

"Okay, *enough*! What is going on? Why is *everyone* offering their condolences? It's just a shoulder wound!"

No one answered him, at first; they were all hesitant to say anything. Cortes was the one to lift his head and look him in the eye.

"It's a death sentence," he said, looking back down at the floor and stepping back to his own seat. Jenkins' brow furrowed at his claim and he turned his head to Carver, who had covered his mouth with his left hand.

"Remember Warner a few games ago?" Carver asked, opening his hand slightly so Jenkins could hear him easier. "I told him to basically commit suicide and tapped my arm. He was shot in the shoulder, do you remember that?"

Jenkins nodded.

"You asked me why he was already dead and I just told you to move. It's because I didn't want to talk about it at the time, but you're going to know soon enough." Carver said before rubbing the bridge of his nose and dropping his hand so there was nothing between them.

"The rough and short of it is that you're not getting out of this one. When you get back to headquarters, O'Brian is going to take one look at you and then sign your death certificate. You're going to die and have to be resurrected," he said, not breaking eye contact.

Although he heard the man, Jenkins did not understand.

"Why would they do that?"

"You've been structurally damaged. If it was just a little graze then they'd let you go, but that bullet hit bone and tore through muscle. They're not going to wait six weeks for you to heal properly, *maybe*, when they can just kill you and get a whole new perfect soldier. I'm sorry," Caver explained, dropping his gaze to the floor.

Jenkins had a dozen questions about his death sentence and they were about to flood out of his mouth before the transport shuddered and started toward headquarters. As they rose through the air, Jenkins realized that it all came back to the Commission. It was just another terrible part of the system tied up in money and a lack of ethics.

It didn't take him long to realize that talking to Carver wasn't going to fix that system.

3

Bedside Manners

Ryan was apprehensive about exiting the transport, aware that his death laid beyond the exit of the cargo bay. He tried to think about what he was going to say to the ones in charge of his demise, but he didn't see success in his future. After looking at the hand lying on his lap, Ryan tried to curl his fingers and was met with a flash of pain.

Most of the soldiers had already walked off the transport by the time Ryan mustered his nerve. Carver had shaken his head and patted his good shoulder before leaving. Cortes hadn't looked him in the eye, and Ryan figured the man had a similar experience in his long career. Now that he was alone, Ryan took a deep breath and set his head against the hull of the ship, but he soon realized he wasn't going to get anything done by sitting on that bench.

Ryan got to his feet and could already see O'Brian flanked on each side of the doorway by officers from the Earth Orbit Security Forces. Both of them were rather intimidating; their bulky, black armor was built to withstand structural damage and protect the wearer, unlike the armor each Crow was wearing. After taking another breath, Ryan walked off the transport and toward the men who would decide his fate.

The official was too busy jotting down some information on his handheld computer to notice his approach, even if his guards were already looking at him skeptically. The older man only looked up when Ryan came to a stop in front of him, hoping to seem normal.

O'Brian looked like quite the bureaucrat. His hairline was receding with a speed only genetics could claim, and his chest had more curves than a woman his age. The man was dressed in regular, drab fatigues and wore a pair of thick eyeglasses with thin frames, which reminded Ryan of the end of a plastic bottle.

O'Brian clearly held substance over style.

Ryan would not have been afraid of him if the man didn't hold power over his very life. However, he *did*, so Ryan kept his helmet on and was grateful he could hide his pain behind the mask. The official looked over Ryan briefly and realized he was the last Crow on his updated list.

"Ryan Jenkins. How did the game treat you?" he asked before accessing Ryan's data sheet from the computer. O'Brian didn't really care about his disposition; he was just being as polite as his bosses asked him to be.

With a shrug from his good shoulder, Ryan looked at the guards flanking the official. They were watching him, and he didn't appreciate that.

"Still alive. More than others can say." Ryan tried to mimic Cortes, as he figured it would help him escape notice. O'Brian looked over his glasses and furrowed his brow.

"Quite right, quite right. Let me take a good look at you. Take your helmet off, please," he said before running his eyes over Ryan's armor.

Ryan had done his best to scratch off the dried blood from his shoulder plate, but he was worried the official might notice anyway. Trying to seem normal, Ryan unclasped his helmet with his good hand, peeling the protective gear off his head with some difficulty. The official's gaze hovered over the soldier briefly, but then continued down to the display on his wrist. Soon enough he tapped a few buttons and gestured for him to move on.

Ryan tried to keep his smile secret and was about to head to the locker room when the officer to O'Brian's left cleared his throat and brought up his hand to tap the official's shoulder. After turning to look at his subordinate, O'Brian saw the man nod back at Ryan and tap his right shoulder, grunting as he did. The EOSF officer was on the tail end of middle-age, but he was still able to see a crippling wound for what it was.

At the hint, Ryan wanted to hurl his fist into the officer's jaw, not caring that he would end up the worse for it.

"You sure you're doing alright, Ryan? Seems like you got shot in the shoulder," O'Brian said before further inspecting it and feeling around the warped metal. Ryan did his best to take the statement in stride.

"Just a graze, sir. Don't expect it to—*ghk*..." he said before wincing. When the official pressed down on the shoulder plate, a small amount of blood had oozed out of the hole. Upon Ryan's reaction, O'Brian pulled the soldier's arm and suddenly his mind was overwhelmed by a maelstrom of pain.

He stood his ground and maintained his consciousness, but the Crow knew he had lost his battle. O'Brian had already stood back up and started to enter information into his computer while he talked down to the wounded man.

"Ryan, faking it doesn't help anyone. We can't help you if you hide it from us. Albert," he said, addressing the young officer to his right. "Can you escort Mr. Jenkins here to Medical? I've scheduled in an appointment with Dr. Kane to euthanize the man."

Upon hearing the man speaking so casually about his death, Ryan suddenly felt the injustice of it all.

"Wait a minute! O'Brian, you don't have to kill me. I can keep fighting like this. It's just a shoulder!" he shouted, gesturing wildly with the helmet in his hand. O'Brian looked back at Ryan and then motioned to the other officer, as well. Albert wouldn't be enough to guide the soldier to Medical, it seemed.

"It's a shoulder that's not your property. The Commission needs it fixed for the next game. Can you do that?" the official asked, speaking over Ryan when he tried to interrupt. "No, you can't. I'm afraid it's clearly stated in your contract that upon any limiting structural damage you are subject to a forced resurrection. You signed the papers, didn't you?"

"*Look*, you've never died here. It's terrible. I'm sure I can play in the next game! We can work something out. I can give you my earnings for the next few games. *Please*," Ryan begged as the two officers walked toward him. He held out his helmet to try to ward them off as they approached, but the official just shook his head at Ryan's futile behavior.

"I make *much* more than you. You have nothing I *want*, Ryan. And even if I could help you," he said before removing his glasses and cleaning them, "it's very much out of my hands. God, this is a filthy planet."

The officers advanced on Ryan and he thought briefly about fighting them off just long enough so he could strangle the life from O'Brian, but then he realized it wouldn't mean a thing. There would just be another official to take his place.

The EOSF loomed over him and were about to grab his arms before Ryan stood straight and lowered his helmet in defeat.

"It's fine, it's fine... I'll go easy," he said, bowing his head and letting the young officer lead him along the pathway to the medical complex. It was only a short walk from the landing zone and the barracks, but for Ryan it was torturous. The other guard stayed behind with the official and looked after him as they departed.

"They always think they're special, Laurence. They can always work something out," O'Brian said before turning back to the computer in his hands. The older officer shrugged and looked out to the ruined landscape.

"Can you really blame them?" Laurence asked as he shifted in his place, tapping his fingers along the stock of his rifle. The official just sighed and continued to tap away at the display.

"They signed up for it. I can't feel sorry for them," O'Brian said dismissively as he wrapped up the checklist on his computer. Laurence looked at the official and disgust flickered in his eyes, though he kept it hidden from the smaller man.

If his friends rescued the planet like they hoped, Laurence would have a hard time trying to justify saving the bureaucrat's life. Laurence looked back at the doomed Crow as they disappeared over a crest in the landscape, and he instantly felt ashamed of himself. He had come here to help them, to save them, but so far, Laurence and his friends were doing a poor job of saving anyone.

And that Crow was just one of many.

RYAN FELT miserable as he waited for his appointment in the medical complex. The oversized officer sat beside him in the adjacent chair and shifted in his seat every once in a while, which he could not help but notice. With the calm whites and blues of the clinic surrounding him, Ryan felt more anxious than when he was on the battlefield, so he noticed every little detail.

It was almost worse to be waiting patiently for death in the clinic instead of facing a hail of bullets from the other team. As they waited for Charlotte, Ryan looked at his shoulder. The official and his guards had not bothered to take off his armor, and he could see a new trickle of blood flowing down the crevice. He sighed, knowing now how such a little thing was a death sentence on Eris.

Albert could sense the young soldier's anxiety. He couldn't help the Crow; not at that time. The best he could do was to try to comfort the soldier, but they never did respond well to his empathy, and he wasn't sure how this Jenkins would react. He wished he could tell the poor slave soldier—just like all the other Crows he had done nothing to save—that there were people out there who wanted to help. That there were people whose plans were in motion to free all these soldiers from their slavery. Albert wanted to tell the soldier that he was on his side; he wanted to tell Jenkins to wait and that everything would be alright.

Yet that was not in the cards. Albert had spent years developing the cover necessary to get this position in the EOSF; Laurence much longer. They had been installed there to help, but they needed to keep quiet until the time was right.

In the meantime, they had to watch as these modern slaves were forced to kill each other. Albert felt the whole thing was unbearable. Every day, he could barely look the Crows in their eyes. He had come to save them; he had come to help.

But Albert looked at this soldier and saw just another man he was leading to death.

Charlotte was distracted as she burst through the entryway. She was just coming back from a resurrection procedure and checked the display, skimming through the details. It had already been a few hours since the first casualties, and Hawkins had left it up to her to deal with their last patients. Since the first resurrection, she had been administering sedatives and gently bringing the dead back to a living hell.

It was tiring work, especially when she could not get a break.

Ryan watched as she typed away on the display and could see how weary she looked, and he immediately felt bad for her. Charlotte was surrounded by this day after day, and he could tell she did not enjoy this clinical purgatory. After a few moments of pity, Ryan realized Charlotte was probably going to be the one who killed him and his spirits sank even more. He sighed, knowing her conscience would not let her come back from that one easily.

Charlotte kept tapping away at the display, finishing up the check list for the last resurrection. Feldman had come through normal as always and his vitals were just the same, but that didn't stop the system from freaking out every time he gained consciousness. Since his frame was so different from the rest of the Crows, his heartbeat was considered abnormal, and the Commission had not updated their software to compensate.

Even after five years.

She smiled as she remembered the giant man's demeanor. Feldman was so understanding and calm while the alarms went off around him, which would have frightened other newly-resurrected soldiers. She needed more men like that in her life, rather than cowards like Hawkins.

Luckily, the two doctors had developed a system of mutual avoidance, so there were some days Charlotte didn't even interact with the man. She had hoped to continue that pattern for the rest of the day.

Then she saw Ryan's name flash across the screen for his appointment. Her heart sank as she turned her head and saw the soldier sitting next to the EOSF officer, a defeated look on his face. Charlotte remembered the last two times he had been resurrected; she remembered hoping at the time that he would never have to experience anything like this.

Without a second thought, Charlotte tapped a few keys and opened the intercom channel.

"What?" Hawkins asked, his resentful voice sounding tinny over the speaker. Charlotte sighed as she looked at Ryan, who looked back at her and pathetically waved with his left hand.

"I need you to prep the euthanasia materials," Charlotte stated before clicking off the intercom and waving back at Ryan. There was a knot in her gut and she felt terrible.

"Hah, one of *those*? Who's the unlucky sap?"

Charlotte could tell that monster of a man was enjoying the idea of killing another person.

"You'll see soon enough," she said before walking over to Ryan. She had trained herself not to cry in these circumstances, but Charlotte gained a small comfort in the fact that the procedure still made her feel like a bad person.

Eris had not *completely* killed her conscience.

As she neared the men, Ryan made motion to stand, making Charlotte's heart ache. He was having difficulty with his shoulder, obviously, so the good doctor put out her hand to gesture that he didn't have to go through the effort. Offering him a sad, conciliatory smile, Charlotte crouched down to look him in the eye.

"I'm sorry, Ryan. It seems like I always have to play a part in your pain." She didn't really understand why she said it. It was something Ryan probably didn't want to hear, but he returned her sad smile and shrugged with his good shoulder.

"You can't help it, Doc. It's this world. It just gets into everything," he said, his eyes starting to glisten.

Ryan sniffed as he held the tears back along with all his emotions. He wanted to head into that room without the world breaking him; he wanted to face death with his head held high. Clenching his fist, Ryan looked at the ground as he mustered his courage.

"I'll try to make it as painless as I can. I'll try to make it better," Charlotte said, her voice nearly faltering at the end, and she did her best to keep her tears to herself.

Looking up at her, Ryan could see that she was already feeling terrible for what she was about to do. He could not stop a single tear from rolling down his right cheek.

"It's okay, Doc. I know how it is," he said before picking himself up. Charlotte tried to reach out and help him, but he warded off her hands with his left. When he stood up to his full height and looked her in the face, it was clear he wouldn't allow another tear to fall.

"Charlotte," she said as she led him to the prep room.

Ryan gave her a puzzled look before realizing she was letting him know her name.

"It's pretty," he replied as she pointed to a table in front of him. After taking a slow breath, Ryan walked over to the table and laid down, gritting his teeth as his shoulder met the surface. He tried to ignore the EOSF officer who had led him to this room. Albert was only present in case Ryan tried to attack the doctors while they euthanized him, but he had no intention of hurting the only person who seemed to care.

Hawkins came in with the medications and needles that would kill Ryan and he seemed to have a nervous glee about him, earning a glare from Charlotte as he hummed and filled the syringes with sedatives and poisons. Trying to pretend the scientist did not exist, Ryan closed his eyes and tried to mentally prepare himself for what came next.

An anxious quiet overtook the room and suddenly Albert felt even more out of place. If he wanted, he could stop this from happening. He could save a largely innocent man from getting killed by a mad scientist. At least, that was the impression that Hawkins gave, and Albert certainly did not want to see what the scientist kept behind closed doors.

No one should take such pleasure from killing a man.

Albert could reach out and squeeze the life out of the scientist. He could watch as the man took his last breath and he could make a mad dash with Jenkins out of the Crows' headquarters. Maybe he could convince Laurence to make a run with him, steal a space transport and fly back to Earth.

He realized that it was all foolish; it was all illogical. They would all die in the process and their sacrifice would be in vain. The best thing for him to do was watch the man die and then head back to guard duty with Laurence.

But Albert didn't have to like it.

After Charlotte prepared Ryan's body for the procedure, she strapped him onto the clinic table and tried to soothe him as she pulled on the restraints. Hawkins brought the syringes and medicine nearby and started attaching the IV drips to Ryan's support system, waited a few minutes for the residual drugs to kick in, and then offered the final syringe to Charlotte.

"You want this one? I know you two are pretty close now, *Charlotte*," he said with a hearty dose of disdain. He was obviously not one to connect with his patients.

In response, Charlotte looked at him with fury and narrowed her eyes.

"You can have it, *Peter*. And while you're at it, burn in Hell," she said before laying her hand on top of Ryan's head and running it through his hair. The medication swirling through his veins prevented him from speaking, but Ryan looked grateful for the comfort.

"You're so touchy. You're going to see him in a couple of hours, *Dr. Kane*," Hawkins said before inserting the syringe into the man's arm and pushing the plunger. He then looked to the computer display as Ryan's vitals began to drop.

Although his body convulsed for a few disturbing moments, the display soon read the absence of vitals. His time of death was recorded by the system automatically, so Hawkins started packing up the euthanasia materials, his hands shaking slightly. He had the appearance of a man who was just barely satisfied, and he quickly exited the room and called the janitorial staff on his receiver so they could remove the body.

For a moment, Albert kept his place at the doorway as Charlotte traced the line of Ryan's cheek and then slowly backed away. She turned to him and saw the EOSF officer still standing there, a hulking representation of all that was wrong with the world. Albert could see the anger brewing behind her eyes.

"What are you still doing here?" she asked, almost violent. Albert was taken off guard by the woman's emotion, forgetting momentarily that he was technically one of the bad guys.

"I was just—uh, confirming that Ryan was dead," he said, instantly cursing himself for using the soldier's first name. He wasn't supposed to know that; he wasn't supposed to connect like that.

"You've done *enough*, I think. You should leave. He'll be back on his feet in no time," Charlotte said as her eyes narrowed, punctuating every word like she was slapping him in the face.

Albert could take the hint and turned to the door, but the doctor called after him.

"You're a monster, you know that? Just like us. You shouldn't judge me. You might not *kill* them, but you're a monster." At the insults, Albert wanted to turn and tell her everything. He wanted to tell her that he didn't want any of this and that he was fighting against it. He wanted to tell her they were just waiting for the right moment.

But he felt like a monster. Albert left the clinic without saying a thing.

RYAN OPENED his eyes and quickly told himself he was just stuck in his resurrection cell. It was a certainty this time. Three resurrections were enough to realize that this was just more of the same. He did what he could do gather his patience and waited for Charlotte and Hawkins to bring him back to the world of the living.

After what seemed like a few minutes, he remembered what Carver had told him about his experiences, how the old Crow had eventually figured out how he could start getting his body used to the outside world while trapped in the darkness. Ryan flexed his arms and curled his fingers; he tried to hum and felt the rebreather resonating with him. It hurt, but the feeling was enough to make Ryan smile.

It allowed him the certainty that he was really alive; he was inside another one of his clones.

He continued on like that for a great deal of time. The exercise wasn't enough to occupy himself fully, so his mind started to wander, and eventually he tried to figure out how the Commission slipped in the first resurrection without him noticing. When he tried to dig deeper and remember his second birth, he found that it was completely absent from his mind. It was disturbing, and Ryan wondered what they did to repress the memory or why he had not woken up in that resurrection cell screaming. He thought that maybe it was just a different procedure. Maybe there was no such thing as an early adoption with the first resurrection.

After a few minutes, he thought about Carver and his endless struggle on the battlefield. Without trying, Ryan thought up a fantasy version of himself at the same age, directing a band of young soldiers who had been fooled into his lifestyle. What disturbed him was that it seemed like a very likely scenario. The two Crows *did* have a lot in common, and the veteran seemed strangely content. Carver certainly wasn't happy, but the man made do with his surroundings. Although Ryan found that peace enviable, he thought it the course of a lost soul.

He wondered how Feldman was able to live with all of it. Ryan still knew little about the man, but he knew enough to realize that the soldier did not belong on Eris. Feldman was kind; he was intelligent. He spent his days reading books when he was not training for war.

Ryan's brow furrowed in the darkness as he realized that the giant was an outlier. Most of the soldiers carried themselves with guilt or the resolve of a soldier—sometimes both—but Feldman held hope for the future while the rest muddied themselves with earthly pursuits. Resolving to find out the truth, Ryan realized he would have to talk to his new friend. There should not be this kind of silence between them.

Soon after that, the light cracked the wall of darkness in front of him and Ryan's cell was moving forward along the line. He curled his toes and stretched out his fingers, anticipating the pain to come. In just a moment, he would see how much difference all of this preparation would make for his therapy.

CHARLOTTE SPED up the retrieval process for Ryan's cell, knowing the man had likely suffered another early adoption and that he would hang there in the darkness, otherwise. Since she could not bear to think that she would be responsible for that, too, Charlotte tapped the display in the main control room and set the railway in motion.

Though she hated the taste, Charlotte made herself drink the coffee in front of her. It had already been a long day and her conscience had been battered. She could not suffer being tired, as well.

She pinched the skin of her forehead as a stress headache started to spread to the front of her brain, and she sighed as she looked over at Hawkins' desk. The man had disappeared after the procedure—Charlotte was grateful for that—and the EOSF officer had left thirty minutes ago without a word. She wondered how the oaf lived with himself.

The ranks of the EOSF weren't exactly filled with honorable men, but only the evil could witness the sins of this planet and do nothing.

The loading bay opened in front of her and—after a few minutes—Ryan's cell emerged from the darkness. After Charlotte tapped a few buttons, the resurrection equipment broke from its mooring in the wall and surrounded the landing area, so Charlotte took another gulp of coffee and steeled herself for the coming interaction.

She was responsible for the death and rebirth of this poor man today.

The biotic fluid emptied out of the cell and the construct was loaded into the mooring in the center. After the cell hissed open and revealed its contents, Charlotte found herself face-to-face with the newborn Ryan Jenkins. The man's eyes were wide open and showed the sadness lying underneath, bringing her new heartache. She sighed as she tapped the display to start the sedation process, but when Charlotte was about to confirm the operation, she saw Ryan shake his head.

At that, Charlotte's hand wavered, and she walked over to him. "You don't want the sedatives?"

She had forgotten the proper protocol and only regretted it slightly. No one could blame her for getting caught up in the moment, since she had just seen this man alive in the other room.

In response, Ryan nodded and weakly pointed at the rebreather. Returning that nod, Charlotte went to work undoing the straps around his head before grabbing at the machine, wishing things were so much different for him. She then looked back at Ryan, who blinked and huffed out of his nose, so—taking this as assent—Charlotte pulled out the plastic tube.

Ryan clearly felt pain as the machine was pulled out of his throat, and that hurt Charlotte's conscience. Once the tube was out of his body, he let out a wet cough before gasping for air and, as Charlotte watched, Ryan breathed with labor for an agonizing few moments. Part of her thought she had made a terrible mistake, but soon after that, Ryan calmed down and turned to her with gratitude.

"Thank you, Charlotte. I... didn't want to feel the drugs this time," he said before trying to sit up. When he faltered, Charlotte jerked out her hands to help him up and Ryan was suddenly staring at her, face-to-face.

Once he was upright, she backed away and looked at him with worry. If nothing else, she was relieved that he did not seem to be angry at her.

"You're speaking much better this time around," she said, uncomfortable in her own skin.

"I was practicing in there. Carver told me it helps out. Seems like he's right," Ryan said before looking around the room. He lifted his arm and grabbed the back of his neck, his hand shaking as he did. As a result, all the wires and electrodes attached to his arm fell around him.

After letting out an anxious laugh, Charlotte started to remove the things from Ryan's body. He laughed, too, although it hurt his new throat. He felt like it was a good idea to just ignore that kind of pain this time around.

It would disappear after a day or two, anyway.

Charlotte took the last of the electrodes off the man's body and gestured for him to lower his feet to the floor. After taking a deep breath, Ryan turned his body so he could drop his feet down. Once he was able to touch the cold tiles, he tried to place his weight on his new legs.

They responded well and—with a little pain and time—Ryan was standing in a brand-new body. Charlotte looked him over in approval and turned back to the display nearby so she could run down a checklist to clear him for duty. Meanwhile, Ryan sat back down on the table and started swinging his legs.

"Hey, Doc, I have a question for you," he said while looking at the floor.

"What do you want to know?" she replied, keeping her eyes on her checklist. After clearing his throat, Ryan continued in a more confident voice.

"Well, why do my legs work at all with this body? Shouldn't the legs be all atrophied?"

It had always bugged him; Ryan had always seen in movies that coma patients would not be able to move if they woke up.

Charlotte continued tapping away at the screen and just shrugged.

"*Modern science*, Ryan." She turned slightly so he could see the slight smile on her face. "All those wires and electrodes I pulled off you were giving your muscles electronic pulses so they could still be used when you woke up," she said as she hit a few more buttons and finished with the checklist. She turned and looked at her patient and found Ryan looking back at her expectantly.

In that moment, Charlotte realized she could not look him in the eye, and he had noticed.

"It's okay, Charlotte. Really. I'm not mad at you," he said while he got to his feet. He grunted through the pain and crossed his arms. "You're just doing your job."

Charlotte looked up at him and suddenly couldn't take it anymore. Tears welled up in her eyes, and she did not care if they fell down her cheeks.

"Yeah, well that's *my* choice, isn't it? I'm a doctor, yet all I do is keep people in a living Hell. And I just *killed* you, or at least I was *part* of it. How can you not be angry at me?" she asked as tears streamed down her face.

Charlotte was sick of all of the death and pain around her and she realized that she was almost grateful for Hawkins. The demented scientist always volunteered to kill the men when they came in wounded.

"It wasn't *you*. It wasn't even Hawkins, *really*. It's all the Commission, and as everybody keeps reminding me," Ryan said just before sighing and looking at the floor, "I signed the contract.

"I'm a thief, Charlotte, or at least I used to be one. I chose this," Ryan said as he tried to comfort her. However, he had no clue if it would work, as the words did not comfort him, at all.

Ryan had *not* chosen the life of a thief, but he just wanted her to stop crying. More than anything, Ryan wanted to reach out and hug her, feel some warmth on this cold moon, but he didn't know if that would be appropriate. He settled for sitting to the side and preaching platitudes.

"It doesn't matter that you were a thief. It's still wrong and I'm part of it," Charlotte said. When he looked back at her, Ryan gave her a smile filled with melancholy.

"At least you know it's wrong. There are a lot of people who just sweep it under the rug or try to justify it. You're better than that, and you know it," he said as he walked past her and into the hallway leading to the training room.

He hoped his speech would be enough to make her feel better, because it didn't make him feel better in the slightest.

RYAN FINISHED his round of calisthenics and had taken another long and lonely walk to the barracks, but his mind continued to work against him. Earthrise had greeted him yet again and although he had tried to sleep, he couldn't keep his eyes closed.

All he could think about were the twenty thousand times in his life where he could have turned it all around. Ryan thought of twenty thousand different versions of himself with little changes to each, depending on his decisions. He wondered if he would have liked those twenty thousand lives; he wondered if he would have been happy.

Ryan quickly realized it didn't matter, as there was no way to turn back the clock. The following morning, he rose with the other Crows when the alarms went off and continued on with his day like nothing had happened.

During breakfast, Ryan had made small talk with the new recruit who was still going through training. Feldman had not been around that morning, so he had wanted someone with whom to pass the time. The recruit—a man named Chang who was around his age—had very little to say, even when Ryan asked him questions about his old life.

He stopped trying to talk to the new Crow once he noticed the man had started crying into his oatmeal.

After that, Ryan went about his daily tasks and logged in his hour in the shooting gallery. He daydreamed the entire time, the allure of virtual combat evading him. At the end of his hour, the computer readout told him he was largely average, and if Ryan wanted to survive in the games, he would need to improve.

With a scoff, Ryan crumpled up the piece of paper and threw it in the trashcan. On his way back to his room, he walked by Feldman's training room and his curiosity got the best of him. He looked inside to find the giant swinging his sword just like the other day.

However, the giant seemed slower, his swings more deliberate and labored. Ryan could tell Feldman was sweating profusely and that his heaving chest could not give him nearly enough oxygen. As he watched, Ryan saw Feldman swing through all of his virtual opponents, but a few had the chance to fire back. The massive Crow could not kill every one of them, and the computer was noting each virtual bullet that struck him with a short blast of an air horn.

Soon enough, Feldman stopped swinging his sword and set it on the ground, paying no attention to the swarming virtual soldiers as he sat down on the floor next to his weapon. The simulation ended, and the room returned to its natural grey color.

Entering through the doorway, Ryan walked up to his friend, his hands in his pockets. Even sitting down, the giant was an impressive height, and Ryan could not peer down his nose at the older man. Joining him on the floor, Ryan sat down and folded his legs in front of him.

"You having some trouble, Greg?" he asked as he flicked at a small clump of dirt on the ground. He was just opening conversation, waiting for Feldman to express himself.

Instead, Feldman shrugged and scratched at his cheek.

"A little. This last resurrection was rough and unfortunately the muscle memory doesn't translate," he said before looking at his weapon. Ryan followed his gaze and imagined having to train with such intensity. Suddenly, training with a rifle for an hour didn't seem so bad.

"Sounds painful," he said, merely making noise.

"It is." Feldman looked to the door. From Ryan's body language, Feldman could tell there was something on his mind.

"What is it, Ryan? You didn't come in here for small talk. Go ahead with the big talk." Feldman lifted himself off his elbows and regained his intimidating stature just by sitting up, and Ryan looked at him and sighed before half-heartedly examining his new legs sprawled out on the floor.

They were responding so much better than they had the other two times.

"You don't belong here, Greg. You can't have committed any crime. You're too nice, you're too noble," Ryan said before looking him in the eye. "And you don't seem the type who would need money or think this was a good way to go about it. You're too smart. It doesn't make sense."

"I've never really told anyone why I'm here. Why do you want to know?" Feldman asked, his brow furrowed and his deep voice tinged with emotion.

"I don't know, it's just," Ryan said before standing up and pacing the room. When he turned back, Ryan felt the injustice of it all. "I think you could have such a better life. I feel like you're wasting it here.

The rest of us were tricked into it, but by all rights you should have been able to stay away."

"This is what you think about? Alright, I'll tell you," Gregory said, reaching out and touching the hilt of his sword. The smile disappeared as he fell into his memories.

"You know I'm from Osmos. Obviously, I have to be from one of the farming asteroids, since the lesser gravity really lets us hicks grow tall," he said before shifting on the floor. "Well, I grew up on one of those hydro farms. My dad tried to instill some work ethic into all of us. If you believe it, I'm in the middle of my brothers. Saul has a good thirty centimeters on me.

"We all grew up to help on the farm. It was a decent man's living. I had no problem with it and I tended to the fields pretty much every day. I didn't get out too much, but sometimes I'd get to go to town and spend some time in the library. My brothers just went to look at all the pretty girls," he said before pausing. Ryan laughed before he was able to stop himself, and he covered his mouth in embarrassment.

"Sorry, it just sounds pretty cliché," he said, trying to apologize, but then Gregory laughed along with him.

"It does, but I was happy. My brothers could have all the girls they wanted. I always wanted someone who got me up here." He tapped the side of his head, and Ryan nodded in agreement.

"One day I was working near a batch of corn stalks and then one of our drones went haywire. It was one of those machines that would just cut down all the stalks and scoop them up so we could take care of them back at the house," he said before looking at Ryan, who had a very serious look on his face. After he noticed, Gregory held out his hand in a halting gesture.

"It wasn't the horror movie it sounds like. Nobody got sliced up. Some of the livestock got shredded, though, and the thing did run me over and broke my spine. The doctors tried what they could, but my family never had much money to begin with and they told us that anything they could do with *any* money wouldn't be very effective."

A meter away from him, Ryan sat down and looked at his friend.

He hadn't meant to bring back such sad memories, but Gregory continued just the same.

"I was paralyzed, Ryan, from about halfway down my torso. It was humiliating in a lot of ways and downright horrible in a lot of others. My mother had to help me with even the most basic tasks. I couldn't help with the farm, either. I felt like such a burden." He placed his hand on his knee and rubbed it slowly.

"I started reading a lot more. We never watched too much television and I had always liked to read. I started to learn a bit, and I'm sure that would have helped me out if I tried to go to school or something, but life was still rough. I wasn't able to really leave the house without someone helping me the entire way. I started to become really angry with myself and thought about all the things I could have done to avoid that drone. I'm sure you've felt something like that before.

"I'd always heard things about the games but I'd never really paid attention. But then I thought about how they brought back these dead people with perfect bodies. That's what got me interested. Sure, they died a lot, but they got to *live* in the meantime. And they always came back. I felt like it was situation where I could take advantage.

"I contacted the Commission Office in Osmos and asked to be part of the games. They told me that they didn't really take handicapped people, but I already knew how they did the process. Like I said, I read quite a bit in those days.

"I told them I wouldn't mind being killed if I was resurrected into a new body. I would sign up freely if they would give me a body that wasn't paralyzed," Gregory said before rubbing his knee again.

Ryan realized that he had done that before and he had not paid it any attention. Now that he understood, the tiny act tugged at his heartstrings.

"Of course, as soon as he knew that was what I was after, the recruiter turned it into a big bartering contest. We negotiated for a while, but in the end, he was able to get me to agree to a lot of things I didn't want, like the sword. He had the upper hand, obviously, so I had to give in. I guess that's why it doesn't bother me when I realize I'm stuck here for a while. It's much better than the alternative," Feldman concluded with a heavy breath, forcing a smile for his friend.

Ryan could see the pain behind it, but he knew Gregory was content with his decision. In the same situation, Ryan would have been hard-pressed to do otherwise.

After Gregory finished his story, Ryan didn't know what to say. A former life as a cripple wasn't on the list of things he had expected to hear. Ryan had guessed the man was involved in one of the doomed resistance movements, but in the end, his story made perfect sense.

In comparison to his own life, the revelation made Ryan feel hollow. He had no heart-warming story to explain his decision; he was just too afraid to be sent to a slave labor camp. While he thought, Feldman picked himself up and grabbed his sword along the way.

"I don't feel better now that I've told you, so I guess I really didn't need to share it. But I guess that wasn't the point. Have I eased your mind, or do you have more questions?" he asked just as he slid his sword back into its mooring in the wall.

Already knowing it was time to go, Ryan stood up with a fair amount of soreness.

"A little. It wasn't what I expected," he said, starting toward the door.

"It is a bit of an odd story. Like you hinted, I'm not the typical soldier," Feldman said as he caught up quickly with his great strides.

Ryan stood near the door and looked at his friend. He realized that there was no way he could ever measure up to the man, physically or with his character. Gregory Feldman was more than he could ever hope to be.

But Ryan left the room and promised to himself that he would try.

Stage Four

DEPRESSION

1

Patron Saint of Painkillers

Christopher Roberts could see the light peeking through the window and realized it would be a few more hours until the alarms would sound off. When he shifted in his bed, he immediately regretted it, his body betraying him in the early light. Gasping and clutching at the pillow by his head, Christopher tried to withstand the pain burning through him. He had learned to hold back the screams, but that didn't stop the contortions that twisted his body like an abused marionette.

After a few labored breaths, he gathered his willpower and tried to sit up in his bed. The pain was excruciating, but the only thing that could help was in his desk across the room. He couldn't lie there any longer if he wanted to rid himself of this torture.

Christopher did what he could to bear with the sensory explosion when his feet touched the floor. He didn't know why this incarnation was hurting so bad—he hadn't even died in the last match. Hawkins and Kane had proven incapable of fixing him, but Christopher assumed his malady probably had something to do with his former career.

Someone or something—probably the head honchos at War World Entertainment—had to be getting back at him for his cyber adventures. Christopher needed something to justify the daily bouts of pain, or he would have to consider that it was just senseless torture.

The desk came at him fast as he stumbled into the furniture, but as soon as he could prop himself up, Christopher wrenched open his drawer and rummaged through its contents. Every package he picked out of the drawer had long since been empty. They scattered to the floor as the man frantically searched for medicine of any sort.

Eventually, he grabbed hold of Goldstein's latest delivery and popped open the box, an amber bottle of pills inside. He pushed his palm against the lid and twisted off the white cover, accidentally spilling the contents of the bottle onto the desk. Five blue and white pills came out and Roberts closed his eyes, trying to gauge how much medication he actually needed. His mind wasn't working correctly from sleep deprivation, and his fingers ached from hastily twisting the lid off the bottle.

Throwing caution to the wind, he grabbed all five pills, craned his neck toward the ceiling and then threw them into his mouth. In desperation, he swallowed them all without any water, and Christopher wondered if he had finally taken enough to overdose this time. If he did, it didn't much matter.

Christopher would just encounter another body filled with a different kind of pain.

He sighed and drifted over to his chair—picking it up from where it had fallen—and then set it down so he could look out the window. Gingerly, he sat and peered out at the landscape beyond the barracks.

From here, Christopher could see the Earth drifting down below the curvature of Eris. As it sank below the horizon, Christopher tilted his head and wondered what all of his friends were doing back in Los Angeles.

When he remembered what they did to him—how they had set him up—he reminded himself that they weren't his friends. Once the EOSF cybercrimes unit caught up to him, he had lost every friend he had ever met. Instead of trying to remember their laughing faces or the times they spent jacked into the datasphere, Christopher closed his eyes and waited.

LIGHT WAS POURING into his room when the alarms finally went off. Trying to blink the sleep out of his eyes, Christopher felt a stinging sensation as he looked around his room. He was still sitting in his chair and quite honestly surprised that he was able to fall asleep without trying.

His balance faltered as he rose, but was on his feet, soon enough. Wavering from side to side, Roberts realized that maybe he had taken a few too many pills, but he tried to be content with the fact that he hadn't killed himself.

It was a small victory to contrast the constant losses.

He went over to his dresser and threw on some fatigues before exiting his room, and he was a few meters along before he realized his contraband was still out in the open. With a shake of his head, Christopher returned and set things in order before heading toward the mess hall.

Christopher's body instinctively knew where to go, but his mind was slow to follow the reasoning. He didn't realize until well into his journey that he was heading for the mess hall, or that he was even hungry. His train of thought was way behind his actions, and that worried him.

After a moment of contemplation, Christopher gave himself a slap across the face. Dulled in every way by the medicine, he let out a pitiful laugh. Whatever bed he had made, now it was time to sleep in it, and a mere slap across the face wasn't going to bring him back to his senses. He would just have to go to breakfast and pretend to be normal.

It wouldn't be the first time.

SOME OF THE Crows gave him odd looks, but Roberts was quick to give them a glare before heading to the line of food in the mess hall. He had a reputation for not tolerating nonsense, and this was one of the few scenarios where he leaned on that reputation. Every fighter had their secret pain, but Roberts didn't want anyone to know what he experienced after every resurrection. There were only two people that he had ever told.

One was his supplier; the other, a saint.

Before he realized, Roberts had walked through the line and his tray was full of things he didn't necessarily want or need to eat. Internally, he scolded his body, but he still picked up the tray. Maybe this new clone body had a desperate craving for grits and artificial cheese. After walking to the nearest empty seat, Roberts set his tray down and fell to the seat in the same moment.

Even now, he felt like he was floating around, and that was enough for him to set down a mental rule that five was too much. The dose was clearly too much for a fresh body—however pain-ridden it was—and three days had not been enough time to build up a resistance. Every time, he had to remind himself that he was always starting over fresh.

He never could remember.

When Roberts looked down at his tray, he noticed a third of the food was gone. He was about to look around for the culprit before he realized there was a taste in his mouth, and it was another moment before he realized it did not taste good.

Roberts sighed and resolved again that he would not take five pills right after a resurrection. After swaying in his chair and muttering to himself, he looked across the table and found Jenkins avoiding eye contact with him. Roberts couldn't call Jenkins a rookie anymore—the Crow had eleven games under his belt—but he still seemed so young.

Then Roberts remembered that *he* was the youngest one on the Crows' roster. Jenkins had two years on him, but something about him made Roberts think of happier times. Maybe it was because he wasn't so far removed from his life before Eris, but Roberts couldn't pretend to know. He just nodded to himself and looked back at his tray.

Rookie or not, old or young; it didn't matter. Every Crow was doomed in their own way, and Jenkins was no exception.

RYAN HAD BEEN WATCHING Roberts from his periphery, careful not to make too much noise. He didn't want to antagonize him, as his erratic movements were probably the result of a drug-induced stupor.

Ryan had tried to eat the food in front of him, but as time passed, the artificial sustenance had only become more unappetizing. It was becoming harder to justify eating, as he had realized that his bodies wouldn't last long enough to starve.

He sighed and looked around the room, observing his fellow soldiers as they ate their breakfast. Norris was only one of them who ever really talked during those times, whether or not anyone wanted to listen.

Ryan had to wonder if it was all an act or if it really was true what they said about him. After Ryan had asked why Norris was always so cheerful, Cortes had mentioned that the sniper had been the product of behavioral experimentation. Now, as he watched Norris tossing food around his table, Ryan was curious.

Still, it felt impolite to broach the subject.

The Crows started to file out of the mess hall, and soon there were only stragglers left in their seats. Except for a few of the drones, it was just Ryan and his addict of a teammate. With a brief glance at Roberts, Ryan's thoughts returned to what went on in the poor soldier's brain.

The thought completely ruined his appetite, and when he looked down at his tray, he found that his food resembled vomit. Ryan picked up the metal tray and deliberately did not look at the Crow sitting across the table before turning to leave.

"It's okay," Roberts said weakly. Ryan looked back and found the addict's eyes filled with a temporary lucidity. "It's okay, Ryan. I understand."

Ryan stood there as Roberts picked up his tray and emptied it into the trash bin on his way out of the room. Ryan didn't quite know *why* the addled Crow had spoken up, but it brought up a dozen questions.

Ryan had felt like he had understood his situation, but Roberts had proved he had understood nothing.

RYAN WALKED BACK from the shower to his room, his muscles aching from the exercises in the training yard. He was still digging in his ear with his pinky to remove some stubborn water when he noticed Carver leaning against the wall near his doorway.

Ryan's eyes narrowed and he halted for a moment—his bare skin cool in the air of the barracks—but eventually he stepped forward. As Carver noticed his approach, he pushed himself off the wall and dug his thumbs into his pockets.

"I wanted to make sure you were alright."

Ryan could tell the old man meant it.

"Yeah, I'm fine. It's just a new body."

"Of course, and we know what happens *there*," Carver said as Ryan opened his door and walked into the room. After setting down his toiletries, Ryan turned and set his hand on the back of his desk chair.

"Yeah, we do. What's this about, Carver?"

The old man was briefly taken off guard, but soon regained his composure and tried to shrug off the confrontation.

"I wanted to see if you were alright, is all," he said before looking Ryan in the eye. It was an obvious bluff, and Ryan crossed his arms and waited until Carver relented. "Fine, kid. I wanted to make sure you're not thinking of anything stupid after that last death. The first time *they* kill you is a little hard to handle."

Ryan could tell Carver felt awkward having this conversation, so he decided to end it as soon as possible.

"Look, I'm not happy about it." Ryan sat down in his chair and crossed his legs out of decency. "But that's how it is. Sometimes it's just not fair. Maybe things will turn around."

"That's... pretty optimistic for you," Carver said with a note of skepticism. Ryan shrugged and rubbed the painted-on wood grain of his plastic desk.

"Greg helped me put it in perspective. Made it seem better."

"Feldman, eh? He's a smart guy, that one," Carver said before turning to leave. "The problem *is*... he's smart enough to convince himself of anything."

Carver departed without another word, and Ryan was left to decipher the veteran's meaning. Cryptic, at best, Ryan wondered how the old Crow could think poorly of someone like Feldman.

Ryan was starting to get agitated that people thought he knew what they were saying. First Roberts, and now Carver. It seemed like every person thought they knew best—that their years on Eris made them experts on everything. With a few paltry words, they could completely alter his life.

He wasn't so sure he should believe any of them.

Instead of dwelling on their supposedly-enlightened opinions, Ryan dressed himself in light fatigues and considered what he would do for the next few hours. Nothing seemed appealing, and laying down seemed like a nice temporary relief.

However, as soon as he fell onto his bed, he discovered his mind was filled with the thoughts and opinions of others. Ryan wished that they would leave him alone and let him think for himself.

He turned in his bed and looked at the window. The sun was currently eclipsed by the moon, but the light bouncing off the other moons was more than enough to see everything clearly. He couldn't sleep if he tried.

But Ryan didn't want to sleep. Once he realized that people were trying to fill his minds with their own opinions, he started to realize that he was not thinking, at all. Ryan hadn't bothered to inform himself on his situation or even the state of Earth or all its satellites. He had forced this ignorance on himself.

Ryan suddenly felt guilty for not giving himself the opportunity to know everything he could. He realized that this was the reason he was on Eris in the first place.

There was only one way out of this situation, so Ryan sat up, grunted and jumped off of his bed before bursting out the door and down the hallway. He didn't close the door behind him, since he had nothing worth stealing.

Once he found himself in the library, he looked over all the dusty tomes on the shelves. One day—he promised to himself—Ryan would read as much as he could, but that would have to be in the future.

Ryan was in no mood for a history lesson. What he wanted to know was what was happening on his planet and on the moons in orbit.

Ryan wanted to know what was happening *now*.

He sat down at a computer terminal just as the adrenaline dumped out of his system, and the search homepage stared back at him. For a moment, he wondered what he would search for and what he should know.

It was becoming frustrating—looking at this empty canvas and a blinking cursor that seemed to taunt him—but then he realized that he just had to start somewhere. Ryan typed in the name of his local paper back in New Chicago, hoping to become informed about the state of his city.

Everything seemed to be marvelously boring. Ryan had forgotten that the *New Chicago Post* was a horrible corruption of journalism, just like most of the news outlets. There were no details hidden in the print about the constant crime or murders or gang fights Ryan was *absolutely sure* were taking place while he waged his artificial war.

Instead, the front page was filled with fluff pieces, business mergers and *human interest* stories. Ryan didn't much care about corporations trading money; they were all the same, and he could hardly remember their names.

Even more damning, another headline summarized an entire article, saying that a whale had beached itself. There didn't seem to be a story, and if there was, it had been detailed extensively in just seven words. Hoping for more, Ryan read another headline but immediately scoffed.

Another celebrity's dog had taken the mantle of best-in-show, and this somehow affected the greatest metropolitan area in the region.

Ryan shook his head, ran his hand through the fuzz on his scalp and sat back in the chair. He realized that he had been kidding himself, just like the rest of the world. No one actually cared about what was happening and—with the exception of trivial knowledge—current events were absolutely useless to the general public.

At best, the front page of any news site could be classified as water cooler talk.

Ryan had wanted to know what was going on, and in just a few moments realized that nobody was going to tell him. This newspaper, just like all the others, pandered to the kind of people who didn't want the truth, to the people who just wanted something to talk *about*.

At the revelation, Ryan closed his eyes and realized that only a few moments ago he had been one of those willfully-ignorant people. He rubbed his right eye and sent the browser back to the search screen.

Ryan typed in a few more words and then the *War World* website was visually screaming back at him. He could see flames across the sides and bullet holes throughout the screen, soldiers actively trading bullets at the top and a large *Enter* button in the middle. Ryan sighed and tapped the display to find the main page, which billions of people visited daily.

He could see tabs for all the information he could ever want about the games. In the middle of the screen, he could see the four anchors for the show, and in his dismay, Ryan had to laugh.

Patrick McEwen was standing off to the side, half-smiling at the camera, and Ryan wondered what the old man felt when he watched the games. It was no secret that he had been a Crow alongside Jonathon Carver, but he had retired years ago while his teammate continued the fight. Although Ryan would not wish for McEwen's addled mind, that career gave him some small hope that he would get out, eventually.

McEwen was half a mummy, but he was technically *alive*.

The old man's face brought a question to Ryan's mind, so he went back to the search engine and typed in *War World Retirees*. One of the first pages led him to the roster of all the teams through the course of the last fifty years; War World Entertainment's records for the entire program.

Hundreds of soldiers had been on each team and the sheer number of deadly gladiators was rather intimidating. Ryan skimmed down the list for minutes—taking note of the more famous names—and his jaw went slack as he went about his task.

Ryan marveled at the thousands of names, especially when he considered that most of them had somehow gotten out of the system.

They might have been old like Patrick, but they had been able to *retire*. Next to each soldier was a small biography and picture, though Ryan couldn't recognize most of them.

If nothing else, it seemed like they had profited from playing the games.

Ryan sighed with gratitude and wondered what he could do from this terminal. He wanted to contact them; he wanted to talk to any of those veterans who had escaped the system.

After navigating through the hundreds of teams on the website, Ryan clicked on the web address of one of the Crows, causing a message to pop up on his display.

No Contact Allowed.

He tapped the address again with the same result. Ryan started to get frustrated and clicked another name, a soldier that had been active within the last ten years. The message popped up again.

No Contact Allowed.

Ryan's eyes narrowed and he wondered if the problem was with the terminal or the website, itself. Ryan was tempted to hit the display with his hand until he heard a book fall behind him.

"Oh, damn..."

Ryan spun around to find Roberts watching him; the mousy, dark-haired Crow had been standing by a stack of Feldman's books. After a sigh at the tome at his feet, Roberts looked at Ryan with a nervous smile.

"Well, sorry about that. Wasn't trying to break your concentration," he said, anxiously scratching the top of his head.

"Were you watching me?" Ryan didn't like being followed, watched or any combination of the two.

"I was. Sorry for that too," Roberts said before walking to the computer terminals and grabbing the closest chair. He turned it backward and then sat down so he could rest his arms on the back of the chair, but Ryan did not appreciate the familiarity.

"Why?"

"Thought you might be going through some shit. I saw how you acted in the mess hall." Roberts lowered his head to rest on his forearms, which clued Ryan in on how medicated he really was. He had never seen Roberts dosed like this.

"Yeah, what was that *it's okay* about? What did you mean?"

"I just meant that I understand. I know how it is. This place is starting to get to you, and I get that. This little addiction of mine isn't exactly fun," Roberts said, looking him in the eye. The movement caught Ryan slightly off-guard, but Roberts sighed while lazily rolling his chin along his arms.

"I figured Feldman probably told you, by now. You two seem to be chatty, and it actually helps me out. I know I can trust you to believe me when I talk about all this. You already have me at a... disadvantage." Roberts turned his eye to the computer display, where the error message was still flashing. "Trying to talk to some of the old soldiers, huh?"

From his tone, Ryan knew Roberts was asking a leading question and sat straight up. "What do you know?"

"Much more than *you*. And stop being so antagonistic. I'm just trying to talk."

After a moment of stubbornness, Ryan looked at the screen and read the message blinking back at him. "Apparently, I can't talk to any of these old members of the Crows. I don't really know why."

"It's because they don't exist."

"What are you talking about?"

"They don't. They *did*, of course—I remember seeing some of these guys back when I was a kid—but when their contract was up, they stopped playing," Roberts said lackadaisically, yawning in his medicated stupor.

"Yeah, they retired," Ryan said, suddenly wary of what that meant. With a sigh, Roberts scrunched up his face, pain obviously filtering back into his senses.

"One way to say it, but you know how the system is. We're in debt up to our ears. At that age, most of the guys can't ever pay it back. And this is where the cruelty of the system is really apparent," Roberts explained before lifting his head back off of the chair.

"If they can't pay the Commission back, the Commission doesn't resurrect them."

Ryan looked down at his hands. He tried to fathom any other possible meaning to what Roberts had said, but his mind had already jumped to the horrible conclusion before he looked back and Roberts gave him an understanding nod.

"Yeah, if we can't pay them back, then they kill us, essentially. For good, it seems," Roberts said, eventually turning to look at the terminal in front of him.

It was off, but that didn't matter to him. It was just something he could focus on so the world would stop shifting around him, and maybe something he could focus on instead of the pain.

Ryan looked at his fellow Crow and contemplated what it all meant. If it was all true, there was no happy ending waiting for him. He would grow old and feeble within the walls of these barracks and then, when the Commission had no use for him, they would just stop letting him live.

One day, some other desperate slave soldier would find a fake biography written next to his smiling picture on the *War World* encyclopedia.

"How do you know all this?" Ryan asked, his fingers trembling after the revelation.

After a moment of consideration—thinking he might tell him the whole truth of how he came to be on Eris—Roberts instead offered a shrug. The movement set off an echo of aches and pains along his spine that made him wince, making him wish he had brought his pills with him. It was a long way back to his room.

Hoping to end the conversation early, Roberts decided to give Ryan the short version.

"Friends of friends. Medical records I dug up. Roster reports and yearly incomes and balance sheets. Basically, a lot of illegally-acquired information. I tried to contact some of those soldiers, same as you, and found out there were no records of the guys after the games. Did a little database mining and found that they had never left Eris, at all. Found incineration orders for their old bodies. I'd show you, but I don't want to risk them finding out that I was rifling through their personnel files again."

Roberts laid his head back on the chair, confident that it was the right choice to leave out the part about how that datamining had started the chain of events that led to his incarceration.

"How do you know?" Ryan asked, and Roberts raised both palms before imitating the tapping of a keyboard.

"I was a hacker in a past life," he said, already regretting the finger movement. "A simple error message like that wasn't going to stop me. I have a problem with... boundaries."

Roberts leaned back in the chair and felt his back muscles starting to strain. Although he knew better, Roberts thought about taking five pills again.

"You're not lying?"

After shaking his head, Roberts decided that he had to get back to his room as fast as possible, so he rose to his feet. He would have entertained Ryan further, but the pain was already running along his nerves, sending tingles and twitches throughout his body.

"What would be the point? I was just trying to break it to you easy. Don't want you getting all suicidal on us," Roberts said before turning to leave.

He was at the doorway when he looked back at his friend, but Ryan was still staring at the team roster on the computer display, his mind elsewhere. Roberts felt horrible that he had to be the one to tell him, but he knew Ryan would have found out, eventually. In that moment, Roberts remembered when he had first realized the brutal truth, all alone with no one to comfort him.

Roberts didn't want anybody else to feel that despair.

RYAN LOOKED at the blinking computer display in front of him. Although Roberts may not have been the most credible source of information, he did have a point.

He really had no reason to lie.

Ryan thought about what he could do to change his fate. If nothing changed, he would simply be retired once the Commission thought he had outlived his usefulness. That brought to mind Feldman and his outlook, something Ryan had hoped to emulate.

As he sat there looking at the blinking cursor, Ryan knew he would never come close. He didn't see any way out of his situation, and he was absolutely sure that no one would come to save him.

Briefly, Ryan thought about all the groups that had tried to save the perpetual soldiers. There had been two protest groups that had been founded and crushed since he had started watching the games. He remembered the riots by the Eris Freedom Initiative in St. Louis and the pictures of scattered pools of blood and mangled bodies. At the time, he thought they were stupid to even try.

As Ryan slumped down in the chair, he desperately wanted them to try again.

Ryan picked himself up and wandered around the hallways of the barracks. Although he saw the odd soldier now and then, he wasn't paying attention. That might have been rude, but Ryan was mired in his own self-concern.

Every time Ryan thought he understood his surroundings, something new came out of the woodwork to kick him right back down. Ryan had promised himself that he would be more like Feldman; he had promised that he would look forward to the future.

The future was bleak and Ryan knew there was no joy to be had. He would keep suffering and he would keep dying; the slave soldier would continue walking through these grey hallways day after day and see all the poor souls who were stuck in there with him.

How could he be optimistic when every life around him was doomed?

Ryan tripped over nothing while he was walking through the East Hallway and threw out his arm in order to stop his fall. Once he regained his balance, he looked over to his right to see what he had grabbed, quickly realizing it was the name plaque for the Crow who lived in the nearby room. Or, more appropriately, *had* lived in that room.

Though the type had been scratched off the plaque, Ryan could see the vague remnants of *P. Roth* displayed on the plastic. He had been the first person to be traded away since Ryan's arrival on the Crows, and although Ryan had never thought Roth was even close to competent, it was sad to see someone go. As he walked past the empty room, Ryan wished Percival Roth the best.

He certainly didn't need Ryan to wish him anything else.

Ryan continued walking for a few minutes—passing by each of his teammates' rooms—but something compelled him to stop in the middle of the hallway. He turned slightly and noticed that the nearby door was open a crack, but there didn't seem to be any movement in the dark space.

Ryan shrugged and looked at the tiled floor at his feet. It was somewhat dingy, but that was normal for the barracks. The corporations that owned the Crows and the nearby teams were not overly concerned with keeping a tidy home for their athletes. They only had to abide by the guidelines that the Commission had provided for them.

Ryan sat down anyway and put his back against the wall—leaning his head back so it made contact with the cool surface—and closed his eyes. He tried to justify his world and his position, he tried to justify the hope that Feldman held inside that big brain of his, but Ryan couldn't see the silver lining.

It was beyond ridiculous to think Feldman was an idiot, but it seemed that the giant was misguided. Ryan could understand his unique perspective—as the games had helped him regain his body—but that was the thing. Feldman was *unique*. Besides him, almost nobody benefited from the games.

Ryan's thoughts fell back to Roberts and his spirits fell even more. He wondered what the kid had done to end up here with all of these career criminals and desperate people. Hacking was a crime, but usually it was just a slap on the wrist. To end up on Eris, he must have dug deep into something *no one* was supposed to know. As he considered his poor teammate, Ryan wondered what he would think about Feldman's perspective.

Then he saw the name placard beside the door across the hall.

Without meaning to, Ryan had hunkered down outside of Roberts' room. He wondered if his brain had subconsciously driven him to this part of the barracks, but Ryan couldn't think of anything worth conversation. What information Roberts had given him was out of compassion rather than any attempt to create any sort of bond. Ryan doubted that a lifelong friendship would come out of Roberts' lesson.

However, subconscious or fate or merely coincidence had led him to the addict's door. Ryan took that as enough of a reason to knock on the plastic surface and see if he was in. The door gave way and creaked open, revealing the inside of Roberts' room. Roberts had never gotten around to closing the door all the way, and it wasn't long before Ryan could see why.

Roberts was curled up on the floor in front of his desk, an amber bottle was lying on its side on the floor and white and blue pills were scattered on the desk and floor. Drool had collected into a puddle near his open mouth, trails of it flitting in and out as Roberts drew in quick breaths. Ryan could see that the tiny soldier was suffering spasms throughout his body. His fingers were curled and the veins in his neck popped out of his skin.

Tears were streaming out of eyes Roberts could not close.

Ryan had not been prepared to see such horror when he knocked on the door, but he quickly regained himself and rushed over to Roberts, trying to put the soldier's arms to his side instead of curled up in the air. Roberts surprised him with his strength, but Ryan had a few kilograms of muscle on the smaller man, so he overpowered the seizure easily.

Yet Ryan could only preach platitudes as he tried to help his thrashing teammate.

"Roberts! It's okay! It's just me! It's just Ryan! I just want to help. What can I do to help?" he asked, trying to keep the urgency out of his words.

Through the pain, Roberts seemed to recognize his compatriot and started to gasp out words between spasms. Although his mind was screaming, his tongue just would not pronounce anything intelligible.

The poor boy used all of his strength to point at the pills scattered near his arm.

It was times like these that Christopher Roberts just wanted to die.

Ryan noticed the gesture toward the pills and grabbed a handful of them before placing them one by one into Roberts' mouth. Although he had no way to tell the usual dose for his teammate, Ryan figured that seven pills would be enough to handle a fit of this severity. If not, he could always give him more.

Roberts didn't bother to count them as his new best friend gave him the medication; he just swallowed as the fire ate away at his muscles and tendons. He would just have to deal with the consequences later, when the pain stopped. There was absolutely no time to think.

After a few minutes, Roberts' body started to go limp, his muscles relaxing from the strain. Ryan figured the medicine had yet to kick in, but the sense of security that it gave Roberts was probably enough to help. Once he was calm, Roberts craned his neck to look at him.

"Thanks, I... needed that," he said, his jaw hurting even more when he spoke. Ignorant of that pain, Ryan offered a weak laugh.

"Sorry, I didn't mean to take so long. I didn't know what to think," he said before looking to the doorway. Ryan had left it open and suddenly felt uncomfortable that some passerby would see him cradling a weak Roberts surrounded by contraband medication.

After a moment's consideration, Ryan wished he had not been the only one to witness all that suffering.

"This time seems a little worse than normal. I've... never had a fit like that. I felt it coming on in the library, which is why I left so early. I don't know what they did to me, but... it's not normal." Roberts coughed weakly and turned his head down to the ground. In that instant, his eyelids drooped and his limbs lost their strength.

"How many... did you give..." Roberts said with a concerted effort. He didn't expect his consciousness to fade so fast; it usually took fifteen minutes for anything to kick in.

"I just grabbed a handful, maybe six or seven," Ryan said, only then realizing his mistake.

Roberts' head sagged as his neck became too weak to hold up his head.

"Damn... that's not..." he mumbled before losing consciousness.

RYAN CHECKED his pulse and was grateful he could still feel it, but he knew Roberts was still in trouble.

Unfortunately, he didn't know what to do with him. Carrying his limp body to medical was out of the question—as he would then have to explain where Roberts had gotten the drugs—and he *definitely* could not abandon him in his room.

After collecting himself and setting Roberts on his side so he wouldn't choke on his own vomit, Ryan tried to figure out who could get them out of this mess. In a flash, he knew exactly who could help him.

It was the only person who would have anything to lose if Roberts died alone in his room surrounded by painkillers.

Ryan ran through the barracks faster than he thought he was capable, especially back on Earth. Luckily for him, he didn't encounter anyone as he ran down the East Hallway and rounded the bend, or when he continued past the mess hall. If anybody had seen him fly through the hallways, there would have been some awkward questions and Ryan didn't know if he could answer them.

He just hoped Goldstein would be able to sweep this under the rug somehow.

He rounded the corner to the West Hallway to find a few of the drones walking back from the mess hall. Fortunately, they were all facing the other way and Ryan slowed down to a normal speed before anyone noticed. His heart was racing and he breathed heavy, but he made it seem like just another day.

Ryan spotted Goldstein walking ahead of him and increased his pace to catch up with him. Once they were side by side, he tapped his shoulder.

"Hey, kid, what's up? You need something?"

Ryan motioned with a nod that they should go to Goldstein's room, not trusting his words to come out in anything other than gasps and staggered breaths. Goldstein chuckled at the gesture and went along with his antics, leading the way to his room.

The door wasn't closed for five seconds before Ryan broke down and started gasping for air, instantly making Goldstein wary. When Ryan looked back up after a few heaving breaths, he prayed the merchant might know what to do.

"I need that favor."

"*What*?" he asked skeptically, crossing his arms.

"I need you to help me with Roberts," Ryan urged, his voice almost a whisper, but it caught Goldstein's attention. His weary face flashed with anger and annoyance.

"Shit. What did Chris do? Tell me anything and everything," he said before walking to his desk, his hand drifting to the drawer. Ryan picked himself up and rubbed his eyes, his breath finally catching up with him.

"He's overdosed in his room. I don't know if he'll make it."

"How much did he take?"

"I don't know for certain. At least seven, most likely more. He had this pain spasm going on and..." Ryan said before trailing off. The guilt for helping Roberts overdose was starting to set in, and he had not prepared himself for it.

"Goddamnit... fucking Hawkins." Goldstein yanked hard on the handle of his drawer, causing its contents to jostle around before he set about finding his transmitter. After a few seconds of rummaging, he picked up the transmitter from beside other paraphernalia and keyed in a contact number. Then he looked at Ryan.

"Thanks for letting me know instead of taking him to Medical. Saves me heaps of trouble. I'm going to need your help here."

Ryan looked at him warily, but accepted that it was something he had to do. This was partially his fault. "What do I need to do?"

Goldstein sighed and looked at his teammate.

"Well, *we* are going to haul his body out of the barracks and *Hawkins* is going to fix him."

RYAN FELT uncomfortable sitting out in the open, the shattered moon above them a constant reminder of the tortured boy at their feet. The only times Ryan had been outside of the barracks were the painful walks back from the clinic or during the games, and the mental link was not a pleasant one. It also didn't help that they were doing something that was certainly illegal.

That's why they couldn't take Roberts to the clinic; the cameras were everywhere.

They were about two hundred meters from the barracks and it was just after Moonrise. The reflected light washed over the three of them on the concrete slab, clearly illuminating Roberts as he suffered through a contraband overdose.

He didn't know the specifics between Goldstein and Hawkins, but Ryan guessed the scientist was responsible for some of those black-market wares. It only made sense, if Goldstein could get the scientist to come out at a moment's notice and come save a miserable life from his own mistakes.

At the same time, Ryan had to wonder what the cruel doctor got out of their agreement.

While they waited, Goldstein was constantly checking the watch on his wrist. Maybe he thought he could will time to move faster and force Hawkins to save the boy. Maybe he was just anxious they were spending so much time outside where the Commission could find them. Maybe he actually cared, or perhaps it was all three.

In any case, Goldstein didn't want to think about it. He just didn't want Christopher to die just because his mad scientist was late.

Looking to the horizon, Ryan watched as a rover left the clinic and bounced along the landscape surrounding the Crows' barracks. He could see from the rover's jerky course that it wasn't on an automated path, which meant that it had to be Hawkins.

Soon, the vehicle screamed down the hillside and drifted toward the little outpost they had created for themselves, kicking up dust the whole time. At his feet, Ryan watched Roberts lying there—not even conscious enough to groan—and felt another blow against his conscience.

No matter what he told himself, Ryan was part of this boy's suffering.

When he arrived, Hawkins threw open the door and jumped out of the rover with his portable med kit. He was not happy about this house call and did nothing to hide it. Walking up to Goldstein, the pudgy man set down the bag in front of him.

"Why the *fuck* couldn't you ration him portions that wouldn't kill him, Zachary?" Hawkins spat out, pushing up his glasses as he stooped down beside Roberts' unconscious body. The scientist was clearly very familiar with Goldstein and seemed to hold some power in their relationship.

At least, that was until Goldstein started yelling back.

"*I'm* not the one who screwed up here. This is *your* fault, *Frankenstein.*"

After eying Goldstein for the insult, Hawkins set to work on his makeshift operating table and started removing instruments from the kit. He brought out a vitals meter and tapped it into the vein on Roberts' arm, sighing with disgust as the meter told him exactly what he had predicted.

"This could have been prevented, Zachary, and I wouldn't have had to come out here. This is *your* fuck-up, and why, may I ask, is *he* here?" Hawkins asked before glaring at Ryan.

He glared right back, suddenly feeling very confrontational.

"Maybe you should just help your patient, *doctor.*" Ryan had never liked the man, but something about this situation was enough to push him over the edge. Hawkins' eyes narrowed behind his glasses, but he kept his anger to himself.

"I'm a scientist, you *child...*"

He went about filling syringes with different medications to counter the effects of the medicine coursing through Roberts' body. Ryan noticed there were a lot more than he would have expected for this kind of procedure, but he trusted Hawkins to only bother with the barest necessities.

Hoping to keep Ryan out of it, Goldstein stepped closer to his business partner and whispered into his ear.

"You need to stop this shit. The kid's already fragile enough and he doesn't deserve it. And this—*right here*—is something that we can't afford."

"You know he's part of my experiment," Hawkins said as he started to tap an IV for Roberts and set the boy up for recovery. Once that was done, Goldstein grabbed at his arm and looked him in the eye.

"I'm saying you should *stop it*," he urged, a hint of rage bubbling up from the depths. Hawkins was alarmed at first, but then laughed at the audacity.

"You know *that's* not going to happen. Now get your hands off me. I have work to do." Then Hawkins shrugged off Goldstein's hand so he could pump Roberts full of drugs.

Goldstein sighed and walked a few meters from the doctor and his patient, knowing he did not have the power to stop Hawkins' evil.

After watching Goldstein walk to the other end of the slab, Ryan suddenly wanted to know what they were discussing, especially when he overheard *experiment*. He followed Goldstein and sidled up to him as the older man looked into the distance.

"What's all this about an experiment?" Ryan could tell Goldstein was taken aback by his statement, but he waited patiently for his response.

"You don't want to know," he said with a sigh before Ryan took hold of his arm and squeezed.

"*I want to know*, Zach. Tell me," he said assertively, hoping the man's first name would engender some kind of camaraderie. Before he replied, Goldstein looked back at the doctor and patient and scratched his arm absent-mindedly.

"Hawkins uses Roberts and the drones for mental experiments. Those poor saps like Corrigan, Sargasso and Haywick who just sit there and stare while the rest of us talk? Hawkins broke them already. Roberts' version is all about pain. *Chris* thinks it's just some synchronization error the Commission forces on him, and he's not that far from the truth. Hawkins..." Goldstein paused, sighing as he thought about the poor soul lying there on the concrete.

"Hawkins wants to know how long until Christopher's mind cracks. He wants to know how much pain us soldiers can take before we go nutty. Or maybe he's just been doing it so long that it's become a game to him. I don't know him *that* well, but sometimes I think he just enjoys it," Goldstein confessed, the burden of the secret finally lifted from him.

When he turned to face Ryan, there was only empty air to greet him. Goldstein kept turning and was just in time to witness Ryan launching his fist into the side of Hawkins' face, his glasses somehow hanging on by one ear after he landed the blow.

Wasting no time, Goldstein rushed over to stop his teammate from going further and tried to hold the furious Crow.

Hawkins shuffled away from the two soldiers in a panic and took a second before realizing that *he* was the one who was supposed to be in charge in this situation. Forcing himself to his feet, Hawkins took on an indignant air as he set his glasses back on straight.

"What are you *doing*, you imbecile? I'm trying to fix the boy here!" He had forgotten his guinea pig's name in the moment, but it didn't matter. Every one of them was the same to him unless Hawkins recognized his own work.

As indignant as Hawkins was for getting attacked, Ryan was practically foaming at the mouth.

"You caused it in the first place! I'm going to give you pain like you give him, *then* I'm going to get your ass fired for malpractice, or whatever they call it now!" he threatened, dragging Goldstein along as he stepped toward the chubby scientist. At his surprising strength, Goldstein was suddenly afraid of what Ryan might be able to do.

Hawkins just looked at the pair of them and laughed.

"That's *rich*, action figure. You're not going to get me *fired*. The Commission *encourages* my... extra-curricular activities. *They* gave me the funds. And something to think about, *soldier*," he said before walking forward to look the man in the eye, fear absolutely absent.

Ryan saw the pale green of them behind the thin glasses and felt uneasy.

"If I can do this to Roberts, what makes you think that I can't do it to *you*? I have the power here. Besides," he said as he returned to Roberts, who had unleashed a puddle of vomit.

"I'm fixing him right now. His pain levels will be back down and he won't try to overdose himself again. In fact, I'm already done." Hawkins withdrew the needles and packed up his things, confident he was safe from harm.

Ryan's fury left him as he contemplated what Hawkins had said. He knew the Commission wasn't the most moral association, but he had thought something like *this* might have been beyond them.

After that revelation, Ryan stopped fighting against Goldstein and sank to the concrete. Meanwhile, Hawkins had stood up and walked to the rover, motioning for Goldstein to join him.

"Follow me, Zachary. Your friend can stay here with his fellow action figure."

Goldstein looked down at Ryan and knew he wasn't going to do anything stupid, not after Hawkins' threats. After following his business partner, Goldstein kept his distance as Hawkins threw his bag into the rover and heaved himself into the cabin.

"So? What? What *exactly* did you want to say?" Goldstein asked with an air of hostility. He was getting impatient with the scientist and his atrocities, and—unlike every other day—this was the first time that he had a first-row ticket.

Now that he had seen it for himself, Goldstein knew it was way past the line.

"Don't let this happen again," Hawkins replied with a sneer. "I mean it. You've forgiven some of my debts in your betting pool, but I don't have to engage in this black market thing with you. I can do without."

Goldstein's eyes narrowed as he looked back at Christopher's body. No one should have to suffer like that.

"Tell me this, Hawkins," he said before turned to the scientist,

Hawkins looking back expectantly. "You told me way back that the pain treatments were permanent for the clone. How'd you fix him?"

The overweight scientist shrugged as he leapt into the driver seat of the rover.

"I didn't. He's going to have to suffer until he dies tomorrow," he stated, tapping the controls for the rover. Unable to conceal his true feelings any longer, Zachary walked up to the man's seat, anger twisting his face.

"You're an *asshole*. And—among *other* things—how do you know Chris is going to die tomorrow? He could have to live with this treatment for a while," he said, but the cruel scientist laughed down at them.

"Oh, I doubt that. I was trying to find the extreme end of the spectrum with this body. This *might* have been an accident, I'll give you that," Hawkins said before starting the vehicle.

"But tomorrow, if he doesn't die from all the explosions and bullets, I'm willing to bet he's going to finish the job, himself."

2

Staring Down the Barrels

Jenkins was flying through the air and could not be bothered by it. After jumping out of transports nearly a dozen times, falling to the surface had become second nature. The wind whipping past his helmet did nothing to his nerves and all the anxiety he had felt from the act in past games was now completely gone. As he opened his parachute, he wasn't worried about falling.

He was worried Roberts would be a burden.

Jenkins released the tethers of his parachute and landed on the surface with a perfectly executed roll. To better understand their situation, he checked his display to see the beacons of the other Crows on the ground. Jenkins could hear Roberts land behind him with a thump and, concerned, looked back to see the boy soldier brushing himself off.

They had been toward the back of the aircraft, but Jenkins could see the last few Crows dropping out of the transport over Roberts' shoulder. After watching the tiny black specks flying through the air, Jenkins looked back down to see Roberts standing there, his chest plate puffing in and out and showing that he was breathing heavily.

Jenkins hoped it was just exertion.

"You okay, Roberts?"

"I'll be fine. Took some meds before we got on the transport, so I'll make it through. How you want to play this?"

As if nothing was wrong, Roberts stepped around the wreckage of their landing zone and walked past his partner. Jenkins decided he would just have to trust his comrade, despite his skepticism.

Before the match, Jenkins had considered telling Roberts the part that Hawkins played in his misery, but had eventually decided to keep it to himself. Roberts already had a suitable boogeyman in place, and telling him Hawkins was the culprit would change nothing.

He still felt guilty about it.

"Well," Jenkins said as he looked toward the beacons of the other Crows. "Did you want to meet up with any of the other guys and travel in a squad?"

"Never been my forte, but considering what we're up against, I might want to go to someone with explosives. Wasn't Templeton trained for that?"

Feldman and Carver were to the north along with a host of others, but none of them were supposed to be carrying heavy ordnance. Jenkins laughed at the question and shook his head.

"Nah, Templeton was given an automatic the first day. They didn't trust him with anything special."

"Well, I can't remember anybody who's trained for it, then," Roberts said, tapping his fingers along the barrel of his rifle.

As he looked at the beacons around them, Jenkins shrugged.

"I'm not sure we have one on the team. They trained Roth to carry an RPG, but he got traded to the Hammerheads after that last game."

That statement prompted Roberts to put his hand on the back of his neck and sigh.

"Are we seriously going into a mech match without explosives?"

Thirty years prior, as a way to increase ratings, the Commission had introduced mech matches into the games. Each team was granted one mechanized suit piloted by one soldier from their ranks. A normal soldier could not hope to fight on equal terms, but that had never been the point of *War World*.

"I guess so. We could try to get up with Abrams. She's piloting for our side," Jenkins suggested half-heartedly, as being near a mech—even a friendly one—was rather dangerous.

Roberts scoffed and shook his head at that.

"What, and end up being target practice? I'd rather not. We could head over to Norris and hope he shoots the pilot before they realize there's a sniper," he replied, and Jenkins bounced the idea around in his head. He nodded and looked for Norris' beacon, which was four kilometers to the east.

If nothing else, being near a sniper would provide for a safer opportunity.

It'll have to do, Jenkins thought before beckoning Roberts to follow him to their teammate. In the back of his mind, he hoped Roberts' medication wouldn't run out before they got to Norris.

JENKINS' lungs were burning through his chest, worse than anything he had experienced in therapy. Every few strides, he thought his heart was just about to stop and that would be the end of his current incarnation. Just as he was about to give up, he saw Roberts increase his pace and that was enough to cause him to despair.

"I'm done... gotta stop," Jenkins said before falling to his knees and heaving as much air as he could into his lungs. Roberts continued for a moment, oblivious, but soon decreased his speed and looked back at his comrade. Once he walked back, Roberts hunkered himself down on a nearby piece of grating.

"Sorry, I just don't like being in the wide open like this. I always have this feeling that there's some guy with a gun waiting for me to let down my guard."

Roberts' eyes narrowed as he thought he caught a glimpse of something fifteen meters to his right. With a grunt, he looked back at his partner, who was still heaving on his knees.

"How do you do it? *Seriously*. I've never run that fast and I have a perfectly good body," Jenkins said before looking back up at the veteran soldier.

Roberts just shrugged and looked toward his right again, determined to find that telltale glimmer. He could have sworn that he had seen one of the Commission's little pets.

"Eh, my body's young, I'm pretty light and I usually have to deal with quite a bit more pain than you old bastards. Plus, I'm hopped up on painkillers, so I can take more of it right now. *There it is*," he said, his voice lowering to a whisper as he caught sight of his prey.

Roberts brought up his rifle slowly as Jenkins watched, noticeably confused. He was still watching when Roberts jerked up his weapon and trained his sights on the flicker to his right. He fired three times before a bullet glanced off what sounded like metal.

After making contact, Roberts smiled and pulled the trigger two more times, and Jenkins saw a small explosion as a machine disengaged its cloaking device and fell to the ground. Seeing the job was done, he yawned beneath his helmet.

"Got it. Knew it was there," Roberts said before turning to look at Jenkins. "I hate those things."

Having no clue what *those things* were, Jenkins picked himself up and walked over to inspect the machine that had fallen out of the sky. It looked like one of the small news robots that had filled New Chicago, pestering everyone who was trying to go about living their petty miserable lives.

"What *is* that?"

"You've never seen one? It's just one of their cameras. It's how they get all of those close-ups for the show. There's a million of 'em floating around here," Roberts said as he kicked the machine. It rolled down the hill and settled against another piece of debris.

Roberts felt the pain echoing throughout his foot and wondered if he really would make it through the game before the pain came back. Although he had brought three more pills in his satchel, Roberts wasn't exactly sure he could muscle through the pain.

After turning to look at Norris' beacon, he was grateful it was only a kilometer away.

"Let's go. It's not much further."

Following behind but lost in his own thoughts, Jenkins tried to remember if he had ever seen any of the robots floating around the ruined landscape. He thought he remembered some flickering or little glimmers as he fought his opponents, but he put it down as wishful thinking. In any case, it was probably best to ignore them all together.

"Why do you do that? Aren't you going to get in trouble with the Commission for destroying all of their cameras?" As they walked, Jenkins watched the landscape underneath so he would not stumble.

Roberts looked over at him and shrugged. Truthfully, he had never thought about it, but it didn't really matter. He was never going to have enough money to get out, not to mention pay all his outstanding debts to Goldstein.

Even if the merchant was bleeding Roberts dry, there was no way he could afford living with this interminable pain. Roberts was grateful for anything Goldstein would give him.

"Well," Roberts started, but he soon found he had no real excuse for his petulant behavior. "I guess they can bill me later. Let's go."

There was not much in the way of cover for the last kilometer—probably why Norris had chosen this spot to use his rifle—and it gave Roberts no comfort. To deal with his anxiety, Roberts was about to increase his speed and try to sprint the last three-quarters, but then the pain hit him.

It was worse this time, worse than anything he had ever experienced. He had thought the seizure in his room was already too much, but this set of spasms made mockery of that thought. Roberts' spine arched as the convulsions made his body go rigid, his body still moving forward from the momentum of his last stride. Whatever thoughts had been in his head were replaced by those of pain. In fact, for a few horrible moments twisting in the air, Roberts forgot to breathe.

His lungs simply would not function during that episode in terror.

Jenkins watched as Roberts stumbled and slid through the wreckage, eventually slamming into a piece of aluminum siding ten meters from his fall. Jenkins rushed to his partner's side and found Roberts had no control over his body.

The way his body twisted and curled was unnatural and grotesque. Jenkins thought of all the things he had seen since coming to Eris. He remembered all of the arterial sprays and flying limbs and the disemboweled soldiers trying to scoop up their intestines; he remembered all of the atrocities and nightmarish images that he had seen play out in front of him.

Seeing Roberts like this was worse than all of it.

Ignoring his horror, Jenkins slid to his knees and tried to help the man control himself. Roberts unwillingly fought against him and his strength was amplified by his power armor. Every time Jenkins pinned his arms to his sides, Roberts would lash out, and he was sure Roberts wasn't even aware he was kneeling nearby.

Jenkins shouted at him, forgetting the private line in the moment.

"Do you have any pills on you? What can I do?"

The second question wasn't directed at Roberts; he was asking the universe. Giving into the despair that had haunted him all this time, Jenkins knew he couldn't fight it anymore. Almost too late, he realized Roberts was trying to speak, fighting through the pain and the spasms.

"Pil... poc... leg..." They were the only thing that could stop this infernal pain.

Jenkins took a second to interpret what Roberts was saying and then checked the satchel attached to Roberts' leg. After a desperate moment, Jenkins had three pills settled in his palm and wondered if it would be enough.

Setting the pills down on the ground—where they gathered dirt—Jenkins tried to unclasp the man's helmet. Roberts' head slammed back against the ground before coming up to greet Jenkins, but eventually he was able to unclasp the helmet and remove it.

When he did, Roberts' eyes were wide open and wild, which took Jenkins off-guard, but then he grabbed the pills from the ground and shoved them inside Roberts' mouth. Two of them went down easy, but he spat out the other one during a convulsion. Jenkins grabbed it from the ground, covered in dirt, and shoved it back into Roberts' mouth, forcing it closed with his hand.

Roberts tried to spit it out again, but Jenkins stuck armored fingers between his teeth to stop him. Even through the mesh of his armor, Jenkins winced from the pain and looked down at Roberts—gums bleeding from biting metal—and he couldn't help but be overtaken by pity.

Jenkins looked around at the war-torn world, wondering what kind of monster could force this on another man. Then he realized that he was surrounded by these monsters. Every person who operated these games cared more for profits than the misery they enforced upon these helpless "athletes." Even the official and the guards who were just doing their jobs couldn't be bothered to think about the forsaken soldiers of Eris.

Jenkins turned toward Norris' beacon in the distance and knew that he had to get there. He also knew Roberts would do nothing to help, but he couldn't possibly blame him for that. For a moment, Jenkins contemplated leaving him, but quickly pushed the thought aside.

He *was not* going to just look out for himself. He *was not* going to be one of *them*.

Even so, Jenkins wondered how he was going to carry Roberts the rest of the way. He had never been the strongest person, before or after his training. Sighing, Jenkins turned his gaze to the horizon and noticed a glimmer ten meters to his left, rage building instantaneously.

Jenkins growled as he realized that the two of them were being filmed for the enjoyment of eight cruel worlds.

Without a word or another thought, Jenkins brought up his rifle and shot at the glimmer. The first shot disabled the cloaking device and from there it only took two more rounds before the machine fell out of the air.

Jenkins looked back down at the crippled man at his knees, tears pooling at the bottom of his eyes, and his words were heavy with emotion.

"They'll bill me later."

SWEAT POURED DOWN JENKINS' face. His helmet was stifling and the added effort of carrying and dragging the semiconscious Roberts the last half-kilometer had been a trial. He would have carried his friend the entire way, but Jenkins had ended up using too much energy.

When he looked up after a burst of activity, he noticed they were only two hundred meters from Norris' position. Even with the power armor helping his motor functions, Jenkins couldn't keep moving across the wasteland with his comrade in tow.

Jenkins wasn't that big; he wasn't that strong.

Figuring the hardest part was over, Jenkins let Roberts slide to the ground. He could feel the cramp lancing through his side recede as he sat on a nearby rock, regaining his strength but already knowing he would ache the next day.

Looking down, Jenkins laughed as he realized it was one of the biggest rocks he had seen on the surface. The landscape was colored with metal, trash, scrap and the occasional dead body or yellow parachute, but rocks were hard to come by.

He looked at the ridge where Norris was set up and cleared his throat before opening the common channel, determined to avoid getting carried away with emotion. Out of his periphery, Jenkins could see Warner's beacon on the other side of the clearing from where he was standing over Roberts.

"Hey, Norris, Roberts is pretty screwed up. I'm bringing him up to your position and maybe we can tide over the rest of the game," Jenkins said over Comms, letting himself breathe easy as he waited for a response. There was a crackle before the aloof sniper laughed over Comms.

"You cowards. Yeah, that's fine. We have a pretty good position up here. Only a few little hills and blind spots. Nothing we can't han— what *is* it, you bloody wanker?"

Jenkins let himself smile as he looked back at Norris' holdout, wondering what choice words he was saying to Warner.

He was still grinning as a rocket slammed into the ridge and bathed it in fire. Jenkins' smile melted away as he watched the flames grasp upward. Still having trouble taking it all in, he slowly turned his head away from Norris' missing beacon to see a metal machine ambling toward their ruined hillside.

Jenkins spiraled into despair as he realized that they had come face-to-face with the monstrosity they were trying to avoid.

"Goddamnit! Jenkins, you there? It's Warner. Jenkins!"

Once he heard the voice, Jenkins broke out of his daze and shook his head. He fumbled with the Comms link in his anxiety, but eventually tapped the interface button.

"Yeah, still here. Is that their mech?"

As he overcame his denial, Jenkins took another look at the metal creature. He could just barely see the pilot beneath all the twisted coils of metal and framework, reminding him of old science-fiction movies, which was where the Commission probably got the idea.

Half of the kibble was likely unnecessary but included for aesthetics, to make it seem more alien.

While looking over the monstrosity, Jenkins could see the still-smoking rocket launcher on the left arm and a minigun on the right. The pilot was exposed from the chest up, but in order to fire at the man beneath the metal support bars and bundles of wires, the Crows would have to face death incarnate.

"What? Of *course*, dumbass. Stop asking stupid questions," Warner said. "So we're kinda fucked here. I'm about thirty meters from you behind some cover and the mech is between us. We could get some good crossfire and distraction going for us. That's the good news.

"Obviously, Norris is burning up there. I told him to move position after he killed those Lion scouts, but *noooo*, the fucker wanted to paint a target on his back."

Jenkins looked back at the mech again and saw that the pilot had two other Lions as support, one flanking each side. It wasn't going to be as simple as running around and trying to take out the pilot.

"So what's the plan? You wanna go for the support or the pilot? They're both going to be problems." Jenkins tried to ignore the panic flooding his senses. He looked back at the Lions and saw they were warily advancing toward Norris' grave. It was exactly what Jenkins would have done, as a sniper always had at least one spotter.

Jenkins gritted his teeth and tried to figure out the best plan of attack before grabbing the grenades from Roberts' belt. *He* was certainly not going to be using them.

"Yeah, no shit. I say pilot would be best. That thing is gonna tear us apart," Warner suggested, but Jenkins didn't see it the same way.

"Well, you can shoot at him if you want, but I think we should throw a chaff and take out the support first. Leave the mech blind. Then maybe we can flank it and plant a round in the pilot's head. I feel like the other two would be able to react faster."

Jenkins dreaded the coming moments. It wouldn't be long before the three Lions were directly in between them. As he squinted at their opponents, Jenkins heard a crackle over Comms.

"You kids grow up so fast. On three?" Warner asked, his voice shaking.

Jenkins grabbed around at the pair of grenades he had taken from Roberts' belt and wrapped his fingers around the chaff.

"Start counting. I'll throw the grenade, just tell me when."

Jenkins pulled the pin on the silver grenade and watched as the three soldiers crept forward to the still-burning wreckage. He could see one of the Lions approaching Warner's cover, advancing with his weapon forward. The other was about ten meters away from Jenkins' position when Warner said *one*, but Jenkins knew the Lions weren't going to be polite enough to wait for Warner's count.

So he threw the chaff and then brought up his rifle, closing his eyes just before the bright flash of the grenade.

The chaff erupted halfway to the mech. All three of their opponents were well within the blast radius and Jenkins brought the sight of his rifle up to his helmet, grateful that the blast didn't affect his or Warner's helmet displays, since they were just outside of its range.

The Lion closest to him was spraying ammunition wildly in his direction, hoping to lay down suppressive fire, and Jenkins knew he would have done the same thing. Aware that he had a very small window of time, Jenkins breathed deep and aimed for the soldier's head.

When he pulled the trigger, he missed. Cursing, he readjusted his aim and steeled his nerve as bullets whipped through the air around him. Jenkins pulled the trigger two more times and each time the bullets flew past the Lion's head.

At that point, the chaff effect was starting to wear off and the anxiety was getting to him. He tried to carefully aim this time and saw the Lion finally doing the same—the static having cleared from his display—which meant Jenkins only had a split-second before they were on equal terms.

Staring down the sight of his rifle and seeing the reflection of light from his enemy's scope, Jenkins breathed out and pulled the trigger one more time. Thankful that he didn't see any muzzle flare from the weapon, Jenkins kept his eyes open and watched as the Lion's head snapped back. A corpse fell to the ground.

Meanwhile, Warner had popped out of his cover and had fired bursts at the soldier closest to him. The clusters of bullets glanced off the soldier's chest and only forced the Lion to stumble backward, and Warner cursed as his machine gun jammed. He yelled in fury as he threw it at the man.

Enraged, Warner grabbed one of the grenades on his belt and chucked it at the soldier, realizing it would do far more damage than his machine gun. Warner maliciously smiled as the soldier stood there unaware that death had been placed at his feet, just watching as the fragmentation grenade exploded into all directions and threw recycled earth into the air.

Warner couldn't stop himself from grinning as dust filled the air where his opponent used to be.

The smoke from the explosion mingled with the fog already present, and Jenkins could just barely make out Warner as he turned his head to look at him. Momentarily relieved, Jenkins watched as Warner was fine one moment and then bullets riddled his body and arterial sprays pumped out of the bullet wounds.

Warner looked like he was having a seizure as he stood there.

Only after Warner's body started to twitch and flail did Jenkins hear the whirring of the minigun. Their small victories had left them with a sense of false security, and Warner had paid the price for both of them. Jenkins watched as Warner's body stood—still propped up by the suit's motor functions—and the rattle of the Crow's last breath echoed through Comms.

Jenkins was about to give into self-pity when he heard the rocket ignite and scream through the air. He didn't even think about ducking behind cover; he knew he was dead already.

However, the rocket was not aimed at him. The missile flew toward Warner's body and exploded upon impact with his chest plate, propelling pieces of Warner in all directions while a red mist took the place of Warner's body. The force of the explosion forced the fog of war toward Jenkins and he struggled to breathe, crouching behind the rock that now served as his cover.

Jenkins realized after stifling his cough that he had probably breathed in a small part of his teammate. Swallowing down his anxiety and disgust, he tried not to think about it. He just looked at the mechanized soldier and wondered what he was going to do.

As Jenkins watched behind cover, he realized the mech's pilot had no idea he was huddled there. He could hear the pilot's muffled voice and guessed that the Lion was trying to speak to his teammates over Comms and—finding life preferable to death—Jenkins wondered if it would be so bad if he just hid and waited out the rest of the game. He didn't think anyone would blame him for it.

When Jenkins looked down to check on Roberts, he found a helmet and a full rifle clip at his feet. In a panic, he whipped his head around and tried desperately to find him. Jenkins couldn't understand where the man had gone, since the poor man wasn't even conscious. He frantically searched for an eternity of a moment, but he eventually turned back to the mechanized soldier that meant certain doom.

He had found Roberts. He was staring down the mech from ten meters away.

CHRISTOPHER THOUGHT he could hear something. He desperately wanted to know what it was, but his thoughts would always be interrupted. Christopher could never get more than a half-second of real, true consciousness. All he knew for certain was pain. It was always there. It wouldn't abandon him just because of a few pills.

Christopher could not see very well. It seemed like it was night and that the moon had disappeared, just like all the stars. He tried to remember when he had gone blind, why he had been robbed of his sight. Suddenly, his ears started to hurt and he wanted to hit them, he wanted to do something to make him know that everything had not disappeared.

An explosion rocked him toward consciousness, and when Christopher opened his eyes, he realized he had not gone blind. Christopher could see the pebbles in front of his display shaking and clattering along the ground. Each tremor brought another spike in pain for him.

Christopher winced involuntarily and craned his neck upward, his pain barely dulled by the medication smothering his senses. He watched as Jenkins looked beyond the ridge, and Christopher knew his partner hadn't noticed his awakening. When he lowered his head back down to the dirt, Christopher hoped his unfortunate partner would forgive him.

He unclasped his helmet and let it roll away from his head. Christopher didn't want to live his last moments trapped in the piece of metal; he didn't even remember when Jenkins had put it back onto his head. When Christopher looked back, he realized from muffled conversation that Jenkins was talking to Warner over Comms.

Letting a sad smile twist his face, Christopher knew the rookie did not need his help anymore. Jenkins was a fine soldier, and it would be best for Christopher to just get out of their way.

Bringing up his rifle from the ground, Christopher hit the release button on its side, causing the magazine to slide out of the weapon. Regrettably, he caught it with his hand, which was enough to start off a dozen echoes of pain through his arm. With a slight wince, Christopher narrowed his eyes and then placed the clip next to his discarded helmet.

Jenkins was still talking over Comms when he decided to crawl away. He didn't want to break cover and ruin their plans, so Christopher stayed below the line of rocks along the path. Every time Christopher brought his elbows down and dragged his body forward, he wondered why he was doing it.

Somewhere along the line, his condition had passed from inconvenient to unbearable and maybe he just hadn't noticed. Christopher wondered again what it would be like to overdose; if it would be the best way to end his life.

Christopher saw his surroundings suddenly illuminated and it made his eyes twitch in pain. Still, he brought his unfocused gaze back to the clearing and watched as Jenkins and Warner attacked the three Lions. Stunned by their effectiveness, Christopher was about twenty meters away while he watched his compatriots kill the mech's support.

Still, he knew they were going to die. Simply put, they were just overpowered.

With sorrow, Christopher watched as Warner was riddled with bullets and then the rocket burst him into pieces. Then he realized Jenkins was going to die next. He would jump out like some hero or the mech's pilot would flush him out.

Christopher looked at the executioner wrapped in tendrils of mist and smoke. After a moment, the fog of war started to obscure the machine and then it was just a black shape in the mist. It didn't look so monstrous then, not when all the sharp edges and horrific wires and weapons were just a silhouette.

Looking down at his hands, Christopher thought about hiding. There was no way he or Jenkins were ever going to take down the pilot. If he wanted, Christopher could probably wait out the rest of the game and then stumble to his painkillers. He could medicate himself to live and die another day, or—if he wanted—he could slip away lying in his bed, a bottle of pills in his hand.

But Christopher realized he didn't much care, anymore. He already felt hellfire within his skin, and he didn't even have the benefit of seeing it. It didn't matter if he died crippled in pain on his bed or if a few dozen bullets tore their way through his body.

He grabbed his empty rifle and tried to stand.

It was pure torture, at first. His legs trembled from his own weight and the reverberations throughout his legs were enough to set off another chain reaction of pain. His mind emptied of thoughts and he was about to fall to the ground when he had a moment of clarity.

It was going to be even more painful to crawl to the mech.

Christopher gathered himself and tried to walk casually to the machine.

He failed. The best he could do was limp to his doom, but he forced his legs to move toward the metallic reaper. It was still cloaked in the fog and smoke, looking suitably grim, and Christopher smiled as he appreciated the image. He could work with grim.

And in the back of his mind, a small part of him hoped this time could be the last time.

JENKINS WATCHED in horror as Christopher limped toward the machine. Although he desperately wanted to shout at him to run away, as soon as a single noise came from Jenkins' position, he knew the pilot would turn and send a rocket his way. He could only watch as the tortured Crow hobbled toward the mechanized soldier.

The fog swirled about Christopher and Jenkins wondered if he knew what he was doing. As he got closer, Jenkins was able to see his face and it all became obvious.

Christopher knew exactly what he was doing. His face was the picture of grim determination; his labored steps filled with purpose. Jenkins' breath caught in his throat as he watched the scene unfold.

The mech's pilot noticed Christopher when he was only ten meters away, but he was only looking up at his opponent and holding an empty rifle by his side. As intended, the pilot had no idea there wasn't a magazine in the weapon, so he scrambled with his controls and moved the shoulder-mounted plasma cannon into position.

In response, Christopher brought up his arm and pretended to aim at his opponent.

A beam of plasma lanced through the air and engulfed Christopher's arm at the shoulder. The beam was wide enough that it took out most of the limb, but the rest of his arm below the elbow fell and landed with a wet thump at his feet.

Christopher staggered as the beam burned off his arm, but soon regained his balance. Still engaged in a soldier's mindset, the Lion fumbled with his controls and accessed the minigun function for the right arm. When he started to aim at his opponent, he finally realized Christopher was still standing, waiting without a helmet on.

He wasn't going to run; he wasn't trying to pick up his weapon or throw a grenade. Christopher was just waiting for the pilot to finish the job.

The pilot looked at his opponent and let his thumb hover over the button that would start up the minigun's rotation. The Lion suddenly felt terribly guilty for all the people he had killed and for this boy he had just crippled. Though fog swirled about Christopher's face, the Lion could see the tears all the way from his cockpit.

"Please."

The Lion—a man named James Kaspar—heard him say it. Still, he desperately did not want to finish this man who reminded him of his young brothers. Kaspar knew he had to do it—this was part of the game—but killing this Crow was the last thing he wanted to do. It didn't matter if the boy was asking him. Kaspar had not come to Eris for this.

"Please. This is too much for me." Christopher's voice seemed to leak out of him.

Kaspar looked at the Crow's eyes and knew this was no longer his choice to make. This boy was already going to die, wanted to die, and Kaspar might as well get a boost to his paycheck.

Kaspar's thumb pressed down on the trigger and the minigun whirred to life.

Jenkins watched as the bullets rained down onto Christopher's frail body. He watched as the life left the poor boy and the smoke from the bullets started to pour out of his body, heating the air around him.

Unfortunately, Jenkins was in too much shock to close his eyes when his partner's body fell and his unguarded head sank into the target zone of the minigun.

The image of Christopher's face being riddled with bullets and eroding away was too much for Jenkins to take. He fell back down behind cover and tried to stifle his urge to throw up.

However, he could not manage to stem the tide and rushed to unclasp his helmet. Jenkins was just in time.

He vomited onto the ground as his helmet was rolling away from his feet.

After a few moments of heaving, Jenkins sat back against his cover and wondered if *that* was what Christopher had truly wanted. He had heard the boy pleading with his executioner—egging Kaspar on—but Jenkins knew that he was just trying to escape the pain. He hoped that was all; he hoped Christopher wasn't suicidal.

He had heard that the Commission took that very seriously.

Jenkins was sitting there against the rock he was using as cover when the last of it left him. He finally realized that there was no hope on Eris. Feldman really was a fool, just like Carver had said. None of them were getting out alive.

Jenkins thought about the five people who had just died in front of him. He knew that those two Lions were in exactly the same boat; they were not Jenkins' true enemies. Norris and Warner and Roberts and those two were dead for *no* other reason than good entertainment.

It was only a matter of time before Jenkins would join them, just like his current "enemy" in the mechanized suit of armor. Maybe it would not be this game, maybe not the next, but probably sometime in the next week. They all had a death sentence hanging over them, and the numbers did not lie.

Jenkins sat there and wondered what he was going to do for the rest of this existence. He had not saved his friends and he wasn't going to get away. The pilot was too paranoid for that now.

From the whirring and beeping of the man's systems, Jenkins could tell the pilot had already initiated the scanning system on his mech. It would only be a short time before Kaspar would know that Jenkins had been hiding like a little rat, hiding while his friend pleaded for death.

Jenkins looked down at his grenade belt and sighed. He decided that even though he wasn't going to live, he could still make it easier for the rest of his teammates. Better this pilot than one of them. Jenkins dropped the sling of his rifle from his shoulder and broke cover.

Scrambling over the rock, Jenkins' boots caught purchase on the dirt and he sprinted toward the machine of death. He counted himself lucky that Kaspar was still looking at Christopher's corpse, but the mech was still about twenty meters away and that was a lot of ground to cover.

Jenkins was about halfway there when the pilot noticed the incoming threat. Abandoning any hope of sneaking up on the Lion, Jenkins knew he just had to make it to the machine and then it was allowed to kill him if it wanted.

His cargo just needed to get there.

Kaspar started up the minigun as the mech's torso rotated to face his enemy, realizing far too late that this was a kamikaze mission. As Jenkins ran, the bullets of the minigun sank into the ground in a vicious arc and he could hear some of them ricochet back at the metal monstrosity, its occupant unharmed.

Jenkins was only five meters away from the machine when he heard the bullets closing in on him. Still, he was just grateful that Kaspar had already used the plasma beam and that it would take time to recharge. As he made his way to the four-meter monstrosity, Jenkins armed his grenades and let them cook in his hands. He briefly wondered if he was going to make it or if they would explode before he reached the machine.

He knew he would die, either way, and it was not going to help anyone in the long-run.

Jenkins was about a meter away from the machine when he could see his adversary in the cockpit. He wondered what the Lion was thinking as he started the kinetic motivators and jumped to his death, his speed surprising even him.

As Jenkins rushed through the air, he could see the pilot scrambling for his sidearm. Kaspar must have known that it was too late, but Jenkins could understand that he needed to do *something*. When

Jenkins landed against the steel frame of the cockpit, he hung there for a moment.

He had enough time to see Kaspar bring his gun to bear and think that this was not so horrible of a death.

Before Kaspar could squeeze the trigger, the grenades in Jenkins' hands exploded around him. His hands split apart from the blast and the force of the explosion slammed him back against the ground in a bloody cascade, shrapnel scattered around his flesh. Kaspar was just as unfortunate; the blasts were enough to crush his helmet against his skull.

There was no living thing left to witness the mech falling to the ground.

However, a remote drone filmed the last of the spectacle and kept the footage rolling as the smoke and fog closed back on the site of the explosion. Soon enough, even the silhouettes disappeared and the remote drone flew on to more exciting things.

After all, there was no point in filming a graveyard.

All Hope Abandoned

Douglas Finnegan sat in the break room as he read the news off his phone. Even though the announcer knew none of the real news ever got through the corporate services, it gave him something to talk about if someone asked him what he thought on an issue. Douglas could at least *seem* like an intellectual.

He was almost done with his lunch when he saw Eric walk in and close the door behind him. Suppressing the groan building in his throat, Douglas tapped at the next article on his phone.

Maybe Eric would leave him alone if he didn't make eye contact, so Douglas grabbed a slice of his tangerine and bit into it absent-mindedly. It was a bit ripe and juice escaped his mouth and ran down from the corner of his lips. Though he grabbed his napkin and quickly tried to wipe it away before Eric noticed, it was in vain.

"Be careful, there, Sean," the head anchor said as he grabbed his coffee and sat down opposite Douglas at the table.

"That's not my name."

Eric laughed and stirred his coffee with his index finger.

"Maybe not, but you respond to it, don't you?"

Douglas looked up at the celebrity and supported his neck on his hand, grabbing a small bit of skin behind his ear and pinching it. He hoped the pain would be enough to distract him from attacking his coworker.

"What do you *want*? I'm just trying to eat my lunch," Douglas said, but the antagonism had not worked out quite like he wanted. Eric Jones—the lead anchor of the most popular television program in the Earth Orbit System—threw up his hands and smiled.

"I'm not trying to stop you, buddy. Just making idle chat."

He peered at Douglas over the rim of his coffee cup with a strange look, which unnerved the antisocial announcer. Trying to ignore Eric's behavior, Douglas looked back to his phone and read the next head-line. He didn't really want to hear about the recall for the new set of pseudo-pets and the parents who were screaming bloody murder.

Determined to find *something* to distract him, Douglas sighed and clicked on the link anyway.

"Anything crazy happening in the world?" Eric asked from the other end of the table. After a quick glare at his coworker, Douglas turned his attention back to the phone.

"Maybe. The news wouldn't tell us if it did."

"The tragedy of our times, Doug. Wouldn't it be great if we *could* know?"

Eric's audacity was palpable, but instead of wearing the smile usually plastered to his face, he was uncharacteristically serious. Douglas could see real concern on the man's face and—for the first time—wondered if he really knew Eric Jones, at all.

"There are plenty of tragedies for our time. We make money off of one of the worst ones," Douglas said before looking back down, this time escaping rather than ignoring. He was even less interested in the toy recall, now.

"You're right. I feel guilty every day," Eric admitted, which was enough for Douglas' eyes to go wide.

He could *not* believe that he had heard those words coming out of Eric's mouth. This was the kind of man who flaunted his celebrity. To hear this man admit guilt—even in the break room—was astonishing and, frankly, unbelievable.

However, when Douglas really looked at Eric, he saw the remorse painted across his face. Either he was telling the truth, or Eric was an even better actor than Douglas had thought.

"If you feel guilty then why do you do this? You're one of the people who benefit the most from the games. Why do you endorse it, if it hurts your conscience so bad?" Douglas needled, unable to keep venom from seeping into his voice.

They were more attacks than questions. He was lashing out at the man he had always seen as the most corrupt and vile of them all.

"I know, Doug. I *know*. It's terrible and I know I seem like the worst kind of guy. But," Eric paused, his gaze flickering as he focused on something far away. Douglas could swear that tears were just beneath the surface. "God, I really shouldn't tell anyone this."

Attacking the man wouldn't lead to any answers, so Douglas set his arms on the table and tried to remove the hostility from his stance.

"You shouldn't tell anyone *what*?"

When Eric ran his hand through his perfectly-coiffed hair, Douglas was absolutely certain that the man was *not* acting. Makeup had teased that thing for ten minutes and this celebrity was not thinking straight.

"It's just so hard doing it by myself like this. I know there are others here, but I have no idea who they are. It's all so secretive. It's just— when I look at you, I know you're not part of it, but I think you can understand. You're not like the rest of them," Eric said, rubbing his forehead with his left hand.

"What's going on, Eric?"

"Doug, I'm... part of the Eris Freedom Initiative," Eric confessed before dropping his gaze to the table and rubbing his eyes.

Douglas couldn't believe that confession. There was no way the lead anchor of *War World* was part of a resistance movement. It just didn't seem possible.

"*How*? *Why*? Why tell me?" Douglas asked, unable to stop himself from asking everything at once.

Throughout, Eric had difficulty looking him in the eye. There was a tense silence before he could answer, at all.

"It wasn't always like this. I was happy being up there in front of the cameras for a long time, but do you remember when I said that

Jenkins kid reminded me of my cousin?" Eric took in a deep breath and wrung his hands on the table before continuing.

"Well, it wasn't my *cousin*. Jenkins reminded me of my half-*brother*. Phil had my mom's last name, so nobody really picked up on it. He got into some bad trouble with a casino and they basically sent him off to Eris. I don't think I've had a bender quite like the one I had after I learned about it," he said before sitting back in his chair and staring at the fabricated wood grain of the table.

"God, he was just a *kid*. He only lasted a few games before he tried to off himself. Something happened then; something changed him. They let me go down to the blasted asteroid for some special and I was able to talk to the guy," Eric said before leaning on the table and beckoning Douglas closer.

"He didn't even *recognize* me. He didn't act like himself. It was like they replaced him with an identical twin. I came back here to Earth and just fucking lost it. I started drinking every night and taking whatever drug was put in front of me, not to mention putting my dick in everything that moved..." Eric groaned and shook his head before sitting back in his chair.

Douglas remembered when that happened. Eric had almost been fired, but since his notoriety increased the ratings for the show, the network heads instead gave him a bonus. Back then, Douglas had just thought him a hedonist, but now he saw the broken man who had committed those acts.

For the first time, Douglas felt pity for Eric Jones.

"That's when the EFI reached out to me. They had done their homework and figured out why I was slumming it like that. They told me to keep quiet about it, but when the time was right, we'd do a special broadcast. We'd take it all back and help all those people. They told me I could bring my brother back," he said before letting real tears fall from his eyes.

"How could I say no?"

Douglas sat back and tried to take in all the information. He wondered how the man had been able to keep up his shiny plastic face all these years when just behind his eyes, he was filled with self-loathing and the desire to see his brother again.

Then he realized the consequences of this confession.

"I sympathize, Eric, I really do. This is actually the first time I've ever liked you, but why the *hell* did you do this here? And what if I was going to turn you in? Did you think this through, at all?" Douglas was wary about what the EOSF might do to *him* just for listening.

Eric shook his head as he stared at the ground.

"You weren't going to tell anyone. I could tell how much you hate all of us. I think that's why I wanted to tell *you*. You're the one decent person here, or at least the only one who's not undercover. Frank and Sam are fucking jokes. Patrick's brain-addled and useless. I have no idea about anyone else. It may seem desperate and stupid, but I knew you were the only one who would understand.

"As far as the whole thing being stupid, well, this is the last place they would look, right? It's the break room of the program designed to advertise the games. I don't think they'd watch us. I'm a face and you're a voice. Outside of television, we're worthless," Eric argued, sitting back in his chair like he had just won a game.

"Well, what *now*? Want me to get you a cookie?" Douglas awkwardly asked, laughing wearily at his own joke as he also sat back in his chair. He was still processing all that information and trying to reassess Eric as a decent guy when Eric leaned in and ruined everything.

"Well, I guess *now* I'm just going to have to recruit you."

CHARLOTTE SIGHED as Ryan's cell emerged from the darkness. She knew he had already been awake for at least an hour and that he was in pain and alone in the black abyss of the storage room. She knew that he was going to face certain death in just another day; she knew there was no way for him to escape this cycle.

And there was nothing she could do.

Charlotte tapped the display and readied all of the resurrection equipment, taking care to avoid excess sedatives. If nothing else, she could try to accommodate some of her patient's wishes. Charlotte sighed as she realized what was in store for Ryan.

It was becoming more and more apparent that he was becoming the next Carver.

As she walked toward the entrance of the resurrection chamber, Charlotte looked over at Hawkins, who was furiously tapping at his display. She had absolutely no interest in reading about his study or his results, so she ignored the man as she left the control room.

Ryan's cell drained while she approached the loading deck and she stood by as the cell hissed into place and opened in front of her. Trying to stay somewhat detached, Charlotte watched Ryan open his eyes and attempt to lift his hands to his face. He was already wiping away some of the biotic fluid as she started the procedures to fill a syringe with base sedatives.

Although Charlotte noticed Ryan shaking his head, she tapped at the display so the resurrection unit would administer the sedative.

"It's just for the rebreather, Ryan. I'm not giving you the full dose. I know you don't want it." The imprisoned soldier relaxed once he understood. Charlotte had lied to him—giving him more than necessary for the rebreather—but she would not have this man suffer needlessly.

Ryan would just have to deal with her compassion.

Charlotte watched as the automated needles sank into his arm and emptied into his blood stream, laying her hand on Ryan's shoulder once the needles were extracted from his flesh. It was not the skin-to-skin contact she would have preferred for this poor man—Charlotte was wearing plastic gloves—but she hoped it was some comfort.

When she saw Ryan relax at her touch, it almost made her smile.

Charlotte rose off the stool and set herself to the task of withdrawing the rebreather. She then removed the straps and lifted them from under Ryan's head before taking hold of the plastic.

"You ready?" she asked, waiting for some sign of consent. After a few more facilitated breaths, Ryan nodded and Charlotte forced a smile before she drew out the tube, hoping it wouldn't hurt too much.

The tube slid out of his throat accompanied by a painful cough, but that was routine. Charlotte placed the tube on a table nearby and ran her hand along Ryan's scalp to soothe him.

"Was it bad this time? I never watch the games anymore."

Ryan turned to look at her, but he was staring off into space.

"It doesn't really matter, does it?"

Charlotte's smile disappeared, and suddenly she was in a deep pit of her own despair. This man deserved better; they all deserved better.

"I'm sorry. I'm going to sit you up now."

She placed her hand under his back and started to lift. Ryan wasn't relying on her so heavily, this time; she could tell that he had been flexing his muscles in the darkness and was trying to move without her help. As she thought about the situation, it became difficult for Charlotte to hold back her emotions.

Once Ryan was sitting up on his own, Charlotte started to remove the electrodes and wires from his body. It was a quiet process. At some point in their relationship, she had lost the ability to speak to him easily.

When she was finished with the process and started to go through the checklist on her computer, Ryan finally spoke up.

"How is Roberts?" His voice was low and despondent.

Ryan wasn't even looking at her; he was looking into the reflective surface of the plate glass mirror in front of him. It was like he knew Hawkins was on the other side, oblivious and tapping away on his current pet project.

"What are you talking about? Did Roberts have a bad death out there?" Charlotte didn't know how much Ryan already knew, and she wanted to make sure she didn't betray Christopher's trust.

"Did Hawkins do it again, or did he tone it down this time?" Ryan turned to her with anger in his eyes.

Charlotte looked him over and wondered if he knew more than she did. The curiosity brewing in her mind was more than enough to push her from morose thoughts.

"What do you know? What's going on with Christopher?" she asked, setting one hand on the table and the other on his shoulder.

Ryan turned his head back to the mirrored glass and sighed. Although she had asked him for the truth, Ryan knew she would not take the news well. Sparing her seemed to be the kind option.

"Nothing, really. I just know he's hurting. I just wanted to know if it was better this time," he stated, his tone becoming apathetic.

Charlotte knew Ryan was lying, especially once he looked back to the mirrored glass.

"Ryan, it's *me*. I'm not going to get you in trouble or anything, and I know you mentioned Hawkins. If there's something happening here, I want to know. I want to help Christopher."

Ryan looked at the doctor and could see the genuine concern in her coffee-brown eyes. That look was worth more than anything else in Ryan's life, and he hoped and prayed this woman would find a way off this rock before it was too late.

In the meantime, he would not weigh down her conscience more than necessary.

"I don't know anything. It was just rumors and stuff. Honestly. Time to go to the training room?" he asked, hoping it would be a suitable misdirect.

Knowing Ryan was trying to shield her from the worst of it, Charlotte turned to her display, aggressively tapping through the menus in order to finish the mandatory checklist. Afterward, she nodded to the door and the training briefs on the stand.

"Go on ahead, I have to grab something from the control room," she said, and Ryan looked sheepishly at her.

Charlotte couldn't blame him for the behavior, but she needed to keep her newfound severity. She watched Ryan limp away and head down the hallway before she stomped over to the door of the control room.

Charlotte burst through the door to see Hawkins smiling as he leered over the display of the computer. Now that she *knew* something was going on behind her back, Charlotte couldn't bear to see Hawkins smiling. She kicked at the man's chair, forcing the scientist to spin to the other end of the room.

"What are you doing, you stupid harpy? I was working!"

Charlotte could see saliva flying from the man's mouth and hated him for it just a little more.

"Working on *what*, Hawkins? What do you do in the dead of night when I'm not here? What do you do to these men?" she asked before closing the distance and dominating his perspective.

"What do you do to *Roberts*?"

Taken off-guard by the nascent hostility, Hawkins only regained his ego at the mention of Roberts. Then rage filtered through his fear.

"What did Jenkins tell you? That fucking imbecile, *what did he tell you*?" Hawkins yelled as he jumped out of the chair and let it fall to its side.

Charlotte was taken aback by the action, but decided to hold her ground. She was going to get answers.

"Ryan didn't tell me a *damn thing*. He knew that I wasn't going to like it. He knew that it wouldn't make a difference, but damn it, Peter, I need to know what's happening in my clinic," she declared, pointing at the floor for emphasis.

Hawkins sneered at the plea before backing off considerably. If the action figure could keep his head around this woman, so could he.

"It's not really *your* clinic, now is it, *Dr.* Kane? It's mine, and I'm going to do what I want with it. Remember, you work for *me*. Now," he said as he walked over to the chair and picked it up from the ground, "excuse me while I get back to *my* work."

Hawkins dragged the chair back to his terminal, past the still-fuming doctor, and then sat down at his workstation.

Charlotte had lost control of this, somehow, and she had not kept the anger she needed to get it back.

"What did you do to Christopher? Just tell me."

She knew the monster would confess even if it was just to hear the merits of his own genius, and Hawkins stopped his tapping and seemed to think about what he was going to say. His wicked smile accentuated his rodent features.

"I make adjustments to his pain sensors and receptors with every iteration, trying to account for every variable. I'm searching for the neurobiological limits of this subject's tolerance for pain before, frankly, he goes insane. I want to see how a man copes with that kind of existence," he said before cocking his head to the side, waiting for his kind assistant's mind to shatter.

He knew Charlotte would not take the news well.

Charlotte walked over to the desk and steadied herself as she considered the heinous experiment happening right under her nose. It was unethical and sadistic. Still in shock, Charlotte could only call the man's science into question; she couldn't let her emotions overcome her senses.

"But, how are you going to get any results if you just do this to Roberts? All of it could be subject to the frailty of one man."

Charlotte desperately wanted it all to end, and she hoped that the mention of unaccounted-for variables could be enough to sway the doctor.

Yet Hawkins still wore that smug grin.

"That's why he's not the *only* one. I've done it before with a few others on the team. Markham, Corrigan and Haywick are all some proud specimens of other experiments. But really, it doesn't much matter.

"*I'm* not the only one. Throughout the clinics on this moon there are similar scientists and similar soldiers, though I must admit they don't measure up to my own intelligence," Hawkins said with a flourish of his pudgy hand. He chuckled, savoring the opportunity to make this ethical doctor suffer.

"Did you really think we wouldn't be careful with *our* data?"

Charlotte gripped the desk harder. This was not the twisted idea of just one man; this was throughout the whole Commission. The whole organization of War World Entertainment was corrupt, and she was an *employee* for these people. Charlotte's world had spiraled into darkness, and she could only focus on Hawkins' little smirk.

"I think we're done here, Dr. Kane. You should go train your little toy soldier. He's going to get lonely over there."

RYAN WALKED through the doorway of the barracks and stood in the lobby for a moment. Evans was gone for some reason—it was still before Moonrise—but Ryan would never have wanted to see the arrogant receptionist, anyway. It would have just been another reminder that the men who should be in prison are *not*, and that if there were any justice, their roles would be reversed.

Except Ryan would not have wanted that, either. No one should have to live on this artificial moon.

Ryan's thoughts fell back to his time during physical therapy, and he knew Charlotte had learned the truth as soon as he had seen her tortured face. He felt somewhat responsible, since she might not have asked any questions if she had not seen his anger. The loss of Charlotte's smile was his fault, and it somehow seemed worse than any of his real crimes back in New Chicago. He had never felt guilty about any of that, but Ryan shoved his hands in his pockets and headed toward his room, feeling like a criminal.

The pain wasn't so bad this time around, or at least he had gotten used to it. The aches, pains and tears had not disappeared completely, but it was more an annoyance than anything. Ryan tried to tell himself that it was a good thing, but he had lost the will to look on the bright side.

This world would keep him in debt until he was not useful anymore. At any time, he could be swept up into an unethical experiment. Eris was a testament to the cruelty of the human race and he had gotten himself mired in its depths, too poor to care about committing any crimes. Once he thought about it, Ryan was not so sure he would be able to live on the outside, even if he somehow made it off of Eris.

Part of him felt as if he had seen too much.

Ryan reached his room and closed the door behind him, breathing deep in the cold air. He stood there for a moment and scanned the four walls and everything between them.

No matter how hard he looked, he couldn't make himself comfortable there; it felt like someone else's room. This was not a proper home, even if it did hold all of his unearthly possessions. It was somewhere he was allowed to live when he was not dying for the collective's amusement.

He trudged over to his bed and sat down. Ryan looked at the wall in front of him and wondered if there was anything worthwhile in his life, if some action he had taken had made someone's life better, if someone would smile if they remembered Ryan Jenkins from New Chicago. He wanted to remember *something*; some memory of when he, as a person, *mattered*.

He wanted to remember that moment, but it wasn't there.

Ryan fell down on the bed that didn't really belong to him and buried his face in the pillow that was not his property. Ryan had always considered that he could get out and maybe get back to Earth. It would be Hell, but perhaps he could pay himself out of his interminable contract and escape. The distant possibility of his emancipation was still there, but now he realized that it didn't matter at all. *He* didn't matter at all.

In his twenty-four years of living, Ryan Jenkins had not made a positive or negative impact on anyone. In his life, he had been a small-time crook whose own friends had sold him out. In his many deaths, he was merely an average athlete.

Ryan Jenkins had not loved. He had not fought for some ideal. He had said no grand speeches. He was no paragon or saint; he was no villain or nemesis.

History would not remember him *poorly*. History would not *remember* him.

Even if Ryan were to buy back his freedom, no one would celebrate. What was left of his family would have moved on or most likely would be dead by the time he could afford it. He had no real friends outside of his compatriots, and even *they* were more like coworkers. They would only mourn a reminder of their own suffering.

Ryan couldn't stop the groan escaping from his throat. It had been so long since his sadness or emotion had been vocalized and he was not in the mindset to stop it. This realization was so much worse than the others; he was not just stuck on this artificial moon.

He had nowhere else to go.

Ryan heard a knock on his door and quickly realized that he did not want to talk to any of the three likely candidates. Instead of walking to the door, Ryan opened his eyes against the pillow and examined the threads holding the pillowcase together. Even with that concerted effort to ignore his visitor, he heard another slow knock and realized they were not going to go away.

When Ryan opened the door, he found Feldman's massive face hovering above him. A two-day beard was scattered across the giant's face, already lending more shadow to the man, and Ryan had to step back from the doorway to avoid craning his neck.

"Hey, Greg. What do you need?" he asked as he retreated back to his bed.

"I wanted to talk to you." Feldman remained at the threshold, but Ryan sighed and gestured that he should get out of the hallway.

"What about?" Ryan asked, crossing his legs on his bed as Feldman stooped down and managed to get himself across the threshold. Once he was back to his full imposing height, Feldman walked over to Ryan's desk and used it as an improvised chair. Once he was as comfortable as he could get, he cleared his throat.

"I know you're upset, but I want you to know that it doesn't have to be like that. We don't have to make our hearts and our minds hard like this. I *know* it's tempting.

"I've watched you change a lot since that first month of training. I know you've learned a great deal about this moon, but I'm hoping that it doesn't change you completely," Feldman said, taking a long, deep breath.

"One of the major reasons I've nurtured our friendship is because you have the potential to not give in. You *don't* have to be like the rest of them. They sleepwalk through their lives, Ryan," Feldman said before making eye contact.

"I don't want you to let yourself fall into a living oblivion. Our lives are difficult, but humanity has had to deal with its dark times before. We just need to seize our lives for ourselves and not let our circumstances destroy our worth. I want you to take that to heart."

This sincerity was all he had, and Feldman obviously hoped he could bring Ryan back from that pit of despair. Instead, he shook his head in dismay.

"Greg, you're a great guy, but how do you do it? You read your history texts and how humanity gets back on track and don't understand that there are thousands and millions of people who are *just* stepped on. They don't have *stories*; they don't have great *ideas* or *grand* moments. They just live, they get trampled on and they *die*. But most of the time the trampling isn't what kills them.

"*Time* gets that honor. They get broken and messed up and have to live with that for the rest of their lives. And you don't seem to realize that it's already happened to us. In the end, we're all just corporate slaves with nowhere to go. Even when we get out, there's no place for us. We're *broken*. We're *trampled*. And to top it all off, we just don't *matter*."

Ryan looked down at his feet before turning back to his friend with a blank face. The absence of tears was what hurt Feldman the most.

"Really. How do you do it? How do you justify your existence here? You're a giant in love with academia, literally *built* for war by a corporation. And just so you know, this *isn't* an attack. I just want to know how you can live here like you do without realizing that it's all for *nothing*," Ryan lamented, eventually turning to stare at the blank wall near his bed.

Letting his sadness overcome him for a moment, Feldman let the desk hold him up. For all his high-minded philosophy, he had not been able to save his friend.

"I know that," Feldman said while looking at the floor. "I know that in the end, we don't matter. We're inconsequential and, in reality, nothing is waiting for us. No one is going to reward us for being the best people we could be. No one is going to care if we hold our heads high or refuse to let ourselves die willingly. I know that the millions of people on this world are meant for nothing, most likely. This isn't something I haven't taken into account."

Gregory faced him and Ryan could see the sorrow haunting his eyes. Even if it was too late, he had to continue.

"I don't live like this for *anyone*. I don't do this to impress people or for people to call me a hero. I don't swing my sword for money or fame. I don't *care* about that. It doesn't matter to me that history will move on without me.

"I am who I am and I have my ideals because *that's* what makes me proud of myself. I hold myself to a higher standard because *that's* what I want from myself. I justify my existence by being the best thing I could possibly be. I don't want a reward and I don't want approval. The most I would ever want is that my example is enough for just one man," Gregory said while narrowing his eyes, "for just *one* person to allow himself to be a better version, to reach *their* potential."

The giant heaved himself off the desk and looked down at his friend from a lofty perspective.

"I shout my character out to the universe. I allow myself to be an example for others, and it is enough that I may hear echoes. *That* is how I justify myself, and I really do hope you can understand that," he said before stooping underneath the doorway and walking away.

Ryan looked after the giant as he departed and wondered how such a man could really exist. Again, he desperately wanted to follow in Gregory's footsteps and be a better version of himself.

But this time, he knew he couldn't.

Stage Five

ACCEPTANCE

1

Uncomfortably Numb

Carver ate his oatmeal with no thoughts of consequence. His new beard—mostly white this time—was starting to itch, and he was doing his best to tolerate it. While off-handedly scratching his cheek, he dug his spoon back into the grey matter and tried to ignore its similarity to mucus.

No one tended to sit next to the old Crow during their meals. Some were scared, but most were just uncomfortable around the man. Not only did Carver have his status as a legendary soldier, but he was just too old. The young gladiators had nothing in common with him.

Most of them had been raised a full generation after he had entered the games.

Sometimes, their behavior made Carver feel lonely, but he knew that the kids playing at war could say nothing of consequence. Barely any of them had more than a hollow existence, and the few who did were just as quiet. Usually, the other Crows sat a few seats away from him—just far enough so Carver wouldn't be bothered by their idle chatter—and that was acceptable for everyone involved.

Carver drew the spoon from his mouth just as he noticed Ryan walking toward his table. After trudging over to the other side, Ryan sat down opposite him and gave a nod of courtesy to the veteran.

Carver returned it and watched as he lazily started to eat the food off his tray, looking like any other man who ate for sustenance rather than pleasure. Finding nothing of interest, Carver looked back down at his oatmeal and lifted up another morsel of tasteless muck.

They ate like that for a time. Only after a few minutes did Carver turn his attention back to his young comrade and watch him eat. Somehow, Ryan seemed even more lifeless and dejected than the last time he had spoken to him.

"Tell me about it," Carver said in his usual brusque manner. He knew some of the Crows did not appreciate it, but he knew for a fact that Ryan wasn't one of them. After looking up from his food, Ryan wiped his lips with the back of a hand and cleared his throat.

"Why do you want to know? It's just another pile of shit."

What unnerved Carver was that he could tell that Ryan wasn't trying to brush off the conversation. He was just indifferent.

"It's on your mind. I want to make sure it's not affecting you. Talking about it helps." Carver grabbed at his tin of water. He hated drinking anything flavored for breakfast, especially the acidic orange juice concentrate the Commission practically threw away on the Crows. It was too much to handle at the beginning of the day.

As he brought his own cup down, Ryan sighed. "Roberts... his *condition*. That was a lot of it, but now I'm just becoming more... familiar with my situation. Just more shit to deal with. You understand."

From the look in Ryan's eyes, Carver could tell something more personal was underneath the surface.

"I'm sorry, kid. That's just part of this world. If it helps any," Carver said before reaching for his spoon, "it's not horrible, once you finally hear all of the horrors down here. The more you deal with it, the easier it *becomes* to deal with it. Obviously, I have a lot of experience with that.

"As the years go on, it just starts to feel like a job. Just like anything else that people are doing these days. I know some people gripe about their work the same way that we complain about having to kill each other. People can get used to all kinds of situations, and if you let it, this place becomes bearable. It's kinda the only thing we got."

Carver placed another spoonful of oatmeal in his mouth and quickly realized he was no longer hungry.

"I think that's what I'm afraid of," Ryan replied wearily, propping up his forehead against the heel of his right palm. Although his eyes were open, he wasn't staring at the sterile table in front of him. His gaze was far, far away, and Carver sighed as he watched the child.

They were more alike than he had thought.

"I can understand that. I was, too," he commiserated before returning to his breakfast, wondering why he had let his life turn out like this. In that moment, Carver thought about the day he had joined up for the games.

The former EOSF captain had just been dishonorably discharged and was looking for work. A life of service had left him with no experience in other professions, since destroying riots and uprisings couldn't be counted as skilled labor. That day—when he had seen the magnificent advertisements for recruitment into the games playing across giant televisions—Jonathon Carver had thought it was a golden opportunity.

And as the old Crow looked at his oatmeal, he wished he could go back and wring that young idiot's neck.

RYAN STARED at the mass of clouds overhead and thought about this world of his. It was practically smog up there; not the sparse sky that he had grown up with in New Chicago. Even if it wasn't nice to look at, the scientists who had transformed this asteroid into an artificial moon had loaded down the atmosphere with oxygen and nitrogen and other binding elements.

Grey clouds stretched out above him, but he could see one of the other moons off to the left. Judging from the orange pigment, Ryan guessed it was Solaria, but he had never really studied all the asteroid constructs. He didn't know how they were kept together; he didn't know why he didn't float off every time he jumped. It depressed him that he knew so little about his prison.

Before he had become so focused on things he did not understand, Ryan had been training in the yard and attempting a bench press by himself. Feldman had not been so keen to keep up their training practices after their confrontation, and Ryan did not blame him. Even though he had regretted how it had concluded, he could not follow Feldman's example. Ryan was beyond those ideals of hope.

Now he was alone in the courtyard, hoping the sky might fall down on him. Ryan didn't want to know any of the bile the news networks would spew out to coddle the populace. He didn't want to read past stories of heroism and might, denying the bleak present. He didn't want to watch any shows that glorified money and product placement. If anything, Ryan wished he didn't have to be awake, but he knew sleep was beyond him.

So he just watched the cloud formations overhead as they passed and wondered at the science behind it to distract him in between sets of weight lifting. After a few sets, the time for distractions became more plentiful than his time exercising. He couldn't bring himself to lift the heavy iron weights, since any temporary gain in strength would be rendered meaningless after his next death.

"What in the bloody hell are you doing out here?"

At the intruder's voice, Ryan's eye twitched, and he turned his head to see who had joined him in the training yard. Norris was approaching from the doorway of the barracks and he had his hands on his hips. After a casual glance at the Englishman, Ryan turned his eyes back to the clouds.

"Stargazing," he said in a dead man's tone, hoping Norris would abandon further questions. Instead, Ryan heard his teammate laugh and come closer.

"You're daft. I like it."

Knowing all hope for solitude was lost, Ryan faced Norris with a raised eyebrow.

"Well, what in the bloody hell are *you* doing out here, Norris?" he asked, adopting his teammate's accent.

"Eh, I gotta get rid of some energy. Jess is busy talking to her sister or something so she doesn't want to spar. Women, right? Problem is I still have this fuckin' adrenaline boost from the shooting yard, so I have to do something. Thought I would get some shadow-boxing in. Make a right show of it," the flame-haired man said before launching into a flurry of blows against an invisible opponent.

"Well, don't let me stop you." Ryan looked to the blank sky. "I'm sure I can pretend-stargaze while you pretend-fight."

Norris stopped jabbing at the air and put his hands back on his hips.

"Ey, you prick."

Ryan turned back as Norris put on a wide grin and gestured toward his chest.

"Why don't we have a go at it? Let's see what you got," he proposed, changing stances as he jumped from side to side. With a laugh, Ryan turned back to his ceiling of clouds.

"Nah, I don't think so. I got enough of that in training, and it isn't even all that useful in the field."

"Oh, *c'mon*. Jess and I don't do it because we need the *skills*. We do it because it's *fun*. Or, at least it is for me. No telling what that slag is thinking," Norris said, lifting his arms above his head to stretch.

"You speak so *fondly* of your girlfriend."

"Not my girlfriend, mate. Sometimes we use each other. All it is. Now get up. I'm gonna kick your ass for a bit," Norris said, a grin plastered on his face like a cartoon character.

After a deep sigh, Ryan abandoned his staring contest with the cloud cover and sat up on the bench. Norris was grinning and bouncing around in the dirt, and Ryan had to wonder how the man could be so happy.

Cortes' whispers of behavioral modification returned to his mind, and Ryan decided it really did make sense that Edward Norris had been a different person. Clearly, this version was insane, but Ryan figured he could do with a dose of levity and picked himself up from the weight bench. Norris offered him an infectious smile, and if he was *that* happy, Ryan wondered if it even mattered whether or not it was artificial.

"So, is this just bare knuckle? How are we going about this?" Ryan asked, never actually having watched Norris and Abrams during their sparring sessions.

Norris looked at Ryan skeptically.

"You're a *special* one, aren't you? Bare knuckle hurts like hell if you do it right. We have pads over there, rook," Norris said in a disappointed tone before walking to the equipment stack and pulling out two sets of shin pads and light gloves.

At his prompting, Ryan walked over to his teammate and grabbed the gloves, which seemed a little small. They were light pieces of black leather and plastic and Ryan could tell they wouldn't stop much of anything. Waving them around, he gave Norris a quizzical look.

"These are supposed to *help*?" he asked, earning a wicked smile from Norris as he slipped on his own set of shin guards.

"*Supposed to.* Don't want bloody knuckles, do you? The shin pads you're gonna want for sure, because without the right conditioning, your legs are going to suffer. Get it all on, ya pansy."

Then Norris danced away and shadow boxed a few meters from the stack of equipment. Dropping the gloves at his feet, Ryan shrugged and slipped the shin pads onto his legs. They were a bit loose, so he did his best to tighten the straps and failed miserably. Once Norris looked over, he scoffed at Ryan's predicament.

"Yeah, that's the problem with those *one-size-fits-all* pieces of shit. Wouldn't mind speaking with the tossers who thought *they* were a good idea. Hurry up."

Abandoning any notion of well-fitting equipment, Ryan wondered if he was going to regret all of this. Once he was wearing his hand-me-down gear, Ryan stood up and walked toward the ridiculous jester. His shin pads slid up and down his feet as he walked, and Norris laughed before offering him an exaggerated wink.

"One word for you, soldier, and that's *pretty*. You ready for this?" Norris punctuated the question by raising his fists to the sides of his face.

Ryan looked at the man and shrugged before getting into a boxing stance.

"Pretty sure."

"See, the correct answer was *no.*" Norris then abandoned his stance and leapt at him.

Ryan was barely able to react as Norris launched his right fist at his face. Twisting to the side, Ryan let Norris' hand sail past his head—feeling grateful for his quick reactions—but for half a moment he was able to see the gleeful smile stretching across Norris' face.

Then the lithe soldier planted his foot and twisted his body to force his knee into Ryan's unguarded midsection, sending out all of the air in his lungs with a painful grunt. Ryan fell down to the ground and—thinking Norris was going to attack him again—instinctively brought his arms up to his chest to ward off the incoming blows.

They never came.

"So that's *pretty sure*, eh? C'mon, get back up." Norris spoke from a meter away, so Ryan let his arms fall to his sides as he sat up. The jester was still bouncing around and striking at the air, unaffected by the first few seconds of their fight.

Realizing he really wanted to bring Norris down a peg, Ryan brought himself back to his feet and raised his hands back into guard. He was glaring at Norris when he finally returned his focus to the fight.

"So you ready, newbie?" Norris teased, holding his hands to his side.

Ryan clenched his fists and heard the leather creaking in between his fingers, holding them near the sides of his face.

"I'm sure."

"Good, but I still don't believe you."

Norris jumped forward again and Ryan wondered how the man would attack this time. After closing the gap, the jester tried to pummel Ryan with a series of crosses that he was able to dodge or parry easily. Norris then threw a left hook which sank into Ryan's ribcage, and those bones creaked in protest.

When Norris backed up a pace and launched his right leg into a devastating round kick aimed for his upper thigh, Ryan knew he was in trouble. He had seen the combination before in New Chicago and knew that he did *not* want to be hit.

Ryan forced himself through the pain and stepped into the strike, catching only a fraction of the blow. Not expecting it, Norris was caught off-guard when Ryan grabbed at his collar and threw a cross with his right hand. It wasn't enough to do any serious damage, but it was enough to shock Norris into reconsidering Ryan's abilities. They held each other in the clinch for a split-second before they pushed off each other and circled clockwise.

Norris was still smiling, even with his newly-developed fat lip.

"*Sure* will be good enough. C'mon then," he said before closing the distance with a proper stance.

Ryan threw a couple of jabs that Norris avoided and he was able to step out of the way of one of Norris' more complicated combinations. They were testing each other now, realizing each other's boundaries.

They traded blows, and for a time, neither side had a complete advantage. For every powerful hook Ryan delivered, Norris threw a few uppercuts. For every one of Ryan's kicks that caught empty air, Norris spent just as much energy attacking the spots where Ryan used to be. The force of their blows was doing little to stop the other person, but after every strike, each Crow used up more and more energy.

After a few minutes their movement became sluggish. Strikes that hit solid flesh were not nearly as strong as they could have been.

Very early on, Ryan's chest was heaving from the efforts and he was drenched in sweat. Even the training he had to go through after every resurrection was nothing to those five furious minutes with the Englishman.

Even so, that smile on Norris' face had not gone anywhere and made him look ever more the jester. Again, Ryan had to wonder if he was legitimately enjoying himself or whether it was some side effect of the rumored behavioral conditioning.

"You got... some fight in you, mate. We might have to do this... more often. Jess is always a good challenge, but we pugilists always need something... new." Norris paused between the words to gasp in air, and Ryan was grateful that the man sounded tired. "So do you want to end this?"

Ryan looked at Norris and lowered his fists slightly. He had not expected the sparring session to end so soon, as Norris and Abrams would usually fight each other for half an hour, at least. Even if he was exhausted, Ryan felt slightly offended Norris would offer the olive branch after only one round.

"It's a bit *early*, don't you think? Are you ready to call it quits?" Ryan asked with a smile. Despite his fatigue, he was actually enjoying himself, but he figured he'd leave it up to Norris, who replied with a weak laugh.

"Not at all, *Mr. Jenkins*. Just thought we'd speed this up and have a victor. We'll just go extra hard, eh?" He even winked at the end, and Ryan's heart sank as he understood the implication.

Norris had been going easy on him.

Ryan only had enough time to raise his hands before Norris rushed forward and unleashed a flurry of attacks. He seemed impossibly fast and even the strikes Ryan *could* block hurt like hell.

As Ryan tried to evade the incoming blows, he noticed that Norris had let the smile fall away. The friendly sniper's face was grim and without joy; he was focused entirely on damaging his opponent. That was when Ryan realized that the man really *could* kill him without caring. The empathy and good nature had disappeared from the man, and a killing machine was slamming his fists and legs into Ryan.

What little doubt he had about Norris' mental conditioning disappeared along with the man's empathy.

Ryan parried a strike from Norris' left arm and noticed the other one was coming from his right, so he ducked underneath the wild hook and jabbed quickly at the man's exposed ribcage. It was enough to distract and delay Norris, so Ryan took the opportunity to strafe around to the man's side and start whaling on his body. He slammed his fists into Norris' midsection twice before attempting to sweep his legs with a low round kick.

Unfortunately, he didn't notice until it was too late that he had let his guard down, that a left hook was coming over his shoulder.

Ryan staggered as the hit connected and he reeled from the blow. Darkness crept into his field of vision and although he tried, Ryan was unable to regain his balance and fell to his knees. He knew that he had to do something and looked around just in time to see Norris' fist swinging around from his right.

As he felt an explosion of pain in his nose, Ryan instantly knew it was broken.

Warm blood flowed from his nostrils and Ryan wondered if it would be an easy fix. Disoriented from the strike, Ryan looked back to where he had last seen Norris. He didn't find the man, but Ryan definitely felt his shin slamming against the side of his head.

Then the darkness swept in from the outer reaches of his vision and covered everything.

"SORRY, mate, kinda lost control there after you hit me. You okay?"

As he heard Norris speak, Ryan groaned as he tried to remember how he had gotten here. He had to blink a few times to shake the bleariness from his eyes, but then he realized Norris was hunkered down on his knees next to him. Ryan then noticed the pain coming from the center of his face and brought up his hand to feel the damage. He hovered over his nose for a while before mustering the courage to endure the pain such a small touch would bring.

Ryan somehow didn't touch it; his nose did not seem to be there. He let his hand drift to the left side of his face and instantly regretted it as the pain shocked him. It would have been difficult not to hold a grudge against Norris for this, and so he didn't even make the attempt. Ryan sat up and turned to face Norris, who had pursed his lips.

"I'm sorry, buddy boy. *Real* contrite. I got so into it that I forgot it was just a friendly sparring match." A desperate smile was on Norris' face, and Ryan glared at him briefly before he was distracted by the pain in his face.

There would be plenty of time to be angry later. For now, he had to get to the clinic.

"Neeb do see da docder." Ryan was going to get much more frustrated if this is how he would have to talk for the next half hour.

Back on Earth, he had been lucky enough to escape the practical initiation rite of breaking his nose. One fistfight on Eris and it was worse than he could have imagined.

"They're not going to do anything special just for something like this, rook," Norris replied, shaking his head. "We gotta fix this one, ourselves."

Ryan slowly turned his head back to face the soldier and made angry eye contact. The throbbing in his nose was not going to be enough to distract him *this* time.

"Wha do you *meen*?"

"I'm gonna have to... well, set it for you," Norris stated, biting his lip. At the claim, Ryan furrowed his brow and regretted it. There was too much connected tissue in that area, and it had set off another flash of pain.

"I cat see docder?" he asked, more than furious, at this point. Still, Norris shrugged and rubbed the back of his neck while looking at the floor.

"Thing is, they wouldn't do anything different than what I'm about to do. It's not exactly like it needs to heal right; you just need to stop bleeding until the next game. One hundred percent probability you're gonna get a new nose at some point, so why fix it, right? I'm *real* sorry about that. Truly," Norris said before he knelt down next to him.

Ryan started to hyperventilate—aggravating the tissue in the center of his face—but after a few moments he willed himself to breathe normally and looked at his compatriot.

"You wa me to do anyding?" he asked, deadpan even through his garbled speech, and Norris laughed awkwardly and motioned to Ryan's sparring glove.

"You might want to bite down on that, mate. It's gonna be a bit hard to deal with."

Without another thought, Ryan undid the strap around the glove and then slid it in between his teeth, making sure to avoid breathing through his nose. Norris put his hands close to the broken appendage and bit his lip.

"Don't hate me too much, now," he said before shoving Ryan's' nose back into place.

It was more painful than he had expected.

Ryan could feel his teeth meeting through the glove in his mouth and all he wanted was for the pain to stop reverberating throughout his skull. After a few moments of intense pain, it lessened until it was just a dull ache.

Once Ryan was brave enough, he reached up to touch his nose and found it in the right place, give or take a few millimeters. Tasting metal in his mouth, Ryan turned his head to look at his assailant-turned-field-doctor. Norris was scratching his head and looking at him with puppy dog eyes.

"Did I mention I was sorry?"

Ryan shook his head and looked at the ground painted red by his own blood, finding it curious that was all the carnage that had come from his agony. After a weary shrug, he turned back to his teammate and found he had no rage left. In another time, he might have wanted to kill the man, but it just didn't matter anymore.

Ryan had already experienced much worse. He would continue to experience much worse.

"I dink... I *think* I'll just stick with stargazing from now on, Ed," Ryan said, spitting blood at the ground.

Norris awkwardly laughed and stood up, feeling like he was free from any sort of guilt.

"That's *more* than fair, rook. I might have done the same back when I was a new recruit. But hey, if you ever want to trade blows again, just let me know," Norris said before launching into more shadow boxing antics.

Ryan thought about laughing, but did not want the pain to bounce around his skull again.

"*Sure.* I'll do that."

RYAN COULD NOT SLEEP with his head pounding like this. He had already spent an hour tossing and turning. Although he didn't want to put any pressure on his nose, he had never been able to sleep in any position other than on his side.

The breathing situation wasn't helping, either. Ryan had blown his nose earlier to get out the clot, but his nostrils had quickly become plugged with a mixture of mucus and blood. After two attempts, Ryan had given up trying to keep it clear and just let the whole area throb. Roberts had let him grab two of his pills and that was helping, but he could still feel the dull ache pulsing from the depths of his brain.

He sat up on his bed and turned to put his feet on the ground, feeling the cold tiles send shivers through his legs. While staring at the empty wall in front of him, he recalled his conversation with Feldman a week before. Ryan wondered if Feldman would ever allow himself to open up like that again, even if it wasn't to him. For the time being, one little expression of despair seemed to have ruined their friendship.

Ryan stood up and started to pace around the room, feeling like it was pointless to sit on his bed like that. After walking over to his desk, Ryan plopped down on his chair and considered writing something, but quickly realized that he had nothing to write and no one who would ever read it.

It would be a useless act, so he put it out of his mind.

Frustrated, Ryan walked over to the window and looked at the ruined expanse in front of him. The entire plain of steel wreckage, trash and dirt would have been swallowed up in darkness if not for the light bouncing around between the false moons. It was still strange—even after another month of living and dying—and once again, Ryan could see the original moon coming up over the horizon in front of him. Somehow, he had spent the entire night in pain without realizing it.

Ryan could see the shattered pieces floating around in front of the ruined sphere and wondered what would happen if just one of them lost its orbit and floated down to Earth. He wondered how the people would react if another shard of the rock fell down and destroyed a hundred square kilometers, just like so many places during the Moonfall. He then wondered what the residents of Old Chicago had felt as the massive pieces of rock descended on their city.

That thought let his mind drift to his old life in New Chicago.

He realized that he didn't miss it anymore. He had not for a long time—now that he thought about it—but he couldn't quite remember when that changed. Perhaps it had been when he had first died, but it all seemed to escape him. Figuring that point of time was too early for him to lose his connection to home, Ryan looked further on in his timeline. Once he started looking back through his wasted days on Eris, he searched for the point where he had stopped grieving his old life.

After a few minutes, Ryan couldn't find that point in time and that made him anxious. He could remember feeling certain emotions during and after different interactions, but his memories didn't evoke the same reaction that they did at the time. They didn't seem like his feelings or his memories, as if it all happened to someone else.

Then the young Crow realized that it *had*. He might have the memories, but this body was a stranger to all of those events that happened in those past lives. He might have had real recollection of the events, but they did not call to anything in him. Just like his habit of pinching the bridge of his nose or the scars that he had acquired on Earth, all the remnants of Ryan's old life had fallen away. That man was genetically identical, but Ryan didn't feel like he was really *there*. He had all of their memories, but lacked the ability to interpret them correctly.

He breathed out and thought about this new development, realizing that he had just *remembered* New Chicago, he had never *missed* it. The only one who would have missed it died back on Earth.

Ryan Jenkins had never *left* New Chicago. Ryan Jenkins was the one who had grown up on those dirty, dingy streets and had been sold out by his friends. Ryan Jenkins was the one who had agreed to pay back his debts to society by fighting in an endless game of war. Ryan Jenkins was the one who was going to miss his home town but had never had the chance to leave. Ryan Jenkins had died there in a medical center after they had mapped his genetic code and his brain.

Ryan Jenkins was in the ground.

The man in the moonlit room stared at his reflection in the window and Ryan Jenkins was looking right back at him. Nothing had changed. He still looked like the same person except for the broken nose. The man looking at the glass knew Ryan Jenkins backward and forward.

He just didn't know if he *was* Ryan Jenkins.

RYAN PONDERED his existence until the morning hours, and the only thing that brought him out of his daze was the blaring of the morning alarm. He realized he would need to eat even if most of the food would have the distinct flavor of blood; another gift from Norris breaking his nose. After throwing on his fatigues, Ryan headed to the mess hall.

He was greeted by the all-too-familiar sight of his comrades half-heartedly shoveling food into their mouths. Ryan's appetite had suffered with each death, and this identity crisis had eradicated what was left of it.

Even still, Ryan went through the motions and threw random food onto his tray. Afterward, he walked over to the benches and sat down where there weren't other Crows, as he didn't want to talk to anyone while he was trying to figure these things out.

Unfortunately for Ryan, it wasn't long before he was joined by Norris. Upon seeing him sit down, Norris had abandoned telling his stories to Sargasso and Chang—who didn't seem to notice—and had quickly moved his tray to the seat across from Ryan.

Although Norris seemed reticent to begin the conversation, Ryan could tell from his anxious squirming that he really wanted to say something, so he pushed his tray forward to give him a clear sign.

"Good morning, Ed. How are you?" Ryan asked, sarcasm drenching his words. Norris laughed awkwardly and then waved a finger to point around his face.

"*I'm* good. How's the nose?" His grin was too large for his face.

Though he wanted to be angry at his teammate, Ryan offered a half-hearted smile and sighed, feeling the pressure in his nose and making a mental note not to sigh again until he had a new body.

"It's wrecked, but don't feel bad about it. It's a temporary thing, after all."

With a nod, Norris grabbed a biscuit off his tray and started tearing at it before opening a package of jelly and plopping it onto the largest half.

"Maybe *not*-so-temporary. Did you see who you're paired with for today's match?" His voice went a little higher to go along with the leading question.

After his existential crisis last night, Ryan hadn't even considered looking at the pairings for the match. He lifted his head off his hand and started poking at his potatoes with a fork before shaking his head.

"I haven't gotten a chance. Anybody special?" he asked, but he already knew the answer. Guilt for a ruined nose wasn't enough cause for Norris to join him at the breakfast table.

"I should say *so*," Norris replied before laughing and popping the biscuit into his mouth. "You get to be my *spotter*, buddy boy. It's an easy job. You find 'em and I pop their heads off."

"If I remember correctly, you haven't been doing so well in the games lately, and neither have your spotters. I recall a few rockets and grenades blowing up around you," Ryan said apathetically, staring at his tray while passive-aggressively teasing his new partner as he lifted a spoonful of tepid yogurt.

To his credit, Norris only gaped for two seconds before laughing and placing the spoon in his mouth.

"You're a *cheeky* one. Explosion's not the worst way to go in these games, you know. It hurts like *hell*, but *only* a second before the force does that funny little thing where you splatter everywhere. Much better than bleeding out, I always say." Norris let hand holding his spoon fall to the table and gave Ryan an encouraging smile.

"*C'mon*, you should be *happy*! I'm not all sad and depressing like those blokes you always hang around. It'll be a nice breath of fresh air for you. Just... make sure you breathe through your mouth," Norris said before laughing and looking down at his tray.

By that time Ryan had stopped paying attention, and when Norris dived into some story of past battles, he did not hear him. He was more focused on his own experiences, or perhaps lack thereof. Whatever he was, Ryan could not rely on memories that might not have been his. He decided that as long as he felt it or he could taste or touch or see it, then it was part of his life.

However, when Ryan took the time to think about it, he realized that *also* made Norris part of his life. It was not *ideal*, but it was enough to lift Ryan out of the murk of his identity crisis. No matter the memories from his past lives, he could still identify the life in front of him. It was *his,* and he could experience that for himself.

Ryan looked around the room while Norris prattled on and saw that most of the Crows were dead quiet. None of them talked very much on game days; they usually kept to themselves and prepared for their dance with death. Some with dignity, some without.

Ryan watched Abrams eat her muffin with a quiet resolve before he panned around and saw Cortes just looking at his food. He never did eat that much food, but today, Ryan could see that Cortes was only pretending. Ryan wondered how long that had been going on, but then he was distracted by Warner and how he viciously cut into his breakfast meat with a desperate ferocity.

Continuing his scan of the room, Ryan saw Goldstein alone at his table, and he did not seem to have a care in the world. From all appearances, he had not died recently; Goldstein had a decent amount of hair, both on his head and his cheeks.

As he watched Goldstein take his time eating French toast, Ryan chewed absent-mindedly on whatever was in his mouth. It seemed like so long ago that he had fought and died with these people eating their breakfast, even if he had only been fighting for a month.

Ryan lost interest in Goldstein and turned to see Roberts sitting across from Templeton, finding the small Crow acting tough like always. If Ryan had not seen it for himself, he would never have believed that Roberts was living in constant pain.

For a moment, he wondered if Hawkins ever felt guilty about what he had done to Roberts and so many of the others, but he thought better of it. That lab-coated monster surely had other things on his mind than his soul. It was just another one of the plentiful tragedies on this war-torn rock.

Ryan was about to look back down at his tray and convince himself to eat, but he realized someone was staring back at him. This was not some vague glance or mistaken eye contact; the man's blue eyes were determined and pierced through Ryan's soul like he was room-temperature butter.

It would have been ludicrous to think Carver did not understand. Considering how similar they really were—considering how Ryan was practically a young version of the old legend—it would be a disservice to think otherwise.

As they all finished their breakfast and filed out of the mess hall, Ryan wondered how much the old Crow knew.

2

After-Life Crisis

After the impact with the ground, Jenkins stood up and looked around his surroundings. If not for the overly generic appearance of every landing zone, he would have sworn he had been on this patch of war-torn moon before. After hearing a thud and a rustling behind him, Jenkins walked over to the new arrival, who had landed gracefully and rolled out the rest of his momentum. Once he was standing, Norris patted down his armor and coughed.

"Always kicks up a storm, doesn't it?"

Jenkins knew an answer was not expected from him, so he didn't bother to provide one. He nodded east and shrugged.

"Easy way out of the landing zone is over there." Though Jenkins was obviously acting impatient, Norris laughed at the gruff behavior while he checked the condition of his rifle.

"Ah, but *where's* the fun in *that*? Sorry, wait a bit while I look this darling over. One time when I landed, I cracked the scope and didn't realize until we got in the thick of it. I'd rather know if I have to start using the iron sight," Norris said as he peered down the scope and smiled.

As cliché as it was, he loved this gun and all the ones like it.

Norris couldn't see anything wrong with this specimen, so he slung the rifle over his shoulder and grabbed his sidearm in order to defend himself if they found a Kraken or two. He walked up to Jenkins and—before the young Crow could react—threw an arm around his shoulders and tapped his chest plate with the barrel of his pistol. Jenkins did nothing to hold back his snarl as Norris spoke from too close.

"*Look*, you need to brighten up. We're gonna have *fun* today, just you wait. All you have to do is tell me where to point the finger of God, here, and if you want, you can throw away bullets like candy. It'll be a right old time." He nodded at the rifle on his back when referring to the *finger of God,* and Jenkins shrugged off his arm with a huff.

"Next time you throw your arms around me, you better have a drink," he said before walking to the pathway, unaware that Norris' antics were already improving his mood.

"*That's* the spirit, mate. And I've already drank a bit today—just so you know—so I guess that means I get to touch ya," Norris teased, winking at the end of the statement.

He knew Jenkins couldn't see it, but the joke just didn't feel right without it.

"I meant a drink for me, you dick. Never mind," Jenkins said as the path opened up to another ruined iron landscape, drawing a sigh out of him. There was a touch of pain in his nose at the mistake, but Roberts had given him another pill, so it was manageable. "So, basically, we're gonna walk around until you see a good spot to shoot at people's heads?"

After a grunt, Norris looked at him and waved his gun around with a flourish.

"*Well*, I figured we could watch some soaps and maybe go to the pub beforehand, but I *guess* we could do our jobs. And the spot's right over there," Norris said while pointing his pistol at a decrepit building off to the south. "How about we play house until the bad guys show up?"

Norris started off to the building—only half a kilometer away—and Jenkins was left to watch as his partner carried himself without a worry.

Understandably, it was a bit of a shock when Norris reached level ground and then skipped toward his destination. Floored by the man's cavalier behavior, Jenkins realized that if he did not follow, Norris was going to be killed by some Kraken that was taking this a little more seriously.

So Jenkins was left with no choice but to sprint after the man.

He reached Norris within a minute, since he was standing in the middle of the battlefield; he had stopped skipping once Jenkins had not joined him on his journey. It seemed impossible that Norris had *not* completely given away their position, but after a moment of frenzied scouting, Jenkins realized they were alone.

"What are you doing, rook? Stop acting so nervous. *That's* what's going to kill you," Norris said, nodding at his own wise remark.

Jenkins' eye twitched at the statement and he almost couldn't believe his partner's antics.

"And skipping's *not*? That was the most idiotic thing I've *ever seen!*" Jenkins half-shouted, trying not to make too much noise in case there was a Kraken hidden outside of view. Norris just laughed and shook his head.

"You *poor* boy. You really haven't lived. I suggest some skipping. It does the heart wonders. I am going to need you to stop stressing out, because *this*," he said before waving his hand to indicate their relationship, "needs to be more light-hearted."

"Norris, you could have skipped your way into enemy territory and gotten yourself killed. Do you not see the seriousness of that? You could have *died*," Jenkins emphasized, hoping to make his partner more responsible.

Instead, Norris stopped in his tracks and tapped on his shoulder.

"I'm *going* to die, mate. Maybe not today, maybe not in the next game—could be a long time considering how good I am—but I *am* going to die," he said, doing his best to relay his smile through his tone.

"And so are you!" he continued with a flourish. "It's something we just have to accept. And the thing is, mate, that I don't want to spend my entire life worrying about how and when I'm going to die next or what I could have done to prevent it. I'm just going to have fun with it. I'm going to skip when I feel like it. I'm going to shoot people's heads off when I'm good and ready. Now, tell me, rook, where's the flaw in that logic, hmm?"

Jenkins glared at him throughout the speech and wanted to interrupt a few times, but now that he was put to the question, he realized Norris was entirely right. The only way Jenkins was going to live through this life of his was if he accepted it for what it was. He was going to die and most likely never make it off Eris again, but this was his life. He had plenty of time to dwell on it, since *retirement* would be so far away.

After his realization, Jenkins looked at Norris and felt ashamed of chiding the man for his childish behavior. Once he saw the shame set in—even if it was just in his body language—Norris cocked his head and threw an arm around his young comrade.

"Aww, don't be like *that*. It's just a life lesson, rook. And, with all that said, it was incredibly foolish for me to skip through the battlefield," he said, nudging the bottom of Jenkins' helmet. "It was a little insensitive of me to do that, and I'm sorry. I could've died and left you all alone and I didn't consider that. I'm sorry for being selfish."

"No, you're not." Jenkins laughed, knowing the truth of it.

"I *am*! I am. Okay, not *entirely*, but I *am* sympathetic. Listen, no more skipping from me in this game, how about that? Now can you cheer up?" Norris asked before lifting his hands up in a light-hearted gesture. Though he scoffed, Jenkins' heart was lighter for all of Norris' nonsense.

"Yeah, I think I can do that."

Norris clapped his hands and grinned beneath his mask.

"*Excellent*, you wanna get some skipping in?" he teased, wishing his partner could see his face.

"You can go fuck yourself, Ed." Jenkins was unaware that a smile had crept across his face during the exchange. Norris laughed and patted the man's back again.

"*Already did*, mate, but don't worry," he said with a wave of his pistol. "Other hand."

"Gross," Jenkins said before continuing to the house and stifling laughter.

"Oh, you can't tell me you don't do it, too. It's healthy!" Norris exclaimed, and Jenkins shook his head in resignation. As they walked, Jenkins looked at the man walking alongside him and knew exactly why Abrams had chosen him.

Norris never let Eris get him down.

It wasn't long before they reached the dilapidated building. It clearly used to be at least three stories tall, but the third level had been torn off by the time it had been transported to Eris. The second floor had an exposed roof and plenty of tumbling walls around the side.

Even in its damaged state, the Commission had provided Norris the perfect sniper nest.

Norris ran over to the stairs and looked at the rotten wood—wondering if it would support his weight—and then shrugged. Getting upstairs was the goal, so Norris would need to take the chance. He gingerly placed his foot onto the wooden plank and could hear it creak, but it accepted his weight and the sniper smiled.

The entire staircase underwent the same scrutiny; he would only progress to the next step after testing whether or not it would tumble away. Eventually the sniper reached the top of the stairs and turned around to let Jenkins know it was safe, but was surprised to see his teammate right behind him.

"*Scared me*, there. Why didn't you wait until I'd tested the entire thing?" Norris asked, the shock too much for him to make a joke.

"If it could carry your lanky ass, I'm pretty sure *I* would be able to get up the thing. Besides, if one of the boards snapped, I wanted to be able to catch you when you fell," Jenkins said with a sarcastic note.

However horrible he had felt in the last night, it was nice to just goof off with this new friend. Norris appreciated the change in atmosphere and laughed heartily.

"Oh, *my hero*, how *ever* should I thank you?" he asked, adopting an impression of a southern belle. Jenkins laughed and pushed past him onto the second floor.

"Maybe you can introduce me to your hand."

Norris exploded into laughter and had to hold onto one of the support beams nearby.

"You're a *dirty* little fucker, aren't you? *This*," he said before waving his hand between them again, "will work. Okay, I'm gonna set up here on the north wall." After slinging his rifle back over his shoulder, Norris walked past him and then set about his task.

Jenkins smiled and wondered if he would ever have thought of that joke with anybody else. In the meantime, he watched his partner tweak the instruments on his rifle and settle himself into position. At first Norris went prone, but then it seemed like he was uncomfortable and decided he was better off hunching down on his ankles. Norris seemed to like that position, and then he sat down with his back to the wall behind him, eventually laying his rifle across his lap.

Then he surprised Jenkins by unclasping his helmet and setting it by his side. The sniper's red hair stood in stark contrast to the bleak browns and greys around them. Although Jenkins was curious as to why Norris would take off his helmet, he didn't say anything.

He didn't need to. Norris saw the man's tilted head and shrugged.

"It's harder to see through the scope like that. The other snipers always rely on the instruments and the relay to the helmet, but I hate switching back and forth like that. I'd rather just have the helmet off." As if they were pests, he waved away his peers' use of technology.

Jenkins walked over to the man and sat down against the support beam so he could look out through the walls around him but still be comfortable.

"Yeah, but isn't it going to be way easier for someone to pop your head off?"

For the obvious question, Norris gave him a disappointed look and shook his head.

"*Mate*, I thought we talked about this. I'm going to enjoy myself and the helmet is certainly no fun. Besides, I'm *way* too good for that," he said before winking again and betraying his excuse. While proud of his behavior, it was just this side of too vain for Norris to admit that he preferred jokes and stories to technical proficiency in combat.

Norris peeked around the wall opening by his side and scanned the horizon. When he did not see any activity and turned back to his compatriot, he noticed Jenkins was still looking through the holes in the walls nearby.

After an anxious moment, Jenkins shrugged and sank against the wall.

"So what now?" he asked, yawning and garbling his words as a result.

"Roast marshmallows. Other than that, we just check to see we're not getting surrounded, but that's pretty much the extent of it."

"Ah," Jenkins said, looking at the rifle in his hand. He wondered if he was even going to use it.

Then Jenkins realized that in the best of circumstances, he wouldn't have to.

"SO THE THING WAS, I had basically skipped out on all these rotten debts and was on the run for a little bit. I made it to Solaria and I was living as a cabana boy before the EOSF got to me. It was a sight, let me tell you," Norris said while laughing at the memory.

They had not been waiting long in their hovel before he had launched into a *very* revelatory story about his past. For Jenkins, it was no surprise, as it made sense that Norris would be the type to run out of a few casinos.

"I was this half-naked gangly ginger being led through the hotel by these fully armored EOSF officers while all these celebrities and rich people looked on in disgust. Fucking *Richard Masters* was there—that motherfucker—and believe you, me, they had the worst looks on their faces. This one codger gave me this look like he smelled a sewer rat, and he might have not deserved it, but I couldn't let that one stand, mate. I headbutted the ponce and I just laughed the whole way to the prisoner transport. I think I had blood all over my face for my mug shot.

"*Anyway*, long story very, *very* short, after I made a few friends on the inside they pulled some strings and I ended up here. I sometimes wonder if that old fucker had to get surgery..." Norris said before looking off into space. He grinned at the thought and shrugged. "That would have made it so much better."

Jenkins laughed at his story and shook his head—the man was certainly unbelievable—but then Norris gave him a look and nodded at him.

"What?"

"Don't you *what*, me. Time for your story, rook. Fair trade and all that jazz." Norris scratched his cheek, which was covered in patches of peach fuzz. Jenkins looked at him for a while, reticent to tell his story —especially since it might not be *his story* anymore—but Norris had just told him his tale. It would be an act of bad faith to let the jester remain ignorant.

Shifting in his seat, Jenkins rubbed his hand along his weapon as he tried to remember someone else's past.

"Not much to tell, really. I was in a gang. My friends gave me up to the EOSF and I took the easy way out." He told the short version, feeling somewhat detached. Norris gave him a moment to continue speaking, but then the sniper made his disappointment evident.

"You're a horrible storyteller, mate. It's *all* in the details. Remember that old man from my story? That's what made it a good one. I'm not even sure if it really happened anymore; I've just always had him in the story. He's part of it, now. You understand?"

Jenkins considered the point. Norris was right; the details were always what made a story good and Jenkins had never been the type to tell a good one. He shifted in his seat again and looked through the hole in the wall just in time to see a pair of enemy soldiers scrambling over wreckage a quarter of a kilometer away. He immediately sat forward and started to get into position.

"Contact! Behind you!"

"*Shit.* Shitting shit, I was just about to get you to talk," Norris muttered before turning to raise his rifle. He was far more concerned with Jenkins' past than the encroaching threat, since he did not have to spend his days with *them.*

After putting his eye to the rifle's scope, Norris watched as two

Krakens advanced on their position. The soldiers had no idea they were about to die, which earned the sniper's smile.

There was something beautiful in that ignorance.

Norris keyed in on the soldier in the background and centered the crosshairs just a dash to the right of the man's helmet. He compensated for the wind resistance and timing, and once he pulled the trigger, Norris felt recoil shudder through his entire frame. Through the scope, he watched as blood spray from the wound arced over the ground.

For a second, the Kraken in front just looked around in a panic and Norris could tell that the poor man had no idea that his friend was already dying. Norris had already centered the crosshairs for the next shot when Jenkins whispered across the room.

"There's a couple over here, too!"

Jenkins had not known what to do with himself when Norris had started his hunt. For a while he had stood there and watched, but he felt awkward the entire time. Before Norris had planted a bullet through the first Kraken's head, Jenkins decided he could at least be the spotter his sniper needed.

Jenkins had crept around the second floor and looked at each avenue of approach. It wasn't until he got to the opposite wall that he noticed there was another pair of enemy soldiers walking toward them from the other direction. From what Jenkins could tell, the Krakens must have been trying to rendezvous at a good landmark, and this house was as good as any.

After the gunshot from the sniper rifle echoed through the clearing, Jenkins noticed that his Krakens had brought up their weapons. That was when he desperately whispered at his compatriot, hoping Norris would finish his business on the other side quickly.

Meanwhile, the sniper was busy trying to hit a running target. After the small distraction, Norris had turned back to aim at the Kraken and found the soldier trying to get to suitable cover.

At least he's not an idiot, Norris thought before trying to lead the man with his aim. The bullet would be fast as hell, but his trigger finger would not, so he had to compensate a small amount.

Taking his time, Norris centered his aim before squeezing his finger and feeling the recoil shudder through his body again. One last glance through the scope was enough for him to see the Kraken holding his neck on the ground. Appreciating his good work, Norris smiled and picked up his rifle.

"Better than a massage," he said before rushing over to Jenkins'. He liked his partner—even if he was a mite too serious—but as he saw Jenkins lifting his rifle, Norris shook his head. There was no way he could trust Jenkins to hit anything past fifty meters.

Norris was almost over to the wall when he heard a creak and felt the floor give way beneath his foot. He tried to catch himself on the ground, but the floorboard caught on something else and his ankle landed on it all wrong.

After feeling the snap of bone and sinew, the pain ripped through his leg soon after that.

"Fuck *me*! Bloody *Hell*! Fu—" he shouted before trying to hold his tongue. Prior to the break, he had been trying to keep their whereabouts unknown. Now that a clandestine operation was a distant prospect, all he could focus on was the pain coursing through his leg.

Jenkins rushed over to his partner as soon as he could. After throwing his arms underneath Norris' armpits, he did what he could to drag his compatriot out of the hole.

However, without knowing it, Jenkins forced Norris through indescribable pain as his ankle bumped up against a number of boards on its way out of the hole.

His face was twisted in agony as he lay on his side, and Norris couldn't hear a word of what Jenkins was saying until shock had set in.

"What's going on? What's wrong?" Jenkins' words formed out of the haze, forcing Norris to bite his cheek so he could focus on his companion. He would deal with the pain later, but for now, Norris grabbed the sniper rifle with one hand and thrust it at the boy in grim determination.

"Ankle. Can't move right now. You blow their heads off for me, why don't ya?" The pain was getting to be too much and Norris couldn't help but wince as he spoke.

Though he grabbed hold of the weapon, Jenkins shook his head and held the rifle like it was some sort of relic.

"I've never *trained* for it. I don't know how to use it…"

"It's a fucking *gun*! Point it at people and shoot them. There's a trigger that you have to squeeze, you bloody wanker…"

"Yeah, but—"

"Sweet Lord *Jesus*, are you *fucking* with me? Just use the vid jack and the digital *goddamn* overlay. It does all the work *for* you, so get to it! Those Krakens are probably running over here, this second," Norris shouted before looking down at his ankle. It was bent at a totally wrong angle and he slammed the ground with his fist at his foolishness. It was such a stupid thing to happen.

No one had even killed him, this time.

Since his partner was out of commission, Jenkins carried the rifle over to the wall and set it up against a pile of rubble next to a caved-in section of the wall. After finding the vid jack near the scope, he pulled it out of the rifle before plugging the cord into the auxiliary port on his helmet. At once, he could see the vast expanse beyond the house. Numbers of calculated distance, trajectories and wind currents were displayed on his display, as well.

Once he let out a breath heavy with anxiety, Jenkins lay flat and readied the rifle before looking for the Krakens. They were running from one piece of cover to the next, and that only made Jenkins more and more anxious as time went on. He had never had to use the sniper rifle before, and this was definitely not the place to learn.

He centered his aim over one of the running Krakens, paying close attention to the advice coming through his display as he pulled the trigger. The recoil was almost enough to make the rifle jump out of his hands, but he held it down and tried to readjust his aim for his next shot.

Jenkins looked for the man he had just tried to shoot and was relieved by what he saw. It was no headshot, but the man had been shot through a gap in the armor by the shoulder and had been spun around by the impact. The Kraken was just lying on the ground and writhing in pain. For now, he was of no concern.

Considering that Kraken out of the fight, Jenkins looked around for their partner and was immediately filled with dread. Not only was this Kraken within twenty meters, but they had been watching when Jenkins had fired the last shot. Jenkins only just happened to notice the muzzle flare of the Kraken's rifle before he instinctively tried to become part of the floor.

After a panicked moment, Jenkins brought his head back up and looked through the scope. He was confused as he realized that there was no enemy in view, but he knew the Kraken had to be *somewhere.*

Jenkins was still looking around the battlefield when he saw the grenade sail past him and Norris, landing in the opposite corner of the room. Exploding louder than he thought possible, the grenade fragmented into a hundred pieces and Jenkins curled in on himself to make himself a smaller target.

Somehow, the fragments did not pierce through his armor, and Jenkins eventually returned to looking through the scope.

He noticed far too late that he could hear his opponent's footsteps echoing through the stairwell. This man was not gingerly approaching like the Crows had before the fight; he was bounding up each step.

Still confused by the explosion and the split overlay of the sniper rifle, Jenkins was caught flat-footed and without an effective weapon when the Kraken rounded the top of the stairs and trained a rifle on him.

Jenkins was dead to rights and he knew it.

Luckily, the Kraken hadn't noticed Norris lying there with his broken ankle—having somehow avoided most of the shrapnel from the grenade—and was entirely surprised when the Crow unloaded half of his pistol clip into the soldier's helmet. The wall behind the Kraken became a gory mess and Norris smiled weakly as the corpse fell back down the stairs, and Jenkins watched as his wounded partner tried to sit up with difficulty.

He's a monster, but at least he's on my team, Jenkins thought.

As he walked over to his partner, he yanked out the vid cable from his helmet and then laid down the rifle near Norris. He offered an appreciative smile at the gesture, but then he slapped Jenkins in the helmet and shoulders as he jumped away.

"You are a fuckin' *idiot*! *I don't know how to use it*," Norris said, launching into an exaggerated imitation of Jenkins' apparent idiocy. "You almost *died* there because you couldn't shoot a weapon right. You're *lucky* I can compartmentalize this shite."

Accepting the blame, Jenkins hunkered down on his ankles and bit his lip.

"How bad is it?"

"I'll put it this way. If Roberts gave you some extra pills, you better give 'em to me," Norris said with a sigh. After killing those four Krakens, they should probably change position, but Norris was not going to be easily moved. It seemed Norris was still coming to grips with all the difficulties they now faced.

"Should we try to set it?"

"No reason to. It'd just hurt like the devil come early and they'd still inject me with their fancy drugs. Just help me get over to that wall," Norris said while pointing at his old position. Knowing what he had to do, Jenkins realized there was no dignified way to get the man across the room.

Jenkins put his arm under the man's legs and the other behind his back and lifted. Norris was heavy, but the suit helped with that part, at least. Although Norris winced at the movement—feeling the weight of his foot pulling at his broken ankle—he did not object.

"*My hero*. Guess I'll have to introduce you to my hand," Norris teased once more, though his voice was weak and the fight had left him.

Jenkins forced a laugh as he walked over to the north wall.

"You can keep her. I'm sure she'll console you," he said before placing Norris near an opening in the north wall. He laughed and motioned toward his rifle, hoping Jenkins would get the hint. Despite what had just happened, the sniper was still trying to smile.

"That she will," he said under his breath, watching Jenkins walk over to the weapon and retrieve it for him. After giving the rifle back to its owner, Jenkins backed off to the support beam. He watched Norris set the finger of God across his lap once more.

"So I guess it's back to story time," Norris suggested as he slid back up against the wall, trying to find some comfort even as pain ran rampant through his leg.

The fall had probably done more than break just his ankle.

"Shouldn't we try to get out of here?" Jenkins asked. Their position had been compromised—just like in the match against the Lions—and there would be another wave of soldiers, soon enough.

They would not be so lucky a second time, but Norris waved it at all away.

"No way I'm going anywhere. I can't even cross the room. I'll just stay here and when they arrive, I'll knock off a few heads. Could be much worse. Anyway—like I said—give me your story again, but do a better job."

Seeing his resolve, Jenkins sighed and felt the pain from his broken nose again. He didn't know what to tell the man.

"It's really just what I've told you, Ed."

"Look, mate, I got plenty of time to kill until those tentacled devils come for me. Just let me know about all the things that lead up to when I saw your bright and shining face in the barracks. But—you know—*details* this time," Norris insisted, and Jenkins knew he wasn't going to budge.

Preparing himself, Jenkins leaned back against the support beam and breathed out.

"I was smuggling some tech—a shipment of megaprocessors—with a couple guys from my gang. Tommy and Jack were their names, and I had known those bastards for six years. We came up through the gang together. It was just supposed to be these computer parts, but the security was pretty hefty for that. Almost didn't go in, actually, and—well, now I kinda wish I hadn't.

"After we distracted the bigger guys and knocked out the little ones, the three of us were off with boxes of processors under our arms. Then, well, things went to shit. The guys who were supposed to pick us up got held up or something, I never got the story from them or at the trial. Cops showed up and threw all three of us in jail."

Jenkins laughed in desperation before starting again.

"I didn't even get a chance to make a deal or anything. My so-called *friends* left me high and dry and I took the blame for the whole thing. I got into the system and the judge was lenient on me because he knew I was just a street kid who dropped out as soon as I was legal. So he offered me the deal to come here, and... I took it. Because I was a dumbass. Shoulda known that Demeter was going to be the better option."

After his story, Jenkins looked at the floorboard and thought about the memories he had just described. They seemed so distant. He didn't regret any of it, because he didn't feel like *he* did it.

The only thing that brought him out of his thoughts was a grunt from Norris.

"Mate, you've either had the most boring life I've ever heard or you're leaving something out."

"There really *is* nothing else. I spent most of my life trying to get money and respect from people who didn't give two shits about me. My life was basically over before I could get it started. Now... it just feels like it didn't even happen to me," Jenkins trailed off, and his partner sighed and looked beyond the wall of the building.

"I can... sympathize with that, I guess. Still, not very entertaining," Norris muttered, reliving his own memories. Jenkins looked at him and knew he wanted to ask something before the Krakens came down on them. He just needed to know.

"Norris, you don't seem like you're all that different from your stories," he began, and Norris laughed at the statement.

"That's because I haven't really changed, mate. Best ones never do."

"They say that you used to be quiet, that you used to be kind and sweet when you first got here," Jenkins continued, knowing he was stepping on some toes. Norris narrowed his gaze and sat back against the wall.

"They say things, don't they? What's it matter to you?"

Jenkins shifted in his seat and realized he just had to blurt it out. It wasn't going to come naturally.

"They say the scientists changed you. They say that they turned you into a monster." Jenkins desperately wanted to throw the words back into his mouth, but he knew that he had tied his hands now, which was the point.

Instead of raging against him, Norris leaned forward and brought his hand to his chin.

"That certainly is a lot to say. Let me ask you, if they did modify my brain or behavior or... *whatever*, why wouldn't they take away my memories or just turn me into a different man? Why would I be able to tell you anything with confidence, eh? Did you think about that before you asked these questions of yours?" he asked, bringing down his hand before waving away the investigation.

Jenkins felt ashamed and was about to speak, but then Norris continued.

"The whole thing is bullshit, Ryan. I've *always* been like this. And not a bloodthirsty sort, that's not what I'm talking about. I'll *admit*, I had a fair amount of depression when I first got here. I tried to make friends by being nice and a whole other load of nonsense. But then I realized that even in this prison of ours, I can still grab hold of my life and make it the best I can.

"It comes back to what I said earlier. I'm going to do what I'm going to do, and I'm going to try to have fun with it. And really, when you turn off the part of your brain that says it's immoral to kill and whatnot, it definitely makes it easier. I accept my role, but that doesn't make me a monster, and I don't appreciate all those rumors about my *behavior modification*. I kill people who get right back up in a few hours, and morality doesn't ever enter the equation. Simply put, I'm allowed to enjoy what I am allowed to have."

Jenkins listened, but he wondered why he had brought it up in the first place. Throughout the entire match, Norris had been doing his best to cheer him up and had done an exceptionally good job. Jenkins realized how foolish he had been to think he was a victim of some conspiracy. This man had just accepted his fate.

After that revelation, Jenkins couldn't bring himself to look him in the eye.

"Now *don't* you get pouty on me, princess," Norris interrupted his guilty thoughts. "I know that rumor is floating around and I guess it's natural for you to ask about it. But no more of it, you hear? And if someone ever talks about it around you, just let 'em know that I'm all me. I'm the original Edward Norris. Nothin' fake behind this smile of mine, get me?"

Jenkins looked at the grinning man and wondered if he could ever bring himself to be like him, to accept this world and live bright in its shadow. Whatever horrible things Norris had done on this planet, it really was no worse than anybody else. There really was no harm in the occasional joke or smile.

"Well, look, the fuckin' squids are already here," Norris muttered, immediately earning his attention. Jenkins looked back up to see him peeking out behind the wall of the building and noticed there were three men from the other team approaching their position.

Bringing up his weapon, Jenkins wondered if he should take pot shots at them, but he heard a soft click before he could decide.

"Time for you to get going, buddy boy."

Jenkins looked down to see his partner giving him a half-hearted smile. He was also aiming his sidearm at Jenkins' midsection, which made it painfully obvious what he meant.

Shaking his head, Jenkins couldn't comprehend the man's reasoning.

"I'm not going to leave you to *die here*. I'm *not* going to be that asshole," Jenkins argued with a newfound determination. Norris just laughed and raised an eyebrow.

"You're not going to *be* that asshole. I'm pointing a gun at you and telling you to leave. And don't push it, because I don't mind shooting you somewhere unimportant. What you don't see is there's another two heading in from the south. I can't shoot that way, and, well, we'll just leave it at that.

"I'm going to stay here, draw them in and then use these fancy grenades on my belt to blow us all to hell. I'm going to enjoy it, and you're going to be half a kilometer away when it happens," Norris explained, wearing a forced smile on his face.

With determination, Jenkins shook his head again and stood to his full height. He didn't believe Norris would shoot him like this, not if he was trying to save his life.

"No, Ed. It's not like I have anything to live for out there. I'm going to stay here and fight."

"*No*, mate, you're not. You don't get where I'm coming from. I can accept that I'm going to die along with these ink-spitters, but I'm not going to let you throw yourself into a meat-thresher just because it's the *right thing to do*. That's *not* how you play this game. There are no heroics or selfless deeds. There's life and what you do with it. You have no reason to die here with me, and I'd prefer if you didn't. I'll see *you* tomorrow."

Jenkins looked down at Norris in frustration. He wanted to do something for the doomed man, but knew that every word was true. There was no point in dying with the sniper; it would just be a needless resurrection when he had the option of getting away. Jenkins huffed and stood there for a second, even though he knew he had to leave.

Seeing the result of his internal struggle, Norris sighed.

"You know what they say about freedom, mate?" he asked, the question sounding familiar. Jenkins just looked at Norris and shrugged, knowing the man already had an answer in mind. After waiting a moment, Norris looked him in the eye.

"It's choosing your way to die. Go on, then. They're almost here," Norris said, his voice almost a whisper, before turning onto his belly and taking aim with his rifle.

Jenkins didn't wait for him to shoot his rifle and instead ran down the steps, over the Kraken's body and out of the east exit of the broken building. As he broke into a sprint, he could hear Norris start shooting at the encroaching Krakens. Although he could hear returning gunfire from the other team, he knew they would not hit Norris.

He wouldn't let something like a potshot do him in.

The explosion from Norris' grenades ripped through Jenkins' senses and hurt his eardrums before he had made the half-kilometer, and a wave of hot air crashed against his back. Knowing he was safe, he turned to see the massive blaze devouring the top of the building and wondered *just what kind* of munitions Norris had been hiding.

There was no way that was standard equipment.

Jenkins was still looking at the flames when he realized he wasn't feeling anything about Norris' sacrifice. Tomorrow, he would be greeted yet again by that big smile full of awful teeth. In a few days, Norris would throw a few punches his way in the training yard. Jenkins realized that none of it mattered; none of the death, none of the pain Norris had just experienced.

But he knew Edward Norris would have wanted it that way.

CARVER COULDN'T GET his mind off what he saw in Ryan that morning. He had seen it before in soldiers who had committed suicide; he had seen it in Washington. If nothing else, Carver didn't want that to happen with Ryan.

It echoed too close to home.

The old man sank a few rounds into the back of the retreating Kraken and made sure the enemy had been accounted for. The Krakens were not the best team, but a stray bullet would kill just as easily as a determined one. With the season coming to a close, some of the *athletes* fought harder, although Carver had never seen that phenomenon in any of his Crows.

Making things worse, Cortes and Feldman were dead nearby. Feldman had been paired with Templeton, but the inexperienced Crow had been killed by a pair of Krakens that had flanked around the giant.

After Feldman made his way to Carver and Cortes, the three of them had done well until this last altercation. Cortes had been too distracted having a conversation with himself to notice the bullet that ended up in his brain. Feldman had been slaughtered before he could reach the enemy. After the smoke had cleared, Carver had been alone in this clearing.

He never intended it, but he always seemed to be the last man standing.

Carver walked to the Kraken he had just killed and sank another round into the man's back, leaving no chance for a dying man's retribution. After kicking over his body, Carver inspected the Kraken. It was just another cookie-cutter action figure lying there in the dirt and metal, a white squid on a blue background painted on his shoulder. When he looked at his dead opponent, Carver wondered what it would be like to exist outside of this constant warfare.

He didn't remember his life before it; he didn't know life without it.

Carver didn't think this was an annihilation match, but if it was, the Crows were well on their way to losing it. He had only heard of problems from the others over Comms, and now the beacons were mostly gone. He thought about joining up with Abrams and Warner to the north, since they seemed to be one of the few pairs still intact, and he was about to move on when he heard a crackle over Comms.

"This is Jenkins. I'm running to your position with two contacts on my heels. I need help."

His voice had been interrupted by desperate breaths, and without needing to think, Carver broke into a running start toward Jenkins' approaching beacon. After a quick scan for Norris' missing beacon, Carver knew Jenkins was alone.

That was the last thing he wanted.

IT HAD BEEN a long time since Jenkins had to run this hard. For some reason, he had thought he was safe after Norris' sacrifice, but he should have known better. Only in ideal circumstances would an explosion like that take out five enemy soldiers.

Jenkins had languished in that spot too long and before he could fully understand, two of the Krakens were running at him with their weapons drawn. Luckily, his instincts had kicked in and he had started sprinting toward the closest ally. He was grateful it was Carver's beacon.

The first thirty seconds were tense as the bullets flew past him, but now that the enemy soldiers had to run to keep up, the gunfire had stopped. Jenkins knew that if he slowed down, he would die. If he turned to fight, he would die.

The only option was to keep running.

He was halfway to Carver when the cramps started. It didn't help that his entire head felt muddy and heavy from all of the clotting from his broken nose. The pain was crippling, but he knew he had to suffer through it.

The Krakens behind him would have no mercy just because he was a little winded.

Pushing the pain from his mind, Jenkins tried to remember that none of those nerves mattered and that it was just his body telling him that it had had enough. He was the boss of it; his body would have to listen to him and keep running. Pain was just something that he would have to endure, for now.

The more he thought about it, the more Jenkins realized that he did not *want* to ignore it. While it was certainly not pleasurable, he recognized that pain as one of the few things that was entirely *his*. This was his experience; it was not a memory from a past life or some vitals meter from a lab. This pain and cramp in his side, this pressure in his brain and the ache in his muscles were all things that were unique to him.

Jenkins chose to embrace the agony that was pulsating through his body, and once he stopped trying to deny it, the experience flooded his perceptions. Suddenly, it was no longer something endurable; it was an avalanche of sensory information. The dull aches and pains from his resurrections—the ones that he had convinced himself weren't all that bad—were now slamming into him with full force.

However, he decided that it was the right thing to do. Jenkins wasn't going to deny any part of his existence now.

He accepted it all.

Although he did not regret letting himself feel that pain, he did regret the timing. Ryan still had two hundred meters to go before reaching Carver's beacon, and each step was now torture. Each intake of breath felt like he was breathing in fire and he gasped with each stride. For a prolonged moment, Ryan started to black out on his feet, but he was able to gather his wits about him and keep running.

He was rounding past a pile of concrete and rebar when he heard Carver's voice over Comms.

"Kid, just get to me and take cover. I'll take care of them."

Jenkins didn't bother with a response. In any case, he didn't have the breath to speak, and Carver probably had the best idea of how to take care of the Krakens on his heels. The old man had been at it long enough.

The pain was screaming around him as he rounded another corner and saw the old Crow training his rifle over an ancient transport. If Carver's beacon had not been overhead, Ryan would have never noticed him. To his advantage, Carver was hiding in plain sight in like-colored surroundings and had hidden the red crow on his shoulder beneath some muck.

Even then, Jenkins heard the soldiers behind him and could tell they were gaining. His decision to embrace the pain had cost him his speed.

He was still sprinting toward the veteran when he saw the muzzle flare from Carver's weapon. Once he felt the air whip around him, Ryan was grateful when he heard a half-hearted groan from one of the Krakens. Without having to look, he knew Carver had shot the man in the head. The old man always took his time and chose his shots accordingly.

Jenkins heard the Kraken behind him skidding on the ground as he tried to stop. Although he was trying to back out of the trap, it was already too late, as Carver had taken aim at the weak point in the armor at the knee and pulled the trigger. The Kraken wasn't going to walk again in this lifetime.

Decreasing his speed, Jenkins was about to jog to the veteran when he saw Carver jump off the car toward the fallen Kraken.

"Keep going, kid! He ain't dead yet," he shouted as he ran past, and Jenkins obeyed without question. After he slipped behind cover, he peeked back to watch his mentor approach the writhing soldier. The

Kraken scrambled for his sidearm when he noticed Carver's arrival, but the old man had already started firing.

Blood erupted from the wounds and let out a fine red mist, but then silence fell. Carver stood over the man for a time with his gun still drawn, ready to fire again at a moment's notice.

Laughing in between breaths—even though he knew it was inappropriate—Jenkins realized that War World Entertainment had sold versions of little green army men modeled after Carver in that exact same pose.

When he was done, Carver let the rifle fall to his side and scanned the horizon, ready for any possible attack. Although he didn't see any more approaching soldiers, he was nervous about turning his back to the field. He never knew where the next bullet would come from.

Once he felt secure, Carver walked back to his young teammate, who was still heaving air in and out of his lungs. As he knelt down, Ryan unclasped his helmet and threw it away, revealing a beet-red face. Carver could see the boy's chest quaking from the effort of breathing and knew that something else was going on. This was *not* just exertion.

"Couldn't... breathe... in that..." he said between rounds of gasps. Carver's brow furrowed as he tried to assess Ryan's problem.

It seemed like he had a new one every day.

"What else? That's not just being out of breath there," Carver stated.

Unable to form the sentences in his mind, Ryan swallowed hard unintentionally and gasped for air again. After a few minutes, Ryan started to breathe somewhat normally, or at least enough that he could speak.

"I started... thinking about the pain. From this..." He paused so he could point at his ruined nose. "And from the resurrections and the running. Everything. Then it... all came back. It hit me hard. It felt like torture."

Ryan looked noticeably confused, but Carver knew what had gone wrong. He could tell that the mental recall wasn't exactly intentional.

"Well... *don't do that*. Do you remember your first resurrection?" Carver asked. "It was Hell, right? The bodies don't get better. We don't get better with them, either. Our brains just trick us into getting used to it. We always hurt like that. It's just that the more we deal with it, the more we convince ourselves it doesn't really hurt. You just fucked it up by thinking about it."

"I guess that's the lesson, then," Ryan said before looking off into the distance. Carver knew there was something else, but he didn't know what he was looking for, so he let it go.

The kid would speak when he was ready.

They sat there for a while as Carver tried to figure out what they were going to do. There were more Krakens out there, for certain, but the old man didn't want to meet them. He was done with death for the day and he could tell his young friend was in the same boat. They would not move unless Ryan changed his mind; they could just stay there for the rest of the game. Carver would allow him that privilege.

It wasn't long after he made that decision that it became obsolete. Carver heard the klaxon blare from within his helmet and watched text roll through his visor display.

"Round over. The Krakens win. Repeat, the Krakens win. Make your way to your respective rendezvous points and return to your base."

Carver sighed at the message, looked at the boy in front of him and saw the despair flickering behind his eyes. Ryan would speak soon. He knew it in his bones.

Instead of prying, Carver rose to his feet and scanned the horizon for the rendezvous point, which was half a kilometer off to the north.

At least it's not too far, he thought.

"It's off that way," Carver said as he nodded toward the landing zone.

Although Ryan shrugged and picked himself up with difficulty, eventually he started to walk. Carver grunted to get his attention, and pointed his rifle at Ryan's discarded helmet.

"I don't want to wear that right now."

"At *least* pick it up. They're gonna charge you for it if you don't bring it back."

Although Ryan let out a disgusted sigh, he eventually stooped down and picked up the equipment. Carver watched as he turned toward the landing zone and walked off, clearly distressed by his place in the world.

Ryan would speak soon, but Carver was terrified of what he might say.

RYAN COULD STILL FEEL echoes of the pain he had experienced in his escape from the Krakens, but they were much more manageable after their break. He ambled toward the landing zone for a while before he realized that without the helmet, he had no idea where it was. Holding his rifle in one hand and his helmet in the other, Ryan let Carver take the lead and meandered behind.

As they walked, Ryan was only somewhat paying attention to the landscape in front of him. Although he had lived through the game, it didn't feel like a victory. Norris had died and it had meant nothing. All of those Krakens had died for no reason, really.

There just didn't seem to be a point to it all.

They walked along the path for a few minutes before Ryan broke out of his daze. He didn't notice how familiar it all was until he looked around. That same feeling from the landing zone permeated through him—like he had seen this place before—but he argued it away. The whole planet looked the same. Eris was all twisted metal and trash and broken buildings covered in parachutes and corpses. Yet this patch of ruined asteroid seemed to call back to an earlier time.

Now that he had noticed, it became difficult to push the thought away.

Ryan noticed the body as they were nearing the box-shaped transport. He could see what remained of his teammates piling into the loading bay, but only in his periphery. For some reason, the dust-covered corpse in front of him was drawing his interest.

Face up and hands placed on its stomach, it was as if someone actually had the decency to lay it to rest.

Though Ryan could not turn away from the eerily-familiar sight,

Carver soldiered on. Since he had seen countless corpses like that, Carver passed by the dead body without a second glance. It didn't matter if the bullets had stopped flying. He didn't have the time or energy to waste on honoring each dead body.

Ryan walked up to the corpse in a daze. It had been there for weeks —dust and grime covered every inch of the thing—and it was impossible to see the original colors of the armor like that. Ryan knelt down and put his hand on the body's shoulder, wiping away the dirt only to find a red crow emblazoned across the upper arm.

This used to be one of them.

Suddenly, the world disappeared around him. The transport did not exist. Jonathon Carver was a distant memory. The only thing that mattered was the dead body in front of him.

Ryan looked the corpse over again and wondered who was inside. There were no nametags or other physical clues. The digital beacons were all they had to tell each other apart, and they were deactivated on death. The only way Ryan was going to figure it out was to take off the helmet. Although he knew that the Crow inside would not look anything like it did when it was alive, he had to know who it had been.

He reached his hand to the soldier's neck and flicked at the clasps to the helmet. It took some force since it had been closed for so long, but eventually they relented. Taking hold of the helmet, Ryan breathed in deep, feeling anxious for some unknown reason. Whoever this had been had already been resurrected; Ryan had probably talked to him.

However, he couldn't shake the feeling that this one was special.

When Ryan lifted the helmet, he found the man's head to be a little worse-for-wear, but it was still completely recognizable. It had been untouched by the fight itself, and the helmet had kept the soldier's head in decent condition.

Ryan looked down at the man's face and knew it was his own. When he reached out, it was soft and mushy to the touch. At the same time, he lifted his left hand to his own face and felt the rigid bones and elastic skin. They were not so different. He felt at the man's lips and looked at the corpse's teeth. He ran his tongue around his own teeth and knew they were the same. He felt the man's nose. *It* was the same as it had always been, but when he reached to touch his own nose, it was different.

His nose was broken and still hurt to the touch.

With that one jarring pain, he realized that they were different people. This was not Ryan in the past; this was someone else. This corpse had the exact same DNA and memories, looked *exactly* like him, but it was a dead man on the ground. Ryan was *alive*.

He was still breathing—even if every breath was painful—but when he looked at the body, he could not reconcile the differences. This man may have looked like him when he was alive, but he was not the same Ryan Jenkins. The man standing there was Ryan Jenkins; that man lying on the ground was not.

That was when it hit him. That corpse had been more *Ryan Jenkins* than he was right *now*. That man lying dead on the ground was the first one on the planet. It may not have been the *first* Jenkins, but he was so much closer to the original. The man who was looking at his corpse was not the real Jenkins. *He* was the copy. *He* was the clone.

Having abandoned his grip on an identity, the young Crow realized he held this Ryan's memories inside him just like all the other iterations. Following that thought, he realized that he was not just the copy of one man. He was the replication of five separate men. They were all genetically identical, of course, and they had the same personality, but they were different men.

The man called Ryan Jenkins realized that he—that *he*—had only been alive for two days. *He* had not lived twenty-four years on Earth. *He* had not been on Eris for almost two months. *He* was just a clone with another man's memories. When he died, he wasn't going to get a new nose. He wasn't going to be able to sleep better and fight with Norris in the training yard, taking turns with Abrams.

He was going to die, and another young Crow would rise in his place.

It was too much for him to handle, his entire existence falling down around him as he stood over the corpse of that first clone. He was having difficulty standing and his eyes were wide. He was holding the side of his head and everything was spinning.

In technical terms, he was just a newborn.

And he was going to *die*. He wasn't going to get off planet. Even if the entity known as *Ryan Jenkins* could somehow muster up enough funds to get off the damned moon, this clone would not. *This* man—who had only been alive for two *days*—was going to die. It was enough to shock tears out of his eyes.

Carver was almost to the transport when he realized there were no footsteps behind him. Turning to see what was the matter, he watched Ryan lean over the dead body and wondered what the boy was thinking. He continued to watch things unfold, and he knew something was wrong once Ryan backed away from the corpse.

He had started by walking, but a few paces later he realized the urgency and broke into a light jog. After a few moments of that, he broke into a mad sprint. Something was definitely wrong here. Ryan had been on Eris long enough to see a dead body.

This was a special occasion.

Ryan was still holding his head when Carver arrived. It only took a second, but Carver soon realized what his young friend had seen. His heart filled with dread as he took in the sight of the abandoned corpse of Ryan's first clone.

"Oh, no. *Ryan*, look at me," Carver pleaded, holding out his hands in surrender. Whatever crisis Ryan had been going through was nothing if not multiplied by this new event. This was something that no soldier was ever meant to see. "Ryan, *look at me*."

The young Crow looked over at Carver, but still held his hand near the side of his head. He needed the support that the physical contact gave him, and he dropped the rifle in his other hand. Seeing that behavior, Carver unclasped his helmet and threw it away. He wasn't going to talk the boy down with that mask between them.

"Ryan, *listen. That's* not you. That's just a corpse. *You* are you. This doesn't make you any less of a person. That's just the game. You can just forget about that clone. You can get *through* this."

Carver didn't want the boy to fall apart like this, not like Washington. After his speech, Ryan let his hand fall to his side and regained his full height and—for a moment—Carver thought he had succeeded.

It was far too early for that.

"I don't want to forget it, Carver. This is part of the game, right? I have to know this. That," he said, pointing at the corpse with the sidearm he had grabbed from his belt, "is not me. I get that.

"Just like I am not *him*. I am *not* the man before me who died blowing himself up on a mech. I am *not* the man who died in the clinic because our owners didn't want to wait for him to heal. I'm not even the man who died by your side in Sudden Death," he said before tears filled his eyes. He laughed weakly and continued.

"Just like I'm not the boy who grew up on the streets of New Chicago. I'm not the guy who Tommy and Jack gave up to the cops. I'm not the guy who sold himself and all his clones into slavery." He turned around and paced around the corpse.

"But the thing is... he's *dead*. Ryan Jenkins died on Earth. I've never met him, but I know everything about him. And I do mean *everything*. I know his entire life. And though I've only been alive for a couple days, I even have a few months' worth of memories from a few other guys who lived here. Who died here."

Carver knew this kind of talk. He had only heard it once before— even if it was four years ago—but he remembered every word of *that* speech. He cleared his throat and was about to interrupt, but Ryan whipped around and waved his sidearm at him.

"*No*, Carver, *I'm* talking. I'm going to just go ahead and do that," he declared before lowering his weapon. "See, that's not even the *big* problem! I'm alive right now and that's something to be thankful for, I guess. All things considered, I had a good time with Norris today before he killed himself in a blaze of glory. You know what he told me?"

Carver looked at the deranged soldier and kept his mouth shut. This speech was not for him.

It was for the man saying it.

"He told me to live my life. He said we shouldn't worry about our next death or how it was going to happen. There's power in that. We can live our lives even when we're trapped down here. We can enjoy ourselves and skip to our heart's content," he explained, turning to the corpse on the ground. Seemingly as an afterthought, he scratched his nose with his right hand and looked back at Carver.

"But that's the thing, old man. I *don't* enjoy this. I've only been alive two days and I've experienced more pain than some have in their *whole lives*. My nose was completely destroyed and I've had to fight for my life. I had to watch a good man *die* just because he broke his ankle. This life is misery. *Why* would I want to stay like this? Why would I want to wait for the death sentence to finally come? I've only been alive two days and I *know* this is Hell."

Carver knew what Ryan had already decided. Although he knew how this would end, Carver didn't have the right words to change the outcome. He didn't have them for Washington. Ryan was still looking at the corpse, and he did nothing to stop the tears streaming down his face.

"You know what they say about freedom?"

Carver kept quiet. They both knew the answer.

"It's choosing your way to die. And this... this is my choice," Ryan said before lifting his sidearm and bringing it under his chin. He let out a deep breath and closed his eyes. He was done with this world.

Ryan Jenkins pulled the trigger and the world vanished for him.

Carver watched as the new corpse fell on top of the old, and he almost didn't notice the tears fall from his eyes. When he finally did, he was surprised at himself for being able to feel like this. Although it hurt, Carver reveled in it. He had denied himself this kind of emotion for four long years.

After he collected himself, Carver walked over to Ryan's fresh body and rolled it off the older clone. Blood leaked from under the young man's chin and from the top of his head, but Carver ignored it. He laid the corpse out just like the other and folded his young friend's hands above his midsection.

He almost couldn't see it through the tears, but Carver picked out the camera from his periphery. After kissing the mesh of his armored fingers and then lowering them to Ryan's forehead, Carver sniffed back his tears and stood up to his full height. Then he walked over to the cloaked machine and grabbed hold of the levitation strut so it could not get away.

Carver looked right into the lens, knowing that Garrison would eventually get the message.

"We need to talk."

MAXWELL GARRISON LOOKED at the quarterly reports for the Northwestern Division and sighed. The advertising revenue was down and the living wage had gone up for all of the support staff, which was its own headache. Casualties and resurrection costs were about the same, but Garrison was not happy.

Along with the fact that he was balding and overweight and had to pay his mortgage—which were *always* reasons that he was not happy —Maxwell would now have to sacrifice something to compensate for the loss of revenue. He would have a smaller bonus now, or at least one of his underlings would. Perhaps Maxwell would have to consider giving up one or two days from his vacation to Solaria in the summer, and that thought was entirely unpleasant.

He was still looking over the reports when Jonathon Carver walked into his office, confident as he approached the bureaucrat. He was followed by Garrison's assistant—pleading with him to stop walking— but one stern look from the legendary Crow was enough to silence the mouse of a man.

Carver walked up to Garrison's desk and just stood there. To Garrison's immense relief, he had enough manners to wait until he was addressed. After a moment of fake disinterest, Maxwell looked up from the reports and motioned with his hand that Jonathon should take a seat, but the old man shook his head.

"You've changed the layout. The couch used to be over there," he said, pointing his thumb behind him. Garrison peered at the man over his glasses and sighed.

"Yes, Jonathon, about *ten years ago.* You've been here since then, back with that business with that soldier you mentored. Now,"

Garrison said before he leaned back in his leather chair, which creaked all the way, "what can I do for you? Are you ready to retire, yet? I swear you're the only one who actually costs me money."

In response, Carver shook his head and took the seat offered him, causing Garrison to raise an eyebrow.

Usually, the soldier was not one for comfort.

"It's about the new kid," Carver said, resisting the urge to twiddle his thumbs. At the mention of a *new kid*, Garrison ran through the archives of his mind to figure out what Carver possibly meant. Garrison came up with a hundred likely suspects and let his derision be known by throwing up his hands and shrugging.

"Jenkins. The suicide," Carver clarified, though he was definitely annoyed that he had to do so.

Garrison could narrow *that* one down. *Those* were not very common. He scanned through his memory and remembered signing off on some papers regarding a Ryan Jenkins just that morning.

"Oh, yes. Well, he's cleared for duty. No reason to ruin the crop. He just had a dissociation episode. Mentally, he seemed to be coping with life on Eris. I've already signed the order."

Garrison was pleased with himself for acting so quickly. Usually, that kind of decision would take a week, at the very least, and Garrison wondered why Carver would even bring him up.

"He's not going to make it."

Garrison furrowed his brow and leaned on his desk with his elbows.

"Now, Jonathon, explain yourself."

"The kid's like Washington. He's just going to keep doing it. It makes sense for him, you didn't hear him..." Carver trailed off, feeling far too much emotion.

"I've reviewed the tapes—"

"Then you didn't *fucking* listen! And this goes *deep*, Garrison. He's been going through the stages since he got here. This isn't just dissociation. He fundamentally *believes* that he is born and dies through the system, that there's no way out. Just like...Washington."

Carver had halted on the name of his other failure. With the mention of the poor suicidal soldier from four years ago, Garrison sighed and leaned back in his chair.

"You mentor this boy, too?" he asked. The old Crow looked down at his hands and nodded.

"He's like me. Early adoptions and everything. Nowhere else to go."

Garrison sighed again and looked at his own hands. Even though they were freshly manicured and pampered, they had just as much blood on them as this legendary warrior.

"Didn't you learn your lesson last time?" Garrison asked before taking off his reading glasses and rubbing his eyes. This was a fiscal *nightmare.* A whole crop ruined just like that, or, *worse,* he held liability for letting him back on the field.

"I tried to do it different. I tried to help, rather than just teach like I did with Washington. But it's too late for that. He's not coming back." Carver avoided eye contact and refused to let the tears fall.

"Ugh... It's going to be a lot of paperwork getting him off the field, now. I hope you know that," Garrison said, already turning to his computer so he could begin filling out the right forms.

"You don't need to do that," Carver replied in a clipped tone. At his opposition, Garrison stopped rubbing his eyes and gave his employee a wary look.

"What are you talking about, Jonathon?"

"Hawkins' behavior experiments. Use them on Ryan and turn him into a monster. It's the best thing for him. He'll be happy being ignorant," he argued, turning back to make eye contact once his tears were under control.

Garrison sat back in his chair again and shook his head.

"Jonathon, I can't believe *you* fell for that. Norris is just—"

"Not *Ed*. The Brit just doesn't care. I know that," Carver interrupted before putting his elbows on the desk, "but I know there are others. You have the capability for it. You map out people's brains and I'm sure you can change the routes, if you want. Tweak memories and all that crap. Just do it for Ryan."

Garrison pursed his lips and looked at the man. Carver was a verifiable legend and he had been all over the network. It wasn't outside reason that he could know about Hawkins' secret experiments, as the scientist was not particularly *coy* about his achievements.

Garrison sighed and started to wipe his glasses with a cloth.

"*Ryan*, eh? Alright, *fine*. We can do it. *However*, it is a very expensive process. We have been trying to use it to create heroes for television. Like you in your prime, but artificial. More marketable. I'm not sure we could even get approval to *use* your Ryan. He has not proven himself yet. And... the suicide does not help," Garrison explained, trying to dissuade the veteran.

Carver just leaned back in his own chair and sighed.

"He'll be all that you need. Remember, you're the ones changing his brain. You can make him whatever you want him to be," Carver argued, causing Garrison to sigh and look at the Crow.

They were not friends, but they held a mutual respect.

"Jonathon, there's still the matter of the expense. This usually has to come from the higher-ups. I am merely middle management."

"C'mon, Max. As a favor to me."

Garrison was shocked at the request; Carver never used the man's first name. It was a sign to his commitment, at the very least.

"I don't think I can *afford* to," Garrison replied, thinking about his vacation to Solaria. The cost would eradicate his bonus and then some.

He might risk getting fired for just *suggesting* it.

"I'll pay it," Carver said softly.

Taken aback, Garrison let out a loud cough and had to gulp down the glass of water he kept to the side. The bureaucrat did *not* know what the Crow was thinking, but Garrison's mind was already number-crunching at the possibility. Before responding, he tried to remember Carver's earnings and the projected cost.

It was absolutely absurd, but it *was* possible. Garrison cleared his throat and looked at Carver with a severe expression.

"Jonathon, that is *ridiculous*. You have been supposed to retire for a while, now, and you still *can*. While you *do* have the funds for this, it would wipe out your savings. You would be back in *debt*, of all things. You would *never* get out and you would *die* here. Do you *really* want that?"

Garrison held no sentiment for Carver, but he held no malice, either. This was a fool's errand.

"It's not about what I want. It's what I need to do. I owe him, Max," Carver said, tears pooling at the bottom of his eyes again. Garrison looked at the legend sitting across the table.

"You *don't*, Jon. You've only known this boy a couple months."

"I *owe* him. I could have saved him. I'm going to make up for it."

Garrison looked down at his desk and sighed. There was no reasoning with the man; it was part of why he was so famous. Garrison shook his head and pursed his lips before looking back at Carver, who had fought down his sadness. His cold blue eyes were looking right back, and Garrison no longer had a choice.

"I will get all the paperwork ready. I'll set it up with Hawkins and we... we will get this done." Garrison breathed out the words in a defeated manner.

Carver was staring off into space as Garrison spoke, but he nodded when the bureaucrat finished speaking. After taking a deep breath, Carver got up and walked to the doorway, but before he left the room, Garrison cleared his throat.

"Try not to regret this, Jonathon. It might be ugly," Garrison warned, his sympathies to the doomed soldier. Jonathon Carver sighed and headed to the door, talking loud enough that Garrison had no issue hearing him.

"This whole moon is ugly, Max. He'll fit right in."

3

Acknowledging the Problem

Albert led the Crow into the clinic and wondered just what had happened to him. In painful detail, the guard remembered the last time he had escorted the man into this clinic. Since then, he had somehow become a completely different person. The way he acted, the way he talked... everything about him was different except his face. As a result, Albert was determined to avoid talking to the soldier as they walked down the corridor, but the man was likewise determined to make him laugh.

He had succeeded once. It was a bawdy joke about a whore, but felt guilty before he even laughed. It seemed far too crude.

No one should laugh right when they are about to be euthanized.

So it was incredibly disconcerting that this Crow had laughed the entire time Albert lead him to death. The undercover agent had hoped it was shock, but it seemed like the man just accepted it all. It only took a moment for Albert to wonder if the slave soldier might have been the victim of one of Hawkins' experiments, but he pushed the thought from his mind.

He couldn't do anything about it, *now*. That was his mantra.

They entered the clinic as Dr. Kane was preparing the euthanasia kit. She wore a vacant expression on her face, and Albert could tell that she was putting up a front. Obviously, the good doctor was holding back feelings she did not want to express.

"Hey, Doc, how you doin' today?" the Crow asked, gleeful as he plopped himself down on the medical table and gave her a wide smile. Charlotte forced a smile for the corrupted Crow and started wiping down his arm with an alcoholic swab.

"I'm fine, Ryan. How are you?" she asked, only *just* keeping up the façade.

"*Dying*. Rough trade out there. Some asshole decided to clip me in the shoulder right before the buzzer. I tell you, they're just out there to spoil my day. Now I have to get all that training in just because some guy wanted to take a *pot shot*. What horseshit, am I right?"

Charlotte forced another smile and patted him so he would lie down on the table. Rolling his eyes, he obliged, but only so he could joke around once he was flat.

"I'll see you in a bit. You know I'm an early riser."

Charlotte surrendered a weak laugh before she inserted the syringe into his arm.

"Are you ready?" she asked with a soft voice. He shrugged and gave her an innocent grin, and her own smile finally left her once she pushed the plunger.

It wasn't long before the grin disappeared and he wasn't able to move. Charlotte then grabbed a second syringe and attached it to the IV connection before pushing that final plunger.

A morose quiet fell over the room as the man's life left him. Eventually, Albert awkwardly tried to leave, but then he heard the doctor quietly sobbing. When Albert turned back to face her, Charlotte was staring at the man she had just killed.

"It looks just like him. It looks just like him... but it's not. It's someone else. That fucking bastard."

Albert looked at her with pity. Now he knew for sure that Jenkins had become one of those tampered soldiers. It was one of the worst rumors he had heard about the games.

The resistance agent shook his head and repeated his mantra once more in his mind. He couldn't do anything about it *now*. They would all have to wait just a little bit longer.

Lost in his thoughts, Albert did not notice the doctor turning her head, trying to fight back her tears and regain her dignity. She glared at him.

"How can you just stand *by* like that? *This*," she shouted as she pointed at the corpse, "is what your employers do! They kill them over and over again and once they've broken their toys, they go ahead and destroy their *souls*! *This* is what you're a part of! Are you *proud* of yourself?"

Albert tried to repeat his mantra, but it was too much for him. He couldn't just stand by.

Not anymore.

Albert walked over to her and stood half a meter away, forgetting his size might intimidate her. He didn't want to get any closer for fear that she would lash out, but he *really* did not want any part of his message to escape the room. Hawkins might be lurking, or the cameras might pick up dangerous information from their conversation.

"I'm *not* proud of myself. Not right now, but this isn't me. This isn't what I'm *going* to be. I'm just playing a part. Just like you, Dr. Kane," Albert stated, standing up straighter in his self-righteousness.

Charlotte's eyes became fearful as Albert continued, half from his intimidating size and half from his dangerous words. It was the most he had ever said to the woman, and it was *not* small talk.

"I'm part of the Eris Freedom Initiative, and I'm not the only one. This time we're taking the fight to them. It's not just Eris we're trying to free anymore. The whole *system* is broken. Once we take back Eris, we're going to take back Earth. We're going to take back our lives.

"I don't know what you'd be able to do..." Albert paused, seeing the desire and fear in her eyes. "But we're not going to turn you away."

Afterword

Watch For...

The Crows return in Phoenix Rising and Swan Song, so you can jump right into the rest of the series as soon as you like!

And if you're curious about some of my other writing, I've re-released my novel Ouroboros, a political standalone about hallucinogen abuse, through 25&Y Publishing, and my second series, first series, the Forsaken Comedy, is a dark fantasy trilogy about the Horsemen of the Apocalypse trying to save Lucifer and the rest of existence.

Currently, I am working for Yoton Yo Studios as the Narrative Director for the Exfinitum TCG, and I have a few titles under contract with 25&Y Publishing. First is Daytrippers, a paranormal science fiction series set in the same world as Ouroboros, and the next one in the queue is Evenin' Flow, a short story collection that covers multiple genres.

And if you literally just want something to watch, I have a YouTube channel based around Beat Saber, where I review custom songs and try to guide new players. Once I get back into streaming, my handle on Twitch, and most platforms, is Kkauffany, so feel free to say hi!

www.ingramcontent.com/pod-product-compliance
Lightning Source LLC
Chambersburg PA
CBHW070830280626
47161CB00015B/431